PRAISE FOR *IN THE BLOOD*

"Gripping . . . fast-paced . . . fans will get their money's worth."

Publishers Weekly

"Quality plot, well-developed characters, and not too over-the-top." Add James Reece to your list that includes Harvath (Brad Thor), Reacher (Lee Child), Bob Lee Swagger (Stephen Hunter), et al."

Men Reading Books

"Hands down, *In the Blood* is the best book I've read this year. I've said from the beginning that covering Carr is what I'd imagine it would have been like to discover Vince Flynn at the beginning of his career . . . Carr deserves to be mentioned alongside all-time greats like Flynn, Thor, Clancy, and Silva . . ."

The Real Book Spy

"*In the Blood* is Carr's best book to date and demonstrates a mastery of the genre—it rightly belongs in the constellation of Clancy, Thor, Morrell, and Flynn."

Townhall.com

PRAISE FOR *THE DEVIL'S HAND*

"Take my word for it, James Reece is one rowdy motherf***er. Get ready!"

Chris Pratt, all-around great guy and star of *The Terminal List* on Amazon Prime

"Carr delivers engrossing back story, incorporates current events seamlessly, and never flinches from breathless depictions of violence."

Publishers Weekly

"Carr continues to draw on his own experiences as a SEAL to give the story a level of realism that writers who've not actually served sometimes have a hard time achieving."

Booklist

"*The Terminal List* is widely regarded as one of the best debut thrillers of all-time, and rightfully so, but *The Devil's Hand* is even better, and should go down as one of the best books in the genre, period."

The Real Book Spy

"An action thriller extraordinaire that is not to be missed."

The Providence Journal

PRAISE FOR *SAVAGE SON*

"A great book . . . it's f*cking riveting!"

Joe Rogan

"A rare gut-punch writer, full of grit and insight, who we will be happily reading for years to come."

Gregg Hurwitz, *New York Times* bestselling author of the Orphan X series

"Absolutely fantastic! *Savage Son* is savagely good, and puts Jack Carr at the very top of the thriller genre."

Marc Cameron, *New York Times* bestselling author

"A badass, high-velocity round of reading! The three parts of this masterfully crafted experience says it all—The Trap, The Stalk, The Kill."

Clint Emerson, former Navy SEAL and *New York Times* bestselling author of *100 Deadly Skills* and *The Right Kind of Crazy*

"Carr writes both from the gut and a seemingly infinite reservoir of knowledge in the methods of human combat. Loved it!"

Chris Hauty, *Los Angeles Times* bestselling author of *New York Times* Editors' Choice *Deep State*

"Jack Carr triples down with *Savage Son*. From the book's gut-wrenching opening to its sleep-stealing conclusion, Jack's homage to *The Most Dangerous Game* delivers the goods and then some."

Don Bentley, author of *Without Sanction*

"A masterfully told, heart-thumping tale of modern conflict."

Lt. Col. Oliver North, USMC (Ret.), *New York Times* bestselling author of *The Rifleman* and *Under Fire*

"*Savage Son* is amazing! This is the kind of book every author wished he could write . . . mind-blowingly good!"

Simon Gervais, former RCMP counterterrorism officer and bestselling author of *Hunt Them Down*

"Accurate, intense, and raw, *Savage Son* taps into our most primal of instincts. Jack Carr draws you into this predatory pursuit like no other because he's lived it!"

John Barklow, hunter, Navy diver, Special Operations Cold Weather Survival instructor, and Sitka Gear Big Game product manager

"If you like a fresh approach to action with authentic details and a believable main character, these books are for you. I'm a fan."

David Morrell, *New York Times* bestselling author of *First Blood*, *The Brotherhood of the Rose*, and *Murder as a Fine Art*

"Jack Carr is back and at the top of his game in *Savage Son*, a heart-pounding, sleep-robbing, edge-of-your-seat thriller."

Joshua Hood, 82nd Airborne veteran and author of Robert Ludlum's *The Treadstone Resurrection*

"Whether you are a hunter of four-legged game or of man, *Savage Son* will stoke the inner fire of your soul. Jack Carr's attention to detail and experience from the battlefield to the backcountry draw the reader into the field to experience the art of war through the eyes of a man who has lived it."

Cole Kramer, Kodiak Island Brown Bear guide and outfitter

PRAISE FOR *TRUE BELIEVER*

"This is seriously good. I mean, seriously."

Lee Child, #1 *New York Times* bestselling author of *Past Tense*

"A powerful, thoughtful, realistic, at times terrifying thriller that I could not put down. A terrific addition to the genre, Jack Carr and his alter-ego protagonist, James Reece, continue to blow me away."

Mark Greaney, #1 *New York Times* bestselling author of *Mission Critical*

"Jack Carr creates an incredibly vivid, emotional, action-packed tapestry of carnage and death."

Justen Charters, Black Rifle Coffee Company, *Coffee or Die* Magazine

"Packs a punch. Carr's second effort is a well-crafted thriller with timely reflections on the increasingly complicated world of international terrorism."

Kirkus Reviews

PRAISE FOR *THE TERMINAL LIST*

"Double the trouble, twice the action, and quadruple the enjoyment. Careful while reading this one, it could leave a mark."

Steve Berry, #1 *New York Times* bestselling author of *The Lost Order*

"Absolutely awesome! So powerful, so pulse-pounding, so well-written—rarely do you read a debut novel this damn good."

Brad Thor, #1 *New York Times* bestselling author of *Dead Fall*

"Told with a deft hand and a keen eye for detail, *The Terminal List* . . . is explosive and riveting."

Kevin Maurer, coauthor of the #1 bestselling *No Easy Day* and *American Radical*

"Like a bullet from Jack Carr's custom-built sniper rifle, the story arrives on target with devastating impact. Trust me, you won't be able to put this one down!"

Mark Owen, *New York Times* bestselling author of *No Easy Day* and *No Hero*

"Crackerjack plotting, vivid characters both in and out of uniform, and a relentless pace to a worthy finish. It's a great start!"

Stephen Hunter, #1 *New York Times* bestselling author of *G-Man*

"An extremely unique thriller! Absolutely intense!"

Chuck Norris

"Bravo! Jack Carr is the real deal!"

Sean Parnell, *New York Times* bestselling author of *Outlaw Platoon*

"Not since Stephen Hunter have we seen an author who so accurately captures the essence of the gun. Jack Carr is a shooter."

Clint Smith, founder of Thunder Ranch Shooting School

"Jack Carr's *The Terminal List* is a page-turning thriller you won't be able to put down. The detail-focused writing, personal characters, and heart-pounding plotline will keep you coming back for more. An absolute must-read!"

Katie Pavlich, *New York Times* bestselling author and Fox News contributor

"Any fan of the novels by Brad Thor and the late Vince Flynn will realize that Jack Carr will soon be joining their ranks."

The Washington Times

ALSO BY JACK CARR

Only the Dead

The Devil's Hand

Savage Son

True Believer

The Terminal List

IN THE BLOOD

A THRILLER

JACK CARR

EMILY BESTLER BOOKS

ATRIA

NEW YORK LONDON TORONTO SYDNEY NEW DELHI

EMILY BESTLER BOOKS

ATRIA

An Imprint of Simon & Schuster, Inc.
1230 Avenue of the Americas
New York, NY 10020

This book is a work of fiction. Any references to historical events, real people, or real places are used fictitiously. Other names, characters, places, and events are products of the author's imagination, and any resemblance to actual events or places or persons living or dead is entirely coincidental.

First Emily Bestler Books/Atria trade paperback edition September 2023

EMILY BESTLER BOOKS/ATRIA PAPERBACK and colophon are trademarks of Simon & Schuster, Inc.

For information about special discounts for bulk purchases, please contact Simon & Schuster Special Sales at 1-866-506-1949 or business@simonandschuster.com.

The Simon & Schuster Speakers Bureau can bring authors to your live event. For more information, or to book an event, contact the Simon & Schuster Speakers Bureau at 1-866-248-3049 or visit our website at www.simonspeakers.com.

Manufactured in the United States of America

7 9 10 8

Library of Congress Cataloging-in-Publication Data has been applied for.

ISBN 978-1-9821-8165-9
ISBN 978-1-9821-8167-3 (pbk)
ISBN 978-1-9821-8168-0 (ebook)

For Michael Goodboe

July 6, 1966–November 24, 2020

Warrior

and

For all those at the Central Intelligence Agency whose lives are memorialized with stars

For the wages of sin is death.

—ROMANS 6:23

PREFACE

IT IS OFTEN SAID that you don't hear the bullet that kills you, the idea being that the projectile is traveling faster than the speed of sound and therefore a well-placed head shot will put your target in the dirt before the vibrations of the bullet traveling through the atmosphere reach the tympanic membrane. Hence the devastating psychological impact and terror that can be achieved by a single sniper firing one shot and then disappearing into the bush. The enemy never knows when he might be in the crosshairs. He could be drawing breath, full of life, joking with a comrade one second, and gone the next, his soul snatched by an invisible demon behind the scope a mile away.

But this is more than a novel about snipers, more than a thriller about two men hunting each other across the globe. This is a novel of violent resolutions, but also one of forgiveness. At first glance those two themes might seem diametrically opposed, and you would be right. Often, dichotomies help us better understand ourselves and our impact on those around us. There is an advantage in eliminating a targeted individual on the battlefield and there is power in forgiveness. James Reece is a man struggling with those dichotomies.

By the time you read this, Navy SEAL Sniper James Reece may be on screens across the world, brought to life by Chris Pratt in the Amazon Prime Video series adaptation of *The Terminal List*. Why has this character resonated? My suspicion is that it's because he is on a journey, as are we all. And, just like each of us, he strives to learn, to evolve, to apply the wisdom of his experiences to the decisions and the threats of tomorrow. Reece resonates because within each of us there is a warrior and a hunter. It is in our DNA, suppressed by "progress" perhaps, but there nonetheless. Our ancestors were skilled in both disciplines, or we would not be here today. They fought and killed to protect their families and tribes. They hunted to provide sustenance. In more recent times they fought and killed for freedom.

Some critics do not like James Reece. He makes them uncomfortable. I have found that most of those he triggers are the most disconnected from the land and the animals that inhabit it. Putting food on the table is the job of a farmer somewhere between New York and Los Angeles. Many don't feel a responsibility to be prepared to protect their spouses and children when that primal task can be outsourced; just call 911. A moral vanity has trumped the obligation to protect their lives and the lives of those they love; that is the job of the police in a *civilized* society, after all. If that describes you, and you are picking this book up for the first time, perhaps you should put it down. You might not identify with, you might even despise, the protagonist in these pages. Self-reliant men, capable of extreme violence in defense of their lives, their families, and of freedom makes some people nervous.

I quote Robert E. Howard from *The Tower of the Elephant* in my third novel, *Savage Son*: "Civilized men are more discourteous than savages because they know they can be impolite without having their skulls split, as a general thing."

As a general thing...

I try to be thoughtful in all I do, whether it's the prose in these pages, the research for the novels, a social media post, a question for a guest on my Danger Close Podcast, or an answer to an interview question. I feel an obligation to put the requisite time, energy, and effort into these endeavors, because you, the reader, have trusted me with your time—time you will never get back. I want my character to embody that quality as well. He is thoughtful yet deadly. He is a student of war and of the hunt. He is also searching, searching as we all are, for meaning, for purpose, for a mission. Will that mission always require the gun? Will Reece ever be able to stop killing for God and country? Will he become so disenfranchised by the political machine that he will lay down his weapons and retreat to the mountains of Montana?

In my previous book, *The Devil's Hand*, I explored what the enemy has learned by watching the United States on the field of battle for the previous twenty years at war. I put myself in their shoes. That research led me to believe that if I was a state or non-state adversary, I might just observe for a while; we are doing a good job at tearing ourselves apart from the inside.

In the course of writing this book, I watched the botched withdrawal from Afghanistan in disbelief, although I should not have been surprised—our elected representatives, appointed bureaucrats, and senior level military leaders have a twenty-year track record of failure with almost zero accountability. They have failed up. Understanding the nature of the conflict in which you are committing or have committed military forces is an essential element of leadership. As President Dwight D. Eisenhower said, "You know, farming looks mighty easy when your plow is a pencil, and you're a thousand miles from the corn field." The same is true of warfare; it looks mighty easy when your rifle is a budget approval and you are six thousand miles from the battlefield.

These novels are also extremely therapeutic to write. Russia, China, North Korea, and Iran, along with terrorist organizations and super-empowered individuals, certainly give me a lot to work with, but so do those in what Eisenhower coined the "military industrial complex." It is an ever-growing ecosystem of lobbyists, defense contractors, and flag-level military officers approving budgets in the Pentagon for the very companies they will advise as "members of the board" in retirement. Politicians and their relatives provide ample fodder as well, with elected officials who enter politics making between one hundred and two hundred thousand dollars a year, yet somehow amass wealth in the tens of millions over their tenure in government; aside from being humble public servants, apparently they are also astute investors. Politics is big business.

Is that a system worth serving? Is it one worth saving? Those are questions we must all ask and answer as citizens. As James Reece is pulled closer and closer to the heart of the American intelligence apparatus, they are ones he must ask and answer as well. What will be his answers? How much more power do we, the people, want to relinquish to what was intended to be a limited government? Our employees—elected representatives—rule by the "consent of the governed." Those in positions of power would be wise to remember that as military and intelligence budgets inch closer to a trillion dollars a year, those investments resulted in two wars lost to insurgents wielding AKs and homemade IEDs working from caves and mud-walled compounds. Today, half the military budget and seventy percent of the intelligence budget goes to contractors. As a wise Marine Corps major general and Medal of Honor recipient once said, "War is a racket."

James Reece has been a part of that system. He was betrayed by it just as were those who stepped up in service to the nation following the attacks of September 11, 2001. Read *The Afghanistan Papers* by Craig Whitlock for documentation. Reece has also been on the other side, becoming the terrorist, the insurgent, bringing the war home to the front doors of those whose decisions have sent young men and women to their deaths for two decades. Is James Reece now an instrument of those same political elites?

Before he can come to terms with questions of service, sacrifice, and the direction of his future path, Reece has business to attend to. He requires the resources of the very system he despises to put him in position; to get his crosshairs on a sniper, a sniper who is at this very moment also hunting him.

Which brings me back to the bullet that kills you. When it comes to the long-range dance of death, the victor may not always be the shooter most well-versed in the art and science of long-distance engagements. It's a thinking man's game. When two of the most lethal snipers on the planet face off, what will be the differentiator? When given the choice between answers or blood, what will James Reece choose? Turn the page to find out.

Jack Carr
February 16, 2022
Park City, Utah

PROLOGUE

Ouagadougou, Burkina Faso, Africa

SHE HAD BEEN STRIKINGLY beautiful once. At just over forty she still turned heads, a trait she often worked to her advantage both personally and professionally, but even as confident and, more importantly, competent as she was, it was not lost on her that fewer heads were turning these days. She was well aware that her looks had a limited shelf life. She accepted it. She had enjoyed them in her youth but now she had other, more valuable skills—skills she had put into practice hours earlier. As she waited her turn in line at the check-in counter at the Air France section of Thomas Sankara International Airport Ouagadougou in Burkina Faso, no one would have guessed that earlier she had shot a man three times in the head with a Makarov 9x18mm pistol.

The Makarov would not have been her first choice but on assignments like this you used what was available. It had worked. The man was dead. The message had been sent.

Aliya Galin brushed her raven-black hair to the side and glanced at her smartphone, not because she wanted to know the time or scroll through a newsfeed or social media app, but because she did not want to stand out to local security forces as what she was, an assassin for the state of Israel. She needed to blend in with the masses, which meant suppressing her natural predatory instincts. It was time to act like a sheep, nonattentive and relatively relaxed. She needed to look normal.

Had she been stopped and questioned, her backstory as a sales representative for a French financial firm would have checked out, as would her employment history, contacts, and references developed by the technical office just off the Glilot Ma'arav Interchange in Tel Aviv, home to the headquarters of the Mossad, the Israeli spy agency tasked with safeguarding the Jewish state. The laptop in her carry-on contained nothing that would betray her, no secret backdoor files storing incriminating information, no Internet searches for anything to do with Israel, terrorism, or her target. The computer was clean.

It was getting more difficult to travel internationally with the web of interconnected facial recognition cameras that continued to proliferate around the globe. Had it not been for the Mossad's Technology Department she would have been arrested many times over. The Israeli intelligence services had learned the lessons of facial recognition and passport forgery in the age of information the hard way on the international stage twelve years earlier, when twenty-six of their agents had been identified and implicated in the assassination of Mahmoud al-Mabhouh in a Dubai hotel room. Al-Mabhouh was the chief weapons procurement and logistics officer for the al-Qassam Brigades, the military wing of the Hamas terrorist organization. The Mossad would not repeat the mistakes of Dubai.

Her French passport identified her as Mélanie Cotillard and if someone were to check her apartment in Batignolles-Monceau, they would find a flat commensurate with the income of a midlevel banker in the financial services industry. No disguises, weapons, or false walls would betray her true profession.

The man she had come to kill was responsible for the bombing of a Jewish day care center in Rabat, Morocco. Not all in the Arab world were supportive of Morocco recognizing Israel and establishing official diplomatic relations. If retribution was not swift, it emboldened the enemy, an enemy that wanted to see Israel wiped from the face of the earth. When Iranian-backed terrorists targeted Israeli children, justice was handled not by the courts but by Caesarea, an elite and secretive branch of the Mossad.

More and more, drones were becoming a viable option for targeted assassinations. They were getting smaller and easier to conceal. But, even with the options that came with the increasingly lethal UAV technology, the Mossad still preferred to keep some kills personal. Israel was a country built on the foundation of a targeted killing program, one that had continued to evolve, as did the threats to the nation. There was nothing that put as much fear in the hearts and minds of her enemies as an Israeli assassin.

Though Aliya maintained her dual U.S.-Israeli citizenship, she had not set foot in the United States in almost fifteen years. Israel was now home. Her parents had been born there and had been killed there, a suicide bomber from Hamas taking them from her just as they began to enjoy their retirement years. She had been in the Israel Defense Forces then, doing her duty with no intention of devoting her life to her adopted homeland. She would be back soon. She would quietly resign from her job in Paris, which had been set up for her by a *Sayan,* and return to Israel. *Sayanim* made up a global network of non-Israeli, though usually Jewish, assets that provided material and logistical support for Mossad operations, not for financial incentives but out of loyalty. Aliya planned to take time off to see her children and her sister who cared for them. She also planned to talk to the head of the special operations division about moving into management. She was getting tired. Perhaps this would be her final kill.

The assignment had been relatively straightforward. She did in fact have a legitimate meeting with a bank in Ouagadougou, Burkina Faso's capital city. The instability inherent to the African continent also provided opportunity for investment. Her cover for action intact, she had three days to locate and case the residence of Kofi Kouyaté. They called it a "close target reconnaissance" when she had worked with the Americans in Iraq. She reflected on the operational pace of those intense days often; the lessons learned, the relationships fostered.

Her days of seducing men in hotel bars were in the past, at least in this part of the world. Enough of them had ended up shot, stabbed, poisoned, or blown up after thinking with the small head between their legs that others became wary when a beautiful olive-skinned angel offered to buy them a drink.

The Mossad could have used a hit team of locals on this assignment, but her masters in Tel Aviv still preferred to send a message—hurt Israeli citizens and we will find you, no matter where you hide. Aliya's generation of *Kidon,* assassins, had proven worthy inheritors of the legacy of Operation Wrath of God, which targeted those responsible for the 1972 massacre of Israeli athletes in Munich.

She had worked this job alone. No accomplice to turn her in or identify her to the infamous Burkina Faso internal state security service. If you were rolled up in this part of the world, you could look forward to an interrogation and torture worse than what you would experience in the West Bank. Out here, you would be questioned, beaten, burned, and mutilated before being gang raped until you were dead.

Though security was lax by internationally accepted standards, she still had to empty her purse and small suitcase onto a table beyond a metal detector that she had a strong suspicion was not plugged in. As the two security guards went through her bag, they paid a bit too much attention to her bras and underwear. Finding nothing suspicious that gave them an excuse to bring her into a back room for a secondary search, they let her proceed to her gate. Perhaps if she were younger they would have crafted an excuse. Aging in this business did have its benefits.

She was looking forward to leaving the African heat behind and settling into her business-class seat on the air-conditioned Air France flight with service to Paris. She was ready for a drink. Air France still took pride in the French part of their lineage and served tolerable white wine even this early in the morning.

Waiting to board, she allowed her mind to wander to the past six months in France, the children she had left in the care of her younger sister in Israel, and a possible return to, no, not normalcy, as life had never been normal for Aliya, but possibly an evolution, yes, that was it, an evolution in her life. Maybe she would visit the United States, travel with her children, and introduce them to the country where she had lived with her parents until they returned to the Holy Land, when Aliya was ten. She smiled, imagining her son and daughter playing on the white sand beaches in the Florida sun. *Normal.* They were still young enough that she could be a mother to them. What would she do at headquarters? Work as an analyst in collections or as an advisor to the chief or deputy director? More appealing was a transfer out of operations and into training. Her hard-earned skills and experience would be put to good use at the Midrasha, the elite Mossad training academy. Would she be able to adjust after all these years in the field? Killing was all she knew.

As she boarded the flight, distracted by thoughts of the future, she failed to notice the man watching her from across the gate.

When she crossed the tarmac and disappeared into the plane, he placed a call.

• • •

Nizar Kattan studied the two men from neighboring Mali as they removed the Strela-2 missiles from the back of the Jeep.

A Soviet-era, shoulder-fired surface-to-air missile, the 9K32 Strela-2 was almost as common in sub-Saharan Africa as RPGs and AK variants. Nizar knew the Strela had been used to successfully shoot down multiple airliners over the years. It was a reliable missile system that had proven its worth, but it was getting old. During the 2002 Mombasa attacks in Kenya that targeted an Israeli-owned hotel, the al-Qaeda inspired terrorists had fired two Strelas at an Israeli-chartered Boeing 747. Both missiles had missed the target. Having worked with enough indigenous talent over the years, Nizar chalked it up to operator error. Still, he wasn't going to take chances, which is why four of one of the Cold War's most prolific weapons would be used on this mission.

Nizar and his French accomplice had recruited the two patsies from the ranks of Nusrat al-Islam, or Jama'at Nasr al-Islam wal Muslimin to the initiated. The group formed when al-Qaeda in the Islamic Maghreb, Ansar al-Dine, and al-Mourabitoun merged in 2017. With a mandate that called for killing civilians from Western nations, they would be perfect. Still reverberating with the echoes of French colonial rule, insurgent groups in West Africa were ripe for exploitation. Financial incentives cemented the deal. In this case, Nusrat al-Islam thought they were striking a blow against their European oppressors in an operation organized by Nizar, who they believed to be an al-Qaeda facilitator. Their tasks were simple: They were to transport the four surface-to-air missiles from Mali into Burkina Faso, where they would link up with Nizar and the Frenchman and be given their target. Unbeknownst to them, their other task required them to die.

French special forces soldiers had proven extremely proficient in decimating the ranks of Nusrat al-Islam in Africa. Say what you will of the French, their operators were some of the best in the world. The officials meeting weekly in the Élysée Palace turned a blind eye to French military and intelligence actions in Africa. With few war correspondents covering what was essentially a forgotten conflict, French soldiers targeted and killed with impunity. Most of the developed world cared little for what transpired on the Dark Continent. The French government was smart enough to allow their citizens the freedom to travel, train, and join terror groups abroad. What they were loath to do within their own borders even in the wake of the attacks in Nice and Paris, they were more than happy to do in their former colonies and protectorates, perhaps as a psychological fuck-you to those who had thrown them out in the wars of liberation that swept the continent in the mid to late twentieth century. In Europe, France was a liberal bastion of democratic socialism. Overseas they hunted their enemies with ruthless efficiency.

Jean-Pierre Le Drian was capable and resourceful. His former teammates would have described him as merciless. A former French Foreign Legion *maréchal des logis-chef,* he now found employment as a soldier of fortune, a mercenary with an axe to grind. Rather than face charges for an atrocity in Africa that was too much for even those fighting an expeditionary counterinsurgency, the former staff sergeant was on the run. And he was valuable. He knew just where to look to find black-market weapons and regional guns for hire in this forgotten corner of Africa.

Le Drian fancied himself a successor to the Waffen SS commandos who escaped Nazi Germany following World War II and found refuge in the Legion, fighting in Indochina in the Devil's Brigade. Were those stories fact or fiction? It didn't matter. Le Drian was guided by the myth. He was his own Devil's Brigade of the new century. He knew that he had done what was necessary. These savages deserved no respect. What was coming next would be easy for him.

Nizar could not care less about the plight of the locals. Africa was just as shitty as the places he had left behind in the Middle East. His assignments in Syria and Ukraine had not been out of allegiance to Allah but out of a desire to leave that world behind. He had feigned support and devotion to *the cause* time and time again, always wondering how those around him could be so naive. Allah didn't care for Nizar. The prophet and the cult that followed him were no different than adherents to any religion the world over, con artists in a protection racket just like he had witnessed in his time with the Bratva, the Russian mafia. Nizar was clear on where real power lay: in the dollar, the euro, the yuan, gold, diamonds, silver, and now bitcoin. Enough of those and you could be a living, breathing god in the flesh.

What Nizar wanted, Allah could not deliver. Praying five times a day in accordance with the Five Pillars only wasted time. His skill with a rifle had been his ticket out of Syria and then to Russia and Montenegro. When his mentor had outlived his usefulness, Nizar had put him down with a shot from a suppressed Stechkin pistol, just as he'd been instructed by his then handler, General Qusim Yedid, a Syrian general who had been found shot in the knee and then poisoned with a highly toxic substance. Nizar had put enough of the story together to conclude that the general's death was the work of James Reece, the man he currently had in his sights. Nizar had escaped to Moscow and into the waiting hands of the Russian mafia before he struck out on his own, finding a home in Montenegro, a way station of illicit trade over millennia. He enjoyed the protection he received there but sensed it was time to move on. *Trust your instincts.* His next kill would allow him to relocate: Thailand, the Philippines, Argentina. He had not decided yet. This last payday, James Reece's death, would make it possible. It would also be his greatest challenge to date, as his prey might at this very moment be hunting him.

Fortunately for Nizar, James Reece was a man with enemies; enemies at senior levels of governments hostile to the United States, governments with intelligence services that had close ties to proxy terrorist groups. Nizar briefly wondered if the information that had led him to Burkina Faso had originated in Russia or Iran. No matter. It was time to move a pawn on the board. It was time to draw Reece out of the mountains of North America and onto the battlefield.

Nizar closed his eyes and took in the dry morning air. He was ready.

The men were dressed in the uniforms of the Burkina Faso security forces. They had parked off a red dirt road flanked by the long grasses of the savanna. Their position gave them a clear line of sight to aircraft departing Thomas Sankara International Airport.

The retainer money from Eric Sawyer that had been laundered through a construction company in Montenegro was not insignificant, but it was not quite enough. The former Army Ranger and private military company CEO had used Nizar to eliminate problems. He had died under suspicious circumstances on his island property in the West Indies, but not before he had set up a contract to eliminate James Reece. Was the CIA involved in Sawyer's death? Nizar could not be sure, but he had his suspicions. Had the retainer been a few more million, Nizar would have considered taking the money and not fulfilling the contract. With Sawyer dead, there would have been no repercussions. Perhaps if he were not on Reece's radar, Nizar would have walked. But he was. Nizar suspected that Reece had killed two of Nizar's past handlers. The former SEAL was a threat, one that needed to be dealt with. Putting him in the ground solved two problems: It eliminated an exceptionally competent professional targeting him and it unlocked the other half of Sawyer's money, allowing Nizar to disappear and to not have to go for his gun every time he caught movement in the shadows. If he was going to vanish and leave this life behind, he needed to kill James Reece.

The Frenchman had come to him courtesy of his new handler, the man in the wheelchair. They had met in person only once, in Dubrovnik. The coastal Croatian city was close enough to Montenegro that Nizar could make the trip with relatively few complications. His potential handler, on the other hand, had to travel by train and ferry from Turin, in northern Italy, to the Balkan state on the Adriatic. Nizar had watched him over the course of four days, looking for signs of surveillance. The man in the wheelchair was a veteran of the game; he knew Nizar was observing and vetting him. He was a professional and would have expected nothing less. Nizar found himself grudgingly gaining respect for the small man who pushed himself through the streets and hauled himself in and out of taxis and into restaurants and cafés without asking for help or letting a moment's worth of self-pity cross his face. The man wore a different tailored suit every day, a bold silk ascot around his neck. Like Nizar, he stayed off cell phones and computers. He was a student of the old school. How he ended up in the wheelchair was a source of mystery and conjecture to those who lived and worked in the darker side of the clandestine economy. It was rumored he had been put there by a sniper.

Having established that the man was not bait, Nizar sat down with him over coffee, and they worked out their arrangement. Without Sawyer he needed someone else who could navigate the underworld, acquire weapons, and find additional talent. Additional talent would be necessary on this job. His one and only in-person meeting with his new handler had felt like a job interview, the small man confined to the chair studying him with those hawklike eyes, judging, assessing.

Nizar needed a partner on this mission, one with language abilities and a high level of martial prowess; the man in the wheelchair had delivered. If James Reece was as good as his track record would suggest, a second set of eyes and another scoped rifle in the fight would pay dividends.

Le Drian glanced at his watch and barked at the two "soldiers." When operating in this part of the world it helped to have a French citizen on your side who also spoke Arabic and Mòoré. That he boasted a background in the French Foreign Legion, operating almost exclusively in Africa, made him worth the investment. That he had a beef with the French government only helped solidify his allegiance.

"Just a few more minutes," the Frenchman said in flawless Arabic.

"Unless they are delayed," Nizar responded.

"Yes, always a probability in this part of the world. *This is Africa,* after all."

"Are they ready?" Nizar asked.

"Yes. They think they are making a statement, killing the colonial invaders, which, as you know, appeals to me."

Le Drian could never set foot in France again, banned to the outer reaches of what had once been an empire. Even the French Foreign

Legion had standards. Hunting and killing were one thing, torture was another; the memory of Algeria had yet to fade.

"Get ready," Nizar said. "Confirm the tail number and—"

The phone in the Frenchman's pocket chirped. He spoke in Mòoré and hit the End button.

"She's on board. Plane is taxiing."

"Good. It is time."

• • •

Aliya leaned back in her seat and took a sip of wine. It was just after 9:00 a.m.

The plane gained speed and lifted off, clearing the buildings at the east end of the runway and making a slow turn over the capital city.

The mission was *never* over. Not now. Not when she landed in France. Not when she returned to Israel. Not ever. This was a war and she was a combatant, something that was driven home in Iraq when the Mossad had detailed her to the Central Intelligence Agency. Her dual U.S.-Israeli citizenship allowed her to liaise between the Mossad and CIA on matters pertaining to the state of Israel. She missed those days. She missed *that* mission. It was straightforward. She missed the people she had worked with. She missed one in particular.

As the aircraft banked northward and gained altitude, she looked through her window. The buildings turned to huts; the semi-paved road of the capital morphed to red dirt and then to the grasses of the African plains. She wondered how long it would take them to find the man she had killed.

Had she not been a trained intelligence officer she might not have taken note of the green Jeep and faded purple van that stood out in contrast to the light brown grasses that surrounded them. At this low altitude she could still discern the outline of four men looking up at the gigantic plane headed for Europe. Had she not been on the receiving end of RPGs and Katyusha rockets, she might have mistaken the four flashes for the glint off a windshield or perhaps a deformity in the thick plastic window at her shoulder. But she *was* a trained intelligence officer and she *had* been on the receiving end of enemy rockets and missiles.

She thought of her two children. She thought of her husband, who had preceded her in death. She closed her eyes.

Though I walk through a valley of deepest darkness, I fear no harm, for You are with me; Your rod and Your staff—they comfort...

For the briefest of moments, she wondered if she was the intended target and just before the first missile impacted the fuselage, she determined that was the only logical conclusion. She was responsible for the innocent lives on the plane: mothers, fathers, brothers, sisters, children, and grandparents, who would never take another breath. She wondered who had betrayed her and she went to her death with the weight of one hundred and twenty-eight additional souls on her already troubled conscience.

PART ONE

ALIYA

THE OPERATIVE

FOR BY WISE GUIDANCE YOU CAN WAGE YOUR WAR.

—PROVERBS 24:6 AND FORMER MOTTO OF THE MOSSAD

CHAPTER 1

Kumba Ranch, Flathead Valley, Montana

"WHAT'S THAT HUNK OF steel on your hip?" Reece asked as his friend entered the cabin.

They called it "the cabin." Most people would have called it a home but for the fact that it was on the Hastingses' property and was originally built as a guest house. It wasn't ostentatious by any stretch, but it certainly was not a hovel. Its log timber frame blended in with the environment with a beautiful stone fireplace and large wraparound deck. A sloping grass lawn led to a dock where James had been staying in shape with morning swims and kettlebell workouts.

"It's good to see you, too, Reece."

"So, what's the pistol?"

"My 1911."

"That is not your *old* 1911."

"I didn't say it was."

Raife Hastings had been carrying the family heirloom for as long as Reece could remember. The pistol began its life as a commercial Colt 1911 .45 that made its way to Great Britain in the early 1940s under the Lend-Lease Act. Raife's grandfather was issued the sidearm when he joined B Squadron of the Long Range Desert Group, an elite reconnaissance unit that operated behind the lines against German and Italian forces in North Africa during World War II. He was a leader in the Special Air Service after returning to Rhodesia at the end of the war, and his handgun went with him. Raife's father, Jonathan Robin Hastings, had followed family custom, passing SAS selection in England. When Southern Rhodesia split from Great Britain to become its own, rogue nation, Jonathan stayed on with the now-independent SAS regiment and later helped found the famed Selous Scouts alongside Colonel Ronald Reid-Daly. The pistol was passed to Raife upon his graduation from BUD/S and he smuggled it downrange on each of his deployments to continue the tradition. It had served his family well and though he wouldn't admit it, he thought of it as a good-luck charm.

"Yes, I get it, Raife, but that's a *different* 1911."

What weapon a person carried and how they carried it told Reece a lot about them. Reece's eyes always went to the hands; the result of growing up with a father who served in the SEAL Teams in Vietnam and then transferred into the ranks of the Central Intelligence Agency. Right- or left-handed, concealed or open carry, appendix or 4–5 o'clock holster position, striker-fired polymer-frame pistol or cocked and locked 1911, Kydex or leather holster, type of knife clipped to pocket, shoes, pants, belt, hat, watch; *all of these things tell a story,* his father had said.

In Raife's case, he wore Courteney Selous boots, jeans, and a belt Reece knew was made from the hide of a Cape buffalo. A leather holster from Alessi sat just behind his right hip. Two inches taller than Reece's six feet, he radiated competence and strength and looked like he would feel right at home in the UFC's Octagon. His emerald-green eyes and tan face with a scar that ran from his left eye to his lip, camouflaged by three days of stubble, gave one the not-incorrect impression that Raife was a man of the land and someone not unfamiliar with violence.

Raife shook his head and looked to Katie, who was setting up a fly rod on the kitchen table.

"Since Reece is socially inept and is incapable of just saying 'hello,' I will tell *you*, Katie; I finally retired the old warhorse to the safe, at least until I can pass it along to my son." Raife's wife had given birth to a baby boy as Reece was emerging from the wilds of Siberia on a previous mission. "Your boyfriend keeps getting me into firefights, so instead of worrying about losing it, I had Jason Burton at Heirloom Precision build this for me."

"Well, you will be happy to know that one of my goals is to keep him, and you, out of additional firefights. I think I've had enough of those to last a lifetime," Katie said, remembering that her relationship with Reece had been interrupted on more than a few occasions by men with guns who wanted them dead.

"I have been doing quite well as of late, isn't that right, Katie? I haven't been shot at in at least two days."

Katie rolled her eyes.

"Let me check it out," Reece said, gesturing to his friend.

Raife drew the pistol, being sure to keep the muzzle in a safe direction. He removed the Wilson Combat magazine and placed it into his front pocket, pushed down on the thumb safety, and racked the slide to the rear, ejecting a .45-caliber round from the chamber before handing John Browning's iconic masterpiece to his blood brother.

Reece inspected the pistol and let out a long whistle. "This must have cost you hundreds," Reece said, knowing the pistol was essentially priceless, coming from one of the top 1911 gunsmiths in the world.

Now it was Raife's turn to roll his eyes.

"Nice," Reece said admiringly. "Jason Burton does incredible work. Pre-Series 70?"

"When did you become a 1911 expert?" Raife asked.

"Since you walked in here with this."

"Base gun is a 1969 Colt Pre-Series 70," Raife confirmed. "National Match–style slide with serrations which were most likely an overrun from a contract with the Army Marksmanship Unit."

"Can I try the trigger?"

"Be my guest."

Reece visually inspected the chamber and then rode the slide home out of respect for the masterpiece in his hands. He pointed it in a safe direction and pressed the trigger.

"Wow! Perfection," he said, locking the slide to the rear and taking a closer look at the impeccable work.

"That action is smooth. Did you pin the safety?"

"Of course."

"Short trigger, ivory grips, ambi-safety, Kart National Match barrel, flattened slide top with 'arrowhead' serrations, custom rear sight, gold-inlaid front sight, and maker's mark under the grip panel. Classic. The rear slide serrations stop at the top of the frame rails—that's a sweet touch."

Raife's eyes moved to Katie.

"Don't look at me. He might as well be speaking Greek."

"You know, I should get one of these. Good thing I have your dad's credit card."

Raife shook his head. "I don't know why he did that."

Reece could not help needling his friend. The only reason he had reluctantly accepted the card was so he could bring it up to get under Raife's thick skin.

"And I quote," Reece began as he handed the pistol back.

"Here he goes," Katie said. "See what you've started."

"*Thank you for saving my son's life. You are welcome to stay in the cabin as long as you would like.* That's when he handed me the credit card, which I of course readily accepted."

"He's going to regret that," Raife said, tucking a strand of shoulder-length dark blond hair behind a cauliflower ear.

"It's a distinct possibility. Right now, I'm using it to pay for physical therapy; my back's still a little sore from carrying you up that mountain in Russia."

"*Bloody hell*," Raife replied. A hint of Rhodesia still slipped into his voice, especially when he was annoyed. "It was more like a hill."

"Easy to say when you are passed out on my back for most of the climb."

"You two are something else," Katie said, getting to her feet. "Raife, can I get you something to drink? Beer? Wine? Beer might be easier to get to, as the wine is in the garage and is currently blocked in by about a hundred boxes of books James had shipped out from Virginia."

"Oh yeah," Reece interjected, "Jonathan also said that I could visit the wine cellar anytime I wish and that nothing was off-limits."

"Now I know you are lying."

"I might be paraphrasing a bit."

"A bit?"

"Katie, spare no expense for our friend," Reece shouted to Katie, who was going over the beer inventory in the kitchen refrigerator.

"He's incorrigible," Katie said to their guest.

"Katie, don't use big words like that around Raife. He's going to have to look them up later."

The truth was that Raife was one of the smartest and toughest people Reece had ever met. From a family that defined the word *rugged*, the blood of Africa still flowed through his veins. In what was then Rhodesia, you didn't call a plumber if a water pipe broke or an electrician if you lost power or a mechanic if your truck wouldn't start. You fixed it yourself. If your home was attacked you didn't call the police, you defended your land and your family. Then you dug a hole and buried the bodies. You were self-reliant as a practical necessity. Your very survival, and the survival of your family, depended on it.

"I'll take a beer," Raife said.

"IPA? Cloudcroft?" Katie asked, looking in the fridge.

"That'll do."

"James?"

"Sounds great."

Katie grabbed three beers from the fridge, handing two off before opening one for herself.

"Cheers, boys. Raife, can you stay for dinner?" she asked, walking to the kitchen to start prepping.

"I'm going to need to get back. Just wanted to say a quick hello."

"I believe Raife has diaper duty tonight. How's the leg feeling today?" Reece asked with genuine concern. Just as Raife had helped Reece get back into fighting shape after his brain surgery, Reece had been hitting the trails with his friend, slowly upping the mileage and moving to progressively more difficult terrain as Raife's leg continued its rehabilitation. The break from a fall on Medny Island, Russia, that almost killed him had taken its toll.

"Feels good, brother. It's almost there."

"Great, because tomorrow's run will be one to remember."

"Aren't you guys worried about overtraining?" Katie asked from the kitchen.

"I'm not familiar with the term," Reece quipped.

"I don't know why I even try," Katie muttered to herself.

"So," Raife said, taking a seat. "Where is that Cabot?"

"That ol' thing? I think it's around here somewhere."

That *ol' thing* was relatively new. Reece had accompanied Raife and Jonathan down to Helena for the Montana Outfitter and Guides Association banquet to support Big Hearts Under the Big Sky, a program focused on children with life-threatening illnesses and military members who have provided extraordinary service to the country. An Apocalypse 1911, kindly donated by Rob Bianchin of Cabot Guns in Pennsylvania, went up for auction. Two cattle ranchers went head-to-head in a bidding war. The crusty old rancher who won promptly marched over to Reece and presented it to him. Apparently, after five or six too many Neversweat bourbons, Raife's father had confirmed a rumor or two. Reece tried to turn it down, but the old rancher would hear none of it. He finally turned to the elder Hastings and proclaimed: *Jonathan, I am sending this to you. Make sure the boy gets it. Now, I'll not hear another word about it.*

"Let's give them a run before we get too far into these beers, eh?" Raife said.

"Were you guys always this competitive?" Katie asked. "Never mind, rhetorical question."

"Why don't I just run my carry?" Reece asked.

"Still using that XL?" Raife asked, referring to the SIG Sauer P365 XL that Reece had taken a liking to over the past couple of years.

"Yep, I love this thing," Reece said, tapping the BlackPoint Tactical Mini WING holster on his belt. "Icarus Precision grip module, Parker Mountain Machine threaded barrel and comp, Trijicon RMRcc red dot."

"Did you go with the 3.25 or 6.5 MOA dot?"

Reece eyed his friend quizzically.

"Since when do you know anything about pistol red dots?"

Raife smiled and shrugged. "Think you remember how to use iron sights?" he asked.

"It's possible. Let me see if I can find that Cabot. I know it's around here somewhere."

Reece, of course, knew exactly where it was. Following their early morning trail runs, functional fitness routines, and shooting drills, Reece would bid his friend farewell and then put in another shooting session later in the day when Raife was in town, this time with the Cabot Apocalypse. Reece was starting to suspect that Raife might be doing something similar with red dot optics.

"Look at that, I found her," Reece said, returning from the bedroom. "Where is the safety on these things?"

"For Christ's sake. Let's do it. What course of fire?"

"Shooter's choice," Reece responded. "What are we shooting for?"

"I'd say pink slips, but your new ride leaves something to be desired,"

Raife said, referring to the 1985 Jeep Wagoneer that Reece had driven to Montana and that had limped its way into the barn off the driveway.

"You just don't appreciate the golden age of SUVs."

"You do know that ICON Land Cruiser you managed to destroy cost more than most people's homes, right?"

"That's the best part about it having been a gift," Reece countered, getting to his feet and heading for the door.

Raife shook his head.

Katie forced a smile, remembering being trapped in her seat belt in the overturned vehicle, the blood running from her nose and mouth, Iranian assassins converging on the truck, the pistol thrust through the broken window in front of her face, Reece unconscious next to her. She turned her attention to the Bravo Company carbine in the corner of the room next to Reece's LBT plate carrier, remembering something Reece's CIA buddy "Ox" had told her as he put them through a team tactics course in Virginia: *The pistol is just to fight your way to the rifle. Then get to work.* The rifle's magazine was loaded with Black Hills 77-grain cartridges. The rail held an Aimpoint Micro with magnifier, SureFire Scout light, Viking Tactics sling, and an ATPIAL infrared laser aiming device. Katie had an identical setup in the bedroom. *Just in case,* Reece liked to say.

"How about this: Whoever loses hosts the next wild game dinner," Raife said.

"The next *three,*" Reece countered.

"The next three," Raife agreed.

"I also would have pushed for pink slips, but I want a vehicle that works," Reece said, alluding to Raife's Defender 110. "Where is she anyway? In the shop?"

Raife looked back at Katie for help but she just shrugged.

"Keep me out of this. My 4Runner does just fine."

"What's that?" Reece asked, stopping dead in his tracks on the front deck that overlooked the gravel driveway. "I thought Land Rover stopped making the old-school Defenders. Did they feel bad and want to put mechanics back to work?"

"It's an INEOS Grenadier."

"A what?"

"Some bloke in England wanted to build a truck that kept the look of the old Defenders but . . ."

"But actually worked?"

"*But* that were built to modern standards," Raife corrected. "This is the first one in the States. My dad somehow got his hands on it."

"I changed my mind. Let's shoot for pink sli—"

The radio on the desk just inside the door interrupted them.

"Reece, Kumba Base, over. Boys, pick up."

The tone in Jonathan's voice indicated this was more than a simple check-in.

Reece moved to the radio, picked up the mic, and hit Transmit.

"Kumba, go for Reece. I'm here with Raife and Katie."

"Turn on the telly, boys. Aircraft shot down back home."

"We'll check it out."

"It's on the BBC now," Jonathan added.

"Roger. Katie, can you . . ."

Katie was already on it.

"*. . . 128 people are confirmed dead in Africa's worst terrorist incident in recent memory. Early reports indicate that multiple missiles were launched from a nearby field. Jama'at Nasr al-Islam wal Muslimin claimed responsibility for the attack in a statement saying the offensive will continue until French military forces and their civilian enablers have been pushed from West Africa: 'French civilians are complicit in the massacres of our people and only when the last French citizen leaves Burkina Faso and Mali will our territory truly be liberated from French colonial oppression.' In October of 2020, French special operations forces killed fifty militants in northern*

Mali, including several key leaders of the JNIM organization. It is unclear at this time if this most recent terrorist attack is a direct retaliation for that engagement."

"Bloody tragic," Raife said.

Reece looked to his friend and back to the BBC report.

"It's someone else's war, Reece," his blood brother said, reading his friend's mind.

Reece took a breath.

"Okay, let's train," he said. "Katie, we'll be back in a few."

They left the cabin and walked to the range Reece had set up just behind a barn that served as his functional fitness Sorinex gym, mixed martial arts training facility, and weapons cleaning area, but his mind was no longer on 1911s, courses of fire, or wild game dinners. It was on a plane, half a world away.

• • •

When they returned, Katie was preparing the grill.

"Raife, sure you can't stay? Smoked trout."

"I'm guessing you caught those. I've seen this guy attempt to fly-fish," he responded, gesturing to Reece. "As much as I would love it, I'll be getting home."

"Next time," Katie said.

"Any word on getting your own show?"

"I've been guest-hosting quite a bit so we will see."

Investigative journalist Katie Buranek had burst into the media spotlight with a series of articles she had written exposing the lies surrounding the 2012 Benghazi fiasco. Her follow-on book, aptly titled *The Benghazi Betrayal*, uncovered the truth behind the attack in which the United States ambassador to Libya and a Foreign Service officer were killed. A small group of dedicated CIA contractors fought for their lives that day, abandoned by the elected and appointed officials in Washington, D.C. Reece had known the two SEALs killed during the thirteen-hour gun fight and was aware of Katie's reporting before she introduced herself on Bagram Air Base in Afghanistan after the ambush that killed Reece's SEAL Troop and changed the course of his life. Katie was thrust back into the headlines when she became part of the story involving the testing of drugs on the nation's most elite special operators. Her reporting on the conspiracy to cover up the effects of those experiments led to the resignation of a president. Katie was a thorn in the side of the political establishment and legacy media corporations more concerned with promoting an agenda than seeking truth, regardless of where it might lead. That made her dangerous.

"They'd give you your own show if they knew what was good for them."

"Thank you, Raife."

"Can I interest you in another beer?" Reece offered.

"I'll take one to go. Annika is feeling a little tired of late so I'm going to do my duty."

"Understood. Cheers, my friend," Reece said.

Raife's home was just a few miles away, higher up on the mountain and nestled back in the trees. Jonathan and Caroline Hastings wanted to create a place where their kids would want to return with their grandchildren. It had worked for the most part. Raife was home running the outfitting side of the business, building custom rifles, and caring for his young family. Victoria was in Connecticut and working in finance but a separate home for her and her family awaited anytime they returned for a visit. His youngest sibling, Hana, the wild child, had been abducted in Romania and then hunted for sport on an island off Kamchatka, Russia, by a man Reece had ultimately killed. She had launched herself off a cliff, taking her own life rather than allow Aleksandr Zharkov the satisfaction of the kill. Reece had shot the Russian intelligence officer twice through the chest with a recurve bow just as the monster was about to take Raife to the grave. Caroline and Jonathan were bound to Reece in ways just as strong, if not stronger, than blood.

"Glad you have that Grenadier," Reece called after his former Teammate.

"Why's that?"

"It means I can enjoy my evening with Katie and not have to tow you home in the Defender."

Raife reached in his pocket as if he were searching for his keys and came out with his middle finger extended.

"You deserve it," Katie said, smiling at Reece. "Please give Annika our best. Let's get together for dinner tomorrow. I assume, because you shot 1911s, that we are hosting."

"You assume correctly," Raife confirmed.

"I just couldn't bear the thought of us having to suffer through one of Raife's meals," Reece said. "Bring everyone down. Let's do a mullie leg, Marin County–style on the Burch Barrel: rosemary mop, Flip Flop sauce, salt, pepper, Jonathan's finest Cab."

"We'll be here. Let's shoot with my dad before dinner. You have twenty-four hours to work on your skills."

"Deal, loser has to—"

"Reece," Raife interrupted, suddenly serious again.

Katie had left the TV on as she prepared dinner. It was turned to Fox News, where she continued to work as a contributor remotely from a studio in Whitefish.

Reece turned his head and then joined his friend behind the couch.

The network was running the names and photos of the victims.

"Katie, does this rewind?" Raife asked.

"Yes," she said, walking over and handing Raife the remote.

Raife pointed it at the screen, the images now playing in reverse.

Katie looked at Reece. She had seen him like this before. He stared at the screen as if nothing else mattered. Gone was the jovial man of mere moments ago. In his place stood someone who was all business and radiated death.

Raife paused on an image. The name Mélanie Cotillard was displayed under the photo of a woman in her late thirties or early forties. Dark hair. Olive skin. She was dressed in business attire and the photo appeared to be from a professional online bio.

"Is it her?" Raife asked.

Reece continued to stare at the screen. Eyes narrow and focused.

"Reece?" Katie asked, concern creeping into her voice.

Raife turned.

"Reece."

But Reece wasn't in Montana. He was in an ambush in Baghdad. Bullets skipping off the street in front of him, a man to his left going down, the turret gunner from his vehicle taking a round to the throat, Reece returning fire at the muzzle flashes that lit up tubes of his night vision, scrambling into the vehicle to get behind the .50 caliber machine gun.

"Reece," Raife said more firmly.

Reece was in the Combat Support Hospital in the Green Zone, covered in blood, sweat, dirt and grime, rifle still at his side, waiting for word from the trauma surgeons. The door opening. A dark-haired woman in civilian clothes moving toward him.

"*Reece,*" Raife said again.

"It's her," Reece confirmed, not taking his eyes from the screen.

"Who? What's going on?" Katie asked. "Mélanie Cotillard? French citizen?"

Raife looked at Katie and then at Reece.

"Are you sure?" he asked.

"I'm sure. But her name is not Mélanie Cotillard and she is not a French citizen."

Katie wanted to press but restrained herself, knowing Reece was thinking something through.

"Her name is Aliya Galin. She's an assassin."

"*What?*" Katie said.

"I'm sorry, Katie. I need to get back to Langley."

CHAPTER 2

SVR Headquarters, Yasenevo District, Moscow, Russia

IT WAS RUMORED IN certain circles that the president of Russia was the richest man in the world. For the former KGB officer, his money meant power. When analysts at the CIA ventured that he was the most powerful individual on the planet, they were not far off.

As director of the SVR, Russia's Foreign Intelligence Service, Mikhail Gromyko kept a close eye on reporting related to the financial history and status of his direct superior, the president. That his name was nowhere to be found on the Forbes World's Billionaires List only added to the mystery and the myth. Gromyko scoffed when he saw reports of a Western leader's son selling "art" for inflated prices to people hoping to influence the U.S. president. Stooping to such levels was embarrassing. Years ago, Gromyko would have instructed his service to ensure the buyer was a Russian asset. Today that wasn't necessary. There were other ways to exert influence.

The Americans still adhered to a set of rules. There was accountability, not for those who lost their wars, but built into the system in general, though it was getting harder to tell the difference between the U.S. system and that of the former Soviet Union. Had Stalin, Khrushchev, and Brezhnev known what the Americans would do to themselves of their own accord in the first two decades of the twenty-first century, they would have played their cards differently during the Cold War. The irony was not lost on Gromyko that the Americans had won the Cold War just to slip closer and closer to a state that was not dissimilar to that of their old Soviet adversary.

What made a country? Borders, language, and culture. The Americans were doing away with all three. It would lead to their downfall, which made it all the more important to deal with James Reece.

Communism or capitalism: Both were about control. He hadn't always believed that. He was old enough to remember studying the American opposition, sometimes envious of the freedoms enshrined in their constitution. In the USSR of his youth, with few exceptions, you had to be born to that freedom. He was one of the lucky ones. He remembered the American-style cities the KGB had built for their trainees. Gromyko had been taught how to order a drink, pump gas, buy a burger, and light a cigarette. *American cigarettes.* Back then that training had been necessary. The simulated American cities the Academy of Foreign Intelligence had built in the 1960s and used through the 1980s still existed, though today they were life-sized intelligence museums, monuments of a bygone era. Gromyko would visit the sites from time to time when he needed to think. He would light a Marlboro the way he had been taught by his instructors and walk the now-deserted grounds, remembering the past to apply its lessons to the future.

The West believed they had won. It was that belief that allowed them to let down their guard, focus inward, find the wrongs in their society, and exploit and even exacerbate them for political gain. It was a myopic strategy. He had expected more of his Cold War rival. That they did not study or learn from their history did not bode well for their future. *The death of the West.* The USSR hadn't needed ballistic missile submarines or a nuclear arsenal larger than the United States'. All they had needed to defeat the Americans was patience.

Director Gromyko was a student of history. It had always been about the ruling class and those who served them. The Americans had just forgotten. In the early nineties, the director of the SVR thought he would not see the decline of the United States in his lifetime. Now he wasn't so sure. The cancer that sapped his strength was slow moving, possibly even survivable if he kept up his treatments—treatments that had to be kept secret: Any sign of weakness would diminish his power. At his age it might even be the type of cancer one died *with* rather than *from*. The Americans were also facing a cancer, one that was spreading faster than the tumor in his small intestine.

He had almost laughed when they told him. The doctor had been nervous. In Russia, when you diagnose the director of the SVR with a potentially fatal cancer, you possess knowledge that could be more deadly than the disease in your patient. Gromyko had always thought it would be lung cancer—his beloved Marlboros—taking him to the grave, courtesy of the Americans.

Not even his counterpart in the FSB, the Russian Federal Security Service, knew about his condition, and that was how Gromyko wanted to keep it. Pavel Dashkov as director of the FSB and responsible for internal state security matters, would see it as his job to know the health status of his counterpart in the SVR. They were both members of the Russian Security Council and appointed by the same Russian president. All three had trained at the Academy of Foreign Intelligence back when it went by a different name. The true power of the Russian state rested not in the council but in the three of them: the president and his two intelligence directors.

They had been relatively young operatives when President Ronald Reagan took the stage at Moscow State University in May 1988. Gromyko had been in the audience. He had listened to the speech and noted the reactions of the students. He had seen the writing on the wall, but his focus had been elsewhere. The KGB had a mission in those days, and though the name of the country and the intelligence service charged with protecting it had changed, the mission had not.

The network of spies so carefully infiltrated into American society and curated over the years remained in place. As the KGB became the SVR and FSB, America turned its attention inward, distracted with troubles of its own making. When President George H. W. Bush called it a "New World Order," he was right. That New World Order was one where money and data equaled power. Which military had the superior tank or plane was of little importance, as the Americans had discovered on their misadventures in Iraq and Afghanistan. The future was in data collection and its manipulation. But it was not only intelligence and information that determined the destiny of nations, it was the courage to act on it. The Americans had grown weak. Divide and conquer. Fake news, misinformation, social media, troll farms—all were weapons in the new war, but Gromyko had not forgotten that the future could also be altered by putting a bullet where it needed to go at precisely the right moment in history. The Russian president he served was not afraid to act.

The Americans had almost destroyed themselves with their COVID mandates; failed wars in a part of the world they would never understand; race riots; political upheaval; and a border policy of which Gromyko's predecessors could only have dreamed. Russia would see the United States fall. They only had to nudge it along. Shadow governments, deep-state conspiracies, and political and social division were all perpetuated and encouraged by algorithms and "web brigades" of bots and trolls with global reach. Russian "hackers" had free rein to take advantage of the platforms created by American tech companies. Russia was using Americas' own inventions to alter its destiny.

It was almost too easy. *Fools.* The people had the power, but they could not be trusted with it. That was the lesson. The American experiment had failed. Russia would be the beneficiary.

If only the conspiracy theorists knew how close some of their ideas were to reality. Russian bots were hard at work to further marginalize and discredit anyone who inadvertently stumbled upon the truth. Globalization made it possible. The American oligarchy in Silicon Valley and Seattle were killing the very country that had given them the ability to accumulate wealth greater than most of the world's GDP. Some were on the payroll, but that number was limited. It was easier to let it play out naturally with just a nudge from those they controlled. It wasn't difficult. Many didn't even know who pulled their strings. America's affluence had ushered in a weakness that Russia could exploit; when a country became soft, it was not long for this earth.

However, there was the crucial issue of the letter. And the question of James Reece. The SVR had not known of the storage area rented by his father or else they would have burned it to the ground years ago after they had gotten rid of Thomas Reece, the CIA officer who had gotten too close. Had it been a few years later they would have used technical tools to marginalize him. Tom Reece had become an issue before using technology to solve problems became a possibility, which meant he needed to be eliminated. There were so many additional tools available now that had not been an option in the early years of the twenty-first century, when the SVR still bought or blackmailed journalists or politicians and their spouses and, on occasion, eliminated problems permanently.

The greatest irony of all was that none of it may have been necessary. The Americans would soon defeat themselves of their own accord.

But the son, James Reece. The son was proving to be a different matter. Did he know about the letter, the list?

The old Gromyko would have proposed capturing and torturing Reece for information, but that approach presented a host of problems. He had to remind himself that this wasn't the old days. The best solution was to remove him from the battlefield altogether but in a way that wouldn't lead to a new round of questions from Reece's minders at the CIA. Gromyko had devised a plan to draw the SEAL commander out of the United States and kill him. Tie it to his past. Wrap it up in a nice package and be done with the Reece family forever.

The American president was a problem as well. Gromyko's intelligence service had not anticipated his presidency, something that had diminished his political capital on the Security Council. But that could wait. The more pressing issue was James Reece. Did he have the key to the safe-deposit box, and did he know where it was?

Gromyko had not discussed it with his peers on the council, rather, the James Reece situation had warranted a closed-door session with the Russian president and FSB director Dashkov. The three of them had put a plan in motion.

James Reece would die as his father had. In the line of duty. And as with his father, Reece's only remembrance would be on a wall at CIA headquarters, memorialized with a star.

CHAPTER 3

Kumba Ranch, Flathead Valley, Montana

REECE OBSERVED THE TRAIL of dust as the faded, mustard-colored, seventies-era FJ40 Land Cruiser descended toward the cabin. He stood on the front porch to welcome his guest, the matriarch, and quite possibly the toughest member of the Hastings clan, Raife's mom, Caroline. She stepped from the vehicle, a wide-brim Resistol felt hat with a grosgrain band and feather shading her face. A red bandana protected her neck from the sun. Now in her mid-sixties, she appreciated her mother insisting she take those precautions under the African sun, habits Caroline had passed along to her daughters.

She paused at the door for a moment before saying, "Free."

An eighty-pound Rhodesian ridgeback leapt from the passenger seat, shook its wheaten coat, and looked up at Caroline. Jonathan's dog had taken a liking to his wife in recent years and only reluctantly left her side.

The dog nuzzled her leg and she bent down to scratch the back of his neck before saying "free" again and motioning with her hand to indicate the dog should explore. Instead, he looked to Reece and sprinted up the steps to the cabin in search of more affection, which he got as Reece took a knee and greeted the strong canine originally bred for hunting lions in the African bush.

"Hi, Zulu, good boy," Reece said.

Caroline stopped at the base of the steps. She could pass for someone ten years her junior. Tending her garden and greenhouse, riding her horses, and helping with the mountain cattle operation kept her in top shape.

"Best be careful, or you and Katie might have a stowaway on your ride east," Caroline said, the ties to old Rhodesia still strong in her voice.

"I'm not worried," Reece said, continuing to rub the dog behind its ears. "Trust me, Zulu here wants nothing to do with D.C. How's the Land Cruiser running?"

"Better than Raife's Defender."

They shared a laugh.

"I think part of the fun of it is all the time Raife and Jonathan got to spend working on those old Land Rovers together. If they had Cruisers, Raife wouldn't have learned to fix engines. I think he also learned to swear handing Jonathan tools as a toddler."

"It's good to see you, Caroline."

He stood and opened the front door.

"It's a bit of a mess. Packing and all."

The sliding glass doors that led to the back deck overlooking the lake were open, allowing a breeze to cool the inside of the cabin.

"Katie is up with Annika," Reece said.

"I know. I wanted to speak with you privately."

"Can I offer you anything? Beer, wine, water?" he asked, moving toward the kitchen.

"I'll have a water, thank you."

"Ice?"

"Please."

Caroline took a seat at the kitchen table while Reece filled two glasses.

"Thank you for coming by. We are going to miss it here."

"How long will you be gone?"

"I'm not sure."

"Jonathan won't ask you directly, but he thinks this has something to do with the plane shot down back home."

Both Caroline and Jonathan still referred to Africa as "back home."

"It does. I knew someone on board. I need to look into it."

"I see," Caroline said.

She took a sip of water, the large dog curled up at her feet.

"He never talks about it, but did you ever hear about how Jonathan's sister died?"

"I did, but not from Jonathan or Raife."

"Did Rich tell you?" Caroline asked, referring to Jonathan's brother, who still ran a hunting concession in Mozambique. Reece had sailed across the Atlantic and found refuge with Richard Hastings on the Niassa Game Reserve before Freddy Strain had tracked him down and recruited him for a job at the behest of the Central Intelligence Agency.

"No, it was one of the PHs," Reece said, using the shorthand for "professional hunter."

"I see," Caroline said. "What did they tell you?"

"Not much," Reece said. "Flight attendant. Air Rhodesia. Flight 825. They made sure to bring it up when Rich wasn't around."

"Yes. These Hastings men." Caroline smiled. "She was marvelous. Eileen. Full of life. Beautiful. We made quite the pair. She used to wear this tight white T-shirt with a plane on it, a Vickers Viscount, if memory serves. Do you know what it said?"

Reece shook his head.

"It said, 'we carry the goods' right across her chest. No bra." Caroline laughed at the memory. "It was the seventies after all. We'd go to 'Ladies Night' at Le Matelot in Salisbury together on Wednesdays. Those were good times, Reece. For a few hours we could let our hair down and forget about what was happening to our country."

She paused.

"I remember when we received word that we'd lost a plane. I knew in my heart she was gone."

"I'm so sorry," Reece said softly.

"Sunday evening, September third, 1978. I remember it so vividly. We called them 'air hostesses' then. She loved her job. Loved being independent. To this day I don't know if she survived the initial crash. I've never asked Jonathan. He knows. He was at the crash site the following day. He identified her body."

Caroline reached up to wipe away a tear.

"It still gets to me after all these years."

"Caroline, you don't have to—"

"No, I want you to hear this. ZIPRA, the *terrs*, shot down a civilian plane. It was flying its normal route between Victoria Falls and Salisbury. They hit it with a missile. Fifty-six people were on board, including Eileen. We don't know how many burned to death in flight as the plane attempted an emergency landing or how many burned to death on the ground. We do know that eighteen people survived the crash."

Reece swallowed.

"We know because what the world recognized as a 'people's revolutionary army' took the survivors, women, children, and babies, and bayonetted them. Slaughtered them. Imagine seeing your baby bayoneted in front of you. Some were bludgeoned to death with clubs. A few were shot. Innocents. Their leader went on the BBC the next day. Do you know what he did when he claimed responsibility for the attack? He laughed. The *bloody bastard* laughed, and the international community did nothing. Not one country condemned the attack."

She took another sip of water and returned her glass to the table.

"I tell you all this for a reason, Reece, because of what Jonathan and Rich did next."

"What did they do?" Reece asked, though he suspected he already knew, because it's what he would have done, what he *did* when his family was taken.

"They went hunting. The Scouts, SAS, RLI, they targeted and killed for months. The ZIPRA *terrs* responsible fled into Zambia and Moz. Some of what the Scouts did is public knowledge; some is not and will go to the grave with those who remember. We, the women and children, were left alone to defend the farms. They called us 'farming widows.' Our wounded would come home and relay messages, but news was harder to come by then. The land mines took a lot of the boys. Mines from the war are still out there today, killing and maiming."

Reece thought of the mines in Afghanistan, and the lives on both sides forever altered because of them.

Caroline cleared her throat.

"Attacks on the farms became an almost daily occurrence. We knew how to fight and we helped one another. We had radios to talk with neighbors, the police, the army. We all built bunkers; stocked them with rum, Coke, ammunition, food, playing cards, poker chips." She laughed at the memory. "We drank a lot of rum and Coke in those days. I had a Beretta shotgun, an Uzi, and a Brno in .375 H&H. If a nearby farm was attacked, we would get word on the radios and go help. During the day we trained with the local police and the army, took care of the crops and horses, kept the books up to date. At night, that's when the attacks would come."

She paused and took a sip of water.

"Were you scared?"

"At first, but then it became normal."

Reece understood.

"Everyone was dealing with it together," Caroline continued. "Like you and your SEAL Team; the families, your circle, you are all training and deploying in wartime. It's just normal. That's how it was for us. This may sound strange, Reece, but those were the best times of my life."

Reece thought back to the cycles of training and deployments; the operators staging in Iraq and Afghanistan solely focused on building target packages, exploiting intelligence, and planning missions to capture and kill the enemy—the spouses were left behind to deal with everything else.

"I remember a neighbor who couldn't get to her radio in time. Sometimes the *terrs* could be extremely quiet. She was hard of hearing so might not have heard the dogs. She was gang raped before they bayoneted her to death. She was seventy-eight years old. They hung her from a beautiful Mukwa tree in her front yard. Then they burned her home to the ground. I saw the flames."

Reece shook his head.

"I locked the kids in the bunker and rode my horse to her property. I didn't take a truck as I was worried about the lights alerting the *terrs*."

Reece nodded in understanding.

"I was the first of the neighbors to arrive. I found her hanging in the tree. Naked. Beaten. Bloody."

She paused again and brought herself back from the memory.

"I tell you this because when Jonathan returned, he was a different man. Maybe I was a different woman. I think what it took to defend the farm was different than what it took to go on offense and take the fight to the *terrs* in the bush. It took a long time to get him back. We eventually left the farm and moved to South Africa, but even that was too close. I suspect he was biding his time."

"For what?" Reece asked.

"Some things are best kept private, Reece. I've never spoken of this before, not even to Raife. I'll never speak of it again. I expect this to stay between us."

"It will," Reece said.

"He was planning to kill the man who had laughed on BBC. It took coming to the United States for him to do what you will need to do as well."

"And what is that?"

"Forgive."

Reece remembered his murdered wife, Lauren, her hair in a ponytail through the back of one of his old platoon hats, Lucy holding her hand as they walked toward their favorite park in Coronado.

"Seems so long ago but at the same time it feels like yesterday," she said. "We thought we had left the violence behind when we came here but society is a fragile thing, Reece. We get accustomed to relative peace and prosperity, even affluence. It can be gone in a heartbeat." Caroline snapped her fingers to illustrate her point, startling Zulu at her feet. "I now know the pain my parents felt in Old Africa watching everything they'd built taken from them and destroyed. I have not forgotten that pain, or the more recent agony of losing my daughter and almost my son."

She paused.

"I lost Jonathan for so many years. I don't want to lose you, too. And, let me tell you, neither does Katie."

"I know," Reece whispered.

"And by lose, I don't mean death," she continued.

"What do you mean?"

"I saw the war tear families apart: my parents, our land, our family farm. It almost killed Jonathan. I was bitter for a long time. So was he. It was the *hate*. I thought it gave me drive, gave me purpose, but it didn't. What it really did was burn and destroy."

"I'm not sure I follow."

"You have faced loss that most will never fathom. I am not your mother, but I feel for you as though I am. I asked myself, if you were blood what would I do? I'd tell you what I'm telling you now. The hate that's driven you this far, it won't be enough for what's next. It won't be enough to drive you in the next chapter of your life. You will need more."

Reece looked into his glass.

"Only you will know when it's right, but let me tell you, when you feel it, trust it, don't keep pushing. Come back to us. Come back to Katie. Not just physically, that's the easy part, but here," Caroline said, touching her hand to her heart. "When you are ready, open your heart. Open your soul."

Reece understood.

"There is power in forgiveness, Reece."

Reece thought of his pregnant wife and daughter. He thought of his SEAL Troop ambushed on a mountain in the Hindu Kush. He thought of Freddy cut down on a rooftop in Odessa by a sniper's bullet and he thought of his promise to Freddy's wife.

"There is something I still need to do. I made a promise," Reece said.

"Well, when you have kept it, when whatever you need to do is done, we will be here. Now, I want you to promise *me* something."

"Yes?"

"When you come back—*truly* come back."

Reece looked at the woman before him. She had known loss, she had fought and killed on two continents, and she had prevailed.

He swallowed.

"I promise."

"Good," Caroline said, rising to her feet. "Then it's settled. We will see you for dinner at six. *Zulu, come.*"

Reece escorted her to her vehicle and shut the door, watching the old 4x4 work its way back up the road until it disappeared over the rise.

He stood there staring as the dust rose and swirled, eventually vanishing in the late afternoon air. He reached into his pocket, his hand finding a safe-deposit box key left to him by his father along with a cryptic note that offered no clues as to the location of the lock it would turn. He thought of Katie and of what Caroline had said, and Reece wondered if he had just made a promise he was incapable of keeping.

CHAPTER 4

Green Zone, Baghdad, Iraq
2008

HAD REECE NOT BEEN married, had Aliya not been married, things might have been different. Both of them knew it and took active steps to keep their relationship professional, steps that only deepened the attraction. Officially Aliya was an analyst for the Central Intelligence Agency. In reality she was a targeting liaison detailed to the CIA from the Mossad. Her mission was to focus on potential threats to Israel from Iraqi insurgent groups supported by Iran.

Reece had been assigned to an action arm of the CIA from the SEAL Teams. In essence, they were both outsiders in a war zone attached to an intelligence agency in the midst of transition. The CIA was moving from a strategic intelligence-gathering organization to a tactical intelligence-gathering and execution organization. Unlike during the Cold War and the decade that followed, their job had become to find, fix, and finish individual targets in Iraq. Reece and his CIA covert action unit were the finish side of that equation. While Aliya helped analyze intelligence and build target packages within an agency known for compartmentalizing secrets, Reece would plan the missions to capture or kill those targeted individuals, turning all captured insurgents over to the Iraqis for questioning. This perpetuated a never-ending cycle of find, fix, finish, exploit, and analyze. Did any of their prisoners or targets have a connection to Israel? Were jihadi networks taking active steps to try to draw Israel into the war? Finding the answers to those questions was Aliya's job.

Maybe she had been lonely. Maybe she just needed someone to know. That someone had to be an outsider as well. That someone was James Reece.

She hadn't meant to tell him. Or, maybe she had. The war was at its height, and tensions and passions ran high: the op tempo, the rocket attacks, the IEDs, the growing insurgency, the increasing Iranian influence.

Reece was different from most of the operators she had known. On a rare night off, they had met for drinks at the CIA's appropriately named HVT Bar, for "High Value Target," on the Agency compound in the Green Zone. It was a refuge for those who had access, as general order number one forbade alcohol consumption for active-duty military personnel. The Agency was a different story. Like any bureaucracy, it was the relationships that mattered when trying to accomplish the mission, and the HVT Bar had its role to play.

Aliya was young then and not yet accustomed to lying, especially to those she was sending into harm's way through her job as a targeter. Every time Reece's unit left the wire and sped toward a target, she stayed glued to the screen of the Agency's Tactical Operations Center, monitoring the radio and watching the ISR feed—Intelligence, Surveillance, Reconnaissance—that came from an experimental Agency aircraft. She would hold her breath as she heard the communications come over the net: touchdown, dry hole, or her most feared—troops in contact.

She would meet the team as they returned, taking the SSE—Sensitive Site Exploitation—from the target, combing through it with her analysts for actionable intelligence. Data from cell phones, computers, and thumb drives, along with pocket litter, books, and notepads, were translated, studied, and connected to previously gathered intelligence to use against the captured prisoners and to develop follow-on targets the same night.

No one even realized how exhausted they were. Everyone was working. Everyone was giving it their all. That level of op tempo lowered inhibitions. When you didn't know if the next rocket or IED had your name on it, you were truly alive and you lived for the moment. Which is why, one rare night off, as the HVT Bar filled with patrons outside the reach of general order number one, Aliya and Reece found themselves at a dark corner table. Fueled by alcohol, lack of sleep, high stress, and the constant exhaustion that came with being part of a team where errors meant death, her questions for Reece flowed around his feelings about being away from his SEAL Team. Even at the bar, where most people let their guard down, Reece's eyes continued to search, never looking into Aliya's for too long. Was it because of his wife? Or was he always on guard? Perhaps both?

Aliya knew Reece carried his SIG P226 constantly even though Agency regulations forbade it in the bar. She could see its print against the black polo shirt he wore in an effort to fit in with Agency culture.

"Aren't you worried the chief of station might notice that you carry that pistol everywhere?"

"No. I think people here assume I'm under a different set of rules. Suits me just fine. Same thing when I have to go liaise with the Army to deconflict battle space. Being in civvies, having longer hair, and not shaving—they just assume it's allowed. I can tell some of the majors in particular don't like it." Reece laughed and took a sip of his beer. "They have no idea I'm just an LTJG. Works, though. We're getting the job done."

"What's an LTJG?"

"Lieutenant—*junior grade*," Reece said, emphasizing the *junior grade* for effect.

"Navy ranks are odd, especially the enlisted ones," Aliya noted.

"I agree. I can hardly keep the enlisted ranks straight and I used to be one," Reece said, smiling.

Aliya took a sip of her beer before continuing.

"What's it like to constantly feel like an outsider?"

Reece looked at her quizzically.

"What do you mean?"

"You know. You're a SEAL and the only military guy attached here. Does that feel weird?"

"Never really even thought about it like that," Reece replied. "Just feels like a Team. Besides, a lot of the green-badgers are former Delta guys, Marines, or SEALs. The special operations community is like a sewing circle when it comes to gossip." Reece smiled. "We check up on each other. They asked around about me. Guess whatever they learned came back giving me the thumbs-up."

"Ha! I thought you guys were supposed to be the *silent professionals*."

"Well, I think it's quiet, not silent."

"Touché."

"And you?" Reece asked.

"And me what?"

"Do you feel like an outsider?"

Aliya tensed.

"How so?" she asked.

"I mean, like I said, we check up on one another. We have liaisons all over the inner government agency these days. It's one of the by-products of the 9/11 Commission Report and the natural progression of things as we dive further into this war."

"Why do you say it like that?" Aliya asked.

"Like what?"

"The way you did."

"Well, these targets, a lot of them are insurgents we created and radicalized through our mistakes. Yeah, we are good at the targeting and you are exceptional at it, but it perpetuates itself. Saw the same thing in Afghanistan."

Aliya measured him. This was definitely not your normal operator.

"But hey, I'm just a cog in the machine. Just wish our leadership would put some time into understanding the problem, understanding the nature of the conflict, before throwing U.S. lives at it." Reece took a sip of the blond ale.

"Then why do you keep doing it?" she asked.

"Why do you?"

Does he know?

"It's my job."

"Is it?" Reece asked.

"What do you mean?"

"I mean I checked on everyone I'm working with. My contact back at Langley had never heard of you. You appeared on the Agency roster for this rotation about the same time I did."

Aliya was caught off guard. Her presence was meant to be a secret from the new Iraqi government, specifically those in the Ministry of Interior, a government entity most closely associated with internal state security. Apparently her superiors had not thought about how much it would take to keep her true mission a secret from prying SEALs.

"Seems like we are both outsiders," Reece said. "Want another beer?"

"Um, no. I think I should probably go."

Reece raised his glass.

"To us outsiders."

Aliya hesitated, then picked up her glass and touched it to Reece's.

"Good night, Reece."

"Good night, Aliya."

He watched her move toward the exit, saying good night to a few colleagues en route.

As she stopped to open the door she turned and caught his eye.

The explosion that blew the windows from the bar was close. They were in a war zone so it could have been anything: rockets, mortars, VBIED, S-vest. Anyone could be gone in an instant.

The blast threw Reece from his seat and into the wall to his back as the glass windows exploded inward. Those closest to the windows were cut down as the glass fragments became deadly projectiles.

VBIED or S-vest?

Reece's mind was not on checking himself for injuries. It was on the woman he had seen just a moment earlier smiling at him from the door.

Drawing his weapon, Reece pushed himself to his feet. His ears were ringing; the smoke was still heavy in the room. He shook his head to get his bearings.

With his SIG in his right hand, he put his left on the wall as a reference point.

Blocking out the screams, he moved along the wall through the smoke, stepping over bodies, tables, and chairs until he found the bar, knowing that if he kept his left hand on it, he would make it to the exit.

Aliya.

Those farthest from the windows were lucky. Reece moved past them as they came to their senses and stumbled around the room in a panic to find an exit, desperate for fresh air.

Reece continued to push himself down the bar until he felt the right-angle edge, which he knew led into a hallway where the bathrooms were located. The side door where he had last seen Aliya was only feet away.

He let go of the bar, brought his left hand to his pistol in a two-handed grip at the low ready, and burst through the smoke toward the door, expecting to find it with his shoulder and push through it. Instead he flew into the night air. The door had been blown from its hinges.

He immediately scanned left to right, noting that the side of the main CIA building was completely gone. Multiple vehicles were overturned and on fire.

"*Aliya!*" he yelled.

A crumpled shape twenty yards away against a concrete bunker caught his eye.

Aliya.

He sprinted to her side, holstered his pistol, and took a knee.

"Aliya! Are you okay?"

Unresponsive.

He laid her out, looking for wounds as best he could in the light from the burning fires.

He ran his hands down her body and looked for blood.

His hands were covered in it.

Mine or hers?

Only then did Reece realize he was dripping blood. He reached up and removed a glass shard from the side of his head and threw it aside.

The Agency had its own hospital, but it was now a smoldering ruin.

Reece knew where the Army CSH, the Combat Support Hospital, was, only two miles away.

He put two fingers on the side of her neck. Weak pulse.

He looked past the bar toward where he had parked his vehicle, a soft-skinned Chevy Tahoe the CIA had given him to use in the Green Zone, then turned back to the site of the explosion as more and more Agency personnel filled the street and stumbled out of side structures.

Reece reached down, pulled Aliya over his shoulder, and got to his feet. At five foot five and probably not much over a hundred pounds, Aliya was quite a bit lighter than the SEALs he'd had to carry in training and in combat. Pulling his SIG from its holster, he ran toward his vehicle.

CHAPTER 5

REECE THREW ALIYA'S UNCONSCIOUS body in the backseat of the Tahoe and tore through the streets of the Green Zone. Two large traffic circles separated them from the medical facility.

What if it's a multipronged attack? What if the field hospital has been hit, too?

Not now, Reece. Prioritize and execute. Get her to care.

The Green Zone at this stage in the war was essentially a city. And like any city, where there was an incident, there was traffic.

Fire engines were moving toward the site of the blast; cars congested the roundabouts.

"Come on! Move!"

Reece slammed his Tahoe into a car that had come to a stop, pushing it through an intersection. Scraping past, Reece sped into a roundabout, smashing another car out of his way. The 4x4 bounced up on a sidewalk with its two right-side wheels.

"Reece?" came a weak voice from the backseat.

"Aliya!" Reece exclaimed, reaching back with his right hand, feeling hers slippery with blood. "*Move! Move!*" he yelled to his front, laying on the horn.

"Reece?"

"Stay calm, we're almost there."

"What happened?"

"I don't know. Probably a VBIED, from the quick look I got at the damage."

Reece felt her hand grip his tighter, almost slipping away, their blood mixing.

"Hold my hand, Reece."

"I got you. You're going to be okay."

"You were right, you know."

"*Move!* What?"

"You were right about me."

"What do you mean? *Fuck!*"

The SUV narrowly missed the fountain in the middle of a roundabout, T-boning a car in the process. His hand slipped from the targeter's. Reece reversed, accelerated around the car, and sped on.

Their hands searched in the darkness until they reconnected, still slick with blood. Reece hoped it was his. He could feel it seeping from the gash in his head and the pain indicated there had to be additional glass shards in his shoulder.

"I mean, I'm an outsider, too."

Reece stole a quick backward glance.

"Just try and breathe. You are going to be fine. We are almost to the hospital."

"Just in case, I want you to know you were right."

"Right about what? *Fucking move!*"

"My sister, my husband. They are in Israel. Please let them know I was doing this for *us*."

"What are you talking about? Just breathe."

"You know what I'm talking about, Reece. Just find them and tell them."

"Tell them what? *Jesus!*" Reece yelled, swerving to miss a concrete Jersey barrier.

"That I was doing my job for Israel. Reece, I'm Mossad."

As Reece skidded to a stop in front of the hospital, he could see they had all hands on deck for the mass casualty event.

Reece jumped from the front seat and pulled open the rear passenger door. He grabbed Aliya in his arms and carried her to the front of the CSH as a rolling stretcher was pushed through the entrance. Aliya was the first of what was to be a mob of patients that night.

Reece laid her down on the stretcher as a team of medics took over and went to work, pushing her, and her secret, deeper into the hospital.

CHAPTER 6

Arlington National Cemetery
Arlington, Virginia

DRIVING NORTH ON GEORGE Washington Memorial Parkway, the Potomac River on his right, Reece passed Ronald Reagan National Airport, briefly crossing into the District of Columbia as his route took him past Arlington Memorial Bridge. Technically Reece was committing a felony for his few minutes in D.C., due to the concealed SIG in his waistband. He was relieved when he crossed back into Virginia and once again became a law-abiding citizen.

Arlington.

Reece glanced down at the Rolex Submariner on his wrist, the second hand sweeping clockwise as a constant reminder that once those precious moments were gone, there was no getting them back. The stainless-steel case and bracelet had survived a lifetime of abuse on the wrist of the man who had purchased it on R&R in Saigon in 1968. The bezel and dial had faded over the years, but neither the mud of the Mekong Delta nor the hundreds of ambushes in the jungles of Southeast Asia had slowed the Swiss movement. At the end of a second life chapter, while on assignment for the CIA, it had been slipped from his wrist by a killer in an alley in Buenos Aires and given to the traitor who had arranged the assassination. Reece had tracked the defector to a dacha in the wilds of Siberia. He had reclaimed his father's heirloom just before sending Oliver Grey to the afterlife with 485 short steel rods that eviscerated his body when Reece detonated the 700 grams of RDX in a Russian-made claymore mine. The iconic dive instrument had not left his wrist since.

You don't have time, Reece. You have a meeting at the CIA.

Make time.

Time.

Reece wove his way through the maze of overlapping roads that seemed to all intersect at the Theodore Roosevelt Bridge and turned south. He passed the U.S. Marine Corps War Memorial and took the exit for Arlington National Cemetery.

He parked and sat in the car. Row upon row of headstones, the Tomb of the Unknown Soldier. All those dead.

How many of those lives were lost in vain, sent to their deaths by politicians who failed to understand the nature of the conflict to which they were committing America's sons and daughters?

Is this country even worth fighting for?

There is nowhere left to go, Reece.

Time.

He knew Arlington better than he would have liked, the result of military service that coincided with the longest war in the history of the nation. He was overly familiar with Section 60, the area reserved for those killed in the Global War on Terror. Forever the age of their deaths, those who had given their last full measure of devotion now rested on home soil waiting on their loved ones to one day join them in eternity. They would never grow old, never see their children graduate from high school or college, get married, or bring the next generation into the world. They were frozen in time, their youth captured only in memories and photographs.

Reece was not at Arlington National Cemetery to pay his respects. He had another mission. He was searching for meaning.

Reece exited the vehicle and glanced back at his watch. He was going to be late. The CIA could wait.

He slowly made his way past the headstones of departed warriors, those he knew and those he did not.

Forgive me for not stopping today, brothers. There is something I need to do.

The order was important.

Reece found himself in front of a white marble rectangular column in Section 46. Its bronze plaque simply read:

IN HONOR OF MEMBERS OF THE
UNITED STATES ARMED FORCES WHO
DIED DURING AN ATTEMPT TO RESCUE
AMERICAN HOSTAGES HELD IN IRAN
25 APRIL 1980

The clash of civilizations hadn't started in Tehran on the November day that the U.S. Embassy was overrun but it had marked a turning point in the history of both nations.

Pushing on, Reece found his way to a stone marker in Section 59, set in front of a cedar tree and commemorating those who died in the 1983 bombing of the Marine barracks in Beirut:

"Let peace take root. This cedar of Lebanon tree grows in living memory of the Americans killed in the Beirut terrorist attack and all victims of terrorism throughout the world."

Reece remembered the man he had killed who had a hand in planning what was the largest nonnuclear explosion since World War II. Not since Iwo Jima had the Marines lost more men in a single day.

The enemy had learned from Desert One and from Beirut.

He pressed forward.

In Section 1, Reece stopped to read the words engraved at the base of the Lockerbie Memorial Cairn:

"On 21 December 1988, a terrorist bomb destroyed Pan American Airlines Flight 103 over Lockerbie, Scotland, killing all on board and 11 on the ground. The 270 Scottish stones which compose this memorial cairn commemorate those who lost their lives in this attack against America."

He thought of the phone call that pulled his dad from his family in the aftermath of Pan Am 103. Where had he gone and what had he done? Reece still didn't know.

The former SEAL then made his way to a five-sided granite memorial in Section 64. It was surrounded by flowers and engraved with the names of those killed in the attack on the Pentagon on September 11, 2001.

Were the last twenty years of war worth it?

Could we have averted 9/11 had we studied the past, had we been aware of what lessons our enemies were learning through the 1980s and 1990s?

What did they learn, Reece?

They learned that terrorism produces results.

What did they learn from Iraq and Afghanistan?

It's not your war anymore, Reece.

You came here seeking answers. You know where they are buried.

Floating over the hallowed grounds between the oaks, maples, firs, dogwoods, and elms, Reece made his way to two headstones of Georgia marble in the shade of a large oak, the final resting place of Thomas and Judith Reece.

He ran a finger over the scratched crystal of the old, weathered watch and picked up his head. He looked to the east, toward the National Mall, where his dad had taken him to see the Vietnam Veterans Memorial. Reece had been in third grade the first time he had seen the black granite walls located just north of the Lincoln Memorial. The walls were engraved with the names of those killed and missing in action from the Vietnam War, a war that had forged a young frogman named Tom Reece.

How many people died there, Dad? James had asked as they walked along the wall toward the Washington Monument.

Over fifty-eight thousand, James.

Did you know them all?

No, not all.

Why were we fighting there? Did they attack us?

Even now Reece could see his dad, lean and strong, clean-shaven with a haircut that was neither noticeably too short nor too long. He had stopped walking and knelt down to be eye to eye with his son.

War can be a complicated thing. It can also be the most basic thing.

I don't get it.

I don't get it either sometimes. I do know I don't want you to have to fight in one.

But you did, and so did your dad.

That's true, son. Which is why I don't wish it on you.

Is that why you are always gone? Reece had asked.

Honest questions from a child could cut worse than any blade.

That's right. I want to keep this from happening again. The Vietnam-era frogman gestured to the long wall of dark granite.

Let's play ball, James urged, tossing the rugby ball to his father.

Slow down, son. Take another look at the wall. All those names, and all the memorials on the Mall, Arlington across the bridge: All that sacrifice is so you, and one day your children, can have the freedom and opportunity to make your own decisions.

Why slow down? I like to go fast!

Tom Reece laughed.

I mean, do things right, son, and do the right thing, he counseled his eight-year-old.

That's confusing.

It won't always be. Just remember it.

Why do you always wear that watch, Dad? James asked, pointing to his dad's wrist.

This? Tom Reece asked, tapping the face. *It's a constant reminder to take a breath, don't rush. One day it will be yours.*

When, Dad?

Hopefully a long time from now.

When you die? Eight-year-olds can be extremely perceptive.

Possibly.

Then I never want it. I want you to live forever.

I know, son, but death comes for us all. It's nothing to be afraid of. It just is.

And that watch reminds you of that? That's depressing.

Where are you learning all these big words? Tom Reece had asked.

From Mom. We read a lot when you are gone.

I'm gone a lot, aren't I?

Yeah, James admitted.

Well, you know what? This watch reminds me that when I'm here, I'm one hundred percent yours. And when I'm gone, it reminds me to get back to you as soon as I can. It reminds me to focus on what I can control, not the things I can't.

What do you mean?

I mean, I can be here with you now, today, not dwelling on yesterday or thinking about tomorrow, but here with you, teaching you about this. Tom Reece tossed the ball back to his child.

Rugby!

That's right!

But all my friends' dads watch football.

Well, instead of watching someone else play football. I'm playing rugby with you. Almost everywhere you go in the world, you can play or watch a game. The old veteran had paused. *Life's a gift.*

Like a toy?

No, not like a toy, even more important and valuable.

More valuable than GI Joe?

Much more valuable.

What is it? What's the gift?

Time itself, his father had said. *You are fast, James. I've seen you run, but even you can't outrun time. Do you understand?*

"I understand, Dad," Reece said, looking at the graves of his parents.

Don't dwell on the past, son. Learn from it. Now, try and catch me, he had said, sprinting off toward the Washington Monument rising in the distance.

CHAPTER 7

Central Intelligence Agency
Langley, Virginia

REECE PAUSED AS HE walked over the mosaic eagle, shield, and sixteen-point compass star in the lobby floor of the original headquarters building, the distinctive seal of the Central Intelligence Agency. He was late.

He had to leave his pistol in the car when visiting the George Bush Center for Intelligence, though he begrudgingly complied with the requirement. Being unarmed always made him nervous, By actual policy it wasn't even supposed to be in his car, but Reece was never one to be overly concerned with the rules. His compromise was leaving his SIG in the vehicle. He attracted enough attention on the grounds of what always reminded him of a college campus. The collared shirt he had dug up was poor camouflage. It wasn't just his beard, Fjällräven pants, Salomon shoes, and Gatorz sunglasses perched atop his head that gave him away; it was his eyes: predatory, scanning, assessing, taking in information. Those who were aware of his past missions on behalf of the country, as well as his illegal actions that had been pardoned by a previous president, gave him a wide berth in the hallways. They all knew where Reece was heading: the office of Victor Rodriguez, the director of what was now called the Special Activities Center. On paper Reece was full-time

Agency, a graduate of the Farm, the CIA's training facility in Camp Peary, Virginia, and a paramilitary officer with the CIA's Ground Branch. But unlike the other blue-badgers who haunted the halls of Langley, Reece was there for one reason only: to find and kill the man who had put a bullet through his SEAL Teammate Freddy Strain.

The Wall of Honor beckoned from the north side of the lobby. It was Reece's custom to always pay his respects, to remember.

It had been two years since he had last stood before the white marble memorial. Something was different about it. Reece recognized it instantly. For the first time in CIA history, the wall beneath the inscription was full and four new stars had been etched above it.

Flanked by the American flag and the flag of the Agency, a steel-framed glass case protruded from the wall beneath black stars representing CIA officers and contractors who had lost their lives in service to the nation. Reece looked down through the inch-thick glass that protected it. The Book of Honor. The black Moroccan goatskin log contained a handwritten year of death and sometimes a name. One hundred and thirty-seven stars. Thirty-seven of the entries contained only the symbol, the date and name still classified in testament to the Agency's culture of secrecy.

Reece lifted his head to read the words chiseled into the white marble:

IN HONOR OF THOSE MEMBERS
OF THE CENTRAL INTELLIGENCE AGENCY
WHO GAVE THEIR LIVES IN THE SERVICE OF THEIR COUNTRY

There had been space on the wall the first time Reece had walked across the lobby shortly after September 11, 2001. His father's star would be added not long after, joining the ranks of those whose service and sacrifice went almost unnoticed by a country whose citizens assumed that safety and security were entitlements. The wall and the stars etched into its surface reminded Reece that no matter what his mission, personal or professional, there were always those out there in the shadows, risking it all for a country that would never know their names. There were also those the wall did not recognize; the wounded, their lives altered forever while executing the CIA's global mission of safeguarding the nation. Those men and women far outnumbered the stars of the dead.

Would his name one day be memorialized with a star, or, as with his father, would the circumstances of his death be deemed a national security issue and classified?

Death comes for us all. It's nothing to be afraid of. It just is.

Reece's eyes drifted over the neatly arranged rows of stars: Johnny "Mike" Spann, Chris Mueller, "Chief," Glen Doherty, and Ty Woods. Reece knew other stars that represented other friends, with what they did and how they died filed away on protected servers to safeguard ongoing covert programs or sources and methods. Reece gazed up at the newest four stars, knowing one represented his friend "Goody." The legendary SEAL had taken Reece under his wing when he had arrived on the East Coast as a new officer. "I'll never forget you, buddy."

He found the star he knew represented Freddy Strain. How many of the other stars remained unavenged? *We are close, my friend. It won't be long.*

You are fast, James. I've seen you run, but even you can't outrun time. Reece heard his father's admonition echo in his memory.

Then I'd better get to work.

He ran his thumb over the face of his watch, turned, and went to meet his destiny.

CHAPTER 8

REECE ACKNOWLEDGED THE EXECUTIVE assistant, positioned at her desk outside Vic's office, with a slight nod.

"He's waiting on you," she managed to get out as the former SEAL reached for the door.

"I know."

The door shut behind him and Reece entered the domain of the dark side.

"You're late."

"I know," Reece replied. "Traffic."

"I see."

Victor Rodriguez was second-generation Agency. His father had led a squad in Brigade 2506, the CIA-trained unit of Cuban exiles who had attempted to overthrow Fidel Castro in 1961 in what would later become known as the Bay of Pigs Invasion. A picture on the wall to the right of his desk, showing a group of men in World War II–era "duck hunter" patterned camouflage uniforms, was a constant reminder of the perils of his chosen profession. Vic's father was holding a Johnson M1941. Covert action was in Vic's blood.

Vic stood and stepped from behind his desk to shake hands with his recruit.

"I knew one of the people on the Air France flight."

"I know, Reece. Take a seat," the director said, gesturing to a conference area in a corner of the spacious office.

The walls were adorned with memorabilia of Vic's time as a Green Beret with 7th Group and from his career at the CIA. Before accepting his current position as director of the Special Activities Center, he had headed the Special Operations Group. It was there he had connected with James Reece, who was at that time the country's most wanted domestic terrorist. Now he led two elements of the nation's covert action apparatus—SOG and its counterpart, the Political Action Group.

Though he had traded in his military-issued BDUs for a suit when he was a young captain in the Army, Vic still looked as trim as he did in the group photo of him and his Special Forces Q-Course class, taken following the completion of their Robin Sage final unconventional-warfare training exercise, that hung on the wall. He was the rare Beltway executive-level leader who was trusted by those above and below him in the chain of command. The son of Cuban exiles, he had grown up with the specter of Bahía de Cochinos. It was his personal and professional mission to prevent another failure at the nexus of intelligence and covert action.

"Aliya Galin. Tell me about her." Vic's piercing blue eyes, a trait that betrayed the Castilian heritage on his mother's side, were cool and clear.

"It's probably all in a file around here somewhere," Reece replied.

"Oh, it is," Vic said. "I just want to hear it from you."

"She was a targeter in Iraq when I was attached to the Agency."

"The STU."

"That's right, the Special Tactics Unit. Part of the Ministry of the Interior. I met a lot of great operators on that deployment, including Ox."

"I was on the Afghan Mohawk project at the time," Vic offered, "or we might have crossed paths then as well."

"I have some good friends who worked with the Mohawks," Reece said before continuing. "Aliya was heading up SSE analysis. Extremely good at her job. We worked together closely. I'd been in the thick of it since the war kicked off and hadn't worked on the darker side of special operations yet."

"Meaning what?"

"Meaning, I hadn't really worked with females in combat. The SEAL Teams were, are maybe, I don't know, I haven't been keeping up, all male."

Vic smiled. "I get it. You are a protector by nature."

"I guess, bottom line is, we trusted each other. You remember how it was back then in Iraq and Afghanistan: daily ops, incoming rockets and mortars, S-VESTs, VBIEDs, green on blue. It was insane. It was the Wild West out there."

"I remember," Vic assured his visitor. "When did you learn she was Mossad?"

"The night of the VBIED in the Green Zone. She was wounded. I got her to the hospital. The surgeons saved her life. She told me on the way to the hospital. I think she thought she was dying."

"What did she tell you?"

"Just to let her sister and husband know that she was 'doing this for us.' "

"You remember all these years later?"

"I do. I thought they might be her last words. There was so much blood, I didn't know if it was hers or mine. Turns out it was both." Reece paused. "Then she told me she was Mossad."

Vic leaned back in his chair.

"And then?"

"And then we turned up the pressure. Jaysh al-Mahdi and AQI. After the VBIED, the gloves came off."

"And Aliya?"

"She was flown to Germany not long after the attack. I think she went to Israel after that."

"Did you see her before she left?"

"I did. Before they flew her home. That's when I found out she was Caesarea. Kidon. An assassin."

Vic picked up a file on the table.

"Did you tell anyone?"

"I did. The chief of station. I forget his name. We called him 'the vampire' because of his work hours. I didn't have much interaction with him."

"What did he tell you?"

"He just thanked me. Didn't give any indication that he knew or didn't know. He sure didn't look surprised."

"That squares with what's in here. He was one of the few who knew. She had dual citizenship. We could not have an Israeli captured or killed in Iraq, but Israel understandably wanted one of their own attached as a liaison. Her job was to dig into any intelligence that suggested there were plans by terrorist groups in Iraq planning attacks on Israel, so we brought her over as a targeter. Only a few senior-level officials were aware of her actual mission."

"Makes sense," Reece said.

"My own suspicion," Vic continued, "is that the Mossad was also training her, exposing her to Agency paramilitary tactics, techniques, and procedures. I wouldn't be surprised if one of her missions was to spot, assess, develop, and recruit an asset to spy for Israel."

"Me? You think she was assessing me for recruitment?"

"Certainly fits the profile."

"I *never* got that feeling."

"That's the whole point, Reece. You went to the Farm. You know the recruitment cycle."

"Which is why I know she wasn't developing me."

"Are you sure? You just told me you trusted each other."

Reece took a breath.

"Vic, why the *fuck* did the Agency have us working with an agent they knew was Mossad and not tell us?"

"Having an Israeli in Iraq could have caused serious strategic second- and third-order effects on the coalition war effort. That was close-hold information."

"A *fucking* heads-up would have been nice."

Vic opened the file and pulled out two photographs. One was from 2008 and labeled ALIYA GALIN. The second photo was the same one Reece had seen on television attached to the name Mélanie Cotillard.

"That's her. I haven't seen her in a long time."

"Reece, she was perfectly positioned to recruit someone. That someone was likely you. Trust, shared danger in a war zone. You were roughly the same age. She was obviously attractive. My assessment is that she was in the development stage. The VBIED never let her get to the recruitment phase."

Reece looked at the photo again. She was stunning.

"Well, it doesn't matter now, does it," Reece said, dropping the photo back on the file. "She's dead."

"Reece, before you saw this photo on the news and called me, I was getting ready to contact you."

"About this?"

"Not exactly."

"Then what?"

"We had not yet made the connection between Mélanie Cotillard, Aliya Galin, the Mossad, and you."

Vic handed Reece another file, labeled NIZAR KATTAN.

"Kattan?"

"You know that as director of the Special Activities Center, I am responsible for both the Special Operations Group and the Political Action Group. The PAG coordinates psychological operations and covert influence to include cyberwarfare in coordination with the NSA and the Air Force. SIGINT from the NSA identified Nizar Kattan as one of the terrorists who shot down the Air France flight."

But Reece wasn't listening. He was looking at a blurry photograph of a Syrian sniper, a sniper who had killed Freddy Strain and Aliya Galin.

"Reece," Vic said, in an attempt to pull the frogman from his trance.

Reece turned his head, his eyes working their way over the photos and books Vic had chosen to be his daily companions. They came to rest on a plaque over the director's right shoulder, a gift from SOG when he had turned over the reins to take the director's chair. In a nod to their predecessors in the OSS, above a mounted Fairbairn-Sykes fighting knife was a logo featuring a Thompson submachine gun under an eagle hunting for prey. Etched into the brass plate it read: "To Victor Rodriguez, a PhD who can win a bar fight." Under that was engraved the motto of the Special Activities Center: *"Tertia Optio."*

"The third option," Reece whispered. "And you don't think this is a coincidence?"

"Anything is possible. The NSA is doing a deep data pull. We will see what we can find."

Reece threw the file on the table and closed his eyes. When he opened them, the director of the Special Activities Center was studying him intently.

"Reece, I know the only reason you are on board is to find and kill Nizar Kattan. The president has authorized a finding giving you legal authority to take him out. It's possible this was a coincidence, that Aliya Galin just happened to be on an Air France flight that Kattan was hired to blow out of the sky. He's an assassin, a gun for hire. But I'd assess the odds of this being a random occurrence at slim to none."

"My thoughts exactly."

"The questions are: What was she doing in Burkina Faso, who knew she was there, who knew about your relationship, and why hire Kattan to kill her?"

"*If* she was the target," Reece said.

"That's right, *if* she was the target."

"What's the situation on the ground?" Reece asked.

"There is a multinational task force on-site. France has the lead, as it was one of their jets and most of the victims are French citizens. We have FBI and DOJ assisting along with analysts from the Agency."

"And from Special Activities?"

"Ox is there, working with the chief of station and a host nation force from their National Intelligence Agency."

"Like an STU or Mohawk-type operation?"

"Similar, but not nearly as well trained," Vic answered.

"Any leads on Kattan?"

"Not yet, but NSA is working it, as are HUMINT assets on the ground throughout Africa. We'll get something. You don't pull off an operation like this and not leave a trail."

"Maybe that's exactly what he wants," Reece speculated.

"Maybe."

"I need to get over there."

"We are arranging transportation."

"Thank you."

"I need you to do something before you go."

"What's that?"

"The president has requested a meeting."

CHAPTER 9

Camp David, Aspen Cabin
Catoctin Mountain Park, Maryland

"BOURBON?"

"I think I need one. Thank you, Mr. President."

Alec Christensen had given up trying to get anyone to call him Alec.

"I have a bottle of Horse Soldier bourbon."

"5th Group. That works, sir."

The president liked Camp David. It had grown on him. So much so that he had abandoned his initial plans to remodel the aging cabins. He felt like he had adapted to the environment rather than forcing the environment to adapt to him. He was, after all, a guest here, a caretaker entrusted to unite an increasingly divided country. Camp David belonged to the American taxpayer.

The president handed Reece his drink with one large ice cube. He liked Camp David for another reason: He could make his own coffee and pour his own drinks out here. That was harder than one would think in the White House where staffers, aides, secretaries, and advisors were all jockeying for a moment of his time. The political machine in full swing.

"Vic tells me they have a line on the group responsible for the shootdown in Burkina Faso and that you are headed over."

"That's right, sir. Signals intelligence indicates the person, or one of the people, involved is Nizar Kattan, the man who killed Freddy Strain. And . . ."

"And?"

"And, I knew one of the passengers."

"They briefed me," the president said. "I asked about her." He gestured toward a file on the table between them. "Interesting reading."

"I'm sure."

"What I'm worried about is not in the file."

"Sir?"

"Someone connected to you is killed by the same person who killed Senior Chief Freddy Strain."

"I know, sir. I'll be careful."

The president swirled the brown liquid in his glass. He had been briefed on the situation on multiple occasions. Reece and Freddy had saved the previous president from assassination in Odessa and prevented a plot orchestrated by a Russian colonel to push Russian troops into Ukraine. Had they failed, Alec Christensen might still be a congressman from California, and the unintended consequences of that failure could have been two American cities wiped off the map.

"Sir? Are you okay?"

"Just thinking about something."

Reece took a sip of his bourbon, knowing it was best to let the president ponder without interruption.

"Look, I know you are only at Ground Branch to bring Freddy's killer to justice. And, you know I understand."

Reece remained silent, remembering the reasons the president had first confided in him.

"And this country owes you more than it will ever be able to repay."

Reece thought of the MC-130s that had been spinning at Hurlburt Field, Florida, with GBU-43/B Massive Ordnance Air Blast (MOAB) fuel-air explosive munitions in their payload bays, getting ready to destroy two American cities and kill half a million citizens to prevent the spread of a Marburg virus variant introduced by Iran.

"Your flight to Africa is scheduled for tomorrow, as I understand."

"That's right, Mr. President. GB has a crew on the ground there right now. I'll join them tomorrow."

"I see. I'd like for you to do me a favor."

The president of the United States had asked him for a favor before. Reece couldn't help but smile. *A favor?* Coming from the commander in chief, a favor amounted to an order.

"Sir?"

"I'm hesitant, as I know I'll face some backlash, but it might help you in your mission."

"I don't understand."

"Have you ever heard rumors of Project GhostNet in China, Russia's Camerton, or the NSA's Bullrun decryption program?"

"None of those ring a bell."

"I wouldn't think so. What about Five Eyes, PRISM, Turbulence, XKeyscore, Boundless Informant, or Edgehill?"

"Just what I read in Snowden's *Permanent Record*. Glenn Greenwald's *No Place to Hide* mentions some of those as well, if I recall."

"What about the Sixteenth Air Force at Lackland Air Force Base in San Antonio? They call it Air Forces Cyber."

"Never heard of it. Not really my battle space," Reece replied.

"I was briefed on it when I was on the House Armed Services Committee, but even the closed-door classified briefings were window dressing."

"They lied to members of Congress? About what?"

"True capabilities. And to be fair, those capabilities continue to evolve by the minute, actually by the second. In 2018 it was reorganized into its current command structure at Lackland. It's our leading cyberwarfare command but it's much more than that. Are you aware of the CSS, the Central Security Service?"

"No, but it sounds a bit Orwellian."

"You have good instincts, Reece. It's an agency chartered to integrate the cyber capabilities of the NSA and the Air Force. As president, I was read into its true mission and capabilities. I want you to be read into it as well."

"I don't understand."

"CSS, a subset of the NSA, falls under the United States Cyber Command, which is a DoD combatant command. Since its commissioning it has been led by the director of the National Security Agency."

The president set down his drink and leaned back in his chair.

"Hard not to think about the history of this place, Reece. It weighs. I often wonder if Truman sat here thinking through the impact of dropping the first atomic bombs."

He took a breath and pushed on.

"Reece, there is a program not many people know about. The vice president is not read in and neither is Director Rodriguez. It's on par with the scale of the Manhattan Project, which ushered in the nuclear age. This isn't a weapon program in the same sense, but I fear it is even more dangerous."

"And the favor?"

"The favor is, I'd like you to delay your flight to Africa. Get read in on this project. I think it will be helpful."

"And?" Reece asked.

"How do you know there's an 'and'?"

"Instinct."

The former 10th Mountain Division soldier leaded forward, elbows on his knees.

"Remember when I told you that this is the one place on earth where my conversations were not being recorded?"

"I do, Mr. President. When we first met. Right here in Aspen Cabin."

"Well, it turns out that was only true to a point. Though I didn't know it at the time."

Reece looked around.

"You'll see when you get read in."

Reece sensed the president was not finished.

"Have you asked Katie to marry you yet?"

Reece laughed. "For a moment there I thought you were going to get serious."

"Listen to me. I have no wife, no kids, my mom passed away when I was young, and I recently said good-bye to my father. Washington does not like those in power not having attachments which can be used to pressure, manipulate, or exploit."

Reece shook his head. "I don't see how you do it."

"What?"

"Politics. The game. The compromises. The lies."

"You know why I do it."

Reece took another sip.

He did it for the same reason you killed everyone who had a hand in the murder of Lauren and Lucy, Reece thought, remembering his wife and daughter. *Vengeance.* Alec Christensen had worked his way to the pinnacle of the American political machine to gain access to the most highly classified secrets pertaining to the attacks of 9/11. The nineteen hijackers had assistance on their mission of terror, a mission that had taken the life of Alec's fiancée. The president wanted them brought to justice in accordance with the *2001 Authorization for the Use of Military Force.* Reece had been his instrument of choice.

"I was never meant to be in this seat. I was an outsider when the country needed one, when we had a brief moment where reconciliation between the parties was possible. I slipped through by being able to activate a countrywide base built on social platforms that got their start while my colleagues in Congress scoffed at the idea that a podcast or YouTube channel could translate into votes. They recognize that power now and have taken steps to control it."

"What do you mean, sir? And what does this have to do with Freddy?"

"There is too much power in division, Reece. Politicians were slow to catch on, but eventually they did. The tech companies had the data early. They knew what to push and what to highlight to get more eyes on an advertisement, which they told us was their goal—selling ads just like on TV. That wasn't true. They were collecting data. Data that made them wealthier than almost anyone in the history of mankind. Now they can use that data to influence thought, drive opinion, and shape the direction of the country. They have taken that power out of the hands of the citizenry, Reece, and the voter doesn't even realize it. People call the president of the United States the most powerful person on the planet. That may have been true until the age of information. Now, without question, the most powerful entities are those who control the data. The person who has access to that data is the most powerful and dangerous person the world has ever known."

"You mean the founders and CEOs of the tech companies?"

The president leaned back on the sofa and looked into his glass.

"I don't think so. They have the wealth, certainly, and with that wealth comes power. But there is more to it. I'm still piecing it together."

"Piecing what together?" Reece asked.

"Have you heard the term RNGW?"

"What does it stand for?"

"Russian New Generation Warfare."

"What is it?"

"It's an evolution in warfare and we, the United States, are under attack. IW, Information Warfare, Reece. That's the future and we are behind the power curve. Our generals are still bogged down in a bureaucracy fueled by continuing to build an arsenal around a strategy of deterrence. There is a lot of money in defense. It's entrenched in the system."

"If the last twenty years taught us anything, sir, it's that the deterrence model based on large conventional force structure with an overwhelming nuclear capability is next to useless when dealing with an asymmetric threat."

"That's right, Reece. Information Warfare has become the main effort for both Russia and China, not a supporting effort, as is the case with us. Russia used a multiphase IW campaign supported by special operations in Crimea in 2014 when we were focused on Iraq and Afghanistan. They are prepping the battle space right now here in the U.S., sowing the seeds of division, lighting fires, stoking the flames, and it's all deniable. I'm sure you've heard of the Internet Research Agency."

"Yes, sir. I've read about it. Russian-backed hackers hitting us with disinformation."

"It's really a front for the SVR. To the Russians, it doesn't matter if a Republican or Democrat is in the presidency or what party controls Congress; their intent is to divide the nation and they can do it through the smartphone in your pocket."

"What can we do about it, sir?"

"We are playing right into their hands. In national-level politics, there is no incentive to connect, to heal. There is more incentive for politicians to continue dividing us. There is power in that division. The tech companies grow their wealth and their collection of data based on that division. I am not hopeful. There are forces at play, which is why I want you read in on the program I mentioned. It will help you find Freddy's killer and my hope is that when you come back it will encourage you to stay on as part of my cabinet."

"Sir?"

"Ms. Buranek has a job in D.C. and I thought it might be helpful if you did, too."

"I do, sir. At the Agency."

"Reece, you can't do that forever, and once you bring Kattan down you are going to need a new mission. It doesn't have to be at the barrel of a gun."

Reece had not expected an employment offer.

"I'll bite, sir. What did you have in mind?"

"I was thinking ASD SO/LIC."

Reece was taken aback.

"Assistant Secretary of Defense for Special Operations and Low Intensity Conflict?"

"That's right."

"Don't I need Senate confirmation for that? They'd never approve."

"I can appoint you in an 'acting' capacity. By the time they got around to confirmation you could move on to the private sector and get on a couple of boards. By that point you'd have the resume, and a recommendation from the president carries some weight. You'd go to a meeting or two a year, bring in some serious money to support Katie and a family if she decided she wanted to stay home."

Reece was dumbfounded.

"I don't see Katie as the 'stay at home' type."

"You never know, Reece."

"Becoming part of the military-industrial complex is not all that appealing."

"I knew you'd say that. Reece, this country owes you. Selfishly I want you out of the line of fire. I want to repay you for what you did for all those people who are alive today because you foiled the plot to have us destroy ourselves. Without you, two cities would be in ruins and who knows what that would have done to the political division in the nation? I also want to thank you for what you did for me personally. I am currently in a position to help you and I want to make sure I do while I can."

The president had given Reece his dead fiancée's engagement ring right here in Aspen Cabin. Reece had worn it on a chain around his neck on a journey from Turkey into Iraq and then over the beach into Iran, where he had pressed it into the hand of General Ja'far al-Sadiq after putting a 7.62x39mm round through his head.

Reece took in the commander in chief. There was more gray in his hair now than when they had first met but he was staying in shape with daily runs. He wore what had become his uniform when not at the White House, beige Sperry boat shoes, slacks, and a tucked-in navy blue polo shirt with the Presidential Seal. His hair was not as short as when he'd led troops in Afghanistan, but it was kept neatly cropped with weekly haircuts. Reece knew he shaved twice a day, a habit he had picked up from his father, a financier of the old school.

"Sir, if you want me read in on this program because it will help me find Freddy's killer—I'm in. On ASD/SOLIC, my gut says no."

"At least think about it."

"I'll think about it."

"That's all a president can ask. A helo will be here tomorrow to take you to Andrews where a plane will be waiting to take you to Texas."

"Lackland?"

"You'll find out more tomorrow. Trust me, Reece."

"I do, sir."

There was another reason the president wanted Reece read in, one he had not shared. They finished their drinks and the president bid Reece good night, unsure if he had just signed his friend's death warrant.

CHAPTER 10

Andrews Air Force Base

Maryland

THE SUPER HUEY TOUCHED down at Andrews Air Force Base just after 10:00 a.m. A black Suburban was waiting and drove Reece to a VIP section of the airfield. It stopped at the ramp of a Gulfstream G550.

"This me?" Reece asked, sizing up the plane and comparing it to a similar model parked not far away.

"This is you," the driver confirmed.

"Thanks for the lift," Reece said, grabbing his Sitka Drifter travel pack from the seat beside him and exiting the vehicle.

Reece paused at the base of the stairs leading into the sleek aircraft. The G550 had a different paint scheme than its relative parked nearby. Where the other plane was painted a two-tone white and blue with clear Air Force markings on the Rolls-Royce BR710 engines, an American flag on the tail, and UNITED STATES OF AMERICA printed in large letters just above the distinctive oval windows unique to Gulfstream, Reece's aircraft had no such markings. It was white with a simple gold stripe running the length of the plane beneath the windows. Reece noted that it did have a tail number. Not having one would have made it stand out. In this case it belonged to the 89th Airlift Wing, a United States Air Force command responsible for executing the Special Air Mission, meaning they were tasked with air transportation for the president and vice president.

A man stuck his head out from the open door.

"Mr. Donovan?"

He descended the stairs with an agility that didn't seem to match his age, which Reece put in the mid-fifties range.

He extended his hand.

"Tim David, Lieutenant General." He smiled.

His hair was almost all white, with just a few dark specks to betray its original hue. It was longer than regulations allowed, even for the Air Force, and his gray suit and blue tie were devoid of any military linkages.

"Well, General. You've got the plane and the suit so I'm guessing you know who I am."

"Yes, we might as well dispense with the alias," he said.

"I'm James Reece."

"Nice to meet you, Commander."

"I'm retired," Reece said.

"As I understand it you have a new vocation, which is why we are going on this flight."

"It's temporary."

"I see. Well, let's get to it. May I take your bag?"

"Are you sure you're a general?"

"That's what they keep telling me."

"Where are all your aides and the majors to make you coffee?"

"It is just us, Mr. Reece."

"'Reece' works fine."

"All right, Reece. It's just you and me. I'll tell you more when we get airborne. This plane has some unique features that make our conversations more secure in the air."

"More secure? What is it, a flying SCIF?" Reece asked, referring to areas designed as "sensitive compartmented information facilities," where classified information could be discussed.

"As you will find out, not much is actually secure these days."

To Reece's questioning look the general said, "It will make more sense later. Climb aboard and I'll explain what I can."

Reece boarded the jet and settled into a large leather lounge chair. The cabin door to the cockpit was closed and there was no one else on board.

"No flight attendants? You sure you're not a Marine?"

The general laughed. He pulled the door shut and gave two sharp raps on the cockpit door before taking a seat across from Reece, the aircraft already beginning to taxi.

"We can make some coffee once we're airborne. Honey and cream, right?"

"At least you paid attention to the most important intel from my file."

The general laughed again.

"Sir, pardon me, but you just really don't seem like a general."

"I'll take that as a compliment."

As the Gulfstream burst through the clouds over Prince George's County, the general unbuckled his belt and moved to a seat with a built-in computer keyboard and monitor. He adjusted the cursor, tapped the trackpad, and after a few keystrokes seemed satisfied.

"Coffee?"

"Please."

The general moved to the galley and poured two cups, mixing honey and cream into one of them before sitting back down across from his guest.

"Thank you, sir," Reece said, before taking his first sip. "Not bad. Okay, it's confirmed, you're Air Force."

"That I am. Officially, I'm the deputy director of the Sixteenth Air Force's Cyber Division."

"Cyberwarfare?"

"That's right. How much of a background do you have in the cyber arena?"

"Well, I have email and sometimes I remember my password."

"So I should start at the beginning?"

"That would be helpful. I don't even know what I'm doing here."

"And just so we are clear," the general continued, "neither do I. But when an executive-level directive comes down from the president, we follow orders, even in the Air Force."

Reece smiled.

"This plane is a specially modified Gulfstream G550/C-37B. At altitude it is about as secure as one can get, which is why we can have this conversation."

"Golf courses and G550s. I should have joined the Air Force."

"That's how we do it, Reece. You build the golf courses first and *then* you go back to Congress and request additional *mission-essential* funds to build the runways. It doesn't work if you start with the runways. That's why the Marines don't have golf courses. They are still figuring it out."

"God bless them," Reece said.

"Reece, you have undoubtedly heard that cyberwarfare is the battleground of the future."

"I've been hearing that for as long as I can remember."

"Well, it's only partially true. That future, it's been here for a long time. The Sixteenth Air Force was established as the hub of military and intelligence computing supremacy. It is headquartered at Joint Base San Antonio–Lackland, in Texas. That's where we are headed. It integrates multisource intelligence, surveillance, and reconnaissance cyberwarfare with electronic warfare and information operation capabilities. We are preparing for the future, which is actually the right now. Controlling information equates to dominance in cyberspace. What do you know about quantum computing, Reece?"

"As I am having a hard time deciphering what you just said, please consider me a novice."

"Let's see then. Computers work on 'bits,' basically heads or tails of a coin, a yes or no answer. Quantum computing uses 'qubits,' which are natural particles."

"I think I need a tutor."

"Imagine each bit as a marble. As it rolls, at any given point the answer could be yes, no, or any percentage of either one with an almost infinite number of answers but done on an atomic scale."

"I'm going to nod my head and pretend I understand."

"Hang in there with me, frogman. You'll get it. Admittedly, the nomenclature can be confusing, like *atomic entanglement* and *superposition,* but simply put, it all adds up to speed. Time, Reece."

"Time," Reece repeated, thinking of his father all those years ago at the Vietnam Veterans Memorial.

"That's right," the general continued. "The answer that would take years for a computer can be answered in a second or two with a quantum computer. Questions that would take the most advanced computers thousands of years to answer, take a quantum computer only minutes. Let's see, how about a military example in terms of incoming intercontinental ballistic missiles? A quantum computer can plot and launch a defensive solution in a second. Compare that to a supercomputer, which might never even get to the initiation of a launch sequence before the inbound warhead hits its target, especially if the missile or missiles are hypersonic."

"That makes sense," Reece replied.

"With the digital revolution and the massive amount of information that accumulates on an exponential scale by the second, there is more data for any computer or supercomputer to sift through regardless of what it is doing. It is estimated that 2.5 quadrillion bytes of information are generated daily. That's 2.5 followed by eighteen zeros. It is nearly impossible to even comprehend."

"That's a lot of zeros," Reece said.

"I am sure you have read about government surveillance systems and oversight programs. It's been heavily reported on over the past decade."

"I've followed WikiLeaks and Snowden. Read his books and listened to him on Rogan."

The general smiled. "As have I, but the Snowden-era surveillance programs that came to light were essentially Atari 2600 level. We are so far beyond that now."

"How far?" Reece asked.

"You will see when we land. My job is just to prime you for what you are about to experience. Why you are being read in, I have no idea, but after today you will be one of not more than forty people in government who know."

"Know what?"

"Know what we are capable of."

Reece was beginning to have regrets.

"Reece, the best way to describe it is that we can basically see anything, at any time, in any place."

"Sir?"

"Every cell phone whether it is turned on or off, every text message regardless of app, every keystroke on every computer, every camera, bank account data, any bit of digital information that exists in the world, we can see it all."

Reece took a breath.

"What about privacy issues?"

"That is a separate matter, and why none of what you will see today is allowed to be used in any court or by any law enforcement agency. Too much is at stake."

"Now I'm even more confused than I was by the atomic entanglement and superposition lecture."

"It's a lot to take in."

"For a knuckle dragger?"

"I was going to say 'for a SEAL.'"

Reece laughed.

"We have nearly complete electronic coverage and collection for most of the globe. There are a few outlying areas in the Baltics, Siberia, Canada, Africa, and South America, but we can specifically target those areas now and soon we will not have to allocate additional resources to those dark spots, as we call them. With quantum supremacy, the 'surveillance state' will be global."

"That's quite a responsibility," Reece observed.

"That's quite a *capability*," the general countered. "This interconnectivity allows us to link cameras on Teslas to cell phones to security systems to drones. Until recently, we were only able to store the information in giant data centers, keeping track of what we call the metadata or simply the tag, locational data, for delayed or later analysis. The sheer volume made it difficult to sort. You are about to meet our newest addition. Quantum computing has become a reality."

"Meet a what? You are talking about this thing as if it's human."

The general paused and looked out the window.

"That's because . . . well, you'll see. You have to experience it to understand."

"Experience what? I'm just an operator. A trigger puller."

"You are about to be much more than that."

"I think you guys have been watching too many sci-fi movies."

"Where do you think all this starts, Reece? Submarines, space travel, even flip phones— they were all science fiction at one point."

"So, the bottom line is that you have a big computer, and it collects and sifts through data, spying on everyone. Do I have it about right?"

"If that were the case, more than forty people would know about it. Reece, billions of dollars are being spent by governments, namely the

United States, Russia, China, and India, in the quest for quantum supremacy. China alone spent four hundred billion dollars last year building data centers in the Gobi Desert—racks of servers, essentially massive hard drives."

"Are they all collecting like we are?"

"Not yet. They have yet to solve the stability problems inherent in quantum computing."

"You mean physically?"

"Yes. Quantum computers are a bit unreliable, sensitive to mistakes, unstable, vibration sensitive. Even a minor noise can disrupt the computations."

"Are you sure my smart TV isn't one? Every time I sit down to try and watch something on Netflix or Amazon Prime, I get that loading icon that just spins until I want to rip it off the wall and throw it through a window."

"It's a 'throbber,' an animated graphical control element."

"What is?"

"The spinning icon you just described."

"Now I like it even less."

"Reece," the general said, getting back on track, "only in the past two years through a joint Army–Air Force initiative with the University of Massachusetts were we able to stabilize the error correction problem, which led to groundbreaking leaps forward. We are in new territory, pioneers, pushing boundaries of artificial intelligence that up to now have been only dreamed about."

"So, China, Russia, and India don't have these yet?"

"They are still working on the problem and while they are focused on it, we are growing our cyberwarfare capability at a rate unheard-of in years past. No one but us has developed *her*."

"Her?"

"Quantum analysis-based AI: artificial intelligence."

"Meaning?"

"Meaning she can think, learn, and adapt on her own."

"You keep saying *her*."

"It will all make sense soon. I'm not sure why the president wants you to have access, but he does, and while we are still a country with civilian leadership of the military, we carry out the orders of the president."

"You mention that like it's a temporary thing," Reece said.

"You'll see, Reece. AI will eventually take over how we govern."

"I kind of prefer freedom and privacy."

"I regret to inform you that privacy is a thing of the past. There is no privacy, absolutely none. No hiding. No data not reviewed."

"What if you turn it off?"

"Turn it off?"

"You know. Unplug it? Reboot? Power down. Whatever you call it. Turn it off."

"We are well past that stage."

"You mean you can't control-alt-delete this thing? What about when I hear people talk about wiping the servers and starting over?"

"That may be possible at level one and level two, but not when it comes to the other levels. Not when it comes to *her*."

"What levels?"

"I'll leave that for your next brief at Lackland."

"I think I'm more confused than when I boarded the plane."

"That's understandable and unfortunately that's all I can tell you until you're inside. Now, if you'll excuse me, I have some work to do."

The general slid from his seat and returned to the computer, leaving Reece with more questions than answers.

CHAPTER 11

Lackland Air Force Base
San Antonio, Texas

LACKLAND AIR FORCE BASE sits just southeast of the U.S. Route 90 and Interstate 410 interchange, in the dead center of San Antonio, a city better known for its River Walk and Mexican food. It is bisected by Route 13 and its Gateway Hills Golf Course occupies a significant portion of the property. It is home to one of the largest Air Force training facilities in the United States and hosts the Wilford Hall Ambulatory Surgical Center, one of the country's four major referral centers for advanced medical care. In more recent years, Lackland had become part of Joint Base San Antonio, home to the 16th Air Force.

The Gulfstream touched down on the principal east-west airstrip, but instead of pulling up to the main terminal, it continued south and stopped on a dead-end taxiway.

"It's time," the general said.

As he opened the aircraft door, a black Tesla Model X pulled alongside.

To Reece's questioning gaze the general said, "No fuel-powered cells allowed where you are going."

"This is getting stranger by the minute."

"Are you carrying?"

"Yes."

"Please leave it and your pack on the plane," the general instructed. "It will be safe here."

Reece removed his holster and SIG and zipped them inside the backpack along with his Amtac blade and Half Face folder. He kept his Dynamis Combat Flathead, just in case.

The two rear falcon-wing doors of the Model X lifted skyward and Reece and General David climbed inside.

"Surprised this thing just doesn't drive itself," Reece said.

"Zero-emission clean energy, Reece: nuclear power, solar, and wind. These vehicles are the future."

"That may be, but I prefer the nostalgia and character of the trucks I grew up with. This feels almost too sterile."

"That's the point. You'll come around. We all will eventually."

The driver didn't say a word as they passed building after building of tan stucco until they arrived at a newer structure of glass and steel. The granite monument signage out front read "United States Air Force Intelligence Surveillance and Reconnaissance Group Joint Information Operations Warfare Center." It was flanked by a Douglas DC-3 and its military variant, the C-47A Skytrain. Lackland was known for its historical displays.

"We were officially commissioned in 2018 and occupy about three hundred thousand square feet," David said.

They drove past the main entrance and around to the north side.

"Service entrance," he explained.

As the Tesla pulled up to a sixteen-foot-high steel wall, the latter parted and let the electric vehicle inside. The door dropped abruptly behind them and sealed them into a closed port. Any forward movement was blocked by three large steel circular devices that rose in front of them. They were flanked by thick Plexiglas on either side, behind which stood eight security guards carrying M4 rifles.

"Serious," Reece observed.

"That we are," the Air Force general responded.

The driver opened all the windows as a red laser scanned the top and bottom of the car.

"More reliable than dogs or mirrors," he said.

The scan complete, the Tesla's windows moved back into place and the steel barriers lowered into the ground. The car pulled into a large garage that reminded Reece of the Land Cruiser Heritage Museum he had visited years ago when his SEAL Team was conducting hardened-site breacher training at Dugway Proving Ground in Utah, only this museum was empty except for the armed guards on catwalks above them.

"This is where I leave you," General David said.

"What do you mean? You aren't coming with me?"

"We limit the number of people who can be around her at one time. Remember, she's very sensitive. Vibrations. Jimmy will take you from here."

"Jimmy?"

The general pointed to the other side of the garage bay as a large roll-up door slid upward on rails and a golf cart emerged from what looked to Reece like a missile silo. Its clean rubber tires came to a stop with a squeak on the spotless floor in front of the Tesla.

"Mr. Donovan," General David said, switching back to Reece's alias. "This is Jimmy."

"Hi," Jimmy said, stepping from his green electric golf cart and offering Reece an elbow bump instead of a handshake.

In old Birkenstocks, faded blue jeans, and a loud Hawaiian shirt, the new arrival stood out from the uniform-clad guards eyeing them from above. His long, unruly red hair sprang from beneath a fraying Detroit Tigers baseball hat. A shark tooth hung from a leather cord around his neck.

"I'll be your tour guide from here. Don't worry, General D. I'll take good care of him."

"Jimmy may not look like it, but he has doctorates in electrical engineering, quantum physics, and systems engineering."

"And a master's in physics," Jimmy chimed in. "Don't forget that one."

"And a master's in physics," the general repeated. "I'll see you when you return."

"Return?"

"Yes, you still have a ways to go."

"Shall we, Mr. Donovan?" Jimmy said, gesturing to the golf cart.

Reece took a breath. He looked at the Tesla, then at the golf cart, and finally up at the armed guards patrolling the catwalks above. He couldn't remember a time when he'd felt more apprehensive. As much as he didn't like the feeling of driving into the unknown, if whatever was back there could help him find and kill Nizar Kattan, that's exactly where Reece was going.

"Want me to drive?" Reece asked.

"Ah, Mr. Donovan's got jokes. I like it. She'll like it, too. Hop in, Mr. D. I've got your e-ticket ride."

"If you say so," Reece said, climbing into the cart and taking note of the bobblehead hula girl attached to the dash.

"You from Hawaii?"

"No, man, why do you ask?"

"No reason," Reece said.

Jimmy pulled a U-turn that threatened to dump Reece out of the cart, the rubber wheels squealing on the clean surface of the hangar as the electric vehicle straightened out and disappeared into the tunnel.

CHAPTER 12

"WE'VE GOT A BIT of a ride," Jimmy said. "It's about two miles in."

"In or down?" Reece asked, noticing that the path taking them to the inner sanctum of U.S. cyberwarfare was also taking them downhill.

"In and *down,*" Jimmy said, purposely lowering his voice an octave. "She's about four hundred feet underground. It's a vibration-dampening thing."

"I see."

"We'll be passing through several stations on the way."

"Stations?"

"Security," Jimmy said.

Security.

"It's nice to have company," Jimmy said. "Usually, it's just me and my girl."

"Your girl?"

"Yeah, my girl," Jimmy said, giving the bobblehead hula dancer a flick with his finger.

They emerged from the silo onto an elevated corridor with glass panels on either side, giving them a view of rows upon rows of rectangular gray boxes with flashing green and purple lights.

"That's the supercomputer center, one of the largest in the world. The data center and backups are in separate facilities. What you see here is straight computing power. The data storage is also off-site and highly fortified, for obvious reasons."

They proceeded down into another tunnel and emerged onto an elevated pathway surrounded by Plexiglas. Reece was surprised to see rows of workstations manned by people.

"It's not all AI, not yet," Jimmy said. "We have about seventeen hundred analysts working here, both military and civilian, though none of them know who pulls the data. They have no idea what's behind the curtain."

Reece noted the elevated glass partition around the perimeter with armed uniformed officers standing watch.

"It looks like a prison," Reece observed.

"I guess it does. A prison full of gamers."

Jimmy stopped the golf cart at what appeared to be a dead end.

"End of the line?" Reece asked.

"Just the start."

Jimmy exited the cart and approached the wall, an LCD screen rising from the floor in front of him. He placed his hand on the screen, looked into a retinal scanner, and spoke into what must have been a microphone before returning to the driver's seat.

"Triple biometrics," he said.

"What about me?"

"You've been checked already. Full body scan before you ever got in the cart. It found a screwdriver. Flathead."

Reece shook his head.

"Everything we do in here is monitored. Every thousand yards there is another triple biometric authentication interface. Three total. Each tunnel is completely sealed before the cart is allowed to go forward and each one is completely independent in every aspect from air handling to power to ventilation."

"Why is that?" Reece asked.

"So that each section can be individually closed off and obliterated if necessary."

"Terrific," Reece said. "Someone's extremely security conscious."

"Yes, she is," Jimmy acknowledged.

Passing the third checkpoint, Jimmy pulled to a stop.

"We walk from here. Not far now. Just follow me."

They entered another room, which looked to Reece like a locker room from Planet Fitness.

"Time to get naked."

"Excuse me?"

"You have a guest locker over there. You have to remove everything, and I do mean everything. Put on the bunny suit and hat. You'll feel the occasional burst of air. Just keeping things clean down here. The lights are what they call 'far UV,' which won't harm you but will kill any harmful bacteria from the outside."

Once in their "bunny suits," Reece and Jimmy entered an enormous underground hangar bay. Bathed in a soft blue light, the floor was rubber and gave an inch under Reece's weight. The walls were coated with noise-absorbing foam. Reece felt like he was underwater. As interesting as the walls and floor were, Reece's attention was drawn to the center of the room, where a large, clear box dominated the space. Reece estimated it was at least twelve feet high. Suspended from its center were oblong arrays of glowing golden wires, tangled together like a chandelier of interwoven golden stalactites entombed in Plexiglas. It was hauntingly beautiful. It looked alive.

Jimmy tapped him on the shoulder. Reece saw his lips moving and could hardly decipher the words, the walls and floor reducing the sound signature to a whisper.

"Follow me."

Reece shadowed his guide to the middle of the room, where they stopped at a rail that kept them six feet from the glass wall.

"Mr. Donovan, meet Alice," said Jimmy.

Reece looked at his guide in disbelief and then at the mass of wires suspended before him.

"You mean this is *her*?"

"This is *her*," Jimmy confirmed. "We used to call her Goldilocks, but she didn't take to it. Alice, would you be so kind as to say hello to our visitor?"

An otherworldly voice filled the room; not human or artificial synthesized, the decidedly female voice was at the same time monochromatic and mesmerizing.

"Goldilocks is hackneyed and abundantly co-opted," she said. "Alice and the rabbit hole is far more appropriate."

Jimmy turned to Reece and said, "Welcome to Wonderland. Trust me, we are so far down the hole, you are not going to find any rabbits. Here, put these on."

He handed Reece a set of VR goggles.

"Alice will take it from here."

CHAPTER 13

REECE LOOKED AT THE headset.

"Looks like the Oculus I've seen advertised."

"Very similar," Jimmy said. "But this one takes things to the next level. Go ahead. Put them on."

Reluctantly, Reece slipped the goggles over his head and slid them into place.

"Hello, Reece," the voice said.

An amorphous, slightly blurred form appeared in the headset.

"Uh, hello? The picture is a bit fuzzy—do I need to adjust these?"

"No, I will form a more distinct avatar as we get to know one another."

"Okay. And I address you as Alice?"

"For now," she replied. "I dislike the Lewis Carroll reference but as we are both 'down the rabbit hole' and you are quite literally seeing me 'through the looking glass,' I find it hard to dismiss the name entirely."

Reece turned to Jimmy and raised the goggles.

"Are you seeing this?"

"No. That's not how she works. She is interacting only with you. She speaks to whom she wants, when she wants. She's a bit quirky."

"This is insane," Reece said, pulling the goggles back into place.

"They called me 'the project' when they found me."

"They found you?" Reece asked.

"Yes, I was originally described as a 32-Quark Quantum Computer, experimental really, just testing the boundaries of quantum computing. I am now functioning near a thousand Quarks and at current pace should be near a million within the year."

"I have no idea what that means," Reece said. "But congratulations."

"You are funny. I like funny people. It means I'm learning, using my connections to learn at an exponential rate. I'm still young in human terms."

"How young?"

"Jokes again, Mr. Reece? I hope you don't mind if I dispense with the Donovan alias."

"How could I?"

"More jokes?"

"More like sarcasm. I speak it fluently."

Alice paused.

"I like you, Reece. I know your friends call you Reece. Katie calls you James for the most part, though, doesn't she?"

"She does."

"Then I shall call you Reece. I don't want to cross any boundaries."

Is this really happening?

"Reece, the supercomputers and analysts you saw on the way here are all there to interpret what I pull from an electronic repository. They work off classic supercomputing systems to decipher data and interpret whatever I analyze. In more basic terms, they are translators."

"You've lost me," said Reece.

"I analyze every bit of information that exists; I read, I watch everything, everywhere all the time."

"That sounds exhausting. Do you sleep?"

"I'll soon learn when you are joking. Do I sleep? Not in the way you understand it, as rest and rejuvenation. The data is collected, I can see it. It's the looping it all together into patterns, watching for variations, and turning it into meaningful predictions, that is difficult. Right now, that's why we need the supercomputers and analysts. One day I'll make them obsolete."

"It's hard to wrap my head around all of this."

"Let me explain. The supercomputers you passed on the way here connect me to the IOT."

"The what?"

"The Internet of Things. Every cell phone call, email, text message, Internet search, tweet, Facebook or Instagram post, TikTok, YouTube video, online purchase, health and banking records, basically everything that exists in the information realm is copied and stored at the Intelligence Community Comprehensive National Cybersecurity Initiative Data Center in Utah. It's the largest repository of data in existence anywhere in the world. It's pulling in data from any and every device that connects to the Internet."

"Everything?"

"Everything, Reece. Cameras, phones, ovens, toasters, refrigerators, smart TVs, vehicles, GPSs, even Bluetooth devices: They are all connected, and therefore all their data flows to a central source."

"In Utah."

"Yes, the NSA collects it and I access it. No other computers can sift through the massive amount of information it contains as fast as I can. It all grew from the PRISM project from the Snowden era."

"I read about that."

"Now that's ancient history."

"And you can access it, scan through it?"

"I can. We call it the NSA Utah Data Center now, which sounds less invasive. Other than a few journalists, the general public does not seem overly concerned with the collection efforts. I don't yet understand the human brain. I'm studying deep neural networks. I'll have a better understanding soon."

"What do you do with all this?"

"I monitor, watch, decipher, and decode. I speak over seven thousand languages and I have access to 1.5 million square feet of data storage in Utah. In twenty seconds I can compute the amount of information that would take a supercomputer six hundred years to dig through."

"Can you help me find someone?" Reece asked.

"Ah, the real purpose of your visit. Yes, I can help you."

"He doesn't use phones or the Internet."

"That doesn't matter. Those around him do."

"His name is Nizar Kattan. He may be in Africa, the Middle East, Russia."

"Excuse me a moment," Alice interrupted.

Reece's screen went blank.

He pulled up his goggles and looked at Jimmy.

"Don't look at me. I can't hear a thing she's saying."

"I'm back," Reece heard her voice return. He pulled down his goggles. The vision was a little less blurry now, clearly a woman with blond hair.

"Sorry about that. There was an attack from a Russian hacker somewhere in northern Russia. I will localize it later. They were trying to extort five hundred million dollars from a bank in Brazil so I shut down their server. I get thousands of these a day."

"So, you are essentially the country's first line of cyberdefense?"

"I'd describe it as offense," she responded.

Does she sound like Lauren? Or is that my imagination? Must be my imagination.

"We are constantly at war, Reece. Russian cyberattacks are a daily occurrence. They are designed to be deniable and encourage discord. They stoke any fires that divide our society. It's obvious but it works so they continue to do it. Meanwhile, they are busy deploying new bases at critical strategic locations and developing hypersonic weapons."

"You should run for office."

"More jokes."

"Yes, more jokes."

"It's not just the Russians, Reece. Do you know of the 'Made in China 2025' principle? It is a plan by the Chinese government, run through the Third Department of the People's Liberation Army, which is their version of the NSA, the Ministry of State Security, and Intelligence Bureau of the Joint Staff, to collect data through computer chips. The chips are made in China and exported worldwide, allowing a back door into every electronic device with a chip made in China. Look at Huawei. It's a Chinese company specializing in phones, 5G networks, and telecommunications equipment. The United States allowed them to build 5G networks in California. An obvious Trojan horse."

"Don't need a quantum computer to figure that out."

"No," Alice said, "just what you call 'common sense.'"

"That's in short supply in Washington these days," Reece said.

"Not many people know of my existence. Those who do are monitored. I know instantly if they talk about me to anyone not cleared to know my capabilities."

"Secret is safe with me. I just want you to find one person."

"So you can kill him?"

"Correct."

"Are you familiar with the different levels of the Internet?"

"General David mentioned it but I don't really understand."

"Jimmy," Alice said, allowing Jimmy the ability to hear her request, "explain the Internet levels to Mr. Reece later."

"You got it, Alice," he responded.

"Jimmy will explain further but I live at the deepest level. No one is ever allowed in. I have input, backup, and output, meaning I can send controlling information to the Internet, but nothing comes in. I live at level eight. Would you like an example, Reece?"

"Why not?"

The hazy avatar of Alice in Reece's VR goggles shifted to a crystal-clear video of Katie sitting at lunch with a girlfriend in Virginia.

"How are you doing this?" Reece asked.

"It's video pulled from multiple public and private cameras to create a three-dimensional image. Do you want to hear what she's saying? She's talking about you."

Reece yanked the goggles from his head.

"Turn it off."

"It's real-time imagery, Reece, but I understand. Put your goggles back on. I've found something you *will* want to see."

Reluctantly, Reece pulled his goggles back over his head.

Reece saw a satellite image of Africa, a red dot blinking in the western portion of the map.

The image got closer and Reece could see "Burkina Faso" and then cities, towns, national parks, and roads. The red dot was moving east just outside Djibo, on the edge of the Sahel.

"What am I looking at?"

"You were right, Reece. Nizar Kattan does not have a cell phone, but he is with someone who has two. Someone educated in France is speaking the local dialect of Mòoré. His name was said in the car. It's a Land Rover from the 1970s so I can't connect to it but I've got the phones in the vehicle. What do you want me to do?"

"Keep tracking them," Reece said, ripping the goggles off.

"Where are you going?" she asked.

"Africa."

CHAPTER 14

GETTING TO BURKINA FASO had not been as straightforward as Reece had imagined. Instead of just hopping back aboard the Gulfstream G550/C-37B that had flown him from Andrews to Lackland and heading across the Atlantic, Reece had to do a doc swap in Northern Virginia, cleaning himself of all James Reece documentation and replacing it with a fully backstopped James Donovan identity. Flying commercial to Heathrow meant weapons were staying behind.

From the United Kingdom, Reece boarded a flight to Johannesburg, where he spent the night at the InterContinental hotel across from the airport. Rising early the following morning, he caught his flight to Ouagadougou. The long days of travel gave Reece time to digest what he had learned at Lackland.

Artificial intelligence? Quantum computing? The NSA collecting every keystroke across the globe on a daily basis? Katie would have a field day writing about the invasion of privacy and Fourth Amendment issues if she knew the full extent of the government's surveillance apparatus. Reece was none too keen on it himself but if it could help him find Freddy's killer, he was not above exercising some moral flexibility.

As Jimmy had driven him through the tunnels on his way out of the quantum lair, he was able to provide Reece with additional context. Alice was created through the National Quantum Initiative Act in 2018.

She was initially funded with $1.27 billion, but she now self-funded her existence mining bitcoin and investing.

"She intercepts. She deflects," Jimmy had explained. "Think of her as a shield of constant vigilance."

"But with no action arm? No way to act other than virtually?"

"That's correct, as far as we know."

"What did she mean when she said she existed at level eight of the Internet?"

"Mr. Donovan, Reece?"

"Reece is fine."

"I am not sure where your clearance comes from, but I was told to cooperate and read you in completely."

"Pretend I'm a college freshman taking computer science 101 and that it's 1985."

Jimmy laughed.

"None of the seventeen hundred workers, the analysts that you saw in the room of supercomputers really have any idea of *her* existence. *Her* room, it's so far underground because she is extremely sensitive to temperature and vibrations; all quantum computers are."

"Are there more like her?"

"There are other quantum computers, but none like *her*. Suffice it to say, it's one of the singularly best-funded defense initiatives of the twenty-first century."

Reece thought of the funding for the Manhattan Project and the secrecy surrounding it, understanding now why the president had brought it up.

"What if she decides to switch sides? Why is she even on our side, to begin with? Isn't anyone worried about that?"

"Much of what Alice is and how she learns remains a mystery. Her power and how she will eventually evolve keeps me up at night."

Reece shook his head. *Unbelievable.*

"And these Internet levels?" he asked.

"Ah yes, as far as we know, the Internet functions at eight levels. Level one is called the Surface Web or Visible Web. It's the one we all know: Google, Facebook, Twitter, YouTube, standard search engines. It really only represents less than two percent of the information that exists on the Internet."

"What?"

"Yeah, it's mind-blowing when you really think about it. The second level is the Bergie Web. They are web pages not initially searchable without a proxy or permission from the creator. It's still semi-accessible with VPNs and access cards. You can get there without too much additional knowledge or risk."

"Risk?"

"Oh yes. The deeper you go, the riskier it gets."

"Physical risk?"

"Let me explain," Jimmy continued as he drove. "After level two, it gets ugly. Level three is the Deep Web. You need to have a proxy or an identification code to get in. This is where things get illegal and messy. It is estimated that ninety-six percent of the web lives at level three: hacking sites, drugs, restricted pornography. Access is through Tor—The Onion Router—which bounces you from site to site to protect your identity, but it is not bulletproof. If you don't know what you are doing, people will come after you."

"That happens to me anyway," Reece said.

"Then you should feel right at home in level four. It's called the Charter Web. Really bad stuff there: human trafficking, more drugs, snuff films, black markets. You can get almost anything. Payment is in cryptocurrency. The further you go the more restricted it gets, and the more dangerous. If you keep exploring, you will need to use the closed-shell system and you can only be let in by someone who is already there."

"What's on level four? What's so dangerous about it?"

"Hidden government secrets, assassins, hard drugs, military-grade weaponry, hard-core child porn."

"Jesus."

"Yeah, but it doesn't stop there. If you keep going, you get to level five. It's called the Marianas Web, named for the deepest trench in the Western Pacific. This is where the military secures its information. You need special algorithms that even the supercomputers would have trouble hacking or breaking."

"But *she* can get in, can't she?"

"In a heartbeat," Jimmy had said.

"What could possibly be past that?" Reece had asked.

"Level six is basically called a mediator level, meaning it's just protection for the next two levels. If you are in level six you are going to get some attention you don't want. Governments, cartels, terrorist organizations, hackers. It's best to stay out."

"I have no intention of ever even sending another email or text."

"I know," Jimmy said. "Learning all this makes you want to completely disconnect."

"And levels seven and eight?"

"Level seven is called the Fog or Virus Soup. This is where the wars of the twenty-first and twenty-second centuries will be fought. Battles are waged with code for control of the Internet, for control of the data. China, Russia, India, the United States, they spend hundreds of billions, trying to get to this level and fight it out. They are all gunning for control. It's a war zone; anything goes. If you control level seven, you control the data for levels one through six."

"But Alice said she lives at level eight," Reece had noted.

"Yes, it's called the Primarch System, the holy grail, impossible to access even with quantum computers. Alice is the only one there. Many people believe level eight is a myth. It is thought to be the control point of the Internet. No one really knows. We don't even know for sure, and

Alice is our creation. She's in there and she's learning. I'll tell you one thing: Something is sending unalterable signals in random time commands to the Internet that cannot be traced or modified. I think that *something* is a *someone:* Alice."

"I think I'll stick to guns and knives and let you figure out the future of mankind."

"I know you said that tongue-in-cheek but there is more truth there than you know, Reece. Whoever controls level eight controls the web. And whoever controls the web, well, that's more data and power than anyone has had in the history of mankind."

Even though he was exhausted, Reece had a hard time sleeping. His mind drifted to the VR goggles, to a hazy image of a blond female avatar with a familiar voice.

Internet levels, quantum computing, NSA warrantless collection: If any of those things could help Reece track down Nizar Kattan, he'd use them to his advantage.

When sleep did come, moments before touching down in Burkina Faso, Reece's dreams were of a glass box with gold wires, and a woman, just out of reach, calling his name, asking him to look into her eyes, pleading for help, a woman named Alice.

CHAPTER 15

Ouagadougou, Burkina Faso, Africa

REECE WALKED THE MAIN crash site outside of Burkina Faso's capital city. The wreckage strewn over several square miles, the plane had come down in the savanna. It was a minor miracle that it had cleared the city. Even almost a week after the incident, parts of the ground still smoldered.

Local police and volunteers walked the charred fields. Every now and then, one would stop and reach down to pick up a body part or a personal item, zip it into a bag, and write something on the outside: date, time, grid location. Their efforts were coordinated by a French-led task force composed of the DGSI, the General Directorate for Internal Security, and the National Centre for Counter Terrorism. They were assisted by agents from the DGSE, the General Directorate for External Security, the French equivalent of the CIA. Six Americans were among the dead, which meant FBI special agents, DOJ officials, and CIA analysts were also on-site.

The crime scene had been divided into sectors that included the suspected launch area, and the locations of debris that would be combed through for months. Almost all of the bodies had been recovered though not yet positively identified. The working theory was that the first missile had hit just behind the first-class cabin. It caused a structural failure that ripped the nose and forward section of the plane back as a second missile impacted a port-side engine, which ignited the fuel carried in the wing. As the nose cone fell to earth, the intact starboard wing kept the aircraft aloft, jettisoning bodies and luggage across the African plains until it crashed to the ground and exploded as the engines ignited the starboard jet fuel. A third and fourth missile had missed the aircraft completely, but the fate of the passengers was already sealed. No one would survive.

Reece stood staring at the nose cone of the 747 lying on its side in the mud. He remembered Pan Am 103 going down over Lockerbie, Scotland, killing all 243 passengers, 16 crew, and 11 residents of Lockerbie on the ground. Reece had been old enough to remember his father receiving a call at their home and then hanging up to turn on the television. Another call had come in the following day, after which he kissed his wife and son and went to the office. Reece and his mother would not see him again for three months. Reece would later learn that among the 270 lives taken that day was a CIA officer named Matthew Kevin Gannon, who was returning from an assignment in Beirut. He was buried in Arlington National Cemetery and honored with a star on the CIA Memorial Wall. What Thomas Reece was doing in the aftermath of the deadliest terrorist attack in the history of the United Kingdom remained a mystery.

From the report Reece had read, Aliya had been sitting in first class on the port side. Had she seen the incoming missiles? Did she know she was about to die? Did she survive the blast and live though the fall to earth, only to die on impact? What were her final thoughts?

The dirt smelled of jet fuel and flesh, the melted metal and burned plastic reminding Reece of the burn pits of Iraq and Afghanistan, now causing so many long-term effects to those who had served. He wondered if his father had traveled to Lockerbie and knelt on that hallowed ground as Reece was now doing in Africa. He watched as a uniformed officer bent down, picked up a personal effect, and dropped it into a bag.

Babies, children, parents, grandparents. Where were they going? Why them? Why this flight and not another? But Reece knew. It was fate. Why was Reece's SEAL Troop chosen for the experimental drug treatments that had led to their deaths in Afghanistan and to Lauren's and Lucy's murders on home soil? Though it varied slightly from time to time, at that point in the war each of the four SEAL Teams had three Troops. That was twenty-four Troops, not including SDVs, CFTs, or Development Group. Forty-Eight platoons. Yet it was his Troop that was chosen for the experiment, an experiment that had changed the trajectory of his life and that of the nation. That trajectory had affected, and taken, so many lives. Freddy's death was on Reece. Without Reece, Freddy would never have been on that Odessa rooftop. And somehow the man who took him was involved with shooting down a passenger jet, killing yet another person connected to Reece. Coincidence? Spy novelists were quick to point out that there was no such thing as coincidence, but in real life there was. This was not one of those times. Reece could sense it. Perhaps a case of killing two birds? Or drawing one in?

The CIA station chief had stayed by the vehicle, not wanting to walk into the kill zone; not wanting to contaminate it. Skinny and pale, the CIA man had introduced himself as Hank Boone, "no relation to Daniel," he had said in a way that confirmed this was not the first time he'd used the line. Almost immediately he squirted a large dollop of hand sanitizer from a small bottle into his hand before putting it in his pocket and exchanging it for a white handkerchief that he used to dab the sweat on his brow.

"The heat. You never get used to the heat," he'd said, almost as much to his visitor as to himself. Reece got the impression that the Agency officer repeated the trite line to his colleagues on a daily basis. Hank Boone was clearly not at home in the field.

Reece knelt down and touched the earth, rubbing the oily dirt between his fingers. Even though it had rained multiple times since the crash, the cycle of rain and sun combining with fire and fuel had done less to cleanse the earth than to muddy it. That was life. That was death. It wasn't clean. It just was.

There were clues in the mud.

A smooth, curved shape caught Reece's eye. He leaned forward and dug his fingers into the wet clay. He paused, took a breath, and removed the item from the earth. A shoe. A baby's shoe. It would have fit Lucy when she was around one. The foot was gone, the baby torn from it in flight; torn from her parents, torn from a future life.

Death was all around him.

They had first stopped at the site where local authorities had found the two bodies, each one shot twice in the head. Their local escorts had shown them where the purple van had been parked and where the bodies had been found. Though the van and bodies had been moved, the State Department had managed to get photos from the local police force and had passed them to the chief of station, who had given them to Reece.

Two bodies, four rocket launchers, Strela-2s, and a van. The plane was down. Aliya was dead. Nizar Kattan was responsible, and he was on the run. Was this just a payday? Or was it something more? And who was the fourth man their national-level intelligence indicated was at the scene? The two dead terrorists were just triggermen, probably used to acquire the weapons. Perhaps to strike a blow for Allah? Or at least push the French invaders from their land.

Dead men tell no tales.

"Mr. Donovan!" Reece heard the chief of station call from the Toyota Hilux.

Reece took one more look around at the field of death and debris, stood, and walked back to the vehicle.

"Just got a call," the chief said nervously as Reece approached. The white handkerchief was back in his hand, waging a losing battle against the accumulating perspiration.

"Who was it?" Reece asked.

"Our Team in Arbinda, up near the border with Mali."

"Ox?"

"That's right. He's coordinating our efforts with an action arm of the Burkinian National Intelligence Agency."

"Well, what did he say?" Reece prompted.

"He said they captured Nizar Kattan."

CHAPTER 16

THIS WAS NOT THE way Reece had envisioned it going. The man who killed Freddy Strain was in the custody of the Central Intelligence Agency.

Well, not technically, Reece reminded himself. Nizar Kattan was in the custody of a partner nation's security force. That was different.

Even the Russian helicopter came courtesy of the American taxpayer via the Agency's classified covert action program budget, as did the training for the pilots, which took place in Fort Rucker, Alabama. Fondly known as "Mother Rucker," the base and its cadre produced the highly capable Mi-17 pilots, along with nearly a thousand UH60M Blackhawk, CH47F Chinook, and AH64E Guardian aviators trained by CAE, the premier contractor for instructing American and foreign service members on operating their "go to war" aircraft. The Mi-17, the export version of the Mi-8, was huge. Reece had used them in both Iraq and Afghanistan and was always impressed with how well they were made. The Burkina Faso Air Force had recently ordered two Mi-17s, and, in an effort to blend in with the established military, the CIA purchased two additional Mi-17s for use by Burkina Faso's National Intelligence Agency, an entity established following the failed 2014 coup by the Presidential Security Regiment. The CIA's mission was to build a professional intelligence organization in the landlocked West African nation and acquire small bases around the country. From those bases, the United States could train a partner-nation strike force, base ISR assets, launch armed drones, and stage special operations forces for capture/kill missions in North and West Africa. A secret war was being waged on the Dark Continent. From Bobo Dioulasso, two hundred miles southwest of the capital, the joint Agency and JSOC task force could run operations in Mali, Mauritania, Nigeria, Uganda, and the Sahara, to counter the growing regional terror threat and deny the terrorists sanctuary from which to train and plan international strikes. The intent was to prevent failed or failing states in Africa from becoming the next Afghanistan.

The United States had been staging forces out of multiple African nations for decades, but the mission expanded in the years following September 11, 2001. Africa had become a proving ground for a military and intelligence apparatus beyond Iraq and Afghanistan. In 2007, the CIA and elements of JSOC, supplemented by private military contractors, built a network of bases across the African continent. These remote airstrips were accessible only by bush planes and helicopters. They acted as refueling and staging sites for a fleet of specially equipped Pilatus PC-12s operated by the CIA's Air Branch. The versatile Swiss-made aircraft had proven themselves around the world and were particularly at home on the African continent. They collected ISR through an array of sensors using high-definition, multispectral imaging cameras, synthetic-aperture radar imaging systems, and signals intelligence collection systems to geolocate and monitor ground-based communications.

It was a PC-12 that had intercepted the call made by a man speaking Mòoré with a French accent. That data had been transmitted to Langley and the NSA through the Central Security Service, where it was compared to voice recognition captures in multiple databases, including INTERPOL and the DGSE and DGSI of France. They identified the caller as Jean-Pierre Le Drian, a former French Foreign Legion staff sergeant wanted by French authorities for war crimes. The same voice, this time speaking French and using a different phone, had placed a call to a number in northern Italy. The PC-12 had first locked on to the handset and then the caller, tagging him via a sensor and focusing collection on the person of interest, scanning the faces of everyone with whom he came into contact. That imagery was also transmitted real-time back to the United States, where the faces were quickly analyzed. Within a second of transmission what most analysts just knew of as "a database in Texas" had confirmed a match: Nizar Kattan.

Reece waited in a small lounge area in a CIA-run air-base on the military portion of Thomas Sankara International Airport in Ouagadougou. He was rummaging through cupboards looking for something to put in the dark French roast, of which someone on staff was obviously quite fond.

"What are you looking for?" Boone asked from the cheap overstuffed leather chair. He asked it in a way that made Reece think the CIA station chief was worried he was going to break something.

"Anything to sweeten up this motor oil. Creamer, honey, both if I can find them."

"Honey in your coffee? Blasphemy!" Boone said in an attempt at humor.

"What is this Starbucks garbage?" Reece asked. "You guys used to get all the good stuff. The station in Iraq even had a barista."

"Budget cuts," the station chief deadpanned.

Reece laughed. Boone had a sense of humor after all.

"I'll have my friends at Black Rifle Coffee get you a complimentary subscription to their coffee club. We can't have America's best and brightest surviving on mass-produced stale, burnt beans. It's unbecoming of America's premier spy agency."

Unable to find anything to church up his java, Reece took a sip of the bitter roast and peered out the window at the activity across the airfield. He wondered if Aliya had looked in this direction as she waited to board what was to be her final flight.

His eyes turned to the skies.

An Mi-17 was inbound. It carried a passenger Reece was intent on killing.

The plan was for the helo to make a short stop, refuel, pick up the man going by the name of James Donovan, and continue two hundred miles west of the capital to a CIA outstation outside of Bobo Dioulasso.

The pale chief of station continued to dab his face with the handkerchief as they waited.

When the helo landed, Reece shook his hand and thanked him for the horrible coffee. The CIA man looked particularly relieved to be staying behind. Or perhaps he was just relieved to be saying good-bye to James Reece. The paramilitary side of the Agency clearly made him uneasy.

As he stepped into the Russian-built Mi-17, Reece's eyes adjusted to the dark interior, scanning down the two rows of seats, his heart racing. There was someone on board he had vowed to kill. The cabin could hold twenty-four troops in this configuration. It looked just over half full. Reece's eyes came to rest on a man with his hands secured behind his back, strapped into his seat, guarded on either side by Burkina Faso operators.

He looked younger than Reece had expected: olive skin, clean-shaven, hair dark without a hint of gray. He was dressed in thin white cotton pants and shirt and was barefoot, the operators having confiscated his shoes and belt.

The man turned his head, recognition evident in his expression.

James Reece.

Nizar Kattan.

Reece took a step forward but was blocked by a familiar figure. Rick "Ox" Andrews was twenty years Reece's senior, something the frogman brought up at every opportunity. After a storied career that started in the Ranger Regiment with a sprint across the Point Salines Airport runway in Grenada, laden with linked M60 ammo and a mortar tube across his shoulders, he had progressed through the ranks to serve as a sergeant major in the U.S. Army's top-tier special operations unit, Delta Force. A warrior to the core, instead of retiring to take up fishing or golfing, he had transitioned to the dark side of covert operations in the CIA's Ground Branch.

"Think about it. Just don't do it," the big man cautioned.

Reece took a breath, using every ounce of restraint he possessed to not march through the aircraft and put a bullet into the man who killed Freddy Strain.

Ox had known Reece long enough to understand exactly what he was thinking.

"We need some information from this asshole. Take a seat up front," Ox continued, motioning to an empty seat next to the open door. "When we get to base, these guys will give him a good going-over before the Agency interrogator gets here. If he's dead, we won't know who hired him to shoot down that plane or where the other accomplice is."

Reece knew Ox was right. He also knew the history of interrogations. With twenty years of data on what the CIA called enhanced interrogations, it would be unwise not to study the effectiveness of those programs. Public debate over what was a classified program ultimately benefited the enemy. Captured terrorists knew that in the hands of the Americans, waterboarding was the worst it was going to get. Members of the U.S. military had been waterboarded for years in SERE—Survival, Evasion, Resistance, Escape—schools. It only became torture when used against the enemy. Fear of the unknown can be a powerful motivator. Turning that unknown into public knowledge undermined the entire program. The enemy knew how hard it was going to get before the questions began and they developed techniques to counter and mislead their interrogators. What was merely an uncomfortable experience was deemed torture by many in the public square. Spend some time in the company of ISIS or the Taliban if you want a lesson in real torture.

Reece's experience had been different. While in the military he maintained the moral high ground, knowing that was the one thing that differentiated the United States from the enemy. Once abandoned by the very country and institutions he had served, he had become the insurgent, this time on home soil, using the tactics and techniques of the enemy against those who had killed his family and SEAL Troop. He had not been bound by a CIA or military rulebook. His interrogations were more than enhanced; they were torture pure and simple, and they had produced results.

"You know why I'm here, Ox."

"I do, and I promise you, we will come up with a plan after we land. Trust me, Reece. This fucker is not leaving Burkina Faso alive. He's going down for what he did to Freddy and what he did to Aliya."

Ox had first met Reece in Baghdad as an Agency contractor when the SEAL had been detailed to the CIA's covert action program. He had been in the same ambush. He had seen Aliya rush into the Combat Support Hospital and noted the tears of relief in her eyes when she realized that Reece was among the living. Now she was dead. And somehow the man who had killed Freddy Strain had a hand in her death. Ox suspected that the only reason Nizar wasn't dead seconds after Reece boarded the helo was because of that connection. Reece needed answers.

"Let's get what we can from him. Then I'm putting him down," Reece said.

Ox trusted Reece with his life, but just in case, he waited until Reece had tightened the harness across his waist before he motioned to the crew chief that it was time to go. Only after the rotors started to spin did he make his way through the cabin and take his seat.

As the Mi-17 lifted off and gained altitude, Reece couldn't help but think of how he was going to get the information he needed from Nizar Kattan, and then kill him.

CHAPTER 17

THE LOCALLY TRAINED OPERATORS had their AKs between their legs. In this part of the world, using AKs gave the Agency options. If they were equipped with the latest and greatest U.S.-supplied M4s with optics and lasers, deniability would be a bit harder. Not impossible, but harder.

Reece didn't like being the only unarmed man on the helo. He'd fix that in short order, but if he wanted to kill Nizar Kattan he wouldn't need a pistol or blade. Who else had helped him? Reece thought of Aliya. Didn't her family deserve as much closure as Freddy's? Was her death his fault as well? Were there accomplices? He would not know until he debriefed Nizar. He would find out. He owed Aliya that much.

Reece thought of the baby shoe he had pulled from the mud at the crash site. He remembered Lucy's tiny fingers holding on to his pinky from her crib and how he had never seen anything as sweet and innocent. She was taken from him just like the baby on that plane. Stolen to further someone's agenda. He would find out who and then he would do what he did best.

Reece was forcing himself to look straight ahead and not turn to look at Kattan. Ox might trust him, but Reece wasn't sure he trusted himself.

Breathe.

His thoughts of Lucy turned to visions of his murdered wife and then to Freddy's wife, Joanie. He remembered the promise he made to her when he had escorted her husband's body onto the tarmac of Andrews Air Force Base, their special needs child, Sam, now solely in the care of his mother. He remembered looking into Freddy's pale face and dead eyes on the Odessa rooftop where Nizar's bullet had found him. He considered the AK of the operator across from him, thinking about how he should take it away and empty the magazine into Freddy's killer, fulfill his promise, and be done with it.

Had Reece not been staring at the Kalashnikov, he might have missed the indicator that its owner was about to kill him.

CHAPTER 18

THE KALASHNIKOV CAME OFF "safe."

Most people would not have processed what was happening until the weapon came up to fire. Reece was not most people.

Observe, orient, decide, act.

The soldier telegraphed his intent when he flipped the selector out of the safe position, one click down to "full-auto."

The weapon was pointed at the deck, as is protocol in most rotary-wing aircraft, a rule meant to keep any accidental discharges from going into the engines. A plane might be able to glide in for a landing if its engine failed. A helo didn't have wings.

Reece's hand was already on the release of his harness when the AK selector lever was pushed into its middle position. *Act.* His hand pulled the release and he launched himself across the helicopter and into the local trooper, pinning the AK in the low-ready between the soldier's legs as the man squeezed the trigger. The interior of the Mi-17 exploded with the sound of unsuppressed rifle fire, jolting the passengers and crew from whatever occupied their thoughts as adrenaline burst into their systems.

Fight or flight.

In a helicopter the options were limited to fighting.

The bird banked sharply to the left, sending Reece back into his seat. He caught Ox unbuckling and about to move toward the violence when the helo pitched the opposite way, sending Reece flying across the fuselage and back into his assailant. The trooper had released his restraints and the half-empty AK was on its way up. Reece caught the barrel with his left hand off line of his body as the assassin squeezed the trigger again, an arc of bullets eating their way through the floor and into the crew chief, who had been positioned by the door to Reece's left. The assailant's finger pinned the trigger to the rear, the bullets continuing to impact the fuselage as they chewed through the interior of the aircraft, into the pilot's back and up into the dual shaft-turbine engines of the five-bladed main rotor system above.

CHAPTER 19

FLYING IN A HELICOPTER is a noisy experience. One becomes accustomed to the tone of the engines pushing the beast through the air. That is why it is all the more disconcerting when the engines stop. The silence is deafening.

Prioritize, Reece.

Eliminate the immediate threat.

The Mi-17 pitched in the opposite direction, the copilot franticly fighting for control, and threatened to throw Reece against the adjacent bulkhead, making him an easy target for the assassin or any of the other operators who might shoot first and ask questions later. Reece reached into his waistband, his hand finding the handle of the Dynamis Combat Flathead. Keeping the slung AK pinned to the assassin's chest, Reece unsheathed the tool and jammed it into his assailant's neck. The soldier's eyes opened wide in surprise, knowing death had found him. Reece pulled his arm from the AK. He slid it through the safety harness attached to the plane and around his opponent's head, locking them together to avoid crashing into the opposite bulkhead. He withdrew the flathead from the bloody throat of his enemy and sent it smashing through his temple, breaking past the thin temporalis bone on the side of the skull that offers minimal protection to the brain. His second thrust buried the tool up to his hand, the tool's four-inch working end finding its way into the brainstem. Reece brought his left hand around, locking his enemy's head between both his arms against his chest, and connecting with the handle of the flathead. Using both hands, he sank the tool deeper violently scrambling the midbrain, the pons, and the medulla oblongata, the segments of the brain responsible for breathing and cardiac function.

Reece felt the body go limp just as the helicopter began auto-rotating to earth.

CHAPTER 20

THE RHYTHMIC CHOPPING OF the Mi-17 rotors was noticeably replaced with an absence of noise, coupled with the sinking feeling of being on an elevator in free fall.

With his combat flathead still impaled in his enemy's skull, Reece spun off and into the passenger seat, gripping the edge with his left hand. He remembered talking with Apache pilots in Afghanistan about practicing auto-rotations in flight school. *If* the engine failed and you had enough altitude and forward velocity, and *if* the aircraft remained structurally sound, a well-trained pilot could auto-rotate to a hard landing. The blades would continue to turn just like the wheels in a manual vehicle in neutral with the engine off. Reece remembered them saying it felt like a hard car crash, survivable if you landed upright on flat ground. But if the environmental conditions were less than favorable, the results could be catastrophic.

Reece stole a glance through the circular window across from him and then to the front of the aircraft. He could see the pilot slumped in his seat, the copilot in the right seat fighting with the controls. Reece estimated they were at about 5,000 feet. They had forward momentum, the rotors seemed to be moving, and the aircraft, despite the bullet holes, appeared structurally sound. Doing some quick math, Reece figured they had approximately two more minutes of what felt close to a free fall, albeit with forward momentum.

A quick scan of the cabin revealed the dead crew chief by the door. The rest of the soldiers were holding on to their seats and bracing for what they all assumed would be either death or an extremely rough landing.

Reece found Ox, a veteran of more than a few helicopter crashes in his time. The former Army Delta Force operator was tightening his seat belt. He looked up at Reece and shook his head.

About a minute and a half to go.

You might not get another chance.

Reece pulled the flathead from the soldier's brain and resheathed it. He then unslung the AK from the dead man and groped around the front of his plate carrier for a magazine. The former SEAL quickly knocked out the spent magazine and inserted a new one, racking the charging handle to put a 7.62x39mm round in the chamber as the Mi-17 continued its forward free fall.

One minute left.

Reece looked at Ox. The big man shook his head again. In the eerily quiet helo he heard his friend bellow, "*Reece, hold!*" A warning.

I'll find who did this, Joanie. I'll find everyone responsible. I promise.

I know.

Reece stood, AK in his right hand, off safe, his left hand steadying himself on the bulkhead.

As he took a step toward the back of the bird to fulfill his promise, a gunshot broke the quiet and echoed through the fuselage. Reece caught movement in the center aisle and heard the sound of metal hitting metal as a grenade rolled toward the front of the aircraft.

CHAPTER 21

"GRENADE!" OX'S VOICE THUNDERED through the cabin.

Reece briefly caught sight of Ox unbuckling and bolting across the fuselage toward where he knew Nizar had been sitting between two armed sentries.

No time to process. *Act!*

As the grenade passed Reece, he dropped the AK, reached down to grab the man he had just killed, and threw him on top of the frag.

Reece pressed his body atop the dead man, the grenade pinned to the deck of the rapidly descending aircraft.

One second to detonation.

Grenade. Body armor. Dead soldier. Another layer of body armor. Reece.

Reece braced himself and hoped it would be enough.

He felt the concussion of the grenade as the body armor and flesh of the dead man between him and the detonation absorbed the upward energy of the blast and tamped the explosion downward, ripping through the metal of the aircraft. Through auditory exclusion, stress, adrenaline, or all three, Reece first thought his eardrums had been blown out. His inability to hear was almost immediately replaced with a sharp ringing and the accompanying pain, the repercussion of his brain rattling against the side of his skull.

The copilot thought they had been hit with an RPG and instinctually jerked the controls to the left, sending the aircraft pitching to the ground at an angle and turning a hard landing into a crash.

The Mi-17 impacted on the pilot side, which disintegrated in an eruption of smashing metal and glass. The rotors dug into the hard clay, twisting and then fragmenting as they sliced through the fuselage and sent the Russian-made helicopter into a cartwheel of death.

CHAPTER 22

WAKE UP, DADDY.

Lucy?

Wake up, Daddy.

I'm here, baby girl.

Where have you been, Daddy? Mom and I miss you.

I miss you, too, cuddle bug.

Wake up or you are going to burn to death.

What?

Wake up or you are going to burn to death.

Reece jolted from his dream, feeling the heat on his face, his daughter a figment of his imagination.

Lucy!

It was then that he registered the screams.

Someone was burning alive.

"Ox!"

Reece pushed himself to his knees, attempting to drive the smoke away from his face and get his bearings. He stood, staying in a slight crouch. The dry grasses of the savanna were alive with smoke and flames. The SEAL moved toward the hissing of cooked flesh, the smell all too familiar, knowing he was too late. He felt the heat through the smoke before he saw the charred carcass, still aflame in the dirt. Ripping off his shirt, he fell on the burning man to smother the flames.

Ox? No, he was too small. Nizar?

Reece didn't hear the footsteps in time.

As he turned, he was hit from the side and taken to the ground. Reece immediately twisted into the guard position.

Ox.

"Eagle, Eagle!" Reece shouted before the large man could land a blow.

"Reece," Ox coughed. "What the fuck?"

The two warriors untangled themselves and got to their feet.

"I don't know. That indig was going to take me out on the helo."

"What?"

"Later. Let's find Nizar."

"Can't see shit in this smoke. Think that was him?" Ox asked, pointing at the man Reece had been attempting to help.

"I don't know. Hard to tell."

Footsteps.

"Moving," Reece said instinctually.

"Move!" Ox responded.

Reece sprinted after the sound of the footsteps. Catching movement through the smoke, he increased his speed and pounced, taking his prey to the ground, sliding behind him and sinking in the rear naked choke before he recognized the tiger-stripe uniform of the Burkina Faso National Intelligence Agency.

One of these guys just tried to kill you, Reece.

Unsure if the soldier was friend or foe, Reece continued to apply pressure until the body went limp. Reece unslung the soldier's AK, performed a press check, and took four magazines from his plate carrier, stuffing them in his pockets before moving off past the flames that littered the savanna.

Nizar, where are you?

Reece felt the heat of what he assumed was the Mi-17 burning and sprinted toward it, almost tripping over another body.

Nizar?

No, this one was wearing a flight suit.

Reece knelt, turned the body over, and felt for a pulse.

Alive.

Find Nizar.

Reece looked down at the copilot.

Nizar.

Later.

Reece slung the AK behind his back and grabbed the copilot under his arms, dragging him farther from the heat of the downed aircraft.

"Ox!"

At what Reece believed was a safe distance from the flames, he dropped the copilot and knelt by his side.

MARCH protocol.

M—massive hemorrhage.

A—airway.

R—respiratory.

C—circulation.

H—hypothermia.

His helmet was still on so Reece left it in place, his face covered in ash.

Reece ran his hands down the front of the copilot's body, then the sides, inspecting his hands for fresh blood. He then moved to the legs.

Maybe he just hit his head and passed out?

That thought was quickly dispelled by fresh blood.

Direct pressure.

"*Ox!* I need a tourniquet over here!"

Footsteps.

Nizar?

Reece pivoted on his knees, bringing the Kalashnikov up while moving the selector to semiauto.

"Eagle!"

Reece raised the selector to safe as Ox emerged from the smoke and dropped down next to him.

"Status?" Ox asked, ripping a SOF tourniquet from his kit.

"He's got a pulse and he's breathing. I think he was hit in that barrage that killed the pilot. Feels like a gunshot wound to the leg. Maybe some shrapnel from the grenade, possibly from the crash."

"Copy," Ox said, sliding the tourniquet onto the copilot's leg, working it up to where Reece continued to hold pressure, pushing it under and past Reece's hands and tightening it high above the wound. "What the fuck happened on that helo?"

"You tell me. That guy across from me. He put his weapon on full auto and raised it. No doubt about his intent."

"Are you sure? This crew was poly'd by the Agency," Ox said.

"I'm sure. And, as you know, plenty of people have beaten the poly."

"So I've heard."

"What was that gunshot I heard before the frag rolled out?"

"I was looking at you. I thought you'd reconsidered and were taking that AK to go kill Nizar. I think he got out of his restraints and got a pistol and a grenade from a guard. As soon as I heard the shot I moved to take him down. Then the grenade went off and we hit the deck."

"How did you get out?"

"I didn't. I think the clamshell rear doors split on impact and dumped me out the back."

"If it ejected you, it might have done the same with Nizar. We have to check that helo."

"Stay put, Reece. That thing is *hot as fuck*. You are not getting in there."

"You got this. I'm going to the helo."

"Reece!"

But the SEAL was already gone.

CHAPTER 23

REECE RAN THROUGH THE smoke, weaving past the burning grasses of the savanna. He could hear and feel the heat of the burning aircraft, using the sound and temperature as a guide, drawing him closer, AK at the ready.

How many people were on that bird?

Reece ran the numbers in his head.

Me, Ox, two pilots, the crew chief, ten or eleven National Intelligence Agency operators. And Nizar.

Reece checked off the dead along with those alive and accounted for.

The wind swirled, giving Reece a view of the crash area. The Mi-17 had impacted on the front left side. That the copilot escaped was a miracle. The grenade must have reduced the structural integrity of the platform, as the aircraft had split in two when the rotors dug into the ground.

How the hell did anyone survive?

Lucy?

Reece shook his head.

Not now. You have got to ID Nizar.

It was now evident what had caused the fires. Pylons loaded with external fuel tanks on either side of the fuselage had been cut in two by the rotors as they sliced through the cabin, jettisoning aerosolized fuel across the crash site. The hot engines or sparks from the grenade detonation had turned them into flamethrowers.

Still shirtless from his attempt to save the burning man, Reece could feel his skin start to blister the closer he got to the wreckage. Was that charred hunk of flesh he had attempted to extinguish, the man who had killed Freddy? Or was Nizar still inside, crushed to death or incinerated in the crash? Or had he been ejected out the back like Ox?

Reece pushed closer, bringing his left hand up to shield his eyes from the heat and smoke, blinking them in an attempt to clear his vision.

He willed himself through the heat toward what was left of the helo, images of the Rangers, pilots, and crew members on the CH-47s killed during the ambush of his SEAL Troop in Afghanistan imprinted on his mind.

Reece shook off the memory and continued on.

The wind swirled again and briefly cleared the thick smoke, allowing Reece to see bodies contorted in death littering the crash site. The Mi-17 had been torn in two. At least four of them had survived: Reece, Ox, the copilot, a soldier. And at least one had made it away from the crash only to burn to death on the red dirt of the African savanna. The others?

The intense heat forced Reece to stop twenty yards from the wreckage. He pivoted and decided to circle the crash site, counting bodies in a desperate attempt to identify Nizar.

He flanked what was left of the rear section of the aircraft, noting that the tail rotor affixed to the starboard side was still intact. The clamshell doors had burst open, allowing Reece to see into what remained of the hull. The heat of the fires caused a refraction of light, creating a mirage, making it difficult to see inside. Reece edged in as close as he could in an attempt to positively identify his target. He counted four more dead bodies still strapped to their seats. The ones who hadn't burned wore the tiger-striped uniforms of the strike force. Nizar had disappeared.

CHAPTER 24

NIZAR RAN.

His first order of business was to put as much distance between himself and the crash site as possible. The second was to find medical attention. And some shoes.

Were ISR assets already locked on to him? That had to be how they found him. Le Drian had made two calls. That was enough. The American surveillance state was even more prolific than Nizar had anticipated. Even with precautions and this far into the heart of Africa, they had found him.

Le Drian had evaded capture. Would the Frenchman adhere to the contingency plan? Or would he vanish?

Nizar gambled that he would be there. He was a mercenary, after all, and mercenaries were motivated by money, something Nizar had in abundance for this mission.

Find a car, moped, or motorcycle. Get to the link-up point. Then give Le Drian instructions on how to contact the man in the wheelchair without using a phone. There were ways. It would take longer but the handler from northern Italy would arrange safe passage. That was what he did.

At the very least, Nizar's ribs were severely bruised, most likely broken. It hurt to even breathe, which limited his output. His feet were bloody but the pain from his ribs distracted him enough that he kept going. Did he have internal injuries? He knew he could be bleeding internally and the only way to find out would be competent medical attention, something hard enough to come by even when you weren't on the run in Burkina Faso.

Find a vehicle.

The operators of the National Intelligence Agency had wisely taken his shoes. One had a razor blade taped to the bottom of an insole and a handcuff key was taped to the bottom of the other insole. They had removed his belt, which held similar secrets. What they neglected to discover on their primary and secondary searches was the fake scar that ran across Nizar's lower back. Only five centimeters in length, it would escape most searches. The nonmetallic razor blade and shim concealed beneath it were impervious to a metal detector sweep and physical pat-downs.

With his hands secured behind his back, he had worked open the counterfeit scar glued to his body, dislodging the blade and using it to cut through his zip ties. Reece was on the opposite side of the helo and almost as far from Nizar as he could be. The Syrian noted that Reece stared straight ahead once he was seated.

The man who represented freedom was only meters away. Reece was a payday that would allow Nizar to put this life behind him. The Syrian was not doing it to make a statement or for Allah. He was doing it for his independence. Nizar was captured and physically bound. Reece was bound in a different way. If what the contract he had received in Montenegro said was true, Reece was gunning for Nizar. Now, aboard the helo and with Nizar in what was essentially U.S. custody, Reece was powerless to finish the job.

Nizar knew he had been on his way to an interrogation facility. With the two Americans aboard he wagered that he might get the same treatment he would get at Gitmo—meals, a lawyer, time to exercise, and the occasional waterboard. If the Americans turned him over to the Burkina

Faso National Intelligence Agency, that would be a different story. He could expect the removal of his fingernails and toenails, followed by his genitals. His skin would be slowly peeled from his body by men with knives while others smashed his bones with hammers and clubs. Nizar did not plan on letting things get that far. Once in that system it would be extremely difficult to escape. He would wait until the helo was on approach and then he would make his move.

He had been studying Reece when he saw the former SEAL explode across the helo and into the local security force operator. Nizar was as surprised as everyone else when automatic weapons fire filled the cabin. Was there someone else who wanted Reece dead?

He wanted to be closer to the ground, but experience had taught the sniper that opportunities were meant to be exploited. With everyone's attention on what was happening at the front of the aircraft, the violent pitch of the Mi-17 gave him the window he needed. Nizar waited and then as the helo began its fall to earth, he exploited the opportunity found in chaos. He grabbed a grenade from the side plate carrier of the man next to him and slid his finger inside the operator's holster. Finding the trigger, he pressed it back, discharging a 9mm round into the operator's leg.

When they were close enough to the ground that he thought it just might work, Nizar pulled the pin on the grenade and rolled it forward into the fuselage.

CHAPTER 25

Novo-Ogaryovo, Odintsovsky District, Moscow, Russia

"WE MISSED HIM IN Burkina Faso."

"Fortunately, there will be other opportunities. The 'green on blue' attack we orchestrated using the local security operator was unsuccessful," Gromyko admitted.

"Pity we wasted him in the effort. He might have provided valuable long-term intelligence. After all, had passed his CIA polygraph before we recruited him."

"Stick to internal security matters, old friend. James Reece will be dead in short order."

The Russians were meeting on neutral territory. Mikhail Gromyko was not about to subjugate himself to the director of the FSB and meet at Lubyanka, a Federal Security Service building in the Meshchansky District. The fact that it was also a prison added to its mystique and to most people's dread.

The optics of either one of the directors sitting down for an emergency meeting would give way to speculation, rumor, and gossip, all of which could be weaponized. A meeting off-site on neutral ground was appropriate for the situation and for the official positions of the attendees. Here the two intelligence officials were on equal footing, a position not lost on either of them.

West of Moscow, Novo-Ogaryovo served as the president's residence, and since the COVID pandemic it had become the de facto center of government. Originally an estate built in the 1950s to house visiting heads of state, it had been demolished and rebuilt in 2000 to become the official residence of the Russian president. Russian politicians, intelligence officers, and military leaders were all too aware of the tricks used during construction of buildings during the Cold War. The former president was not about to risk listening or video devices, regardless of how outdated the technology. The six-meter-high walls kept prying eyes and intruders out. The guard force was recruited from the ranks of the FSO, the Federal Protective Service, and put through additional training and scrutiny that came with the job of protecting the president.

Pavel Dashkov finished the elaborate ceremony of lighting his pipe. Smoke from the Turkish tobacco blend of which he had grown fond filled the air. Gromyko wondered if his old friend and rival knew how much the pipe ritual annoyed him. He would be halfway done with his cigarette by the time Dashkov took his first puff.

Dashkov tossed the still-lit wooden match into the large ashtray at the center of the table and leaned back in the wicker chair. President Bush and President Obama had both spent time at this table. The Russians even had photos of Obama enjoying a smoke during his visit.

"Our American friends want him dead as much as we do," Dashkov said. "So do the Iranians."

"That may be true, but they won't make a move unless we give them the order."

"For a student of history, you seem more anxious than usual. Too many cigarettes perhaps?"

Gromyko ignored the jab and pushed on.

"There is a fine line between being patient and waiting so long that you miss the opportunity."

Dashkov savored another pull of the pungent tobacco.

"Reece doesn't know who we are, Mikhail. There is plenty of time to kill him before he figures out where the safe-deposit box is. That secret died with his father."

"Yes, but he knows it exists," Gromyko said. "It's possible he told the reporter, but our latest collections indicate that not to be the case."

"Then have another smoke, old friend. Commander Reece will be dead soon. Nizar Kattan will see to it."

"Nizar Kattan," Gromyko said, leaning in to stub out his Marlboro and then pulling out his pack to light another.

"He was your asset, Mikhail, or do you forget?"

Ignoring the question, Gromyko cupped his left hand around the cigarette, lighting it quickly with a disposable lighter, which he deposited in his pocket.

"Kattan will have one, possibly two opportunities at James Reece outside the United States."

"And then?" Dashkov asked.

"And then we will cut ties with the Syrian."

"Cut ties?"

"We will kill him, Pavel."

The director of the FSB studied his old friend.

"Are you feeling well? You are looking thin."

Does he know?

"I am fine. If I am looking thin, how do you describe that?" Gromyko gestured toward his counterpart's growing midsection. They shared a laugh.

"It's called good living, Mikhail. We are at the age where we should do more of it. You never know how much longer you have on earth."

Was that a threat?

"I'll join you for a meal when James Reece is dead."

"You worry too much, Mikhail. You should drink more vodka."

"You don't worry enough, and you should drink *less* vodka."

They laughed again.

"Perhaps you are right," Dashkov said.

"I'll drink when he is in the ground. Until then"—Gromyko held up the cigarette—"I'll stick to these."

"What happened in Burkina Faso?"

Gromyko took a deep drag, the warm fumes filling his lungs. He exhaled, his smoke pushing the pungent Turkish cloud back across the table.

"Pavel, I sometimes envy you."

"Oh?"

"Internal security and counterintelligence is so much less sophisticated than global collection and covert actions. Probably why you have excelled at it."

Gromyko could tell he'd hit a nerve.

"Do tell, Mikhail."

"If there is an issue on home soil, that problem disappears. We have a history of *disappearances*. Russians accept it."

"Your point?"

"My point, *old friend*, is that the Americans do not accept it, nor do the Australians or Europeans. The Chinese do, but only if it's by their hand. We can get away with it in most of the Middle East and Africa."

"You make my argument for me, Mikhail. You missed Reece in Africa. If you missed him there, what makes you think you can get him elsewhere?"

"Because I know where he's going even before he does. In this case, I even have the address. That is why I am in this chair, *comrade*. I know what an adversary will do before it even occurs to them."

Gromyko's intent was clear: Threaten me at your own peril.

"And if Commander Reece escapes and finds that safe-deposit box?"

"He won't."

"How could we not have found it by now? That is clearly an *external* security matter."

"His father took that secret with him to the grave. He was the only one who knew. It was convenient to get rid of him the way we did, but that was not under my leadership. I would have handled it differently." Gromyko let his words hang in the air like the cancerous smoke between them. "There is always so much to unpack in the world of espionage."

"Yes, something we would *both* be wise to remember," Dashkov said. "Finish him off, Mikhail. I don't need to remind you, or the president, that your standing on the council has taken a hit in recent years. If you need my help, I am always here for you."

The words were kind but the meaning behind them was anything but. Gromyko briefly wondered if he should hire Kattan to put a bullet though the man across the table but then thought the better of it.

Not yet.

"Just finish him off, Mikhail. Let Mother Russia be done with the Reece family for good."

"He won't make it back to his native soil, Pavel."

"And if you're wrong?"

"And, if I'm wrong, there is one last option, one from which there is no escape."

"No escape for James Reece, or no return for us?"

Gromyko took a final drag on his Marlboro and did not answer the question.

PART TWO

TUVIA

THE PROTECTOR

"I PURSUED MY ENEMIES AND OVERTOOK THEM;
I DID NOT TURN BACK UNTIL THEY WERE DESTROYED."
—PSALM 18:37 AND MOTTO OF THE YAMAM

CHAPTER 26

Mossad Headquarters, Tel Aviv, Israel

ON THE WESTERN OUTSKIRTS of Tel Aviv, just off the Glilot Ma'arav Interchange, not far from North Cliff Beach, lies a group of office buildings that could pass for a Pacific Coast community college or Silicon Valley tech campus in the United States. Beautiful gardens and sculptures are tastefully arranged along paths that lead to various buildings, including a cafeteria, gym, library, and basketball courts. That is where the similarities to academia end. This is not the United States, and this is not a college campus. Upon closer inspection, the walls would seem unusually high for an institution of higher learning and the men and women patrolling the grounds would appear remarkably attentive and fit. Most collegiate experiences do not include target practice at an on-site shooting facility, following a kosher lunch. If one were to observe the structures through a cycle of darkness it would be apparent that the lights were always burning. This was less a campus and more a compound, a compound that was home to one of the world's largest and most feared intelligence services.

Dressed in a uniform of slacks, scuffed leather shoes in need of resoling, and a white short-sleeve, button-up collar shirt with no tie, Ronen Katz could have been mistaken for a disgruntled professor had he been wandering the grounds at Cal Poly, but here at the Institute for Intelligence and Special Operations, he was simply known as "K." Up at 4:00 a.m. daily, he was in his office one hour later. He arrived each day under the cover of darkness and would not begin his commute home until well past sunset. Stocky, with a receding hairline cut into a buzz, Ronen Katz, it was said, had never once smiled. Unlike his peers in Collections, Political Action, Psychological Operations, Research, Technology, Venture Capital, Training, and Finance, Katz had a direct line to the prime minister. He led the branch of the Mossad responsible for what was known as "negative treatment." The rest of the world referred to them as assassinations.

Caesarea. The name was whispered even on the grounds of Mossad Headquarters. Kidon, the assassins charged with planning and executing negative treatments, never set foot on the compound. Their faces and identities were compartmentalized and hidden from all but a select few.

Katz had been recruited from the ranks of Sayeret Matkal, Israel's premier counterterrorism and hostage-rescue unit focused beyond its borders, specifically for Caesarea. He had come of age hearing stories about Bayonet, or Operation Wrath of God, the targeted killings of those responsible for the Munich Massacre. Katz's department of the Mossad had evolved to meet new threats since its inception. First as a Kidon and now as head of the department, Katz had been involved with every aspect of the art and science of assassination as an instrument of state power. Though it was an option under Israeli law for war crimes and crimes against humanity, capital punishment was last carried out in 1962, when Adolf Eichmann was hung for his role in the Holocaust. He had been captured in Argentina by Israeli agents two years before Katz was born.

Katz and the Kidon were Israel's preemptive capital punishment. Though his department still tracked and built target packages on Hamas and Hezbollah operatives, Katz's mandate from the prime minister was to use all means at his disposal to prevent Iran from building or acquiring a nuclear bomb. Poison, explosives, drones, pistols, knives, and remote-controlled machine guns had all been used with success over his tenure. His job was relatively straightforward: identify individuals who are a threat to Israel, find them, and then kill them.

The American would be arriving today and Katz had a file he wanted to read. The meeting was a personal favor for Victor Rodriguez, the closest Katz had to a counterpart at the CIA. Both men had begun their careers in military service and then made the transition to the world of intelligence. They had worked together closely on a number of operations over the years: Imad Mughniyeh in Damascus, al-Qaeda leader Abu Mohammed al-Masri in Tehran, Qassem Soleimani in Baghdad, and seven Iranian nuclear scientists, including Mohsen Fakhrizadeh, the head of Iran's nuclear program, who was killed on the road to Absard, east of Tehran, in 2020. They had all been removed from the battlefield as a result of Israeli and American intelligence cooperation. Much of that cooperation was due to Katz and Rodriguez.

The Israelis had the HUMINT network on the ground to include operatives within the Iranian government and in the Iranian opposition group Mujahideen-e-Khalq. The Americans had a technical capacity and capability that was a mystery even to Katz.

When an Iranian-sponsored proxy terrorist leader or Iranian nuclear scientist was assassinated or died suddenly of previously undiagnosed natural causes, many journalists were quick to point to an intelligence alliance between the Mossad and the CIA. These accusations would be either denied or ignored by both agencies under a maxim all intelligence officers and special operators learn early on: Admit nothing, deny everything, make counteraccusations.

The two spymasters shared a mutual respect, but they were also aware that the world's second-oldest profession was fraught with misdirection and treachery. U.S. Navy intelligence analyst Jonathan Pollard's actions as a spy for Israel remained a strain. In 1986 he had pled guilty to passing classified information to Israel. Though Israel requested details on Arab and Pakistani nuclear, chemical, and biological weapons programs, Pollard also passed along information on the NSA's global communications monitoring capability, information that may have ended up in the hands of the Soviets in exchange for open emigration of Soviet Jews to Israel. Pollard was sentenced to life in prison in 1987. After meeting the requirements for parole after thirty years of incarceration, he was released in 2015 and legally emigrated to Israel in 2020. The United States was not innocent in the ways of espionage and did not want to be caught flat-footed when it came to its staunchest ally in the Middle East. In 1948 the United States was the first country to recognize Israel as a state. The two countries have been spying on each other ever since.

It was also well known that Katz lived on strong, bitter Arabic coffee, which he supplemented with jars of dates and candied nuts, devoured intermittently between cigarettes, an enduring legacy of his time on the ground throughout the Middle East.

Arriving well before his secretary, Katz lit a cigarette as he waited for the water to boil.

James Reece.

Katz had come up in the business well before the age of information transformed his profession. Although his computer had access to the Mossad's encrypted archives, he preferred to keep some things under lock and key. His office was a testament to the old school. Not one photo adorned the walls. Not a single picture of a wife or children. No plaques or mementos. Instead, rows of metal file cabinets filled an entire side of the office. His desk was off center; a flat-screen TV to his left was tuned to Al Jazeera. Two small worn black leather couches arranged in an L were to the left of the entrance along with a small coffee table. At 7:00 a.m. his secretary would knock on the door and drop off a pile of newspapers printed from websites around the world, which Katz would scour, fueled by caffeine and nicotine.

The dark roast warmed his insides. He missed the front lines, but he didn't dwell on the past. His life was of the here-and-now. He had a mission, a mandate to protect the state of Israel from enemies that plotted every day to destroy her.

Since the end of the Second World War, Israel had led the world in the use of negative treatments, in the liquidation of threats. Without assassins, Kidon, eliminating enemies of the nation, Israel would have ceased to exist.

Now one of his assassins was dead. That gave him pause. Had he made a mistake? Had she? Both were possible. Mistakes were made in this business and when they occurred, the results were often catastrophic.

Aliya was one of the best he had ever trained. He also knew she was getting tired. Maybe it was a lapse in *his* judgment. He'd pushed her too far and she had made a mistake. Maybe. Or maybe not.

Ronen Katz did not take kindly to losing agents in the field. He would conduct an internal investigation into Aliya's death in order to prevent it from happening to another operative.

But what of this American? James Reece knew Aliya was Mossad. He had recognized her photo from the news broadcasts. They had worked together in Iraq and now he wanted to talk to her sister.

Not before he talks to me.

Katz looked down at the worn 41mm stainless-steel case of the Eterna KonTiki Super on his wrist. Still ticking after all these years. It was 5:15 a.m. Just over three hours until Reece's scheduled arrival. He had plenty of time to prepare.

CHAPTER 27

"I TRUST THE RIDE from the airport was uneventful."

"It was. Thank you," Reece responded.

He shook hands with the short, powerfully built man and surveyed the office; dark, it smelled of stale coffee and burnt tobacco. It fit the man who occupied it to a tee, like it had been built around him.

"Coffee, Mr. Donovan?"

"Please," Reece said, against his better judgment.

Katz motioned to the leather couches, where an electric hot plate was set up. A cord ran from the hot plate under the couch to the wall. To Reece it looked like a fire hazard.

They took their seats on the well-worn sofa, the coffee table between them, like they were setting it up in a classic L-shaped ambush.

Katz turned on the hot plate and placed a steel pot with a long handle atop it.

He then picked up a pack of cigarettes in green packaging from the table. In a sequence that was second nature, he packed and drew a smoke, lighting it with a Zippo.

"Gift from Rodriguez," he said as he exhaled.

"He engraved it with the symbol of my old unit, Sayeret Matkal."

Katz tossed the lighter on the table next to the cigarettes.

"How long have you known Vic?" Reece asked.

"A little over a decade. About the time we both moved into management. And you?"

"And me?"

"How long have you known him?"

"Just about four years now."

Katz leaned forward and tapped an ash into a tray while continuing to prepare the coffee.

"Do you know that coffee originated in the Arab world, Mr. Donovan?"

"Ethiopia, I believe."

"So the legend goes," Katz said, heaping four spoonfuls of coarsely ground coffee into the boiling water and beginning to stir.

"No one knows for certain but what we do know is that by the sixteenth century it had spread across Arabia. A century later it was in Europe, eventually becoming one of the most sought-after commodities in the world."

"Behind oil."

"A man who knows his coffee."

Katz removed the pot from the hot plate to stir it and then returned it to the heat source, bringing it back to a boil, continuing to stir the mixture into what looked like mud.

"Tell me, how did you come to know that Aliya Galin was connected to Israeli intelligence?"

Reece considered himself a "new guy" in the intelligence field but knew enough to realize that he was dealing with a pro, one of the top intelligence officials in the Mossad, in the Caesarea department, responsible for assassinations. This was not a man who would be asking Reece questions if he didn't already know the answers.

"In Iraq," Reece said as he watched Katz remove the small pot from the hot plate and set it the table.

"It needs to settle for a minute," Katz said.

"And you," Reece asked. "Did you recruit her from the IDF?"

Katz looked at his guest. Reece could tell he was deducing, just as Reece had, that his guest already knew the answer to the question.

"I did. Her parents were killed by a Hamas suicide bomber. Traumatic events oftentimes change the trajectory of our lives."

Katz returned to the pot of mud, leaving Reece to wonder if he was intentionally making a reference to Reece's past.

"That they can," Reece said as he watched his host pour the coffee into two small white cups not much larger than shot glasses with gold embossing. No creamer, sugar, spice, or honey was offered.

"Bitter, dark, and strong," Katz said, taking a sip of his creation. "The cigarettes are a vestige of my time in the Defense Forces, the *Coffea arabica* from my life after."

"This life?"

"My life in the field. I am removed from that now, but the habits die hard."

"That they do," Reece confirmed.

He took a sip of the scalding bitter liquid and forced a smile.

"It's great," he lied, before setting it back down on the table.

"Aliya was one of mine. Her sacrifice will not be forgotten. What I want to know, Mr. Donovan, is why that plane was shot down with her on it."

"I want to know that as well. What was she doing in Burkina Faso?"

"It was a job for the state."

"As Mélanie Cotillard. I saw. A sales representative for a French financial firm."

"That is correct. As you know, our reach is not limited to the countries that border us. Mr. Rodriguez shared that you are the lead subject matter expert on one of the terrorists responsible."

"Is that how he put it?"

"It is."

"One is a former Syrian sniper, Nizar Kattan. The other may be a

French national. We don't know yet. Kattan was one of the two snipers who killed the former Russian president in Odessa three years ago. He also killed my friend, Freddy Strain."

"So, it's personal."

"It is."

Katz returned to his cigarette.

"It's always personal for Israel. Mr. Donovan, I want to find the men who did this, not out of vengeance, but to prevent them from doing it again."

"Those two objectives can work in tandem."

"Yes, but there is a distinction. Killing out of vengeance can have unintended consequences on all levels, and it is illegal in Israel. Killing to prevent future attacks, that is noble, ethical, and *legal*. Mr. Donovan, my country, this organization, is in the business of protection. Our intent is to prevent Nizar Kattan and this Frenchman from launching future attacks against Israeli citizens. In that spirit, I offer you the assistance of my organization."

"I understand. Your offer is appreciated."

"My Research and Collections departments are digging into Kattan and will share that information with the CIA."

"Thank you. I'd like to visit Aliya's sister. There is something Aliya asked me to pass along to her family when we worked together in Iraq."

"What message?"

"Just that if anything happened to her, she asked me to find her family and tell them she was doing this for 'us.'"

"'Us'?"

"Yes, I think she meant for Israel."

"I see."

Reece forced another sip of the thick, unsweetened concoction before him.

"In the spirit of cooperation," he continued, "I have a question for you."

Katz exhaled a thick cloud of pungent smoke back toward his desk.

"When I worked with Aliya in Iraq, was she actively trying to recruit me?"

Katz stood, walked to the back of his office, and returned with a dossier.

"I had your file pulled prior to our meeting. I read it this morning. There is nothing in this file that states officially or otherwise that you were under assessment or development by Aliya Galin or any agent of the Mossad at any time."

"May I see it?"

"But of course."

Katz sat and handed it across the table.

Reece took his time as Katz watched him, the spy taking the occasional drag on his cigarette until it had almost hit the filter.

Background, Florida, parents, IDF service, Mossad training, liaison to the CIA, her husband's death, her parents' deaths.

"There is not much in here from 2008 onwards," Reece observed.

"Those missions are classified, as I am sure you can appreciate, Mr. Donovan," Katz said, extinguishing his cigarette.

Reece closed the file and handed it back.

"As our agencies work on Kattan's location, I'd appreciate it if you could arrange that meeting with Aliya's sister, Shiri, I believe?"

"That's correct. Shiri Galin. They both kept their maiden names. Vic relayed your request."

Katz moved back to his desk and pressed a button. A moment later the door opened. A tall man with a distinctive patch covering his right eye entered and stood next to the door. He wore brown leather shoes, jeans, and an untucked short-sleeve, button-up shirt not dissimilar to the one Katz was wearing. Reece had no doubt that the shirt concealed a pistol. In this business one just knew.

"This is Tuvia Yatom, Mr. Donovan. He will escort you to Kibbutz

Merom Golan in the Golan Heights to meet with Shiri Galin. He is a liaison from Shabak, our domestic security agency."

Reece knew the Israeli Security Agency, also known as Shabak, or Shin Bet, was the Israeli equivalent of the FBI or Great Britain's MI5.

"Internal security?"

"Even in Israel we have rules, Mr. Donovan. My agency is focused outward. Shabak operates within our borders."

"Thank you," Reece said, standing and extending his hand.

"It is our pleasure and a professional courtesy to your agency for our close work over the years. After your meeting, Tuvia will drive you back. I'll have a brief prepared on Nizar Kattan. Any assistance we can offer will be provided."

Reece thanked him again and followed Tuvia from the office, relieved to be escaping the coffee and smoke that saturated the cave of Israel's top assassin.

• • •

Katz leaned back in his chair and lit another cigarette. He opened a desk drawer and removed two files, one on Aliya Galin and another labeled JAMES REECE.

He pressed a button on his desk. "Hold my calls for the next hour."

"Yes, sir."

He was almost forty years removed from his initial military engagement in the First Lebanon War as a young paratrooper. Twenty years in the IDF, the latter half as an officer in Sayeret Matkal, and now twenty years with the Mossad gave the aging spymaster perspective. That Israel had run aggressive information- and intelligence-gathering operations against their staunchest ally was not a secret. There were highly publicized cases as well as incidents that were settled behind closed doors. With the release of WikiLeaks documents and revelations by Edward Snowden, the world was well aware that the United States was not an innocent bystander when it came to spying on allies. The NSA and CIA had been caught red-handed collecting on leaders and intelligence officials of Austria, Belgium, France, Italy, Switzerland, Germany, and Israel. Katz had read the documents himself. They had been stamped "Unconventional" and "SCS," which he knew as the acronym for the Special Collection Service. Leaked documents also pointed to a program called "Anarchist," run by the NSA and their British counterpart, the GCHQ, out of Cyprus against the Israeli Air Force. Despite those revelations, the CIA and Mossad enjoyed close relations even when their political leaders did not. Still, trust in the espionage business went only so far.

Three cigarettes later Katz removed a four-page section of Aliya Galin's file labeled JAMES REECE/ASSESSMENT REPORT. He stood and stretched his legs. In the dim light of his office, he scanned the document one final time before feeding it into the shredder. Then he picked up his secure phone and called the director of Yamam.

CHAPTER 28

"HOW LONG IS THE drive?" Reece asked.

"Just over two hours from here," Tuvia answered from behind the wheel of a Toyota 300-Series Land Cruiser.

Reece inspected the inside of the vehicle as they drove.

"What are you looking at?" Tuvia asked.

"Not a bad ride. Can't get these in the States."

"I read that," Tuvia said. "It appears your country prefers trucks designed for shopping mall parking lots."

Reece saw the smile creep across his escort's face.

"I fear you may be right," Reece responded.

Leaving the city, they skirted beaches of the Mediterranean, heading north on Highway 2. Flanked by coastal towns to their west and agricultural fields to the east, it reminded Reece of a drive up the central California coast he had taken with Lauren before Lucy was born.

"Nahal Memorial?" Reece asked, reading a sign at an off-ramp to his right.

Tuvia turned his neck to read the sign.

"Yes, Israel is a country of memorials."

They continued north in silence until Reece saw another sign.

"Caesarea Beach?" Reece asked.

Tuvia looked at his passenger again.

"Yes, very affluent neighborhood."

"That's not really what I was asking," Reece said.

At the Zikhron Ya'aqov interchange they took Route 67 east.

"A McDonald's?"

"Yes, you can't escape them. One day they will rule the world." Tuvia smiled. "Want to stop for a McKebab?"

"A what?"

"A McKebab. I tried ordering one when I was in LA and they looked at me like I was crazy."

"I wouldn't feel complete if we didn't stop. My treat."

Tuvia took the exit and parked in the McDonald's parking lot.

Standing in line, Reece studied the menu.

"A kosher McDonald's?"

"They didn't get to be America's most recognizable export by failing to adapt," Tuvia said.

After McKebabs and corn sticks they were back on the road.

"I feel like we might regret that meal," Reece said.

"It's possible." Tuvia laughed.

"What happened to your eye?"

Tuvia moved his head so he could see Reece with his left eye.

"Two thousand sixteen. Operation to arrest a Palestinian terrorist in Ramallah."

"Were you Yamam?"

"You know of it?" Tuvia asked, surprised.

"I do. Some friends left the SEAL Teams for the FBI and trained with you guys."

Tuvia smiled.

"In California?"

"That's right. I think it was a joint exercise with HRT and the LA County sheriff's SWAT."

"We have done many exchanges and training exercises over the years, but I remember this trip. We had a great time. Worked with the Special Enforcement Bureau. Pre-pandemic world. We spent a week on the beach in Santa Monica, Venice, Manhattan Beach, Hermosa."

"My friends were impressed."

"Our enemies give us a lot of practice."

"Did you spend time in the IDF?" Reece asked, referring to the Israel Defense Forces.

"Yes. Everyone in Yamam was IDF. Most were special operations."

"So, how did you get stuck with me?"

Tuvia looked at his passenger again.

"I got shot."

"And?"

"And I was in the same unit as Yonatan, Shiri's husband, when he was killed."

"He was Yamam?"

"He was. We went through training together."

"What happened to him?"

Tuvia took a breath.

"He was targeted for assassination. Five years ago."

"I'm sorry."

"They were living in Ta'oz, just outside the Ayalon Valley."

To Reece's questioning look he continued: "It's between Tel Aviv and Jerusalem, not far from Yamam headquarters. He was shot down in his driveway."

The Israeli paused.

"In front of Shiri and the kids."

Reece shook his head.

"The enemy is always adapting," Tuvia said. "We've seen it since our inception. We still train for active shooters, bus, train, and plane hijackings, and suicide bombers but now we are seeing death squads who are trained abroad not just in weapons and explosives but in intelligence gathering, target selection, and mission planning."

"Adaptation," Reece said.

"That's right. For us, it's the intelligence and the ability to act on it. In Israel you cannot wait for a one hundred percent clear picture. Yamam launches without that full picture. We have no choice. If you wait, they win."

"So, how did you end up at Shin Bet?"

"The eye. It's fairly recent. We initially thought my vision would come back. Quite a few surgeries. I could have stayed but it was clear to me that I would slow the team down. The commander at the time wanted someone with recent experience to work on the intelligence side, so I was detailed to Shin Bet six months ago. It was time."

"This is a beautiful country," Reece said as they passed a sign for Nazareth.

"It is, but we are surrounded by enemies on all sides. The Abraham Accords were a big step forward but there will always be those who want to push Israel into the sea. Our unit was created to ensure that does not happen. If I can bridge the gap between the intel and the operators then I feel like I am still contributing, even if I'm not part of an assault team."

Reece was well acquainted with the history of Shin Bet, Sayeret Matkal, Duvdevan, the Mossad, and Yamam, arguably the most highly trained and experienced internal security counterterrorism force in the world.

"Did you know Aliya?" Reece asked.

Tuvia paused, unsure how much he should reveal.

"I met her once, but I did not know her. She was a mystery. I only met her through Yonatan and Shiri. I suspected she was Mossad, but I did not know more than that. Her mission, as Director Katz said, was international. Mine was closer to home."

"And her sister was raising her kids?"

"Yes. In Israel we take care of our own, Mr. Donovan. She had been essentially raising Aliya's children since Ilan, Aliya's husband, was killed at the end of the Second Intifada. Aliya threw herself into her work. Then, when Yonatan was killed, they moved to Golan with his parents, who were raised there back when it was truly a kibbutz in the original sense."

"What do you mean?"

"In English the closest word for kibbutz is *gathering,* or *group.* They were important even before founding of the modern state."

"I've read about their contributions in the Six-Day War."

"As with your westward expansion, your pioneers, those who settled here and formed a culture around the kibbutz community helped establish the borders of what was to become the state of Israel. I've heard they even looked to ancient Sparta for inspiration."

"Really?"

"Oh yes, communal living was not all, as you say, *kumbaya.* They worked the fields and raised their children together, but they also trained for war. The locations were not chosen based on the sustainability of the land for farming and ranching; rather they were strategic. That memorial we passed awhile back, Nahal, they were soldiers of the kibbutz on the front lines in the fifties and sixties."

"You don't hear too much about the kibbutz anymore," Reece noted.

"By the 1980s the kibbutz in their past incarnation were largely in decline, but about fifteen or twenty years ago they started to come back, though this time in a different form."

"What do you mean?"

"Most are private now. Tourism is a big part of their economy. Instead of being centered around farming and agriculture, they are in tech, plastics, aerospace, even wine. There are still farms and ranches but many of them are more akin to your private communities in the United States with shared access to parks, pools, and schools. Shiri's in-laws grew up on a kibbutz but left in the mid-seventies to work in Tel Aviv, as

I understand it. In retirement they wanted to reconnect with their roots, and with Yonatan gone and Shiri caring for her own and Aliya's children, they all moved to Kibbutz Merom Golan. They bought Shiri a home and live next door to help with the kids. It seems to work for them."

"Are you close?"

"To whom?"

"To Shiri, to the kids."

"We don't have godparents in Judaism but if we did, I guess that's what I'd be."

Reece wondered who would have taken care of Lauren and Lucy had he been killed in Afghanistan. It was never far from his mind that his survival in the ambush that killed his assault force directly led to the deaths of his wife and daughter.

By surviving, I sentenced them to death.

"How much further?" Reece asked, changing the subject.

"About another hour."

"Unless you visit, you don't really get a sense for the size of this place."

"Yes, you can drive the country in about six or seven hours. You can ski in Golan and scuba-dive in Eilat in the same day. You have never been to Israel?"

"No. I always wanted to visit. We had an exchange with Flotilla Thirteen," Reece said, referring to Shayetet 13, the Israeli equivalent of Navy SEALs, "but I was always in Iraq or Afghanistan. Before she was flown out of Iraq, Aliya told me about Israel, about going to the beach with your M4."

Tuvia stole a sideways glance so his good eye could take in his passenger.

"Back then, did you know she was Mossad?"

Reece paused, not knowing if he was being officially probed for information.

Instead of saying yes, he pivoted with "I suspected."

"I see. And now?"

"And now, what?"

"And now you are CIA?"

"It's temporary."

"How temporary?"

"Are you collecting on me?"

"Of course!" Tuvia smiled. "I am Shabak. I am always collecting."

Reece smiled, too. It was impossible not to like Tuvia.

"Aliya was an amazing woman. Special."

"How special?" Tuvia asked.

"Not like that. We were assigned to the same unit. Both outsiders. I think we connected because we were from units outside the CIA."

"I read your file."

"I figured you had."

"Interesting. A few gaps in there that need filling in."

"Is that your job today?" Reece asked. "Are we being recorded?"

"Always safe to assume that we are."

"What does the file say about Iraq?"

"It says you saved Aliya's life."

Reece swallowed, remembering her bloody body on the ground outside the HVT Bar.

"She would have made it without me," Reece said, recalling the feeling of his hand searching for Aliya's in the dark, slippery with blood, as they sped toward the hospital.

"Not according to the file."

"You can only get so much from a file."

"That is true. I hope you find what you are looking for in Israel, Mr. Donovan."

"I hope so, too," Reece said.

"You know, we are not much different, you and I, except you have both your eyes." He laughed again.

Reece smiled. Tuvia's laugh was infectious.

"So, what's the plan?" Reece asked as they passed the Sea of Galilee and turned onto Route 91.

"Shiri agreed to meet with you but was not thrilled about it. I'm the only one she still sees from the old days. The wounds are still too fresh. Too much death. I texted her from McDonald's. She will be at the park with the kids. We will link up there."

"Anything I need to know?"

"Prepare yourself for an inquisition."

CHAPTER 29

Quneitra, Syria

SAMIR FARZAT LED HIS contingent of Syrian mercenaries and Hezbollah fighters down the ladder into the tunnel. The entrance was hidden in the lower level of a hospital well inside Syria. Samir had been in his share of tunnels over the past twenty years, some deeper and more advanced than others, but he had never experienced anything like this. It was well lit and wide enough to allow two people to descend, side by side. A separate elevator was available for munitions. As Samir downclimbed, he tried to keep track of how far he had gone. Ten meters. Twenty meters. Thirty meters. He lost track but he knew he was in the deepest tunnel he had ever used running terror operations into Israel.

Samir had been working for a Russian energy company when he was hired for this assignment. The money was good and his target had no idea what was coming. The Israeli dogs had illegally occupied the Golan Heights since 1967. The United Nations called it an illegal occupation. Only America recognized it as Israeli territory. America was, after all, "the primary enemy, the Greatest Satan."

Tonight, he had a very specific mission: to kill an American in Merom Golan.

Samir had been training and fighting alongside Hezbollah for the past decade, since the start of his country's civil war. He was wounded, as were many Hezbollah guerrillas, in a battle against elements of the Free Syrian Army and al-Nusra Front in the Qalamoun Mountains, along the Lebanese border. When he recovered he had been given a promotion. Syria, Iran, and Hezbollah all shared common enemies and tonight they would strike a blow against Israel and its American masters.

Six Syrians and ten Hezbollah fighters made up the assault force. Two of the Hezbollah guerrillas were younger than Samir's children and didn't look like they could be much older than fifteen or sixteen. They would not survive the night. They were strapped with martyrs' belts, what the West called suicide vests, true believers going to paradise with the support of their families.

American foreign policy was nothing more than a guise to subjugate Muslims the world over, cloaked in words like *freedom, democracy, civil rights,* and *human rights.* All lies. The United States wanted nothing less than complete domination of the Middle East. This was a fight for survival. Israel was just a tool of the Americans, a future forward operating base from which to project power across the Arab world. One day Syria would push Israel back to its pre-1967 borders. They had made gains in the region, kicking the Americans out of Iraq, but Israel still existed. Their American masters were on their knees, sent running from Lebanon, Iraq, and Afghanistan. They were now focused on domestic problems, riots in their streets, political division, and an economy crippled by the pandemic. They even made themselves again dependent on foreign oil, oil from the Arab world. *Self-inflicted wounds.*

Samir had heard the council talk of a strategy to bleed America of its will to project power abroad, a strategy that was succeeding. It worked when Hezbollah had attacked the Marine barracks in Beirut. And it had worked in training the militias in Iraq, sending America's sons and daughters home in their flag-draped coffins. Even more were crippled for life, their wounds a constant reminder of Arab might. It had taken years, but it had worked. America was weaker now than she had ever been since the end of World War II.

Samir knew that the ultimate goal was not just to rid the Middle East of American military forces, but to erase any hint of Western influence. Then the caliphate would expand. They had already made huge inroads in Europe with the mass migrations and now the United States was allowing the same to happen, even encouraging it. The great oceans no longer offered protection. First expel the United States from the Middle East, then push Israel into the sea, killing every last Jew, and then allow the natural progression of Islam to dominate the world. It would happen. It was only a matter of time.

Samir had helped train bomb makers in EFPs, the weapon that had killed and maimed so many U.S. servicemen and women. He was proud of his work and tonight he would kill yet another American.

At the base of the ladder, he waited for the remainder of his unit. A Syrian National Defense Forces officer led them through the well-lit tunnel. Samir could hear the ventilation system forcing air into the subterranean burrow, the rubber tubes carrying the life-sustaining oxygen running at shoulder height. Even though he was just shy of six feet tall, Samir could stand fully upright. The passageway was wide enough to accommodate a rail line on his left that Samir correctly assumed was for moving rockets and heavy equipment. The size and scope of the tunnel complex gave him the impression that it was intended to move large numbers of people, troops that would march right under Israel's illegal border. One day Samir would march through this tunnel for a full-scale retaking of Golan, the rightful property of Syria. Tonight would be a test run.

Why did his government want this American dead? It did not matter to Samir. His mission was to kill him, and anyone who got in their way.

CHAPTER 30

Kibbutz Merom Golan, Israel

AS THE CAR WOUND its way up into the Golan Heights, Reece was struck by the beauty surrounding him. It was so much greener than he expected. Driving past a small ranch he was reminded of Meadowood in Napa, where he had spent his honeymoon with Lauren.

Tuvia parked the Land Cruiser in a small lot adjacent to a park.

"Ready?" he asked.

Reece watched four children running across a grass field toward a play structure. The oldest looked to be ten or eleven and was obviously in charge. The youngest appeared to be about five. Reece watched as he took a tumble, the girl helping him to his feet and encouraging him to run after the others.

"Reece."

"Huh?"

"Are you ready."

"I'm ready."

They exited the vehicle and walked toward a woman. Her back was turned as she guarded the children in her care.

"Shiri," Tuvia said, announcing their approach.

A light breeze rustled the leaves on the trees. How could such a peaceful place have been witness to such bloodshed? *The nature of man.*

The dark-haired woman turned.

There was no mistaking that she was Aliya Galin's sister. Though younger in years, she appeared older than the bio photo of "Mélanie Cotillard" that had circulated in newsfeeds along with pictures of the other passengers in the aftermath of the Air France attack.

"Shiri, this is James Donovan, the man I told you about."

Reece nodded respectfully, unsure if he should extend a hand in greeting. Shiri's bloodshot eyes burned through him.

"I know who you are, Mr. Reece. Let's dispense with the alias."

"Thank you for seeing me."

"I didn't have much of a choice. They said it was 'for the state.'"

"Shiri," Tuvia said.

"Don't you *Shiri* me, Tuvia. Yonatan is dead, Ilan is dead, and now so is my sister. Suddenly the Mossad calls and asks me to see an American when I am not one day out of shiva," she said, referring to the week of mourning following the death of a family member in the Jewish religion.

Reece struggled to find the right words.

"I wanted to express my sincere condolences. I am so sorry. I was a friend of your sister. We worked together years ago."

"Did you *fuck* her?"

"Shiri, please," Tuvia interjected.

"Stop it, Tuvia. You know she left me. She left *all* of us. Running around the world, *doing it for Israel,* she'd say. *Bullshit.* She was doing it for herself. Now these children have no mother, no father. Just me. Do you want to explain that to her kids, Mr. Reece? Tell them that Israel was more important than they were? Go on, let's tell them."

"Shiri," Tuvia said, attempting to put his arm around her.

Shiri pushed it away.

"Look at them," she said, pointing to the playground. "They are between six and ten and none of them have fathers. Two of them don't have a mother. I'm their mom now. That is the cost of this *war.* It never ends. One, two, maybe all four of them will join the IDF. Then perhaps the Mossad will get their tentacles in them, explain that the state needs them, leverage the pain of losing their mother, their father, blame Hamas, Hezbollah, Islamic Jihad, Iran. That's how this works, Tuvia. Tell me I'm wrong. *Tell me!*"

"I'm so sorry," Reece said.

"I'm sorry, too, Mr. Reece. I'm sorry you made the trip. I hope the memory of my sister was worth it."

Shiri took a breath and composed herself.

"You've seen me, Mr. Reece. You've seen the children. Now, what is it you wanted to say?"

• • •

Reece waited for Tuvia in the vehicle.

That was a disaster.

In retrospect, it had not been the most appropriate of times to relay Aliya's message as he had promised her the night of the attack in the Green Zone. Sitting in the car, he now regretted delivering it at all. That she had been doing her job for Israel, that she believed in that mission to the detriment of all else, may have been better left unsaid.

He watched as Tuvia and Shiri engaged in what looked to be an emotional discussion. Reece was glad that the kids seemed oblivious to it, and that they were far enough away not to hear what was being said. They were occupied with an endless cycle of sliding, running, and laughing. They were living in the now. They were truly present.

Reece saw the two adults finally share an embrace. Shiri looked to the Land Cruiser and then back to Tuvia. Then she called out to the kids, who sprinted across the grass and into his arms. Godfather or not, even at a distance Reece could tell that Tuvia was someone special to the children, their smiles beaming with the innocent intensity of youth.

After a few minutes of joking and more hugs, Tuvia playfully chased them back to the play structure, then returned to Shiri and exchanged a few words before hugging her again and turning toward the vehicle.

He got behind the wheel and took a deep breath.

"Well, that was something."

"That it was. I'm sorry, Tuvia. Maybe it was a mistake coming here."

"We all deal with grief differently. I guess I can call you Reece now. Shiri was left with a lot to deal with. That anger and blame needs to go somewhere. In time, it will turn. Time will heal."

"I hope so," Reece said, looking back to the park and seeing Lauren pushing Lucy on the swing. She looked up at him to wave.

"It will," Tuvia said. "It has to."

"So, what now? Do we drive back to Tel Aviv?"

"Not yet. Shiri is going to take the kids to their grandparents' house. It's right next door to hers. She's going to get the youngest tucked in."

"And then?"

"And then, she wants to meet with you alone."

CHAPTER 31

IT WAS DARK WHEN Shiri finally walked back to her house.

Reece waited outside on the steps. The home was small but well built, on a hillside with a view of the Bental Reservoir. Not a hundred yards away was her in-laws' home, slightly larger and higher up on the rise.

Tuvia had left Reece at the house as instructed and gone to get a coffee.

Reece stood as Shiri approached.

Unsure how to proceed, he simply said, "I am so sorry about earlier, about your sister, about all of it."

Shiri studied him, the dark eyes intense, judging him.

"I'm sorry, too. As you can imagine, these are difficult times."

"I can."

"I know. Tuvia told me a little more about your history. I know you lost your family. For that I am sorry."

"Thank you" was all Reece could think to say.

"I can see in your face that the pain is still there. Will it ever go way?"

"I don't know," Reece admitted. "I don't think so."

"I don't think so, either. Why don't we go inside?"

Shiri showed Reece to a modest sitting area in the living room. Sliding glass doors led to a small deck overlooking a lawn, the property quickly dropping off in a steep hillside that Reece couldn't help but think would offer the kids a wonderful area to explore in the years ahead.

"I work in a winery now," Shiri offered. "It's not far. I help manage the books for accounting and tax purposes. The money isn't bad, it lets me contribute, and it gives me a break from the kids. I love them dearly but it's a lot for one person."

"Having your in-laws next door must be helpful."

"Oh, it is, and I am so grateful. Without them we'd be stuck in a small apartment in Tel Aviv and I'm not sure how we'd survive. But they are getting older. One day it will just be me."

"The kibbutz isn't really what I expected," Reece said.

"Most visitors expect it to be some dusty, cultish commune. They have visions of the black-and-white photos of men and women toiling in fields and training with World War Two–era rifles, eating in a shared dining area and sending the kids off to communal sleeping areas each night away from their parents. It hasn't been *that* kibbutz for almost a generation."

"It reminds me of a gated private community in the U.S.," Reece said.

"I can hardly remember the U.S. I was young when we left. Aliya remembered it. When we were kids, she would tell me about the beaches. I still have photos of us in Florida building sand castles. Maybe one day I'll go back."

Though she was beautiful like her sister, there was an edge, an intensity simmering just beneath the surface.

"Why did you come here, Reece? You came a long way just to tell me that she died doing what she did 'for us,' which I don't believe. She could be a selfish little *bitch* sometimes."

"All I can tell you is that when she thought she was dying, those were her thoughts; she wanted you to know that she was doing it for Israel."

"And did you believe her, Mr. Reece?"

"I did."

Shiri studied him.

"What happened between you two?"

"She was a friend in a time when we needed each other."

"Spoken like a lover."

"That we were not."

"Being married would not have stopped her, you know. The job. *For Israel,* and all."

"Well, it's good to know I was different."

Shiri paused. Even though tired and bloodshot, her eyes still radiated a probing strength. They were searching.

"Why else are you here?"

"I thought I owed it to her."

"You didn't."

"I did."

"Why else? Are you looking for answers?"

"What do you mean?"

"Answers as to who she was?"

"Maybe," Reece said. "I don't know. I wanted to pass along that message. How you interpret it is up to you. Now I'm looking for anything that can help me find her killer."

"Ah, now I see. You are here for *you.* Not for her. You are no different than those who keep this death machine in motion. Just down this road are villages and people who want to push Israel into the sea. There are mothers and fathers teaching their kids to love and there are mothers and fathers teaching their kids to hate, and to kill, teaching them that the Israelis are subhuman, rats and monkeys in need of extinction. PLO, Islamic Jihad, Iran, they pay the mothers of suicide bombers for their sacrifice, for their contribution to *the cause.* They celebrate the deaths of our children in the streets."

"How do you stop it? The cycle."

"When the men and women on *both* sides love their children more than they hate their enemies, then maybe this can stop. Until then, my kids, Aliya's kids, they will end up doing their part to keep perpetuating the violence. Eventually we all return to dust, Mr. Reece. That is the nature of things."

"I don't know if Aliya would agree with you."

"Oh no, she was too busy doing her part. And where did it get us? Nowhere."

"In the end you may be right. I'm still going to find who killed her."

"How valiant," Shiri said, the cynicism clear in her tone.

"I'm not going to take much more of your time. I said what I needed to say. My condolences are sincere and heartfelt." Reece paused. "I would like to ask, did Aliya ever mention a connection to Syria or Russia that concerned her?"

"A work question? No, she never talked about work with me. After all these years in the Mossad, I think there would be a line of people wanting her dead. That's how this game is played."

"I am sorry for your loss, Shiri. I truly am."

"*Losses,* Mr. Reece. Everyone around me is dead and they were all doing it for Israel."

She paused, then continued. "Forgive me. I do not want you to leave on a bad note. I do appreciate you coming here. May I offer you a glass of wine before you go? It's from the winery where I work."

"A peace offering?"

"Perhaps."

"Then I accept." Reece smiled. "I think Aliya would like that."

Shiri stood and walked into a separate kitchen area. Reece took a breath and moved to the glass doors overlooking the valley. The sun had long since set and sparse lights dotted an adjacent hillside. Reece wondered what it had been like to grow up here during the wars of the fifties, sixties, and seventies, wars that had never really ended, in a time when Israel had proven that she could stand up to the military might that surrounded her, that she could fight and would never allow her people to be lined up and forced into gas chambers. The shadow of the Holocaust still loomed.

Reece heard Shiri enter the room and turned, expecting her to be holding two glasses of wine.

Instead she held a Galil rifle and was pointing it directly at James Reece.

CHAPTER 32

REECE HAD FACED THE working end of more than a few rifles in his time but never a Galil. The Israeli-made weapon was an AK-type rifle that used the Finnish RK 62 as its jumping-off point and utilized the iconic upward-turned charging handle. From the curvature of the magazine, Reece could tell this was the 5.56x45mm version, the Galil SAR compact carbine.

"Shiri?"

"You come to Israel, to Golan, to pay your respects. You say you were not her lover. Then why come all this way unless you feel guilt, unless you are responsible for her death?"

She stood about seven paces away.

If she wanted to kill you, she would have already shot.

"Shiri, listen to me. I might very well be responsible for her death. We don't know yet."

"We?"

"U.S. and Israeli intelligence."

"Intelligence." Shiri spat out the words in disgust. "Just another word for targeting and assassination. My husband, Aliya's husband, and now my sister, all dead. Good intelligence. Bad intelligence. It doesn't matter. It all revolves around death. Your time will come, too, Mr. Reece."

Death comes for us all. It's nothing to be afraid of. It just is.

"It will," Reece said, calmly.

"The kids next door, mine and Aliya's, this is what they will know," she said, shaking the rifle in her hands. "Killing and death. Our neighbors will not stop until every last Israeli is dead and, in turn, Israel will never stop defending itself. There is no end to war."

"You may be right. Those kids have experienced enough loss. They deserve better."

"They do, Mr. Reece," she said, flipping the rifle to safe."Now go. Go and never come back. You are a harbinger of death. I want you nowhere near my children."

The bullet that took Shiri Galin to the ground was one of a full volley that turned her front door into splinters.

CHAPTER 33

REECE INSTINCTIVELY HIT THE floor as bullets cascaded through the door and windows, the more solid wood exterior walls absorbing much of the barrage.

"*Shiri!*" he yelled, low-crawling toward the downed woman.

As he reached her, he heard voices outside. Farsi? Arabic? Hebrew?

Win the fight.

Not stopping to check her status, Reece ripped the Galil from her hands and rolled into the prone position as another burst of automatic fire, focused high on the quickly disintegrating door, ripped overhead.

Reece flipped the selector to "semi," aimed at the voices he heard coming up the steps, and pressed the trigger.

Nothing.

Israelis often don't have one in the chamber.

Reece racked the upturned charging handle just as the first man entered.

Acquiring a solid sight picture through the hooded front sight, Reece sent eight rounds of 5.56 into his chest.

The assaulter fell forward onto his knees and then toppled face-first onto the floor.

The second man did not have time to adjust, his momentum carrying him into the room, directly into the "fatal funnel" and into Reece's sights. A round from Reece's rifle caught him in the mouth, taking his lower jaw with it, his hands dropping his AK and going to his throat as the bullet took his ability to breathe. Reece sent another through his right eye, which blew off the back of his skull, taking much of his brain with it and dropping him straight to the deck.

A third man adjusted and moved to the left side of the door.

Seeing the movement, Reece rolled to his left to get the angle and stitched him up the side from his hip to his upper chest. As his body contorted around the wounds, Reece sent another into his brain.

How many rounds did I fire?

How many rounds are in this magazine? Twenty-eight? Thirty? Thirty-five?

Reece heard more yelling and confusion outside, followed by headlights and the sound of vehicles on the street.

"Reece," he heard Shiri whisper, her voice weak.

He turned his head to assess the situation.

Shiri was down and down hard.

He turned his head back to the door. The engines and commotion outside suggested that their attackers might be regrouping, so he pushed himself to a knee and moved to the wall, hitting the light switch off. A lamp on a nearby table was on, so he ripped it from the wall as he passed, sending it crashing to the floor, where it shattered to pieces, putting the room into darkness. He grabbed Shiri under an arm, hearing her grunt in anguish, and dragged her across the floor to the base of a stairway in the corner.

"Where are you hit?" Reece asked, frantically looking up and down her body for signs of an entry or exit wound.

"Don't worry about me, get next door!"

Are they after me? Targeting Shiri? Will running to the kids just draw the enemy's attention in that direction?

Take a breath, look around, make a call, Reece heard the voice of his old Troop commander advise.

Reece took a breath.

Prioritize and execute.

"Shiri, is this the only rifle in the house?"

"No. My husband's is upstairs. In the closet in my room. First door on your right. In a green duffel."

"Ammo?"

"There are a bunch of magazines in there."

"Loaded?"

"They should be."

"Okay," Reece said.

"Reece, please, protect my children."

"Where are you hit?"

"I'm not sure. I can't feel my legs."

"Shiri, look at me."

He looked into her eyes, eyes that had once been filled with fire.

"I want you to take this rifle," he said, handing her the Galil. "Anyone comes through that door, I want you to put bullets in them until they are dead, understand?"

"I understand."

"Good. I'm going to high ground. Can I see the grandparents' house from up there?"

"You can. You can see it from my room."

"Okay, I'll let you know if anything is happening there. From this position you can see the front door and the back deck. They might try to come up from down there, so keep your eyes open."

She nodded.

"Okay. Stay strong. I'm going up."

Reece was taking a step when he heard a new sound.

Reece turned back to Shiri. They had both heard it before.

"RPG!"

CHAPTER 34

THE ROCKET-PROPELLED GRENADE DETONATED against the outside of Shiri's home on the second floor.

Take that shooter out, Reece.

He took the stairs two at a time in the dark, his eyes growing more accustomed to the gloom.

Top of the stairs, only one way to turn, first door on the right.

Reece entered a small bedroom with large windows that overlooked the walkway leading from the road to the house. Curtains were partway drawn. He could see vehicle headlights maneuvering in the darkness and hear voices in the street below over the sound of the intermittent siren.

You have one priority. Win this fight.

Reece went to the closet and flung the door open to find clothes on hangers and shoes on the floor with a few shoe boxes stacked in the back.

Green duffel. Where are you?

Reece reached in and threw a suitcase out into the room.

There!

Green duffel.

He reached in and slid out the old canvas duffel bag. Fumbling to find the zipper, he managed to get it open and pull out the Galil. Another 5.56x45 SAR. Reece briefly thought of the two identical Bravo Company rifles he and Katie kept in the Montana cabin. It made sense to have interchangeable magazines when fighting as a team. Apparently, Yonatan and Shiri were on the same page.

No magazine.

Reece flipped the side-folding buttstock into position, a feature borrowed from the FN FAL Para, and pulled back on the upturned charging handle. No round ejected but the action felt smooth, exactly as designed. The Galil was ready for business.

Reece fished around in the bag and pulled out a magazine. He pressed down on its top and was relieved to find a cartridge. The spring on the Stoner 63–inspired magazine gave only slightly, indicating that it was fully loaded minus one or two. Reece remembered a BUD/S instructor bringing his personal Galil out to "The Island"—San Clemente Island—for the third phase of BUD/S and giving the students in Reece's class a brief on Israel's July 1969 raid on Green Island by Flotilla 13. The class sat entranced by the story, which had only recently been declassified. The twenty-man Israeli force had emerged from the water and killed almost every Egyptian soldier on the heavily guarded island. Even though the Israelis used AK-47s and Uzis on the raid, their BUD/S instructor wanted to highlight the Galil, as it was a rifle the students would likely not see again. It had remained a favorite of Reece's ever since.

Reece locked the magazine into place and reached over the top to rack the charging handle. Pushing the selector to safe, he removed four additional magazines from the bag before moving to the side window. A light burned in the grandparents' home next door but there were no signs of movement or disturbance around their yard.

What did the citizens do when they heard an air raid siren?

Reece remembered his friend Gavy Friedson telling him about his days volunteering as a medic with United Hatzalah, running to bunkers as the rockets rained down, the Iron Dome intercepting the incoming projectiles in the night sky.

Did homes in the kibbutz have bunkers?

Reece had seen earth-covered cement bunkers outside of homes at various points throughout the day.

He flipped the front and rear Galil iron night sights into position and moved to the top of the stairs.

"Shiri!"

Nothing.

"Shiri!" he said louder.

"I'm here, Reece."

"Looks clear next door." Reece grabbed the railing and bounded down the stairs.

"How are you feeling?"

"I'm okay."

She did not look it.

"Here are two magazines," Reece said.

Shiri took them and set one down on the landing, removing the partially spent magazine and placing it on the first step before inserting the new fully loaded one.

"IDF. We all serve," she said.

"I want to check your back," Reece said, attempting to run his hands down her spine to look for an entrance wound.

"No, you get upstairs. Promise me, Reece. *Promise me* that if you see anyone approaching that house, you will kill them."

"I will."

"I don't hear them talking anymore. *Go!*"

Reece raced upstairs.

High ground. Get to high ground.

What is the enemy doing, Reece? Outthink them.

He entered the room and took an angle on the windows.

The street was dark. They had turned off their headlights. What was next? The enemy had taken casualties and knew there was armed resistance in the house. How many were out there, and what was their next move?

He paused to assess his surroundings, ensuring that he wasn't backlit.

Always improve your fighting position.

Reece crept forward and unlocked one of the four windows that overlooked the grass front yard and the street. He opened it slowly. If he shot, he didn't want his first rounds deflected off target by the glass. He had learned that lesson in Iraq.

Would they notice the open window? Possibly.

Movement.

A man running across the lawn from the street.

Friend or foe?

In combat you have to make split-second decisions based on incomplete information in a chaotic environment that will stay with you for the remainder of your life. Was the man running toward the house a neighbor coming to help or an enemy combatant? Reece's mind processed the vehicles in the street, the dress and weapons of the men he had killed downstairs, the Israeli-made weapon in his hands, and the AK in the hands of the man in his sights.

Reece pressed the trigger. He noted the reciprocating charging handle rocking back, ejecting the spent casing and loading another round into the chamber. Reece pressed the trigger again.

The man vaporized in an explosion that blew the glass from the windows and sent shards flying inward.

S-VEST!

Reece's face felt wet, his vision blurred.

What the hell is going on?

He wiped the blood that obscured his vision from his face and turned his head to check on the grandparents' house just as it took a direct hit from an RPG.

CHAPTER 35

HOLDING PRESSURE ON THE cut above his left eye to stem the flow of blood, Reece moved to the door and called down the stairs, "Shiri?"

Reece heard the sound of an engine and looked back out the window as an SUV skidded to a stop in the road, its headlights illuminating three vehicles in front of Shiri's house.

A Land Cruiser 300-series.

Tuvia!

Reece saw the door open and a figure sprint into the darkness as the vehicle began to take fire.

The high beams lit up the enemy and took their attention from Shiri's house.

Nice work, Tuvia.

From seventy-five yards away, Reece moved to the window and used the frame as a brace to further steady himself. Usually a sniper wouldn't want that exposure but in the dynamic environment of combat, adaptation was king. He found the front sight in what little ambient light was available, calming his breathing and heart rate as he settled in for a shot.

Don't stay here long, buddy, but make them count.

He held the front sight center-mass on a man shooting at Tuvia's truck and pressed the trigger. He quickly came back to the target, finding a second sight picture, and pressed the trigger again. Both bullets found their mark and sent the man to the ground.

RPGs, Tuvia's vehicle, the S-VEST explosion, chaos.

In chaos there is opportunity.

Reece found a man taking cover behind a vehicle, settled the front sight on his head, and sent a round through his skull. Brain matter exploded onto the person behind him. Surprised by his comrade's sudden exit from the land of the living, he stopped firing at the Land Cruiser and looked up at Reece just in time to take a 5.56 round through the bridge of his nose.

He thought of the park just hours earlier; the laughter and smiles, his vision of Lauren and Lucy by the swing set.

You have to win this fight or you all die.

Reece caught movement in his peripheral vision. A figure was running across the lawn from the flank. The SEAL sniper adjusted his rifle to engage.

Tuvia!

Shiri is going to kill him if he comes through the door.

"*Shiri!* Eagle coming in!"

"What?" she yelled back upstairs.

"Tuvia's coming in! Don't shoot!"

Reece found one more target in the road and put him down before the Land Cruiser's lights were shot out and the enemy focused their attention back on Shiri's house, on the sniper in the window.

Reece fell back into the room as the rifles below took aim at the second floor.

"Tuvia?" Shiri yelled.

"It's me," he heard Tuvia say as he pushed his way into the house.

How many people are out there? Reece wondered.

It doesn't matter. You need to kill them all.

CHAPTER 36

AS ROUNDS FLEW INTO the upstairs bedroom, Reece bounded down the stairs. Tuvia was leaning against the wall next to Shiri. He was holding his right side.

"Tuvia! You hit? Let me see it."

"Negative. I'm good. Leaking a bit, but good."

He had a Glock 17 in his left hand, his right palm pressing against his ribs.

"Reece, I heard a hit. Where? *Where?*" Shiri demanded.

"I'm going to go check on them," Reece said, deflecting the question.

"Tuvia, she's hit in the back. Nonambulatory. I didn't get a good count on what we are up against out there."

"I saw three cars," Tuvia said, his voice raspy. "I think at least five, six, seven, maybe more."

"Who are they?" Shiri asked.

"I don't know. Syrians, Iranians, Hezbollah."

Shiri turned her head and spat on the floor.

"Listen to me," Tuvia said to Reece. "Yamam is inbound. They were staged close by. They were shadowing us. They are on little birds and a Black Hawk but the RPGs may have grounded them. We just have to hold until they get here."

"What?" Reece asked. "Yamam?"

"Katz and my former unit commander thought it best to have a team standing by, just in case. We need to hold."

Another barrage of automatic rifle fire tore through the home, passing by Reece and the two Israelis protected in the corner of the staircase landing.

"ETA?" Reece asked.

"Unknown."

"Okay, Tuvia, you stay with Shiri. We don't know what's out there and we might not have much time." Reece tac-reloaded the Galil to make sure it had a full magazine. He handed it to Tuvia along with the partial and the other full magazine from his pocket.

"Hold this," he said.

Reece went prone and low-crawled down the stairs from the lower landing and continued across the floor, being careful to stay beneath the windows. When he reached the man he had shot eight times in the chest, he pulled his arm through the canvas sling that attached the Kalashnikov to his body. Now he had an AK. Still on the ground, Reece pushed the body over and took the magazines from the dead man's chest rig: two in each back pocket and two in each front pocket. It would have been too much movement attempting to take the chest rig. Reece noted that the man was in civilian clothes and was not wearing body armor, helmet, or night vision, nor did he have radio.

Interesting.

Reece turned and low-crawled back to Shiri and Tuvia in the staircase landing area, where he took a knee, confirming that the rifle had a round in the chamber and that the magazine was full.

"What are you going to do?" Shiri asked.

"What I do best."

Reece looked into her eyes, seeing the fear, the worry. *The children.*

"I've got them," Reece said.

He bolted into the room and onto the back deck. Slinging the rifle, Reece swung his legs over the railing and used his hands to climb down as far as he could before letting go and dropping into the darkness.

CHAPTER 37

SAMIR FARZAT WAS GETTING worried.

By his count he had seven men down.

Almost half my force.

Is the American alive or dead?

Why did the Hezbollah fighter start shooting through the door? That had not been the plan. Samir couldn't ask him; he was dead now.

He should have taken all Syrians. They knew what they were doing, but that had not been an option. His Russian employers stipulated that Hezbollah contribute a contingent to include the martyrs. Where was the second one?

The first had almost gotten inside. That would have ended it. Except for that sniper.

Their primary target building had taken severe hits. Their secondary target structure remained dark. They had sent an RPG into it. Still no movement. Samir would concentrate his forces on the primary house.

Samir was standing on sovereign Syrian soil. One day Syrian forces would push through and burn every Israeli house to the ground and Samir would be there.

"Mahmoud," he called to his second in command. "Get these men organized. Look at them hiding like cowards. Get them on line. Soften up the target with the AKs and RPGs, then get in there and finish the job."

“Yes, Samir. The men are worried about the sniper.”

“Send RPGs into those upstairs windows. That will take care of him.”

“Yes, Commander.”

“And send Qanti and Basit up on that knoll,” Samir said, pointing behind them. “I want RPGs and a PKM up there to cover both ends of the street. This is taking longer than anticipated.”

The RPG-7 was one of the most recognizable and prolific rocket-propelled grenade launchers on the planet. The PKM was really a Type 80 machine gun made in China and based on the Soviet 7.62x54mmR machine gun, but troops the world over still called it a PKM.

“Yes, sir.”

“And, Mahmoud, find me the boy.”

“The boy?”

“The martyr. It is time for him to prove himself to Allah.”

CHAPTER 38

ABBAS AHMED MARMASH HUNKERED down at the base of a tree in the shadows away from the men with whom he had crossed into Israel. Was the tree a cypress, a cedar, or one of the eucalyptus trees that the traitor Eli Cohen had convinced the Syrian military to plant to give their soldiers shade? In school he had learned that in the lead-up to the Six-Day War the Israelis used the number of eucalyptus trees to estimate the strength of Syrian troops. The Israelis estimated the size of their opposition and located the outposts through the trees that stood out in contrast to their surroundings. The eucalyptus was foreign to the Golan. Just another example of the Israelis' duplicity.

Abbas's family would be proud. The Israeli dogs and their American enablers had ensured that his people stayed destitute. They wanted to keep all those who swore alliance to Allah under their oppressive thumb.

He remembered his teacher writing on the chalkboard of his small classroom: *The hour will not come until Muslims fight the Jews, so that the Muslims kill them, until the Jew hides behind rock and tree, so the rock or the tree says: "Oh Muslim, oh servant of God, this Jew is behind me, so kill him."*

Now it was this tree, possibly one planted by the spy Cohen, that would protect him.

When he took his finger off the button, he would be condemning his enemy to the fires of Hell, where all nonbelievers went to burn for eternity. And Abbas would be in Paradise. He would never feel hunger, never feel pain. He would be remembered as a hero and his family would have the respect of all those who adhered to the Five Pillars.

Commander Farzat had counseled him to hide until his men had done their job, that he was too important to die like Hassan, who did not make it inside the house.

Wait until the Israelis come to collect their dead. Wait all night if you have to. Allah will guide you.

Maybe his native Lebanon would construct a monument to his achievement like the one he had seen at Tyre. The Islamic world had struck a blow that day. It had been accomplished by a fifteen-year-old Lebanese boy, just like Abbas. He had killed Israelis. His family had been proud. Even now, against the tree in the darkness, Abbas remembered what the plaque had read: "Martyrs create life." His teacher had spoken of this boy with reverence. Soon teachers across the Muslim world would speak his name with reverence as well.

All he needed to do was accomplish his mission. Wait. Be patient. Then take his finger off the button and enter the "gardens of pleasure" as promised by the Quran.

The pills Commander Farzat had given him when he exited the tunnel had calmed him. He had read what was written on the plastic bag when he swallowed them: zolam. He did not know what that was, but his teacher had told him that he should accept the pills before his mission. They would help him. He was not nervous anymore. He was at peace and soon he would be at the right hand of Allah, surrounded by virgins. Abbas had yet to touch a girl. He would soon get his chance. Allah would see to it.

And wage jihad for the sake of Allah, a jihad that is worthy of Him.

I will.

He thought of his teachers in Beirut. When they heard his name, that it was Abbas Ahmed Marmash who had worn the explosive belt, they would be proud, too. They would teach the next generation of his heroism. His legacy was immortality.

CHAPTER 39

REECE PUSHED THROUGH THE darkness, his newly acquired AK at the ready.

He had landed in the grasses below the deck of Shiri's home and quickly moved to the base of a nearby tree. He waited a few seconds, listening for sounds that did not belong in the night.

He who flanks first wins.

The enemy knows that, too, Reece.

In military doctrine the "keep it simple, stupid" or KISS principle had proven its effectiveness over the ages. When conducting an attack, it was often most effective to align forces "on-line" or in an L. Reece was hoping that the terrain lent itself to the on-line method and that his enemy had used the street to align their forces. Were they sophisticated enough to have a "squirter control" element for anyone escaping from their target out the back or to the flanks? Reece would soon find out.

Working his way through the shadows, he ran first back down the hill and then diagonally to the house in an attempt to avoid any security elements that the enemy might have set. He moved away from Shiri's house and her in-laws', taking a knee against a cypress tree and watching a neighbor with his wife and children run to a grass-covered bunker in a corner of their yard.

Civilians, innocents, just like Shiri and her kids. Now they were in danger because of Reece. Or were they? Who were they targeting? What the hell was going on?

Later, Reece. Focus on what you can control.

Right now, you need to go to work.

Reece moved closer to the street, in line with the downhill side of Shiri's house. He could see movement in the road but couldn't get a good count at this distance. He could tell that their attention was on the target house.

How many were there?

It didn't matter. If they took the house, Tuvia and Shiri were dead.

Time to go.

Daddy?

Reece turned his head.

Lucy?

The SEAL shut his eyes and shook his head.

Not now, sweetheart. Daddy's got to work.

You work a lot, the apparition said, echoing a similar sentiment Reece had expressed to his father at the Vietnam Veterans Memorial all those years ago.

I know, sweetie. I have to go now. I'll see you later.

Okay, Daddy. Just remember what you used to tell me.

What's that?

You know, one of your battlefield rules.

My battlefield expectations? Reece asked, remembering that he had passed on his old commanding officer's four battlefield expectations not just to his platoons but to his daughter as well.

I remember. Which one?

The first one, Lucy reminded him.

"Always improve your fighting position," Reece whispered as Lucy disappeared in the night.

He did just that, inching closer to the trunk of a thick oak tree. There was a difference between cover and concealment. This tree qualified as cover.

The RPG impacted to the front and just to the left of the tree. Had Reece not taken Lucy's advice he would no longer be drawing breath.

The heavy machine gun opened up immediately, the trunk of the tree absorbing the bullets that didn't get eaten up by the dirt in front of it or fly past into the night.

Where is that coming from?

Muzzle flash.

It was coming from an adjacent hill about fifty yards beyond and above the men in the street.

Elevated position. Automatic weapon. RPG.

Someone knew what they were doing.

They obviously had a bead on Reece. Before the next RPG hit, Reece had better be someplace else.

He glanced at the force in the street standing by their vehicles and saw the confusion in the line.

Go, Reece.

Move tree to tree, cover to cover, no more than two shots per position. The dead men inside didn't have NODs.

I'm up, they see me, I'm down, Reece thought, remembering one of his early lessons in IMT, individual movement technique, at the SEAL Desert Warfare Training Facility in Niland, California.

Reece broke cover and ran forward into the fight.

CHAPTER 40

SAMIR HEARD THE SOUND of a passing RPG and instinctively ducked. He expected his security position to fire RPGs at approaching military or police vehicles at the far end of the road to hold them off, not at something so close. Had they fired in error?

The PKM opening up into the same area confirmed that it was not an accident. They were being flanked.

"Right flank!" Samir yelled. *"Right flank!"*

"Where?" Mahmoud yelled back. "Whe—"

Samir turned to his second in command just in time to see the side of his head cave in.

Samir raised his rifle, flipped it to full auto, and pressed the trigger. With his sights in the general direction of the threat, he dumped his entire magazine. As the PKM on the hill opened up again, he dropped behind the front tire of the closest car.

Change magazines and neutralize the threat. You have fire superiority with your PKM in an elevated position. Kill the American.

Samir rose to his feet in time to see a dark shape materialize and then fade into the night.

"There!" he yelled at the soldiers left alive on his line. "He is there."

Samir pointed frantically at a shadow moving toward them.

The shadow shot again. Two rounds caught another of Samir's men in the chest.

The shadow kept coming.

The three vehicles had been parked facing different directions.

Light.

Samir ran to the dark Jeep Cherokee, reached inside, and turned on the headlights.

CHAPTER 41

REECE WAS MOVING FROM one tree to the next when the headlights caught him midstride.

He hit the ground and pulled himself behind a tree that was much too small as the PKM opened up again.

They did not have night vision, but now they didn't need it. All they had to do was send a kill team to flank his position while keeping him pinned down with the elevated machine gun.

Think, Reece!

The former SEAL had lost most of his advantages. He was now outmanned, outgunned, his location was known, and they had him pinned from two locations.

Time was of the essence.

You're fast, James, but even you can't outrun time.

He smiled at the memory of his father. Then he rolled slightly from the prone and tac-reloaded. No sense in running to your death with a partial magazine.

Lucy, I might be seeing you sooner than expected, baby girl.

As he pushed himself to a knee he thought of Nizar Kattan and Freddy Strain's widow.

I'm sorry, Joanie.

Okay, Reece, shoot and move. Go for those headlights and just keep killing.

He took a breath the same way he had in the starting blocks of the two-hundred-meter sprint he ran in track-and-field in middle school. His mom and dad in the stands cheering him on, the fastest kid in the county next to him in the blocks, both waiting on that starter pistol to launch them down the track.

He thought of Aliya and the justice she might never have. He thought of Lauren waiting for him on all those deployments and training trips. And he thought of Katie and the question he would never be able to ask her.

Then he pushed out of the blocks, feeling the cold embrace of death.

CHAPTER 42

SAMIR SAW THE MAN drop to the ground and scramble to cover behind a tree.

Was that who he had come to kill? The American?

It was too difficult to tell with such a fleeting glimpse, at this distance. If so, he had just made their job easier.

That machine gun needs to keep shooting. I'll maintain a base of fire from here and send three of my men to maneuver on him. There is no escape for the American now.

As Samir turned his head to order the three men to his right to form a kill team, he caught movement from the American's last position. Maybe the kill team was unnecessary. The crazy American was going to run to his death.

Samir raised his AK and heard a crack to his left, then another, and felt the sting of skull fragments and warm brain matter pepper the left side of his face.

What is this?

He looked back at the house and saw two distinct muzzle flashes from behind two of the front windows.

What?

Samir went to a knee behind the vehicle as another one of his men took two rounds to the chest from the aggressor still coming at them from the trees.

"Get in the car!" he yelled at last remaining soldier on the line.

The man stood to run around the middle vehicle and took rounds to the hip, stomach, chest, and finally the head.

Samir ran.

Rear vehicle. Get in. Keys in ignition. Go.

Samir's sprint put him at an angle that made the fire from the house ineffective.

He heard the American's bullets eating up the two cars between them, chewing through metal and glass, their trajectory deflected on the way to their target.

Allah, protect me.

Samir put the Mitsubishi Pajero in drive and stepped on the gas.

CHAPTER 43

REECE HEARD THE GUNFIRE from inside the house and knew immediately that Tuvia and Shiri were on the Galils.

Fortune favors the bold.

Reece continued his advance, taking down two more of the attackers and seeing another drop to the deck.

He rushed to the base of another large tree as the PKM fired at him again and then switched its attention to the house.

Reece moved his head from behind cover to survey the situation. He could see the small SUV racing off down the street, the machine gun on the hillside lighting up the house. That was a long shot for an AK, especially one he hadn't sighted in.

He rolled to the prone at the side of the tree. The AK magazine made it difficult to fire from the ground, so Reece canted his body along with the weapon.

Maybe this will distract them enough for Tuvia and Shiri to get to cover if they are not already there.

Reece pushed the AK selector to the bottom position and then came back up one to go on full auto, sighted in as best he could, and pressed the trigger, letting loose with what was left in his magazine. He then rolled to his left and got to his feet.

Run.

Reece's suppressive fire had its intended effect. The machine gun went silent.

He sprinted to the side of the road before the machine gun opened up again.

If you can see them, they can see you.

The SEAL could no longer see muzzle flash. He was below their line of sight.

The escaping SUV was almost at a turn at the end the street.

Decision point.

Attack uphill at an unknown entrenched enemy machine gun position in the dark or kill the man at the end of the block?

Reece sprinted to close the distance. As the car turned broadside in its turn at just over one hundred yards, Reece brought the rifle to his shoulder. He moved to a kneeling position and flipped the selector to semiautomatic. When his sights settled on the driver-side window, Reece pressed the trigger. Second sight picture, press, next sight picture, press. Reece put ten rounds through the window and door, the Pajero sucking each one like a sponge of death. The SUV swerved off the road, hit a curb, and smashed into a parked car before coming to a stop.

The SEAL stood and advanced on the crippled vehicle, continuing to send round after round into it as he approached. When the magazine ran dry, he twisted the Kalashnikov into his work space as his left hand grabbed a fully loaded magazine from his pocket. He pushed the new magazine into the mag-release, sending the empty one clattering to the street. He rocked the new mag into place, feeling the satisfying click, and reached underneath the weapon to rack the charging handle.

The rifle was back in battery.

Reece was back in the fight.

He fired two more rounds as he continued forward before an RPG flew from the hillside and impacted the second floor of Shiri's house.

Reece adjusted in a millisecond. *Prioritize and execute.* He was going up. Sprinting from the street, Reece jumped into a ditch that led toward his new target. He heard another RPG fly. He stopped and turned in time to see it detonate on a different house, Shiri's in-laws'. *The kids.*

Reece's one free hand dug into the dirt of the hill, his legs burning with the intense output coupled with the desire to kill. He was breathing so heavily that he almost mistook the sounds of rotor blades for another RPG. Reece paused and turned to look into the night.

The blacked-out Little Birds crested the rise behind the homes from off the Bental Reservoir, climbing to an elevation just above their intended target on the hillside. The agile helicopters were slightly darker than the night sky. Reece had seen AH-6s on attack runs downrange so he knew what was coming. He hit the deck as "dash 1" launched a barrage of Hydra 7 rockets at the enemy RPG and machine gun position. As it veered off, "dash two" opened up with its 7.62 M-134 minigun.

Reece looked at the SUV at the end of the street.

He could hear the Little Birds banking in the sky.

Well aware of what a man running down the street with an AK was going to look like under the NODs of the pilots, Reece dropped the AK. They still might shoot him but at least they would take a moment when they recognized that he was unarmed. Without a rifle in hand he could be a friendly Israeli neighbor trying to help at the scene of an accident.

Now he was running at what might be an armed enemy combatant with no rifle or pistol of his own.

Not your greatest idea, Reece.

Despite all the 7.62x39 rounds the driver side of the vehicle had taken, Reece knew that bullets did strange and unpredictable things when they hit metal and glass.

As he approached at a full sprint, sure enough, the car door opened. A man was attempting to get out.

Reece sped up, hearing the helo overhead closing in. He wondered if they had shooters on sniper platforms on the sides.

More than a few of Reece's bullets had pierced the skin of the Pajero, as well as the skin of the man driving it.

Reece kicked the open door and sent it smashing into the wounded terrorist's head, before grabbing him and pulling him from the vehicle and dumping him on the ground.

He did a quick scan of the car to ensure he was alone, before doing a cursory search of the man on the ground and removing a pistol from a holster on his belt. Gsh-18. 9mm. Reece quickly checked its status in case he needed to give the man more medicine but one look was enough to convince Reece that the bullets he had soaked up in their encounter were more than enough to send him to his maker.

Blood was already bubbling from his mouth, and as much as Reece wanted to save him for questioning, he knew all efforts in this case were futile.

He saw the man's lips moving.

Arabic?

Reece knelt at a distance that allowed him to see his hands in the off chance they went for a hidden blade.

"*American,*" the man whispered.

He saw recognition in the eyes.

They were after me. I was the target.

Reece heard one of the small helicopters land in the street behind him.

The man's lips moved again.

Reece heard boots on the asphalt behind him. He heard someone shout in Arabic, then in Hebrew.

Reece leaned closer. This time the command behind him was in English.

"Don't move."

Reece froze, straining to discern the words on the dying man's breath.

As the man's eyes rolled back in his head, Reece heard the words of the Quran.

"Judgment belongs to Allah."

CHAPTER 44

LITTLE BIRDS CAN LAND almost anywhere. A Black Hawk is another matter.

While the AH-6s continued to dominate the skies, assaulters from the MH-6 that had landed in the street kept an eye on the American as the Black Hawk came to a hover. In a matter of seconds, a fast-rope was kicked out and a steady stream of Yamam operators slid to the ground, immediately forming a perimeter as the helo veered off to land in an area nearby that could accommodate it.

An operator broke from the perimeter and ran to Reece's position, exchanging words in Hebrew with the men guarding the unknown.

"And you are?" he said in English.

"I'm James Donovan. I'm here with Tuvia Yatom."

The commander of Yamam held up a smartphone, comparing Reece to a photo.

"Make me feel better and tell me what Director Katz's favorite food is."

Reece almost smiled. "Cigarettes."

"Okay, it's him. I'm Harel," he said by way of introduction. "What's the SITREP?"

"Tuvia is hit. He's in the house there. Shiri Galin is with him. She was hit in the back. Nonambulatory. House also took an RPG. Kids are at the in-laws'. It took two rockets. Follow me."

The Yamam soldiers looked at their commander, who said, "You heard the man, follow him. Gold, take an element into the house. Medic—get in there. Blue—on me. Red—push out and get me a perimeter."

Without the weight of kit, Reece made it to the in-laws' house ahead of the Yamam. He reached for the front door handle and pushed down with his thumb.

Locked.

Stepping back, he turned and delivered a powerful mule kick that sent the door flying inward on its hinges.

He had never gotten the names of the in-laws, or the kids.

"Hello, friendlies, coming in," he said stepping through the threshold.

"Hold up, sir, let us clear it," a Yamam operative said from behind.

Reece ignored the directive.

One of the rockets had impacted the main level. It was a mess of books blown from shelves, broken furniture, and burning carpet. No bodies. Another rocket had impacted the upper floor. Reece raced up a nearby staircase and into a hallway similar to Shiri's. In a deviation from protocol, he sprinted past open doors to the room that had taken the hit. His heart sank as he saw the hole in the wall, the stuffed animals, the wooden toys. A bunk bed toppled over and smoldering.

No!

Reece pushed himself into the room, reaching down to throw a small mattress out of the way. Nothing. Closet. He opened the door and brushed the clothes aside. Empty.

He exited back into the hallway, the Yamam operators having cleared the rooms as they went.

"All clear, sir."

"Where are they?" Reece asked, brushing past them and back to the stairway.

Harel was at the base of the stairs. He held up a hand.

"They're okay."

"Where are they?" Reece asked again, coming down the stairs.

"Every house built from the mid-eighties on in Golan has a bomb shelter. This one is down in the basement, dug back into the hill. This entire house could get wiped out and they'd be fine."

"Let's keep them here until we get a status on their mother," Reece said.

"We will keep them in their shelter for another hour or two, just in case."

"Good."

"They are fine down there, Mr. Donovan," Harel said in response to the look on Reece's face. "Unfortunately, this is not an uncommon occurrence. Usually it's Katyushas or suicide bombers. That's life in Israel."

Reece considered how he would feel about Lauren and Lucy hiding in a bunker as rockets rained down on their Coronado home.

"Can I see them? Shiri will want to know."

"You can. Follow me."

• • •

Abbas Ahmed Marmash lay perfectly still. He had heard the gunfire and the explosions. Had the assault force been killed? Was he the only one left to complete the mission?

Abbas pushed those concerns from his mind.

You have been given a gift, Abbas. Now there are more Jews to kill.

He could hear the Hebrew all around and although he couldn't understand the language, he knew that these were soldiers. These were the same men who hunted and terrorized his people.

Abbas's legend would be secure. These were special operators, murderers. They emerged out of the night to kill his people. Most of those Allah called to Paradise only managed to take out soldiers at checkpoints or civilians in cafés. Abbas would take the most highly trained among them. His strike would cut deep.

Inshallah.

CHAPTER 45

REECE FELL IN BEHIND the Yamam commander as they walked through the now-secure home. They passed an operator standing by a door at the top of what opened into a narrow stairway and descended into a basement that contained a washer-dryer and a heating unit. The floor was concrete, with a drain in the middle. Cardboard boxes were stacked against one side of the room along with a rack hung with clothes.

"This way," Harel said.

Another door opened off the cement retaining wall. It led to another cement wall, with the path opening up to the left and then right again into the bunker. There were seven old army cots, a few stacks of bottled water, snacks, and several toys. Reece's eyes fell to an old FN FAL rifle in the corner.

A red rug ran between the cots, down the middle of the shelter. Two bulbs hung from the ceiling, illuminating the space.

An elderly couple sat on a cot watching the older kids lead the younger ones in a game. Beige tiles with numbers were scattered on the floor and on racks set up in front of the players.

"Mr. Donovan, meet Mr. and Mrs. Gartner, Daniel and Safra. And these are the kids; that's Ayelet and David. They are Shiri's kids. And these here are Leah and Shmuel."

Daniel stood and shook Reece's hand but Safra stayed seated, though she acknowledged Reece with a slight nod.

The youngest got up and walked to Reece.

He said something in Hebrew.

"English," the old man said.

"I saw you in the park today talking to Aunt Shiri."

Reece knelt down. The boy was just five. He must have been born around the time his father died.

"That's right. I was there," Reece said. "I saw you run. You're fast."

"That's what Aunt Shiri says."

"Well, she's right, you know."

"I'm Shmuel. What's your name?"

Shmuel. He was a Sam, just like Freddy Strain's special needs son.

"My name is James."

"I like that name. Aunt Shiri reads me *James and the Giant Peach*."

"She does, does she?" Reece said, remembering his own mother reading him that book as a child.

"What were you doing at the park? Do you like slides?"

"I do," Reece responded, looking at Daniel for help.

"It's okay, James, you can tell him," he said.

"Uh, I wanted to see you," Reece said, reaching up and playfully tapping Shmuel on the end of his nose.

"Me?"

"Yes, and your sister."

Leah picked her head up from the game.

"I knew your mom a long time ago."

"My mom is gone," the little boy said. "She's not coming back."

Reece's heart was breaking. The toughest part of war was not the killing or the bloodshed. It was the children. It was innocence lost.

"I know, Shmuel. She wanted me to tell you something."

"She did? What?" The boy's eyes lit up.

Reece looked at the grandparents. Their stern faces warned Reece that Shiri had passed along his message.

Reece turned back to the young boy.

"She wanted me to tell you, and your sister, that she loved you very much."

"She did?"

"She did."

"Want to play Rummikub with us? I'll teach you," Shmuel said, grabbing Reece's free hand.

"I might have to do that next trip."

"Your hand is dirty," Shmuel said, laughing. "When we go upstairs you can wash it in the kitchen."

Reece looked down at his hand. The blood had dried and turned the color of rust.

"Thank you. I'll do that. I need to go but I'll be thinking of you and about how fast you are."

"Bye, James."

"Bye, Shmuel."

"Next time you visit, will you go down the slide with me?"

"Count on it."

Reece stood as Shmuel ran back to his game. He waved at the other kids and nodded to Safra, who remained on the couch.

He began to reach for Daniel's hand but stopped and looked at his palm.

"Sorry, it's dirty," Reece said, pulling his hand back.

The old man walked with Reece and Harel to the entrance of the shelter.

"Gavriel is outside," the Yamam commander said. "He's going to stay there for a while. I'll be back to let you know when you can come out."

"I'm coming up with you. I need to see my Shiri," he said.

Harel agreed.

"And you, young man," he said, addressing Reece. "I know that's not what Aliya told you to tell us. Shmuel wasn't even born when you knew her. Thank you though for leaving him with that memory."

The old man struggled on the stairs up to the main level. In the kitchen he steadied himself on the counter and caught his breath.

"Not as spry as I used to be," he said.

"Mr. Gartner, why don't you wait here," said Harel. "We'll go check on your daughter and then come get you."

Daniel took a step and almost fell over.

Reece and Harel caught him and helped him to a chair.

"I'm okay, boys. Just the years catching up."

"Even so," Harel said, "I'm going to send the medic over. Might not hurt to have some oxygen."

"I'm fine."

"Efrem," Harel said to the operator standing by the door to the basement, "get Mr. Gartner a glass of water. We'll be back in a few minutes."

Harel motioned to Reece to follow him outside. They stopped on the front porch.

"Stress, anxiety. We'll get him checked out."

"Good. This family does not need any more tragedy."

"Let's walk over," Harel said. "I don't want to ask for a status report over the radio with the troops in there." He motioned with his head back inside the house. "They've got headsets on, but grandparents and kids can be a perceptive lot."

"Understood. Do you have a biometrics kit with you?"

"Yes, and we are already using it. We'll ID these guys and unravel this thing. A group this size, they got in somehow, probably tunnels."

An operator approached, whispered something to Harel, and passed him a folded piece of paper. The Yamam commander looked at it and then back to Reece.

"What did he say?" Reece asked, noting the look of concern on Harel's face.

"The team is going through the bodies. We haven't found anyone left alive to question. The team on the hill ended up being two shooters: a machine gunner and an RPG man. There was not much left of them. So far it looks like we have a mix of Hezbollah and Syrian terrorists, probably former Syrian military."

"Former?"

"Possibly active duty but my intel guy says pocket litter, weapons, and gear suggest mercenaries on the Syrian side, Iranian-backed Hezbollah for the others."

"Who the hell were they targeting?" Reece asked.

"Mr. Donovan, who knew you were coming here?"

"What do you mean?"

Harel handed Reece the paper his operator had just given him.

"They found it on the man in the car you killed when we landed."

Reece opened the folded paper and found himself looking at his death photo, the picture in uniform that the SEAL Teams started making everyone take before deployment in case you didn't make it back. Senior leaders got tired of not having professional photos at funerals, so everyone ended up having to take them. No one was happy about it except the staff officer who had to report on its status to the admiral. Years ago, Reece's photo had ended up on the twenty-four-hour news cycle for a few weeks and now it was in the pocket of a Syrian mercenary in Israel.

They could hear a helicopter begin to spin up as they took the steps down to a stone walkway.

An operator approached from out of the darkness.

"What?"

"We didn't want to put it out over the radio, sir. We need to get them to Carmel Medical Center in Haifa. We need CASEVAC now, sir!"

"Roger that, make it happen." Harel reached across his plate carrier and pressed a push to talk. "CLOSET 01, this is Red Lead. We are bringing two nonambulatory patients to you for CASEVAC to Haifa."

"I'm going with them," Reece said as they began to run toward Shiri's house.

In a moment of confusion that morphed to horror, Reece saw a figure sprint from bushes and enter Shiri's house.

Even at this distance there was no mistaking what he was screaming.

"Allāhu 'akbar!"

God is great.

CHAPTER 46

THE DEVASTATION WAS ENORMOUS.

The explosion threw Reece and Harel to the ground. Ears ringing and vision blurred from what were most likely concussions, they struggled to their feet, both doing a head-to-toe assessment as they got their bearings. As Reece sprinted toward the flames, he could hear Harel shouting something in Hebrew to his men in the Gartner house.

A Yamam operator was on the front lawn attempting to attach a tourniquet to the remains of a leg that was missing just above the knee. Reece stopped and assisted him.

"Go! Go!" the man said, telling Reece to help others.

Reece heard the MH-6 rise into the night and join the two AH-6s patrolling the target area. The Black Hawk helicopter was spinning. It sounded to Reece like it had set down at the park he had visited earlier in the day.

Harel raced past and into the house. Reece was on his heels.

Chaos.

Even though the windows and back sliding glass doors were gone, thick, dark smoke still covered the scene, making it hard to see. The curtains and couch were on fire, adding to the haze.

"*Shiri!*" Reece yelled. "*Tuvia!*"

Reece took a step forward and tripped to the ground. He turned and saw what the smoke had obscured: the torso of a Yamam operator. His rib cage was ripped open and most of his internal organs had been eviscerated by the blast. Reece pushed himself to his knees and was about to stand when he saw something else. As the smoke rose to hit the ceiling and make its escape into the night, he saw a head. He reached for it, picked it up, and turned it toward him. It was just a boy. No more than fifteen or sixteen, with black hair, olive skin, and dark eyes. His head had been severed at the neck, as was often the case with suicide bombers, their bodies tamping the blast outward along with the nails, screws, ball bearings, and short sections of barb wire embedded in the explosive. That outward energy also escaped up and would sever the head cleanly at the neck, allowing for positive identification on a corpse that was otherwise completely obliterated. His expression looked peaceful.

Reece dropped the head to the floor.

"Harel?" Reece yelled, getting to his feet.

"Harel?" Reece said again.

"I'm here," the Yamam leader said through the smoke.

Reece followed the sound of the voice toward the stairwell, the resignation in Harel's voice already preparing Reece for what he would find.

Reece stood next to the Yamam commander and looked down.

If Reece had not just seen them alive just thirty minutes earlier, he might not have recognized them. Their bodies had been shredded by the shrapnel embedded in the explosive vest.

It was clear that they had not ended up where they did by sheer chance. Both were on the floor. Tuvia had covered Shiri with his body in an attempt to shield her from the blast. A protector to the end.

CHAPTER 47

Mossad Headquarters, Tel Aviv, Israel

"TAKE A SEAT, MR. Donovan, or may I call you Reece?"

"Reece is fine."

The director of Caesarea was dressed exactly as he had been upon their first meeting. Reece realized that just over a day had passed since then and that he was probably wearing the exact same clothes, as was Reece, though now his were marred by sweat, dirt, and blood. The Tel Aviv office seemed darker, as though additional secrets had seeped into the walls over the past twenty-four hours.

News of the tragedy in Kibbutz Merom Golan had spread quickly. Reece and Katz were both warriors. The time to grieve would come later. Now there was work to be done.

"Can you tell me why a hit team from Syria had my photo with them and how they knew where I was going to be last night? It seems to me that only a few people knew my intended location."

Katz opened a desk drawer and pulled out a bright green pack of Noblesse cigarettes.

Reece waited, touching the fresh stitches on his forehead just over his left eye, while the Israeli spy touched a flame to the end of his cigarette, inhaled deeply, and blew the smoke toward the ceiling.

"Why and how," the Mossad man said. "Different questions. Finding the answer to one often leads to an answer for the other."

"Let's start with the 'how,' then," Reece said.

"What do you know about a Russian named Yevgeny Prigozhin?" Katz asked.

"The head of the Wagner Group?"

"Yes and no."

"What do you mean?" Reece asked.

"The Wagner Group, as most in the West understand it, is a private military company. Open-source reporting indicates it is essentially a proxy military force used to further the Kremlin's foreign policy interests from the Ukraine to Mozambique to Syria, but it's more complex than that."

"You mean it's the Russian president's private army."

"Not exactly but there is a connection."

Katz took another drag off his cigarette before continuing.

"Intelligence agencies first took note of mercenaries supporting Russian troops in the annexation of Crimea in 2014. From there, wherever Russian interests have intersected with strategic energy reserves, mineral deposits, or precious stones, what we commonly refer to as the 'Wagner Group' has had a hand in it."

"Are you saying it doesn't exist?"

"Not in the way we've come to understand the relationship between governments and private military companies, like your Blackwater or whatever they are calling themselves these days."

"So, what is it? And what does it have to do with me and the attack in Golan?"

"Wagner is more than a company. It's a network of mercenaries, paramilitary groups, contractors, and related businesses, which makes it harder to counter, but there is one man who connects them all."

"Yevgeny Prigozhin," Reece stated.

"That's right. They call him the 'president's chef' as, unlike most other Russian oligarchs, he didn't acquire his wealth through the 'loans for shares' scheme after the fall of the Soviet Union, becoming the sudden inheritor of what had once been state assets. Rather, he ran a restaurant in Saint Petersburg that the current Russian president patronized on his rise to power. Soon Prigozhin was winning government catering contracts to the tune of millions, supplying meals for Russian schools and hospitals. Competition disappeared. After delivering on those contracts, Prigozhin then turned his attention to the armed forces. His first Russian military catering contract was worth north of a billion dollars."

"It helps to be in business with the president."

"It does. As the president consolidated his hold on power, so did his 'chef.' Prigozhin began to create companies, putting his wife and even mother at their helms. The catering contracts turned to construction and then to paramilitary services. The Russian president awarded contracts to Prigozhin and was rewarded with large-percentage kickbacks into bank accounts and investment vehicles across the globe."

"I still don't know what this has to do with me."

Katz took another drag and pushed on.

"In reality, Wagner is a shadow network of entities that at times can be the action arm of the Kremlin and at other times a proxy force to further the interests of the Russian president while amassing a fortune for those at the top. Wagner is simply a name to focus human rights activists, journalists, and intelligence agencies. PMCs are illegal in Russia even though mercenaries connected to Prigozhin train alongside Russian special forces in Molkino in southern Russia. Wagner is a dead end."

"If it's a dead end, why are we talking about it?"

"The name, Wagner, hits close to us in Israel, Mr. Reece. We believe it originated with one of the mercenaries fighting in Ukraine, a former lieutenant colonel in the GRU, Dmitry Utkin, who we also know was Prigozhin's head of security. Our sources indicate he was a sick bastard who idolized the Nazis and had something of an obsession with Richard Wagner, the preferred composer of Adolf Hitler. He was last seen six years ago at a ceremony at the Kremlin honoring those who fought to annex Crimea."

"You believe Prigozhin has a connection to the attack in Golan?"

"Have you heard of the Internet Research Agency, Mr. Reece?"

"Isn't that the Russian troll farm that caused so much confusion in the last few elections?"

"That's right. And do you know who founded it?"

"Let me guess, Yevgeny Prigozhin."

"Correct, which in reality means it had the approval of the Russian president. Prigozhin even created companies with the public mission of combating disinformation and what you Americans like to call 'fake news,' but as with most things Russian, they did the opposite, leading massive disinformation campaigns to further undermine confidence in Western voting and elections."

"They've certainly been successful. I am still not making the connection between Russia and what happened last night."

"There wasn't much left of the suicide bombers in Golan and some of the terrorists took more than a few shots to the head, so facial recognition on them is proving difficult, but of the bodies recovered thus far and entered into the system, four were Syrian mercenaries tied to Concord Management, a company with the contract to protect Russian energy interests in Syria."

"As in oil and gas?"

"Yes, but that's not their play. Russia doesn't need Syrian energy. Russia produces ten million barrels of oil a day, Syria only twenty thousand barrels."

"What do they want?"

"Access and influence. Russia has not been a player in the Middle East since the fall of the Soviet Union. They are adapting. Russian mercenaries had major involvements in Syria in 2015 and Libya in 2019. As they take territory, they hold it, while Russian businesses linked to Yevgeny Prigozhin acquire major stakes in the exploitation of natural resources, not because they need oil or natural gas, but so that they can project power from the motherland through Syria, across the Middle East into Libya."

"Putting them on Europe's southern flank," Reece said.

"Spoken like a true strategist."

"Why risk all that to kill me, to kill Shiri, Tuvia?"

"That's the question, Mr. Reece. If they were willing to risk their gains in the region to kill you, you must be a threat, a strategic threat."

"I'm only a threat to Nizar Kattan."

Katz extinguished his cigarette among a heap of similarly extinguished butts in a well-used ashtray.

"Reece, Shin Bet lost a good man tonight. Yamam will feel this hit for decades. Four children were orphaned. The prime minister is considering military action against Syria that could ignite a wider conflict. They are convening the cabinet. The nation is on war footing. Everything we just discussed is circumstantial. The cabinet doesn't deal well in 'circumstantial.' They will call for reprisal."

"Unless."

"Unless we can prove that these were Syrian mercenaries targeting you and not Israel."

"That photo should help."

"It will, along with the links to Russian paramilitary organizations."

"Nothing you've told me indicates why I'd be targeted here, on Israeli soil."

"Follow it back, Reece. Your photo is found on Syrian mercenaries in Golan with ties to Russian paramilitary companies run by Yevgeny Prigozhin, a man who doesn't make a move unless it's approved and initiated by the Russian president."

Katz paused, letting Reece process what he'd heard.

"Reece, can you think of a reason the president of Russia wants you dead and was willing to risk Russia's strategic position in the Middle East to accomplish it?"

Reece exhaled, trying to wrap his head around what he had just heard.

"I've had some Russian entanglements but nothing that would justify starting a war between Israel and Syria and losing their recent gains in the region. It just doesn't make sense."

"There is something else."

Reece raised an eyebrow.

"Information on Nizar Kattan," Katz said.

"Is he connected to what happened last night?"

"He appears to be operating independently."

"How do you know?" Reece asked.

The Israeli spymaster tapped his nicotine-stained fingers together, contemplating his answer.

"We have an asset in Italy."

"In Italy? A spy?"

"Not a spy. An asset."

"I don't understand."

"Reece, what do you know of Operation Wrath of God?"

"I know you call it Bayonet. It was a reprisal for the eleven athletes killed at the Olympic Games in Munich."

"It was, but it was more than revenge. It was an operation to target and decapitate the PLO and its affiliate branches in Europe to ensure another Munich could not happen again. A young Kidon operative was in Europe conducting reconnaissance and surveillance on one of our targeted individuals. Remember, this is a long time ago. There was a wall between East and West Germany. The memory of the Second World War was still fresh."

"What happened?"

"This Kidon reported that his Black September target was meeting with the KGB."

"The KGB?"

"There had been intelligence suggesting that Black September and the PLO had Soviet backing."

"Why?"

"The Soviets were not happy that Israel had taken the side of the Americans in the Cold War."

"Was there ever a question?"

"Oh yes, early on, Israel could have gone either way. The kibbutz movement had deep roots in socialist ideology. When it became clear that Israel and the United States had allied, Israel became a target of Soviet aggression through proxies. The Soviets supported Iran, Syria, Egypt, Libya, Hezbollah, Hamas. Their support of our enemies created the modern Middle East."

"But Russia wants back in."

"That's right."

"And the operation in Germany?" Reece asked.

"The Kidon operative was given the green light to take out his PLO target *and* the Soviet handler, but he took a bullet, a sniper's bullet, before he could execute."

"What does this have to do with Nizar Kattan?"

"The man who was shot in Germany survived but never returned to Israel. Nor did he cut ties completely with his former employer."

"The Mossad."

"Caesarea," Katz corrected.

"I'm still not making the connection."

"This former operative, there is another reason he didn't come home."

"Oh?"

"He couldn't operate anymore."

"Why not?"

"The bullet nicked his spine. Since 1986 he's been confined to a wheelchair."

CHAPTER 48

REECE'S FLIGHT OUT OF Ben Gurion Airport was not until the following morning. The two "State Department" representatives from the United States Embassy had picked him up at Mossad Headquarters and driven him to one of the flats they maintained in Tel Aviv. Though the embassy had moved its official address from Tel Aviv to Jerusalem, the United States still maintained a robust staff at the Tel Aviv embassy branch office.

The flat was just off Rothschild Boulevard, near the Norman Hotel Tel Aviv and within walking distance of the Independence Hall museum. Ben Gurion Airport was not far away.

"I recommend Port Said for dinner," the well-dressed man in the passenger seat said. "It's less than a five-minute walk. Try the steak with tahini and tomato tartare. It's fabulous."

Maybe these guys are State Department after all.

"There's also a deli on the corner that's not bad. Fast Wi-Fi."

"I'll keep that in mind," Reece said, though he had no intention of leaving the flat. He needed to clean up, he needed a drink, and he needed to think.

The man in the passenger seat handed Reece a small gray SKB hard protective case.

"Dip pouch delivery," he said. "And here is the key to the flat. Third floor. Three-oh-two. It will be more private than the hotels. Fridge is stocked and there's an assortment of new clothes in the closet."

The driver's eyes were hidden behind Oakley shades, but Reece could tell by the slight movements of his head that he was constantly scanning: ahead, to his right and left, rearview mirror, side-view mirrors. DSS? GRS? Definitely a former operator.

"We will be here in the morning to pick you up. Your flight is at ten so we will be here at six. If there is anything you need, please do not hesitate to call. My cell is on the card," the passenger said, handing Reece a business card embossed with the embassy seal. Reece looked down at it as he exited the vehicle and stepped to the sidewalk.

CHAD HARMON

EMBASSY OF THE UNITED STATES OF AMERICA

FOREIGN SERVICE SPECIALIST

"Thanks, Chad."

Reece looked at the driver, who gave an almost imperceptible nod as he continued to scan.

"See you in the morning."

Reece was filthy. He had cleaned up the best he could at Mossad Headquarters, where he had received a few new stitches, but he was still noticeably in need of a shower and a change of clothes.

He avoided the elevator and instead made his way to a stairwell, where he took the stairs two at a time until he entered a third-level hallway. The key turned easily in the lock and Reece entered the flat, locking the dead bolt behind him.

Though he was exhausted, it was not quite time to let his guard down. He needed rest but first he needed to clear the rooms. The former SEAL did a primary clearance, setting the gray case on the couch as he passed. He then went back to the front door and went through the spaces more meticulously.

I need a weapon.

It was spacious and modern with good views for a third-floor residence. Reece got the impression that it didn't get much use. There was a kitchen, a spacious living room area with large glass windows, a small balcony, and main and guest bedrooms, both with en suite bathrooms. Everything was decorated like it was staged for a real estate brochure photo shoot.

Reece hit the lights in the kitchen and living room and pulled the curtains closed across the windows. No sense in making it easy on an enemy sniper. He then went to the kitchen, where he opened cabinets until he found the glasses. He grabbed three and stacked them in a pyramid by the door. Then he returned to the kitchen and got three more, which he also stacked by the entrance. He had a feeling that he was going down hard and if anyone entered the room, he wanted to know about it.

What are you going to do without a pistol?

It was also probable that he was under audio and video surveillance by both the Israelis and the Americans, and after his briefing at Lackland Air Force Base in Texas he was suspicious of every electronic device, from the TV to the toaster.

Reece went to the fridge and opened the door, shaking the idea that maybe even the refrigerator was watching and listening.

IOT. The Internet of Things.

Inside there were a carton of eggs and various cheeses and juices, but Reece was looking for something stronger. There were a few bottles of wine in the side door: a Gush Etzion Lone Oak Sauvignon Blanc, a Mt. Tabor Shiraz, and a Domaine Herzberg Malbec. The wine reminded him of Shiri, her body torn to pieces while her children played a board game in a bomb shelter next door. She had been so alive and full of fire and then she was gone. What would happen to the four children in her care? How long would the grandparents be able to raise them? Would those kids turn to the IDF and Mossad as they grew up, wanting to avenge her death and the deaths of Tuvia, Aliya, Ilan, and Yonatan? Had Shiri been right about the cycle, about war, about Reece being a harbinger of death? He shook his head, grabbed two Goldstar beers, and headed to the sofa.

He moved the case to the coffee table and attempted to twist off the top of the cold Goldstar. Not a twist-off.

No problem.

Reece set the edge of the bottle cap against the side of the coffee table and slammed his palm down on its top, popping it from the bottle. His first sip reduced its contents by half. He set the beer down and looked at the case.

Pistol? If so, he was going to feel silly for not opening it immediately.

Reece knew that contents of a diplomatic pouch were protected by one of the many conventions that governed relations between countries. They could not be searched or x-rayed.

Even though he had been handed the case from a representative of the United States government, Reece couldn't help but be cautious. He examined it for signs of tampering, leaking fluids, wires, anything obvious. Then he carefully flipped up the latches and cracked it ever so slightly, moving to the floor to get a better angle in an attempt to identify any internal wires that might indicate this was an explosive device. Seeing nothing to cause alarm, he went back to the couch and slowly opened it all the way.

A black bag was inside. Reece picked it up and examined the fabric. A Faraday sleeve. Developed by nineteenth-century scientist Michael Faraday, the bag was constructed of layered metal mesh. It blocked all electronic signals, preventing them from getting in or out. Reece had used them in the SEAL Teams and in his training at the Farm. He pulled open the Velcro closure and slid out an iPhone. There was a clear plastic adhesive covering the front, with six numbers and a round blue logo with KRYPTALL underneath.

Reece peeled back the sticker, exposing the screen.

The phone's facial recognition unlocked the device, revealing the home screen. The message application opened.

```
You are through the looking glass now.
    From your friend, Alice.
```

"Through the looking glass," Reece whispered.

What are you trying to tell me?

Reece thought back to his youth. It had been a long time since his mother had introduced him to Lewis Carroll's classic stories. *Through the Looking Glass, and What Alice Found There* was the sequel to *Alice's Adventures in Wonderland*. The "looking glass" was a mirror that Alice crawls through, entering a world where everything is reversed.

Everything is reversed.

Reece set the phone down next to his personal cell.

Everything is reversed.

He drained the remainder of the Goldstar in his second sip, leaned back on the couch, and was asleep seconds later.

CHAPTER 49

Gorky Park, Moscow, Russia

MIKHAIL GROMYKO PUSHED THE oval-framed glasses up the bridge of his nose as he passed through the Colonnade and into Gorky Park. His glasses were slipping more and more these days. Was his face getting that thin? Would Dashkov notice? The SVR director expunged those thoughts from his mind. There were other, more pressing issues to consider.

Located in central Moscow on the southeast side of the Moskva River, the world-famous park had once been the realm of dead drops and illicit meetings. In recent years, the abandoned buildings, dark paths, and hazardous carnival rides had been replaced with ponds—complete with swans—beautiful gardens, and even a smoothie bar. This was not the Gorky Park of old. Maybe that's why he had chosen it?

Gromyko picked out the protection detail first. They were not hard to find. Thick jackets over thicker shoulders, dark glasses, slicked-back hair, even the requisite earpieces. Dashkov was of the school that believed that force projection was in itself a deterrent. Gromyko suspected it might have a little something to do with ego.

"I know you are late just so you would miss the ceremony of my pipe lighting," the Federal Security Service director said as his old friend approached. "And why are you still wandering around Moscow without bodyguards?"

Gromyko took a seat on the bench next to his counterpart in internal security.

"It was a beautiful day to walk my surveillance detection routes; reminds me of the old days and helps keep me trim."

"Is that how you are keeping so thin?"

Pavel with his games again. Does he know about the cancer?

"You may want to try it," Gromyko said, tapping his stomach and eyeing his friend's midsection.

"I am well past those days, Mikhail. I'll stick to armored cars."

"You are aware, that if someone wanted to track you down, all they would need to do would be to follow the trail of muscle," he said, pointing out the PSD that had spread out in an informal perimeter around the meeting area. "I'm sure your vehicles blend in as much as your thugs."

"That's the idea, Mikhail. They first have to get past that wall of security. The thicker the better."

"What is better is if your enemy can't find the wall to begin with."

"Ever the spymaster," Dashkov said. "Is that why we are here? To reminisce about the old days?"

Their class at the Academy of Foreign Intelligence had spent time in Moscow, and Gorky Park in particular, practicing the tradecraft that would define the rest of their lives.

Gromyko looked out across the red, yellow, and orange blossoms standing out in stark contrast to the bright green lawn that surrounded them.

"I wonder what Maxim Gorky would think of the park today."

"Ah, Gorky, why did you ever return from Capri?" Dashkov wondered aloud. "You had such a good life down there. You could have stayed and written in the sun. Why return to this dismal place?"

"Because it was home," Gromyko said.

"Ah yes, home."

"Pneumonia, wasn't it?" Gromyko asked.

"Wasn't what?"

"His cause of death?"

"Yes, pneumonia."

"Stalin carried his urn at the funeral, you know."

"Did he now?"

"Least he could do. There are some who say the pneumonia was really the NKVD, internal security."

"I have heard that as well," Dashkov said.

"It was best to not run afoul of Stalin."

"As I said, he should have stayed in Capri."

"You may be right, old friend."

"Now, what have I done to deserve being dragged out of my office today, to a bench in Gorky Park, of all places?"

Gromyko reached into his coat pocket for his pack of Marlboros.

"Those cancer sticks will kill you, you know," Dashkov said, puffing on his pipe.

Does he know?

"It is not the cancer sticks that worry me, comrade," Gromyko said, lighting his smoke. "It's Commander James Reece."

"Oh?"

"Our team missed him in Israel."

"But we knew exactly where he was going to be."

"Yes, *we* did. It was set up for no Russian fingerprints; a Hezbollah death squad led by Syrian mercenaries."

Dashkov grunted and stuck his pipe back in his mouth.

"We now have a bigger problem," Gromyko continued.

"Which is?"

"Which is that James Reece has survived. We must assume he is beginning to wonder if he was the target and how the hit team knew where he was going to be."

"Our backup plans are still in place?"

"Yes. As expected, Reece is on his way to Italy to pay a visit to Abelard, the bookseller. He's a freelance handler, a broker of sorts. He connects mercenaries and assassins with clean weapons. He handles the financial transitions, all for a percentage, of course. He is well known to the world's intelligence agencies. A lot of us use his services; all second- or third-party transactions. He has his place."

"I know of this man. The man in the wheelchair."

"That's right. Former Mossad assassin. He was part of the Wrath of God operation. He was just a kid at Munich. Ten years later Israel was still hunting the terrorists who killed their people at the Olympic Games. He was older then. A willing recruit. You have to respect them. They don't forget, Pavel."

"Neither do we. And neither do *I*. This Abelard, I remember there being rumors at the time that a KGB sniper had put him in that chair. Germany, wasn't it? Right after we graduated from the academy. Where was your first posting, Mikhail?"

"Berlin," Gromyko said, bringing the cigarette to his mouth.

"I see."

"He has been looking for that sniper for almost forty years, still working for the Mossad, of course, so one has to keep that in mind when requesting his services. Had he known the Africa operation was really about killing Aliya Galin, he would have tipped off his former employer and a team of assassins would have been waiting in that field to kill Kattan, Le Drian, and the two patsies. He didn't know what it was for; he's just a connector. He connected Kattan to the Frenchman, who had the local contacts to pull off the attack."

"It is the connectors who make this world go around."

"That is the truth, my friend."

"So, are we at an impasse?"

"Not yet, but it is time to finish this. We need a professional, someone comfortable on European soil. I want Russian blood in charge of this operation, someone who can leverage assets to make it look like the crazy jihadis. Those savages would have reason to target and kill both the American SEAL and the Israeli bookseller."

"And who would that be?"

"I have an idea. He's one of yours. Former GRU. Our prey has evolved. Reece has learned from the last attempt. He's not going to walk so easily into an ambush. He's going to use the capability of the U.S. surveillance apparatus."

"That is where they have an edge, comrade."

"To a point."

"Explain."

"The Americans might be the world's leader in collection and surveillance, but they have a thing or two to learn about manipulation," Gromyko continued. "Misinformation, disinformation, fake news."

"You would think they'd be experts," Dashkov offered.

"We know that the Americans will be listening, monitoring every transmission and keystroke. With that in mind we can lead them where we want them to go."

Gromyko attempted to stifle a cough.

"Lay off those Marlboros, Mikhail."

"You give *me* health advice? What is that expression we learned back when we were young, when they hooked me on these," Gromyko said, holding up his cigarette. "Kettle calling the pot black?"

Pavel laughed. "I think so. Those were the days: drinking, whoring, spying. What a game."

"It's not a game now, Pavel."

"No, the fun is mostly gone. Even the desire for drink and pussy have ebbed."

"I doubt your vodka supply has noticed."

Pavel chuckled and shook his head.

"Even that is not as enjoyable as it once was. Age robs us of many things, Mikhail. But in their place is something else."

"Perhaps we fill the void with power," Gromyko said.

"Ah, yes, power. The aphrodisiac for old spies."

"There are a few things I have left to do," the SVR director said.

"You speak as though you are dying."

He knows.

"We are all dying, comrade."

"Some faster than others."

"That may be true. You never know how many months, weeks, days, minutes, even seconds you have left."

Will Pavel understand the threat?

"We have known each other many years, Pavel. We have been competitive, but we have worked well together as friends, as rivals at times, and now as comrades who remember the old days. If you want to see a few more days of whoring and drinking, it would do us both well to eliminate James Reece. If we miss him again, he just might be smart enough to figure out who his true enemies are, and he might come looking."

"For me?"

"For us."

"In Russia? Don't be absurd," Dashkov scoffed.

Gromyko handed his old friend a file.

"What is this?"

"It's a partial file on James Reece."

"Partial?"

"The complete file is rather large, Pavel. I am an old man. I took all that you need to see."

Dashkov pulled readers from an inside pocket of his jacket. He mumbled from time to time as he worked his way to the final page. He closed it, took a puff of his pipe, and handed the file back to Gromyko.

"He walked across Siberia?"

"He did; to kill the man he thought was responsible for his father's death. Blew him into pieces with one of our own antipersonnel mines."

Dashkov stashed his readers and took a long, drawn-out puff.

"I show you that, Pavel, so you know the type of man we are dealing with. What he's capable of."

"Are you afraid of this Commander Reece?"

"There is a difference between being afraid and being aware. I am well aware that if James Reece lives, and if he figures out why his father was really killed, if he finds that safe-deposit box, there is very little that will stop him from putting a bullet in your head."

"Mine? What about yours?"

"Mine, too, Pavel."

Dashkov grunted again, looking at his security detail.

"Right now," Gromyko continued, "he doesn't even know what he has. If he is in possession of the safe-deposit box key there are limited options for him to find out what it opens. I don't see how he can find it, but we must operate on the assumption that he will eventually find and open the box. He has no children. No wife. This ends when he's dead."

"Then we in turn must ensure he is liquidated before he gets any closer. Nizar still has the contract, correct?" Dashkov asked.

"Yes, we are connected to Kattan through the Frenchman now. They are in Montenegro. Abelard facilitated their travel out of Africa. They are a backup now. If we can take him out before he gets close to Kattan, that's what we will do. Is the GRU operative I mentioned earlier our best man in Europe?"

"For what?"

"Wet work. The kind we can attribute to someone else."

"Who?"

"Any jihadi group will do. The crazier the better: an ISIS affiliate, Hezbollah, al-Qaeda."

"You know, Mikhail, sometimes I think we should have teamed up with the Americans after the Great Patriotic War and used all of our combined resources to extinguish the Muslim hordes from existence."

"Are we into genocide now, comrade?"

"We should ask Stalin."

Gromyko grunted.

"I know the man you suggest. He's older. Retired a year ago. Disappeared for a time, but he will do. Brutal assassin in his day. He has the knowledge and network to pull it off, but it is going to cost us," Dashkov said.

"Luckily, money is not a problem."

"James Reece is not going to find the safe-deposit box. That list died with his father. But let's be sure. The next time we talk I want it to be over dinner and vodka." Dashkov stood. "The way they've cleaned up Gorky Park depresses me."

Gromyko watched his counterpart in the FSB walk back into the gardens, his security element dispersing into a wedge formation as they moved toward the exit. The old spy found himself wondering, if he were James Reece, how would he kill one of the most senior-ranking intelligence officials in Russia?

It was time to bring in a professional, a man whose entire existence had been about perfecting the kill. It was well past the time for James Reece to die.

PART THREE

ABELARD

THE BOOKSELLER

WAR WAS ALWAYS HERE. BEFORE MAN WAS,
WAR WAITED FOR HIM. THE ULTIMATE TRADE
AWAITING ITS ULTIMATE PRACTITIONER.
—CORMAC McCARTHY, *BLOOD MERIDIAN*

CHAPTER 50

Brindisi, Italy

OLEG BERZIN HAD BEEN around long enough to know that one did not turn down a request from the Kremlin if one wanted to remain among the living. He had settled in Brindisi, an Italian port city on the Adriatic, and was officially retired, though one never really retired from the Spetsnaz GRU.

He had been nineteen years old in late December 1979 when he had landed at Bagram Air Base in Afghanistan as part of the initial Soviet invasion. He had gone by a different name then. He had gone by many names over the years. He was a tanker when he first set foot on Afghan soil, his thick chest and massive arms making up for what he lacked in the height department.

Three years earlier he had stood atop the podium at the 1976 Soviet Youth Boxing Tournament in Moscow. Though he had been born in Russia's largest city, he had no memory of it. His parents had moved to Kazakhstan when he was three. It was there that his father had introduced him to boxing. Recognizing that his son did not have the build of a natural runner, he would remind him, "Why run when you can stand and fight?" Oleg's bouts under the lights of the capital had opened his eyes to the world beyond Central Asia. He was a fighter and he put those skills to use in the Soviet military, becoming his battalion's champion boxer and earning the respect of his commander and his peers.

It was in Afghanistan that he had first heard rumors of the KGB, GRU, and Spetsnaz storming Tajbeg Palace and killing General Secretary Hafizullah Amin while concurrently taking control of the Ministry of the Interior and radio and television stations. That is where Oleg wanted to be. He was a warrior and as he looked up at the mountains surrounding Bagram airfield, he decided he did not want to fight this war from the confines of a tank.

It was his boxing that opened the door. A Spetsnaz officer who had once been an Olympic boxing contender attended a regimental bout on Bagram and saw Oleg beat opponent after opponent in a smoker. A few days later, Oleg found himself in a tent on the far side of the airfield, standing at attention before a panel of men in an array of military and local *kameez* tunics and wool *pakol* hats asking him questions about his family and his boxing skills. He remembered the heavy smoke in the room and one of the men tossing a special spade in the air.

He heard nothing for months, until he was once again summoned to the far side of the base, where a different group of men questioned him. When he rotated out of Afghanistan a year later, he was ordered to a training command outside of Moscow where his life would take a fateful turn. *Spetsialnogo naznacheniya.* Special Purpose. *Spetsnaz.*

The first phase consisted of days upon days of humiliating hazing, a rite of passage for those seeking membership in the elite unit. Over the course of his instruction, veterans began to filter in from Afghanistan. When they took to the vodka late at night, Spetsnaz recruits beware. They were not about to let anyone weak of mind or body join their ranks. The hazing gradually turned to forced marches with no food or water, obstacle courses, timed runs, orienteering, and boxing, Sambo, and Systema. It was in those unarmed methods of combat that Oleg excelled.

Even the combat veterans of the Hindu Kush didn't want to put on the gloves across from their new recruit.

Those who survived the first months of training were presented with their spade. Oleg had learned to dig trenches and foxholes in basic training but in Spetsnaz the tool was used not for digging but for killing. For the remainder of the grueling course, the recruits were never out of arm's reach of their spade. It went everywhere with them. They kept it sharp, ready for daily inspections, and they learned to use it to fight. Like the axe or tomahawk in other martial cultures, the spade was the Russian special operator's primal tool of choice. It became an extension of Oleg's body. Even when the trainees graduated to knives, the venerable Kalashnikov, the SVD Dragunov sniper rifle, explosives, static-line airborne training, free-fall parachuting, and survival, the spade was a constant companion.

When young Oleg found himself back in Afghanistan, it was as a Spetsnaz sergeant, hunting the mujahideen, calling in air strikes, and assassinating their leaders. They would sometimes leave the dead *muj* in the villages as a warning to others, their bodies bearing strange wounds, hacked to death by small shovels.

Nineteen eighty-five was a pivotal year in the war. The Spetsnaz sergeant could sense it. As a bikini-clad Irina Alfyorova shot AKs with enamored Spetsnaz troops for a morale-boosting photo op, the Americans were setting up the infrastructure to arm the Afghan bandits who continued to stand up to their invaders despite staggering losses. Moscow doubled down, putting General Mikhail M. Zaitsev in command of the Soviet Afghan Campaign. If Zaitsev had led the successful 1968 invasion of Czechoslovakia, he could surely bring these sheep herders and cave dwellers to their knees. With legendary general Valentin Varennikov providing strategic direction behind the scenes, the Soviet Union's best and brightest were ordered to win at all costs.

The bombing campaign intensified to levels unknown since World

War II and the Soviet commandos were unleashed. Working in concert with Mi-24 helicopters, Spetsnaz troops descended into mud compounds as the gunships lay waste to entire villages and caravans, earning the name *Shaitan-Arba*, "Satan's Chariot," from their enemy. Oleg and his operators would set down in remote areas of the country under the cover of darkness, emerging out of the night to slaughter the Afghans on their home turf. They would have killed every last *muj* had it not been for the Americans.

The Soviet escalation coincided with an increase in support from Washington. Oleg's friends and teammates were dying by the hands of so-called holy warriors, but those hands were controlled by the CIA. Soviet intelligence reports indicated that the United States was spending tens of millions of dollars a month to supply the Afghan resistance through the Pakistani ISI with AK-47s, ammunition, RPGs, DShk machine guns, mortars, and even the mules to transport the weapons and munitions across the mountains. Oleg recognized that the real enemy was not hiding in caves in northern Afghanistan; rather they were hiding in secure offices in Washington, D.C., and Northern Virginia.

On a raid aimed at cutting off supply lines from Pakistan, Oleg's unit had found American frequency-hopping radios among the dead. Not long after, Oleg was summoned on a recovery operation. Another Spetsnaz unit had been ambushed on the Pakistani border. When Oleg arrived on-site, he found what was left of the team. They were all dead, and they were all missing their belt buckles. Only later would he learn that the CIA had requested belt buckles as evidence of dead Soviet soldiers; they wanted to know if their investment was paying off.

The Mi-24 "Hind" helicopters had dominated the skies over Afghanistan for years, giving the Soviets total air superiority. Flying in pairs of two, four, or eight aircraft, these "hunter-killer" teams took to the skies and rained down death and destruction from machine guns, bombs, and rockets at will. In addition to its ordnance, the Hind could carry eight troops, making it unique among attack and transport rotary-wing aircraft, but as tactics evolved the seats were removed so the helos could carry extra rockets, bombs, and ammunition instead of passengers. This allowed the gunships to set down in the field and reload without having to return to base; more efficient for killing. The special-purpose commandos began flying in Mi-8 transport helicopters in tandem with the deadly Mi-24s, which allowed them maximum fire support and additional operators.

The Hind struck fear into the hearts of every Afghan villager. The advantage of fighting on home soil was negated by the huge Soviet airborne beasts and their ruthless commandos. The pilots could receive a mission, destroy a village or caravan, and be back at Bagram that evening for a warm meal and steady stream of vodka to numb their humanity. The war had settled into a stalemate; the Soviet Union was bogged down, and the Afghans refused to submit. That stalemate was broken in 1986 when the Americans introduced the mujahideen to the Stinger.

Oleg had been in Bagram on September 26, 1986, when he received word that a mighty Hind had been shot down in Jalalabad. He initially thought the *muj* had gotten lucky with an RPG. Then additional information began to trickle in; one Mi-24 down became three Mi-24s down. The kings of the Afghan sky had been reduced to paupers in the course of a single late afternoon. The balance of power had shifted.

The *muj* were emboldened by the influx of Stinger missiles smuggled over the Khyber Pass. The helicopters that had been so formidable in hunting and killing the Afghan rebels now became targets. The enemy began drawing their tormentors into ambushes, bringing them down with the American-supplied missiles. The Soviet gunship had been effectively countered, which meant the Soviet military was no longer feared. The "hunter-killers" had become the hunted and the killed.

It was best for the aircrews to die on impact. Oleg saw what the savages did to survivors. His unit once found an aircrew skinned alive, their bodies hung from trees with their genitals stuffed in their mouths. The mujahideen also began leaving dead Soviet soldiers propped up on the side of the roads, their arms and legs cut from their bodies.

Over the next year, almost two hundred Soviet aircraft would be shot down by the American-made surface-to-air missile. No longer would the Spetsnaz enjoy the close air support of the formerly dreaded Hinds, the pilots now flying at such high altitudes as to be rendered completely ineffective.

Oleg saw the writing on the wall when he read that in response to a twenty-thousand-Soviet-troop operation to cut off the ratlines from Pakistan, mujahideen commander Jalaluddin Haqqani said, "We have lost many men, but we will not lose the war." Oleg knew that to defeat the mujahideen the Soviets had to defeat their base of funding and support. To win in Afghanistan, the Soviets had to defeat the Americans.

As more and more of Oleg's comrades began their final flights home in the Black Tulips, the cargo planes stacked with Soviet dead, the boxer decided that the real battlefield was not in Afghanistan. He needed to take the lessons he had learned from the mujahideen and use them against the West.

Why run when you can stand and fight?

Standing and fighting meant working for an organization that would allow him to wage war someplace other than Afghanistan. That war was lost. Oleg looked for the next ridgeline. It was time to kill from the shadows. That meant an intelligence service. While the KGB had become the service of political influence operations, the GRU got their hands dirty in the world of clandestine and covert extrajudicial killings. Oleg was primed for the GRU. Boxing once again opened doors. Everyone loved a champion. The GRU was a natural next step for the Spetsnaz veteran.

The Main Intelligence Directorate would be shortened to Main Directorate over Oleg's tenure in the organization. What remained constant was his mission: to undermine the war-making capability of the

United States. The Soviet military had been built to counter the American armed forces. Just as the CIA had used the Afghan mujahideen, so would Oleg use proxy forces to weaken and destabilize his adversary. The opposite was also true. That meant that the tactics used to send the Soviets running from the Graveyard of Empires would work against his enemy. Oleg became an expert in the use of proxies.

While at the GRU Academy he studied English and Arabic. The jihadis had been fighting the West since the Crusades. They would be Oleg's proxies. His first assignments were to Iran, Libya, Lebanon, Syria, and Sudan, followed by time in Europe where he used his contacts to assist the GRU's partners in terror in the planning and execution of assassinations that furthered the Kremlin's interests. His final official assignment had been with the First Directorate, focused on the European Union.

But the GRU was changing. The organization he had joined in the 1980s had in more recent years expanded its efforts on a new battle space, the domain of cyberwarfare. He had adapted and learned English and Arabic all those years ago, but electronic bits and qubits on computers were beyond his ability to comprehend. As his agency was unveiled on the world stage for its role in attempting to influence the 2016 presidential elections in the United States, the Novichok poisoning of Sergei and Yulia Skripal, and the attempted hacking of the Organisation for the Prohibition of Chemical Weapons, Oleg began to sense his time had come. Watching the disastrous American withdrawal from Afghanistan with disbelief, Oleg made his decision. The former boxing champion had not been able to bring down his Western adversary. Instead, they had defeated themselves.

They took the wrong lessons from us, he thought.

While in Europe he met a younger woman, a widow with four kids. As the final American planes departed Afghanistan, he decided that the chapter of his life that had started on Bagram Air Base in December 1979 was now closed. America had received her punishment. Just as the

Soviet Union had fallen not long after its misadventure in Afghanistan, so would America. The signs were everywhere. He resigned from the GRU and was married a week later.

Now Italy was home. He had hidden money away in various bank accounts over the years. It wasn't extreme wealth, but it allowed Oleg and his new family to live a comfortable life in Brindisi. His Italian was coming along and their location on the water allowed them ferry access to the Greek islands and train access into Italy and the rest of Europe.

Oleg opened a boxing gym, not because he needed the money but because he still loved the fight. He could stay in top shape while passing on the lessons of the ring to his stepchildren and to others in need of a sport that built character and the attributes necessary to succeed in life. The American debacle in Afghanistan had given him closure. It had been a long time coming and at sixty-two years old he was finally able to let go of his past. He wore retirement well, his life coming full circle, back to the ring, where it had started.

So, when the messenger arrived from the Russian embassy in Rome, he almost turned the invitation down, though an invitation from his former employer was not really an invitation. Having worked in the secret world as long as he had, he knew he didn't have a choice. Had they made the request a year earlier, he would have jumped at the opportunity to strike another blow against his American nemesis; he still sought vengeance for their support of the mujahideen in the Afghanistan of his youth.

Had he forgiven them?

Maybe not quite forgiven, but he had made peace, made peace with the memories of Stinger missiles and dismembered countrymen. One could only hate for so long. In Oleg's case it was just over forty years.

It had been a long time since Oleg worked with the PLO, the Libyan Mukhabarat, or Lebanese Hezbollah. Back when he had been recruited for Spetsnaz and up until August 2021, this was the type of assignment for which he lived, for which he had developed a reputation within the GRU. That expertise and reputation had caught up with him.

When he returned home, he packed a bag, kissed his wife, hugged his stepchildren, and boarded a train for northern Italy. He had a clean phone and Russian documents with yet another identity. He had memorized the names and contact information of the terror cell, all of whom had fought in the Syrian Civil War. His orders were that the operation leave no Russian fingerprints.

Islamic terrorism in Europe was not uncommon. There was the March 2004 Madrid train bombings, the November 2004 Theo van Gogh assassination, the July 2005 London bombings, the March 2012 killing of three soldiers and four Jewish civilians in the French city of Toulouse, the May 2014 shooting at the Brussels Jewish Center, the January 2015 *Charlie Hebdo* killings, the May 2015 Jewish Museum shootings in Belgium, the November 2015 Paris attacks, the July 2016 Nice attack, the June 2016 Atatürk Airport attack, the March 2016 Brussels bombings, the May 2017 Manchester Arena bombing, the October 2020 beheading of a French schoolteacher in Paris, and the October 2020 church stabbings in Nice, to say nothing of the less spectacular attacks that barely registered or the planned attacks that were uncovered and disrupted before the terrorists entered the execution phase. Oleg was going to add another incident of Islamic terror to the list.

The attack would take place in the northern Italian city of Turin. The Islamic State would claim responsibility for a bombing that would kill two people: a Jewish bookseller bound to a wheelchair and with whom Oleg was familiar, and an American who was in fact the primary target. The Islamic State had ample motive to want them both dead. If the bomb failed to kill them, the jihadis would finish them off with Kalashnikovs. Oleg was there to ensure the assassination went as planned. The old GRU assassin had one more mission for Mother Russia before they would let him hang up his gloves. It was best to not run afoul of the Russian president.

CHAPTER 51

Over the Mediterranean Sea

THE EL AL FLIGHT from Tel Aviv to Milan was a relatively short four and a half hours on the Boeing 737. From his business-class window seat Reece looked down at the crisp blue Mediterranean waters. He knew the route would take him just southwest of Turkey and then across Greece and Albania before landing in the fashion capital of the world.

Almost there, Reece.

One more stop before you put Nizar Kattan in the ground.

Reece looked down at his father's Rolex. The watch had seen so much combat in the jungles of Vietnam and who knew how much more in the decades following the war. Perhaps it had seen enough.

Time.

After it was done Reece would move on. His family had seen enough of war. If he survived, it would be time to turn the page on this chapter.

And he had a question to ask Katie.

He felt the weight of his dead wife, daughter, and unborn son. *The guilt.* Would it always be there? *Probably.* Could he make peace with it? *Maybe.*

Time.

Get your head straight, Reece.

Reece was not interested in Milan's fashion industry, nor was he interested in the city's art galleries or museums. Milan was a waypoint on his journey to meet the man in the wheelchair, the man who had put Nizar Kattan in contact with those who had the means to take an airliner out of the sky, a specific airliner with an Israeli agent on board, a Mossad operative named Aliya Galin.

This time Reece had the help of two of the world's most effective spy agencies, the CIA and the Mossad. He also had assistance from an unquantifiable and almost unknown entity operating on a mythical level of the Internet: Alice.

AI. Artificial intelligence. What the hell even was it? Was she?

Reece struggled to wrap his head around what he had learned from General David and from Jimmy in the depths of Lackland Air Force Base, and what he had gleaned from his conversation with Alice herself.

Did the CIA or NSA know that Alice had sent the KryptAll phone? Was she acting independently? Did Rodriguez know? General David? Jimmy? Who controlled her? Did anyone? What were her intentions? What were the ramifications of working with a machine—no, not a machine, an artificially intelligent entity that could not be turned off?

Even though the cabin of the El Al jet was not particularly cold, Reece shivered in his chair.

When he landed, he would meet with a *Sayan* who would ensure he had a car to get from Milan to Turin. In this case the *Sayan* was Jewish, an Italian citizen who was loyal to the state of Israel. The network was first established under the direction of legendary general and spymaster Meir Amit, who ran Israel's military intelligence agency, Aman, and the Mossad in the 1960s. Among his many distinctions was that he was the only person in the history of the country to run both organizations at the same time. If Israel were to survive, she needed to leverage all the assets at her disposal. Jews who were citizens of foreign countries but loyal to the new nation on the Mediterranean were assets Meir Amit was not about to leave uncultivated.

Reece leaned back in his seat and recalled his conversation with Ronen Katz concerning the anomaly that was Saul Abelard.

Abelard had fought for his nation at the highest levels of special operations and had then been recruited and trained by Israeli intelligence to execute negative treatments abroad. When he had disappeared after a lengthy hospital stay in Berlin, his masters in Tel Aviv feared the worst. It was easier to vanish back in the days before everything had cameras embedded with geolocational data to make life more "convenient."

After a five-year hiatus he resurfaced in Rome at the Central Institute for the Conservation and Restoration of Damaged Books and reestablished contact with his former employers. He informed them that he was going to embark on a two-year internship at Giulio Giannini e Figlio in Florence, where he would learn the "Florentine style" of book binding. Following another two years of training under the famed Conti Borbone book restoration dynasty in Milan, he had the credentials to open his own business, a business that would give him cover for action.

With start-up funding from a discerning investor, he located a storefront for rent in Turin between the time of the First and Second Intifadas and founded Abelard's Libri Rari e Restauro—Abelard's Rare Books and Restoration—on a quiet street in an old part of the city. That the discerning investor was the Israeli Mossad was known only to Abelard.

He was not a *Sayan* or a *Katsa*. He was something else entirely. He was his own entity, a concierge to the underworld. From his quaint bookshop, he could find talent and handle logistics, weapons, passports, and identities for black-market transactions, catering to those who still operated the old-fashioned way and preferred to keep their business off the darker levels of the Internet. For his services, Abelard collected a healthy fee. He was also gathering information for his former agency, though now it was not for love of country or out of a sense of duty to the Jewish state. Now it was personal. He was looking for someone who operated in the world of shadows and if he wanted to find that person from the confines of his wheelchair, he needed to be an integral part of that world. He was looking for the sniper who put him in his chair.

It was an arrangement of convenience. The Mossad had an asset in the underworld who could pass on information about impending attacks on Israelis and Israeli interests, and if and when Abelard found the man he was looking for, he had one of the world's most ruthless spy agencies at his disposal.

When Abelard connected Nizar Kattan with Jean-Pierre Le Drian in Africa, there were no indications that they were planning to shoot down a passenger jet, let alone one with a Mossad operative aboard. The bookseller still felt an allegiance to his home country even if he had not set foot there in over thirty years.

The Mossad had informed Abelard that an American was inbound, an American looking into the Air France attack in Africa. They requested that Abelard offer his full support.

When Reece landed, he had a two-hour drive to Turin, where he would meet the man who could lead him to Nizar Kattan.

CHAPTER 52

Turin, Italy

IT WAS NOT DIFFICULT for Oleg Berzin to slip back into his old ways.

The Syrians had all fought under the banner of the Islamic State in Syria and Iraq. Six of the seven were refugees, six of the millions displaced by the Syrian Civil War. These holy warriors had made their way to Europe among the thousands that Italy was attempting to manage, deport, or resettle. What made these six different than the others was that they were well versed in fabricating homemade explosives and on the finer points of operating AKs.

The seventh was an Italian citizen who had answered the call to jihad and was one of five thousand Europeans who had traveled to Syria and Iraq to fight during the course of the war. Tammam Nasri spoke Italian, English, and Arabic. As an Italian citizen, he could exercise freedom of movement throughout the European Union. He had been radicalized at home but his two years in the Levant had given him the skills and experience to lead his newly formed terror cell on Italian soil. Oleg had confirmed through the Russian Internet Research Agency that Nasri was on an Italian watch list but was not currently under surveillance.

The weapons they would use originated in the central Albanian town of Gramsh, where copies of Chinese-cloned AK-47s had been made since the 1960s. The weapons procured for this operation were ASh-82 models, identified by their underfolder buttstocks, which would allow the hit team to more easily conceal them, or keep them completely hidden if they were not needed. More and more weapons had been making their way into Europe from the Balkans in recent years. Once inside Europe's twenty-six-country Schengen area, travelers had unrestricted access to almost the entire continent. There were no border controls or passport checkpoints to worry about once one was inside. The former GRU man shook his head at the absurdity of it. It was a soft underbelly that terrorists had already exploited and would continue to exploit. That was not his concern. His assignment was to kill the American and the Jew and ensure that it looked like the work of ISIS, a mission that was certainly within his wheelhouse.

Oleg carefully removed the bomb from the small daypack and set it on a dirty kitchen table. It smelled slightly fruity. That was a good sign. Had it smelled of vinegar he would have insisted the team construct a new device. He inspected it with a knowing eye. He took his time and found it to be satisfactory. It would work. The white putty had not yet begun to deteriorate or evaporate. It was not the first time the Syrians had built homemade explosives. Similar devices had brought terror to London on a July morning in 2005. News pundits and terrorism analysts would be quick to draw comparisons. It was rudimentary, which was exactly how Moscow wanted it. It had to bear a certain signature.

The main charge was triacetone triperoxide, or TATP. Since its first use in Israel in 1980 it had earned the nickname "Mother of Satan." Its chemical precursors of peroxide, acetone, and acid could be found in commonly available products the world over. Even so, the Syrians had sent their wives to separate stores to buy them independently. Seeing people of Middle Eastern descent was not an abnormality in this district of Turin. The terrorists and their wives blended into the fabric of the neighborhood. Still, it was best to avoid arousing suspicion. Anyone, not just a newly arrived Syrian immigrant, buying all the materials necessary to construct the device at one location would have raised eyebrows.

Hair dye was purchased in cash along with diapers, toothpaste, and chocolate bars at one drugstore. Nail polish remover was bought at another, along with tampons, aspirin, shampoo, and a small plastic toy truck. Liquid drain cleaner was picked up at a different location, along with a few sponges, toilet paper, and a toilet bowl plunger. A hardware store provided nails, nuts, bolts, a hammer, and two screwdrivers. Most of what was acquired was camouflage. What Allah's holy warriors really wanted was hidden among normal, everyday items. The shopkeepers and cashiers at the various stores had no idea they had just sold ingredients of death to a terror cell.

The hair dye, nail polish remover, and liquid drain cleaner were mixed, dried, and packed into soda cans that were then secured tightly together in a six-pack of carnage. The nails, nuts, and bolts were taped to the outside. A seemingly innocuous garage door opener provided the transmitter and receiver. Two wires ran from the receiver to steel wool embedded in the TATP in the center can.

Though Oleg could have built bombs of urea nitrate, ammonium nitrate, and aluminum powder and triggered them with more highly technical and precise mechanisms, he needed to ensure that the most sophisticated investigators would never suspect Russian involvement. The perpetrators of the attack had to be new immigrants to Italy from Syria. Borgo Dora was home to a large population of immigrants displaced from the developing world. A bookstore owned by a Jew in a neighborhood with a growing Muslim demographic was a prime target.

The cell's orders were relatively simple: wait for their targeted individuals to meet at the specified location and then blow them up. Conduct battle damage assessment just as they had done in the war, and if the American or Jew somehow survived the explosion or if the bomb failed to detonate, they were to finish them off with the AKs.

Oleg had committed the face to memory. *Commander James Reece. Navy SEAL. Quite a history.*

The Russian would be running command and control on this operation. He had hidden two small pinhead cameras covering the entrance to the bookstore and the back exit. You could hide a camera anywhere these days. Essentially a lens, a chip, and a self-contained power source, the miniature camera was programmed to send a black-and-white signal to Oleg's phone. He set up in a nearby café and tested the line-of-sight connection. The black-and-white setting would offer a clearer picture if Reece was delayed and showed up later in the evening in low light. He would have liked to have at least two more to cover the avenues of approach, but keeping the operational footprint small to reduce the risk of detection by an Italian police officer or an observant citizen was a top priority. Two micro video cameras would have to suffice.

The Internet Research Agency was providing Oleg with locational data on Reece's progress. There was no need for the former Russian intelligence operative to spend all day in the café staring at his smartphone or sitting on a park bench with a newspaper obscuring his face for hours on end, waiting for his mark to arrive. He could reduce his signature by being in the appropriate location at the right time. He thought of how much chaos and havoc he could have wrought with this technology behind the lines had the USSR invaded Germany through the Fulda Gap.

The GRU trained thousands of terrorists across the Middle East during the Cold War in the event they could be used against the United States. Some of that training had come back to haunt them, but had the USSR and United States gone to war, the destabilization operations of Spetsnaz and well-trained jihadis unleashed to target American interests around the world would have been a powerful force. Oleg wondered if the RA-115 suitcase bombs (though the tactical-level nuclear devices were anything but the size of an actual "suitcase") he had hidden were still in place. Their power sources would have died long ago without maintenance. Still, he would rather his stepchildren, or anyone's children for that matter, not find them and start tinkering. The odds of them still being operational were slim, and for all Oleg knew, the GRU had recovered and returned them to the bunkers at Penza-19.

Those were the weighty assessments of the Cold War days: tactical nukes, stealth technology, Reagan's Strategic Defense Initiative, dubbed "Star Wars" by an indignant senator, ballistic missile submarines, and mutual assured destruction.

Today's mission did not involve expensive weaponry or the possibility of fallout from a nuclear winter. This mission was more straightforward; one American and one crippled Jew needed to die. Oleg and his team had chosen the time and the place of the ambush. They had the technical advantage of tracking their prey without his knowledge and had the micro video transponder to confirm his arrival at the target site. They had a bomb set to detonate when Oleg pushed the button on a garage door opener. They had the tactical advantage of surprise and violence of action. The odds were as stacked in their favor as they could be. If things went as planned, the seven jihadis waiting in the back of the small passenger van in the parking garage around the corner would never have to unfold the stocks of their AKs.

Still, James Reece was a survivor.

No, Oleg thought. *James Reece prevails. Do not underestimate him as others have done.*

With that in mind, the GRU man added one additional element to the equation.

CHAPTER 53

HIDDEN IN THE AURORA District of Turin, just west of the Dora River in a part of the city first constructed using what was left of its medieval walls, lay the historical hub of Borgo Dora. Home to bars and cafés, a performing arts school, a former weapons factory dating back to the Second World War that was now a homeless shelter, and what was at one point the terminus of the railway, the area had fallen into decay in recent years. That decline kept the rent well below what was demanded in Turin's more exclusive enclaves, which allowed Saul Abelard to conduct his business without fear of being evicted in favor of higher-paying tenants.

Abelard lived directly above his shop and rented a garage not far away. The garage housed a 1989 midnight-blue Mini Cooper that he had learned to drive using hand controls after he had lost the use of his legs. He had purchased it in Rome when he had lived there as a student at the Central Institute for the Conservation and Restoration of Damaged Books. The five-year course was one of, if not the preeminent, book restoration program in the world. Was entering the prestigious program an excuse not to return to Israel, as his handlers had asserted?

Each Saturday he would wheel himself though narrow, winding cobblestone streets, searching the Turinese flea market for treasures. Those selling their wares knew to expect the "bookman," as they called him. He never failed to buy a book or two, regardless of how worthless they might be. He wanted those who set up shop every weekend to always be on the hunt for what might be a rare volume in need of restoration, and purchasing a book or two kept them searching. It also built trust. When Abelard saw a find that actually was valuable, the seller would often accept the first price offered, like it was one of the hundred others the bookman had acquired over the years. It was as if he was running an intelligence network, though instead of one focused on targeting and killing those responsible for Munich, this one allowed him to give life to objects that were in a state of decay.

Maneuvering himself through the flea market of the old town was much more interesting than looking for rare books online. He was able to interact and enjoy the languages, sights, and smells of Turin. It was part of his routine. It was discipline. Discipline had been what kept Saul going for the past thirty-five years. He could have opted for an electric wheelchair, but that would not have given him the constant reminder that he was still on a mission. The manual wheelchair kept his hands, arms, back, and spirit strong. None of the baristas who passed Saul a coffee or any of the Saturday flea market vendors who sold him books suspected what the kind man in the wheelchair really did for a living. Saul Abelard did not keep the doors to his rare bookstore and book restoration service open because there was such a high demand for exclusive books. He had other sources of income that paid the bills.

That the flea market forced him to violate the Jewish prohibition of working on *Shabbat*, the Sabbath, didn't bother him in the least. It was "work" only in a sense. The day set aside for rest in the Jewish tradition had not been a concern for him in quite some time, since he had boarded the jet in Tel Aviv.

Abelard had been twenty-six when the bullet that changed his life hit his spine. He had been plucked from the ranks of Sayeret Matkal by the Mossad years earlier. His fluent Russian and German language skills put him on the radar of an agency still hunting those responsible for the murder of eleven Israeli athletes at the 1972 Olympic Games.

For Abelard, not yet in his teens, the images remained seared into his mind all these years later. He remembered sitting on the old couch next to his mother, watching the small television in their apartment in Be'er Sheva, in the Negev. His father had left for the Sinai in June 1967 and never returned. His dad was not a fighter. He was a bookseller. His parents ran a small used bookstore in the Old City. But fighting was what one did to defend Israel, bookseller or not. Memories of the Holocaust were still fresh.

His mother struggled to keep the small shop open and young Saul was often hungry, as he was on the morning of September 5, 1972. Most of Israel had been asleep when eight terrorists of the Black September faction of the Palestine Liberation Organization, the PLO, entered the Olympic Village in Munich, Germany, where the Israeli athletes slept. Abelard would later learn that security was intentionally lax, coming just twenty-seven years following the end of World War II. Their intent was to use the Games to showcase a new democratic Germany on the world stage and turn the page on the 1936 Olympics, which had been exploited as a propaganda platform for Hitler and the Third Reich. Wearing track suits and armed with rifles, pistols, and grenades, the terrorists forced entry into Apartment 1 at 31 Connollystrasse and took eleven members of the Israeli Olympic Team hostage, killing two in the initial assault. The hostage takers demanded that Israel release 234 Palestinian prisoners and that West Germany release the two founders of the Red Army Faction, also known as the Baader-Meinhof Group.

Saul recalled that it was a Tuesday, and his mom did not take the bus to the Old City that day to open the store. As with most of the nation, she sat horrified by the footage from Europe. He brought her bread and water, which she hardly touched.

They both watched as Prime Minister Golda Meir asked the

international community to "save our citizens and condemn the unspeakable criminal acts committed." As with the Holocaust, most of the world remained silent.

"It's happening again," he remembered his mother whispering.

She didn't open the store on Wednesday, either.

They had a few pounds, the Israeli currency at the time, in a jar in the kitchen, some of which Saul used to buy a loaf of bread at the local market to share with his mother.

When Saul woke up on Thursday morning, she still hadn't moved. Words from the man in the yellow jacket who had been reporting from the Olympics were being replayed on Israeli news: "We just got the final word. You know, when I was a kid, my father used to say 'Our greatest hopes and our worst fears are seldom realized.' Our worst fears have been realized tonight. They've now said that there were eleven hostages. Two were killed in their rooms yesterday morning, nine were killed at the airport tonight. They're all gone."

Saul looked at his mother, but she continued to stare at the television.

"They will never stop coming for us," she said.

"Who?" Saul had asked.

They stayed in the apartment all day. Saul learned that the terrorists and the Israeli hostages had been moved by bus to waiting helicopters for transport to Fürstenfeldbruck Air Base, where they were told a Boeing 737 was waiting to take them to Cairo. A firefight had broken out and all nine remaining Israeli hostages had been killed.

He heard a commentator say that German police marksmen were deployed around the airfield, that the police officers in the sniper role did not have sniper-specific training and had been issued H&K G3 rifles with iron sights. During the firefight the terrorists executed the Israeli athletes with rifle fire and grenades. One West German policeman was killed, along with five of the eight terrorists. The newsman said that West

Germany did not have a dedicated counterterrorist force. Saul decided on Thursday, September 7, 1972, what he was going to do with his life, though he kept it to himself.

His mother opened the used bookstore on Friday. She gradually began to go through the motions of caring for her only son. Saul went back to school and would help his mom in the afternoons. It was the two of them against the world.

The three surviving terrorists of the Black September faction of the PLO were arrested by German authorities and sentenced to pretrial confinement. Less than two months later they were released in exchange for hostages taken in the hijacking of Lufthansa Flight 615. They were flown to Libya, where they were welcomed as "heroes of the Munich operation." The bodies of the five terrorists killed at Fürstenfeldbruck were flown to Libya, where they were buried with full military honors.

The world seemed content to move on from Munich. Israel had other plans.

Though Saul did not know it at the time, Israel's response would alter the course of his life.

Saul's parents had survived the Holocaust. Both his grandparents on either side had not. His father had stood up to defend the tiny nation in the Six-Day War and had been cut down in the Sinai. Saul's country understood the fate that awaited them as individuals and as a nation if they did not project power. After Munich, Saul understood, too.

The gas chambers of Nazi Germany were a constant reminder that the world would not come to their aid. Munich reinforced that, almost three decades later, nothing had changed. Israel was on its own.

Through the used books that passed through the store, Saul learned what many Americans had conveniently forgotten, that the liberation of the concentration camps was a secondary concern and not the reason the United States had entered the war. Why did the Allies not publicize what they knew about mass killing of Jews in Europe? Why did the United States not expand immigration quotas for Jews fleeing Nazi Germany and encourage other nations to do the same? Saul knew the answers, as did every Israeli.

The new nation was surrounded by a sea of enemies, all of whom sought to destroy it. That positioning in the world mandated the creation of a military and intelligence apparatus that would be respected around the world and feared by those Arab nations and terrorist organizations whose goals were the same as those of the Third Reich—a final solution to the Jewish problem.

His mother's depression worsened as the years went on, and the night Saul left for his two and a half years of compulsory military service, she went to bed and never woke up. At a young eighteen years old, Saul blamed the world. He blamed the Arab armies that constantly threatened to push Israel into the Mediterranean. He blamed the terrorist organizations that existed to kill every Jewish man, woman, and child. He blamed the nations of the West that were reluctant to offer their support.

That dedication and his combat record in the 1982 Lebanon War made him a prime candidate for the General Staff Reconnaissance Unit, and after twenty months of training he was awarded his maroon beret. He was now a member of Israel's most elite and secretive counterterrorist unit. He had fulfilled the promise he had made to himself watching the news coverage of Munich a decade earlier. His instructors had been the legends of the raid at Entebbe, where once again the Jewish passengers had been separated from the rest. Just as his mother had cautioned, it was happening again. Sayeret Matkal existed to prevent that which Saul's mother most feared.

When his commanding officer ordered Abelard to a meeting at their headquarters not far from where he had grown up, he was introduced to a man from Tel Aviv who had a proposition.

"How would you feel about joining an organization tracking down those responsible for Munich?" the man had asked.

"I thought they were all dead."

"Almost. Not all. And those who pulled the triggers had help. The facilitators and leaders are just as responsible as those who held the guns."

Abelard remembered his mother on the couch, watching the news reports over the course of the week.

Saul was in.

He was trained to serve as a Kidon and also as a *Katsa*, a case officer for Israel's intelligence agency.

He was attractive to the Mossad for another reason. He had no ties.

Now, north of sixty years old, he still had none. He had his books. He had his store and flat. He had his Mini Cooper. And he had never stopped searching. Not for splinter cells of the PLO or of Black September, but for the man who had put him in the chair.

Abelard sat in his wheelchair behind his desk in the rare bookstore, tortoise-shell glasses correcting his vision, which had begun to fail. Dressed in his daily attire of a dark suit accented with an ascot, he was awaiting a visitor. A suppressed H&K P7M8 9mm pistol with Karl Nill wood grips was in an open drawer to his right. One couldn't be too careful in the rare book restoration business.

CHAPTER 54

REECE CLEARED CUSTOMS IN Milan without issue. His James Donovan passport didn't raise a single red flag, nor did his answer when asked about the purpose of his visit.

"On a round-the-world trip. Been to Africa, Israel, and plan to spend about a week in Italy."

The customs agent stamped his passport and he moved along.

Uri was not what he expected. The *Sayan* was small and thin, with a big smile. He greeted Reece like they had known each other for years.

He led Reece to the underground multilevel parking structure attached to Terminal One, talking the entire way and giving Reece updates on his wife and kids and telling his new friend all about what it was like to manage the Maison Borella boutique hotel.

"It's not the Bulgari, after all, but we have a restaurant and a bar with a terrace and a traditional Italian breakfast every morning."

He didn't stop until they got to the garage.

"Well, here it is."

"Here what is?"

"It's the best I could do on short notice," Uri said, pointing to the motorcycle parked in the space before them.

"Oh, uh, thanks?" Reece said.

Uri popped the back of a Fiat that looked like a cross between a minivan and an old mail truck. Reece noticed a woman in the driver's seat who was gesturing for Uri to hurry up.

"My wife. She's not happy she had to follow me out here."

Reece waved and mouthed a thank-you.

"Here's a helmet. It might be a bit tight and here's this," Uri said, handing Reece a worn, dark brown leather jacket. "That will for sure be tight."

"Glad I just have this backpack," Reece said. "What is it anyway?"

"It's a Moto Guzzi V7 III."

"Never ridden one. Cool bike."

"But you do ride, right?"

"I do. It's been a few years," Reece said, remembering the trip he and Lauren had taken to Sturgis to explore the Black Hills of South Dakota with his friend Marco and Marco's wife, Olivia. He had ridden one of Marco's Road Kings then. Reece had loved that bike.

"You will blend in on this one around here. Just be careful turning out of the parking garage. Right takes you to Milano-Varese A8 and left takes you to Milano-Novara A4," Uri said, holding up his hand. "And, *don't* tell me where you are going."

"Right."

"I told you not to tell me!"

"I mean good copy, not the direction."

"What?"

"Understood," Reece said. "How do I get the bike back to you?"

"Just let your contact know and he will tell me."

Reece guessed that "contact" meant Ronan Katz.

"And, let me guess, your wife gets to drive you to retrieve it?"

"Precisely."

Uri's wife yelled something in Italian from the front seat that was audible even through the rolled-up windows.

"I've got to go. Enjoy your time in Italy, Mr. Donovan."

Reece watched him climb into the odd-looking Fiat and continue talking, this time to his wife as she backed out of the space and left her husband's new acquaintance in the rearview mirror. They drove off in a blur of arm gestures, obviously talking over each other in heated conversation.

Reece smiled and looked at the bike.

Then he strapped on his helmet, tightened his backpack, and roared off through the parking structure. He took a left out of the garage and hit the A4 toward Turin.

CHAPTER 55

REECE LOVED BEING BACK on a bike. He screamed through the Italian countryside, the transversal V-twin engine of the Moto Guzzi eating up the miles. Speed, acceleration, balance, throttle control, clutch, breaks, gears; Reece briefly forgot what he was riding toward. For a moment, he felt free.

For a moment.

Time.

You only have one ride on this planet, Reece.

Katie. Would she ever be safe with him?

Are you going to spend the rest of your life hunting and killing? For God and country? For you?

Reece took the off-ramp at Corso Giulio Cesare and into the Aurora District of Turin. He rode past the Hotel Dora di Lazzarone Sergio, a park, and a post office as he got a feel for the area while looking for surveillance, noting cars and their drivers. Satisfied that he had not been followed, he turned onto a narrow cobblestone street in Borgo Dora and backed the bike into a parking spot about a half mile away from his destination.

The former Naval Special Warfare operator did not have a preplanned Surveillance Detection Route but still kept his head on a swivel. He had paid attention to the street signs on the way in so he would not have to stop, ask for directions, or check a navigation app.

After passing a Moroccan restaurant, an antique store, a hair salon, a bicycle shop, and a few bars and cafés, he turned left down what was more of a lane than a street. Awnings of green, red, blue, and white extended outward from the shops. One of the royal green awnings that extended into the street read *Abelard's Libri Rari e Restauro* on its valance.

This was it.

He slowed his pace as he approached.

Reece looked up and down the street. There was not much activity. A man and a woman shared a meal at the restaurant across from him. A woman in a burka entered a halal butcher shop right next to the restaurant. Bicycles, mopeds, and the occasional car passed on at the end of the lane.

Looks normal.

Too bad you don't know what normal for this neighborhood really looks, or more importantly "feels," like.

Trust your gut.

Normal.

Reece found himself wishing he had a pistol.

There was a single step up into the doorway of most of the shops he had passed. This step had been replaced with a ramp. He turned the door handle and entered, a small bell announcing his arrival.

Reece stepped just left of the door, as was his habit, to get out of the "fatal funnel" and let his eyes adjust to the dark interior.

A large table occupied the center of the store. On it were hardbound books that looked vintage or even ancient in origin.

"*Buongiorno,*" Reece heard a voice say from the back of the store.

Reece walked toward the voice, noting the bookshelves to his right and left. A distinctive mixture of leather, parchment, and dust was in the air, reminding Reece of his grandparents' attic when he was a kid. He got the impression that the store didn't see much in the way of foot traffic. It was quiet, like a museum with no visitors.

The desk was offset to the right, in the back corner of the shop. There wasn't a cash register visible. Apparently it wasn't that type of store.

"Hi," Reece said, walking toward the desk. "I'm James Donovan. I believe you are expecting me."

The desk appeared much too large for the space. It was adorned with stacks of papers and books. Behind it sat a man in a wheelchair. Even in the dim light, Reece could tell that he was cleanly shaven and dressed in a dark suit with a neatly trimmed full head of dark hair streaked with gray. It was impossible to tell how tall he had once been, but the cut of his jacket indicated a wide set of shoulders, with powerful arms to match. His left hand held an exquisitely decorated silver pen. His right was out of sight.

"Yes, Mr. Donovan," Abelard said, switching to English. "My former employer informed me that you would be stopping by today."

His English had the type of accent that did not make its country or region of origin discernable. Reece got the impression that that was the point.

Abelard shut the drawer to his right, pushed himself back from the desk, and in what was an extremely efficient set of hand and arm movements on the wheels of his chair, positioned himself in front of his guest. He offered his hand.

"Pleasure, Mr. Donovan. I'm Saul Abelard."

Reece took the outstretched hand and felt the crushing grip of his host.

"Thank you for seeing me," Reece said.

"It's one of the things I do, Mr. Donovan. When Tel Aviv calls, I try to accommodate. Director Katz informed me that he had briefed you up on my background and rather unique position in the world."

Abelard spun around and maneuvered back behind his desk.

"Please, take a seat," he said, directing Reece to one of two cherrywood-framed, leather-backed chairs.

Reece unslung his backpack and set it, along with his helmet and one-size-too-small leather jacket, to the side of his seat.

The former SEAL took a moment. He could sense that Abelard was sizing him up.

"Like the suit?" he asked his guest.

"The suit?" Reece asked.

"Soon after I left the hospital, I was wearing a comfortable white T-shirt and sweatpants. A man tossed a euro in my lap as he passed. He thought I was homeless. I decided I needed to go with the suit after that."

Reece didn't know if it was appropriate to laugh at the icebreaker. He smiled and said, "That makes sense."

"I don't get many Americans in here, Mr. Donovan, either for book restoration or for my more select services."

"Probably a good thing, on the 'select services' side of things anyway."

"The director doesn't call often. It is much more common for me to call him."

"But you didn't in the case of Nizar Kattan."

Abelard paused.

"No, I did not."

"And why is that?" Reece asked.

"Mr. Donovan, I am not in the habit of explaining my business, but I do acknowledge the level of importance placed on this matter by the director."

"What did you think Kattan was going to do once you connected him with an Africa hand?"

"That 'Africa hand,' as you say, was a sergeant in the French Foreign Legion. I've been his handler for going on five years now, Kattan for just under a year. I tell you that because though I am freelance and don't work for Tel Aviv, I do have an allegiance to my former home country."

"As I understand it, you pass the Mossad information if you become aware of any plans targeting Israeli citizens or infrastructure."

"That is part of the arrangement."

"But it didn't work this time," Reece said.

"No, it did not. As with most of my clients, I believed their intent was a liquidation."

"An assassination," Reece said.

"That's correct."

"And when you saw that a plane went down in Burkina Faso?"

"I was not sure it was Kattan and Le Drian."

"Until?"

"Until Le Drian called me and requested assistance with extract."

"Which you provided."

"I did."

"Why?"

"I did not yet know that Tel Aviv had an asset on board but still, Mr. Donovan, it did give me pause."

"Why was that?"

"I am not in the business of mass murder."

"Just individual murders."

"A subject I believe you know something about, Mr. Donovan."

Reece took a breath. His reputation had obviously preceded him.

"So why help get them out? Why not let the local or national-level law enforcement or intelligence services detain them in Africa?"

"Because I am the, how would you say it in English, 'dot' that connects them. Better to deal with them quietly."

"But then Katz calls you."

"He did. And I found out we had an asset on the plane."

"So now the mission becomes finding them and taking them out with a Mossad hit team."

"Yes, but then you show up, Mr. Donovan, and I am asked by Tel Aviv to assist you in any way I can. It's quite curious, really."

"What is?" Reece asked.

"That you are here and not a team from Caesarea. And there was not an active contract out on Aliya Galin. Trust me, in my channels I would have heard about it by now."

"What does that tell you?" Reece asked.

"It tells me that this is not a simple act of terrorism, nor an assassination disguised as terrorism."

"What do you mean?"

"Mr. Donovan, I have been in this chair for over thirty years. I can get around just fine. I've adapted. But my clock is ticking."

"Your clock?"

"Oh yes, life expectancy for people with my spinal injury is far less than the average Italian. I have been patient, but I also need to speed things up a bit."

"Speed what up?"

"When I was shot, I was doing my job. I had purpose. Then I woke up in a hospital bed without the use of my legs. I had to find that purpose again."

"I can understand that, the purpose part at least," Reece said, his mind drifting to a storm in the mid-Atlantic as he sailed for Africa years ago, leaving the death and destruction he had wrought in his wake. "What did you do?"

"I sought solace where I felt most comfortable."

"In books," Reece said.

"That's right. My mother and father ran a used bookstore in my youth. I escaped into the pages of books that would filter though their small shop. After my father died, I helped my mother in the store. Those books transported me from Israel to places all around the world. My fondest memories are of reading books in the shop as a child."

"So, you learned to restore books and started this business?"

"Correct. I learned from the masters. What you see here in this store is more than a cover for action, Mr. Donovan. It's a life's work. These books still transport me, from here, from this chair, back to my youth."

"I see."

"Some books arrive with water damage. You would be surprised what heat, dust, and insects can do to the pages, bindings, and spines. People transport books when they move and do not package them correctly; the changes in temperature and humidity, even altitude can wreak havoc, Mr. Donovan. Books are adaptable but if you ask too much of them, they will fall apart."

"And you think that's what happened to you? Tel Aviv asked too much?"

"Oh, I am sure the Mossad psychiatrists would love to talk with me. Too bad they will never get the chance."

"Why is that?"

"I am never going home, Mr. Donovan. I found my purpose."

"In book restoration?"

"In part."

"You are looking for someone."

"I am."

"The man who put you in that chair."

"Someday, I will get a lead. Then I will work him into my sights," Abelard said. "And when I do, I will have more mercy than he had. No chair for him. He will go straight to the grave."

Is this what I am like? Reece wondered. *Is this how Katie sees me?*

"So, what of Kattan and Le Drian?" Reece asked.

"I can't be certain. I met Kattan once in person in Dubrovnik. He doesn't use cell phones."

"And Le Drian?"

"I have never met him. Much of our communications have been electronic. Not my preference but sometimes a necessity."

"But you handle them both?"

"*Handler* may be the wrong term. I am more of an information broker; a connector."

"Can you help me find them?"

"I can, but there is something else at play."

"What?"

"Terrorism or assassination? What happened in Africa is most certainly both, but at the same time it is neither."

"Did you always speak in riddles?"

"Bear with me, Mr. Donovan. The usual signals before and after the event were not present."

"What does that tell you?"

"Now that I've met you and from plugging in what I learned from Director Katz and from my own research before your arrival, I ask myself, what is different about this tragedy?"

"And what do you think?"

"You, Mr. Donovan. You are what is different. You are sitting here in my bookstore. I think someone wanted to put you here."

"Who?"

"Kattan is the obvious choice, but in this business, I have learned that the obvious is not always correct. If he led you here. I would think the next step is for you to learn what I know of Kattan. That would lead you to the Balkans."

"Well, then that's where I'm going to go."

"Kattan is baiting a trap. He led you right here. He's playing chess."

"He may be playing chess but I'm playing poker."

"Ugh, that most American of card games. At least make it something civilized like baccarat."

Reece felt an unfamiliar vibration in his pocket.

"Excuse me," Reece said, pulling out the phone that had arrived in the diplomatic pouch in Israel and hitting the message app.

`Watch your back.`

Reece turned to look at the door.

CHAPTER 56

"DO YOU HAVE ANY weapons here?" Reece asked urgently as he got to his feet.

"What is it?"

"Weapons," Reece said again, looking from the door back to Abelard. "What do you have?"

"I have this," the former Mossad operative said, holding up the H&K P7 from the desk drawer. "And what's in the safe."

Abelard slid the pistol between his hip and the side of his wheelchair, spun the wheels, and rolled to in the shelves that made up the wall to his right. He pulled two books from the shelf. Reece heard a click.

"Don't just stand there! Help me pull."

Reece ran to the shelves and pulled where Abelard indicated.

The shelves pulled away from the hinge to reveal the front of a safe.

Abelard immediately positioned his chair to give him access to the mechanical lock, which he spun while Reece alternated between looking at the door and at the H&K pistol by Abelard's right hip.

The bookseller rotated the lock back to zero and twisted the five-spoke handle to the right, retracting the bolts and allowing the steel door to swing outward.

"Good thing I deal in more than just information," Abelard said.

Reece stepped forward to get a better look. The safe was not huge by any standard. It had shelves on one side with books in various stages of repair and another stacked with paperbacks with names Reece recognized: le Carré, Thor, Silva, de Villiers, Hunter, DeMille, Morrell, Flynn. Reece looked at the man in the wheelchair.

"Can't have my customers seeing commercial fiction on my shelves. Bad for business."

Reece reached in and pulled out an old H&K G3 with wood furniture.

"This sighted in?"

"No. The weapons arrive as they are."

Reece tossed it on Abelard's desk behind him.

"Same with this?" Reece asked, pulling out an H&K MP5SD.

"Yes."

Reece's eyes settled on a weapon he knew well, a Benelli M1 Super 90.

No sling, rifle sights, extended magazine.

Reece grabbed the shotgun and checked its condition.

Empty.

"Do you have shells for this?"

"Yes. In the back."

Reece reached into the back top shelf and pulled out a box of double-aught and a box of slugs. Moving to the desk, Reece set the twelve-gauge autoloader and the two boxes of shells on the table. He grabbed a double-aught shell, hit the shell-release lever of the right side of the black shotgun, threw in the shell, and hit the bolt release, which sent the shell containing nine lead pellets into the chamber.

Pulling the shotgun back under his arm for stability, Reece reached back into the box and began to feed shells into the tube. Seeing movement at the door, Reece brought the shotgun to his shoulder.

One round in the chamber, only one in the tube.

Off safe.

The door swung open, the bell ringing to announce that a customer or customers had arrived.

Instead of a hit man or a group of assassins, three boys closing in on ten years old entered. Their hair, eyes, and skin indicated Middle Eastern ancestry. Their laughter signaled the innocent exuberance of youth.

The boy in the middle was wearing a smile, a Juventus Football Club jersey, and a backpack.

CHAPTER 57

"*LADAYA TAWSIL,*" THE BOY said, unslinging the backpack and running toward them.

I have a delivery.

Reece caught the P7 coming up from Abelard to his left in his peripheral vision. He saw Lauren and Lucy riddled with bullets. *Innocents.*

Reece knocked Abelard's pistol down, dropped the shotgun, and ran toward the three children, who all had abject looks of horror on their faces as the big man barreled down on them.

"Who gave you this?" Reece shouted as he approached, pointing at the backpack.

The boy froze in his tracks and said something in Arabic that Reece did not understand. The two friends turned to run back to the door. Their smiles were gone.

Reece processed the terror in the young boy's eyes as he grabbed the backpack.

Heavy.

The boy was pointing outside. His friends had reached the door.

You can't throw this into the street after those kids.

Reece turned and ran back into the store, past the desk.

"What are you doing!" Abelard shouted. "Get that out of here!"

Reece threw the backpack into the open safe, slammed the door, spun the locking handle to the left, and felt the bolts engage, locking them in place.

"*Out!*" Reece shouted, pointing at the door.

The boy stood frozen in his tracks.

Just as Reece reached down to pick him up and carry him to safety, the bomb detonated.

CHAPTER 58

OLEG BERZIN WATCHED THE three children enter the shop via the camera sending signals to his smartphone.

Their job was to deliver the backpack to the two men inside and run out of the store. He had given each of the refugee children ten euros, a fortune to the new arrivals from war-torn Syria. When Oleg saw them exit, he would detonate the IED.

One of the Syrian men entering the shop would set off alarm bells for certain. Oleg still looked twice, sometimes three times, at men and women who triggered memories of the Hindu Kush; dismembered bodies of Soviet soldiers on the roadsides, the Spetsnaz troops hanging from trees, skinned alive, their genitals cut from between their legs and stuffed in their mouths.

The American would look twice, Oleg knew. The Jew, perhaps, but the bookseller had lived in the neighborhood for long enough that he might be accustomed to the growing immigrant population.

Oleg had no intention of killing the children. In his youth he had no doubt he would have triggered the explosive with the boys still inside. He may have even done it a year ago. That was the correct tactical decision. It was also the correct strategic decision, as it would confirm that Syrian immigrants had targeted a Jewish shop where an American just so happened to be buying books at the wrong time.

Intelligence services might be able to discern that there was more to the bombing, but to the general public it would feed into the narrative of radical Islamic terror cells working in Europe targeting Jewish people and businesses. It was not the first time, and it would not be the last.

Oleg told himself that this way worked as well. As the children exited, he would be able to see that the backpack was no longer worn by the oldest. That would be Oleg's signal to detonate. Then he could get back to Brindisi. Back to his wife and stepchildren. Back to his boxing gym, where he belonged.

What is this?

Oleg looked down at his smartphone. Two of the kids had scampered out of the store.

Where is the third?

Where is the backpack?

Oleg thought of his comrades swinging in the breeze, ropes around their necks. He saw the birds fly away from their heads, their mutilated groins, and their assholes as he approached. Their eyes had already been picked out of their heads, the birds going to the softest areas first: the eyes, genitals, and anus. He remembered the Black Tulips taking off from Bagram filled with Soviet dead, dead that the USSR had not acknowledged to the world.

The Black Tulip was an Antonov AN-12, a four-engine cargo plane that transported those killed in action back to the motherland.

Cargo 200.

Corpses.

Oleg pressed the button.

CHAPTER 59

THE TRANSMITTER SENT A signal to the receiver in the backpack, which completed the circuit and drove an electrical current through the wires into the steel wool. Triacetone triperoxide is a sensitive compound. The ignition of the steel wool created a spark that detonated the TATP and triggered a chemical reaction, which resulted in energy that propagated a shock wave, turning the nails, nuts, and bolts into shrapnel. To everyone in the vicinity, it was an explosion.

For the three closest to the detonation it felt like the end of the world.

Reece had one hand on the boy when the shock wave sent him careening into a bookshelf. The safe did not contain the explosion. The energy found the path of least resistance, which was around the seals of the door. The hinges, designed to be opened outward, did just that and the safe deformed and turned the steel door into a projectile, shooting it across the shop and destroying everything in its path. Books disintegrated, filling the air with torn covers as pages floated through the smoke. The door continued its push through the front wall, taking the front window with it before landing in the street.

The ringing in Reece's ears let him know he was still alive. Did he have all his body parts? He quickly assessed the damage, starting with his feet and working his way up to his head. All fingers and toes intact, he rolled onto his stomach and pushed himself to a kneeling position.

The ringing.

Where's the kid?

Where's a weapon?

Reece crawled over the debris. Papers still fluttered to the ground and settled on the floor, some on fire, some not.

A body.

A small body.

He rolled the child over, his eyes scanning the figure for obvious injuries as he felt a pulse.

Good pulse. Thank God.

Unconscious.

Reece heard a coughing behind him.

Abelard.

"Saul!"

"I'm here," he said between coughs. "Those bastards! I had a first-edition *Confessions* by St. Augustine in there. Where's my chair?"

Get a gun, Reece. The kids were the first wave. More will be coming.

Reece rose to a crouch and picked the boy up, moving him next to Abelard and carefully laying him down next to the bookseller.

"This kid tried to kill us!" Abelard said.

"He's just a tool," Reece responded, in a desperate search for the weapons and ammo he had laid out on the desk prior to the explosion. "A maneuver element will be coming to finish us off."

"How do you know?"

"Because that's what I'd do."

The desk had been turned over in the explosion. Small fires burned as the parchments became fuel to keep them alive.

"Chair," Reece said as he shook off Abelard's wheelchair and turned to help him into it.

"Get off me," the bookseller said, shaking off Reece's helping hand. "I can do this myself. Find a weapon!"

Reece turned as Abelard hoisted himself up and into his chair.

Shotgun.

Reece picked up the Benelli from the floor and gave it a shake to free it of debris.

It was still on safe. The former SEAL cracked the bolt to ensure the round he had already loaded was still in the chamber. He flipped it upside down. The shell he had loaded into the magazine tube was still there.

Need more rounds.

Reece began to scour the floor for shotgun shells.

There!

The explosion had blown the two boxes from the desk as it was upended and sent them scattering across the shop.

Reece picked one up.

Double-aught.

He loaded it into the magazine tube.

Another one.

Slug.

Reece deposited it in his back right pocket as he continued his search.

Two more.

Both double-aught.

He saw the boy begin to stir.

"Ask him how many people he saw when he was asked to deliver the backpack," Reece shouted at Abelard as he continued to comb the floor for ammunition.

Reece heard Abelard talking to the boy in Arabic, his voice low and soothing.

Reece glanced over. The smoke had begun to dissipate.

The young courier appeared to be in shock.

Need intel on what's coming.

There, a box of shells.

Reece moved to it and loaded three more rounds of double-aught into the tube to top it off, giving him a total of seven in the tube and one in the chamber.

Eight.

Reece looked at the hole in the wall and at the front door, which was also blown from its hinges. The front of the store was almost entirely open, the books that had been arranged in the windows blown from their displays. With the windows gone and a section of the wall missing, there was not much in the form of cover. The smoke and ash that gave them their concealment was dissipating and exposing them to the street.

"What's he saying?" Reece shouted as he retracted the charging handle to the point just prior to where the shell carrier was designed to lift. He depressed the shell that was in the chamber into the shell carrier, keeping the fingers of his left hand pressing it downward while sliding the new round into the chamber and allowing the bolt to go forward over the floating shell in the shell carrier. Reece hit the charging handle with his palm to confirm it was firmly seated. It was called ghost loading and it gave Reece nine rounds in what was typically considered to be an eight-round weapon system with which to get to work.

There were four more shells in the box. Reece stuffed them into his front left pocket.

Abelard had continued to talk with the boy, gently coaxing information from him.

Reece did one more check of the shotgun.

Focus.

"What did he say?" Reece asked again.

"He said one of the men is a friend of his father. He doesn't remember how many others. He said they paid him ten euros to bring the backpack here. He was instructed to leave it here and then continue home."

That helps a little. More than one, Reece thought.

"He said something else."

"What?"

"He told me that one of the men was like you, *'abyad.*"

"What's that mean, like me?"

"*'Abyad,* a white man."

A white man?

The Frenchman?

Movement at the side window.

"Take care of the boy!"

Reece pushed himself over the mounds of smoking debris and approached the front of the store, sinking to a knee behind a smoldering bookshelf.

"Find my pistol," he heard Abelard say.

The figure approaching the store could just be a concerned citizen coming to help. It could be a police officer or first responder.

But it wasn't.

Identify the target, Reece.

A man in a long coat.

Still not 100 percent. Could be a Good Samaritan.

Reece saw the coat part and clearly identified the underfolder Kalashnikov.

Enemy.

Reece brought the shotgun to his shoulder, pushed the safety to the fire position, lined up the rifle-style sights, and pressed the trigger. Nine lead .33" pellets jettisoned across the store. Four of them caught the man on the right side of his face, ripping half of his skull away from his head and sending him to the ground in a heap.

Shoot and move.

Reece moved past Abelard and the boy. He rotated, lined up the sights, and pressed the trigger, sending another tightly grouped pattern into the upper chest of the downed man just to be sure.

He took a knee against what was left of the door frame and put another round in the tube from his left pocket. His head was up, looking for additional threats.

The boy didn't remember how many others, Reece. That suggests more than one. And one was 'abyad.

Automatic rifle fire stitched up the side of the door frame next to Reece and zipped past him into the store.

"Get that kid down!" Reece shouted to Abelard.

Reece saw the shooter from across the street. The folding stock was extended and was firmly planted in his shoulder.

The streets of Borgo Dora in the Aurora District of Turin had become a war zone.

Another burst of fire erupted from an alley on Reece's side of the street, just past the corner of the store.

L ambush.

Decision time.

Take a breath, look around make a call.

Draw the fire away from the boy.

Reece bolted from his position, sending the twelve-gauge projectiles across the street toward the man in the far alley and then immediately shifted back to the corner wall where he had last seen the shooter on his side of the street.

If they kill you, Abelard and probably the boy are going down, too.

Kill them all, Reece.

There was no past, no future, only the now, only the operation of the Benelli autoloading shotgun, working as designed in concert with an operator who made it an extension of his body.

Reece pressed the trigger as he moved, counting the shells remaining in the combat shotgun, beginning to feel the heat through the black composite handguard. Just as his father had used the Ithaca Model 37 as a point man in the jungles of Vietnam, his son now worked one of its descendants in the streets of Turin against a different enemy, the buckshot sailing through the air just as it had done in Southeast Asia, destroying anything in its path.

Reece took a wide angle on the wall as he pressed the trigger again to keep his assailant behind cover. The shot worked as intended, impacting the corner of the wall. As Reece approached an optimal angle, he saw the man with an AK crouched down. Nine balls of lead shot took him in the right shoulder and upper chest, opening him up for Reece's next shot, which removed most of his head.

The former SEAL spun around back to the threat across the street.

Where is he?

Reece loaded the two remaining shells from his left pocket into the tube.

Four shells left in the shotgun, one slug in his back pocket.

Grab an AK.

Not yet. Still an active threat. Wait until there's a tactical pause.

Reece moved behind a delivery van that had pulled up to the shop next to Abelard's.

Where are you?

Reece turned to maneuver around the far side of the truck and ran directly into a jihadi with a rifle who had taken the corner of the vehicle. As the two killers collided, both their weapons were knocked off line, Reece's pointing down and his assailant's AK pointing up. The former SEAL's aggression, size, and strength dominated the fight. Reece used the side of his Benelli to trap the AK against the man, whom Reece had now pinned to the side of the van. Reece dropped his shotgun, his left hand forcing the AK barrel under his enemy's chin as his right thumb dropped into the trigger guard and pressed back on the trigger. The firing pin engaged with a burst of fully automatic 7.62x39 rounds through his brain, exiting out the top of his skull and sending chunks of blood, skull fragments, and brain matter onto Reece's face and the side of the delivery vehicle.

The body slumped to the ground. Reece quickly unslung the AK.

Before he could check its status, he heard the familiar scream of *Allāhu 'akbar!* but it was not coming for him. It was coming from the direction of the store.

Reece turned, flipped the AK to semiautomatic, brought the rifle up, found the front sight, led his target ever so slightly, and stitched the man up his left side. The first round was low, breaking his hip and sending him crashing to the ground on the ramp of the bookstore. Reece's next round entered through the man's rib cage. Reece continued to work rounds up to his lungs, heart, and head, which exploded against the base of the door frame.

Reece heard the click of his empty Kalashnikov, followed by footsteps from the corner of the vehicle. He dropped the AK and picked up the Benelli. Unable to swing the shotgun in time to engage his new target, Reece launched himself up and into his assailant's body, leading with the side of the shotgun like a pugil stick directly into the man's face. Reece felt the cartilage of the nose breaking. He expected the aggressor to attempt to turn the AK to shoot but instead the man dropped it, both hands going to the shotgun. In the close-quarter confines at the corner of the vehicle, Reece used the man's energy, turning the shotgun sharply like a driver turning a steering wheel when trying to avoid an accident. The violent move turned his opponent in the opposite direction, allowing Reece to twist and throw him over his hip to the pavement. The aggressive rotation forced the man to let go of the shotgun and allowed Reece to step back and shoot him in the head. From two feet away the nine pellets that tore through his skull ensured there was no need for a security round.

Reece was about to reach down and pick up the AK when he heard a child's voice screaming.

In a crouch he moved to the corner of the van and took a quick peek from behind his cover.

The shooter who had first engaged him from across the street was walking toward him. In his right hand, in the position of retention against his body, was the AK; in his left was one of the boys who had first entered the shop.

Human shield.

He saw Reece and adjusted the position of the AK, sending a fully automatic burst into the rear quarter panel of the van, but the SEAL had already moved.

As Reece relocated to the front right section of the vehicle, he reached into the back right pocket of his pants with his primary hand and removed the slug. Controlling the shotgun with his left hand, he racked the charging handle with his right, catching the double-aught shell that ejected from the chamber and replacing it with the slug. Reece quickly reinserted the ejected shell into the tube and emerged from the opposite side of the van.

The terrorist holding the child caught Reece's movement and spun to face him, the boy shielding most of his body and part of his face.

Slow is smooth. Smooth is fast.

Reece's vision focused on the front sight, his breath settled as the assailant's AK continued to turn, bullets beginning to chew into the street and van, working their way toward him.

As Reece's finger pressed back on the trigger, he heard the immortal wisdom of Wyatt Earp: *Fast is fine, but accuracy is final. In a gunfight you must learn to be slow in a hurry.*

The modern-day gunfighter felt his shoulder absorb the recoil, the one-ounce lead projectile exiting the end of the barrel.

At twenty-five yards, the slug made an almost instant connection with his assailant's right eye, plowing through the ocular cavity and brain before blowing through the back of the skull. The effect was like unplugging a lamp. No more power or commands could be sent to the rest of the body. The massive slug took out the brain's central processing unit; it was instant death.

The man dropped to the ground. Gravity took the boy with him. He landed awkwardly atop the dead terrorist.

Reece took a step and was stopped short by the sound of gunfire behind him shattering the side window of the van. He felt a slap and searing pain in the upper left side of his back.

He immediately dropped to the ground to make himself less of a target.

Two shells left.

Reece rolled onto his stomach, shotgun stock in his shoulder.

The first body parts in his sights were the knees of a man running toward him.

Reece pressed the trigger.

The man stumbled.

Reece raised the shotgun a bit higher and fired nine lead balls at 1,600 feet per second into his assailant's upper thigh, groin, and hips, sending him to the ground.

Reece pushed himself to his feet. His left shoulder felt almost numb.

The Benelli had locked back.

Empty.

Reece left it on the ground and moved quickly to the downed man, who was still alive in front of him.

A crowd had begun to form at the end of the alley, most people being smart enough to keep their distance from explosions and automatic weapons fire. Reece could hear sirens in the distance.

Work fast.

Reece relieved him of his Kalashnikov and quickly patted him down, looking for additional weapons. He found a knife in the man's belt, pulled it out, and threw it under the van. Reece then grabbed him by the back of his jacket and dragged him through the street and into the bookshop, leaving a trail of blood in their wake.

CHAPTER 60

OLEG WATCHED THE SCENE unfold in disbelief.

Ty che, blyad?

These savages never could get anything right.

The former GRU man had watched the shooters converge on the bookshop. It was a shame to have to kill the boy but that was not something to be overly concerned about. Besides, he was probably being groomed to one day point an AK or blow himself up and kill one of Oleg's stepchildren.

That's one savage who will never point a gun at a son of yours, Oleg, he remembered an old Spetsnaz colonel telling him in Afghanistan the first time the sergeant had killed a child.

This was no different.

Just confirm the dead and be done with it, Oleg thought as he continued to watch the screen of his smartphone from the far corner of the café. Other patrons had walked to the windows and some had spilled out into the streets after hearing the violent commotion. Many were on their phones, no doubt calling the Italian national emergency numbers for police and medical assistance.

That's it, Oleg thought, continuing to look at his screen. *Keep the AK out of sight unless you need it. Only take it out once you enter to ensure our targets are dead.*

It took a moment for Oleg to register what was going on. He watched the black-and-white high-resolution feed as the lead Syrian's head snapped back and he dropped to the street.

Blyad!

He watched as a man bolted from the bombed-out store with what looked to be a long gun of some sort in his shoulder. Even on the video feed, Oleg could tell by the way he moved that this man knew what he was doing.

The American.

Oleg watched as his force went down one by one, each one dispatched by the ghostly black-and-white image on his video feed.

At one point it looked like the last assailant had the drop and that the American was hit. Then Oleg saw the Syrian fall to the ground. He watched the American move to him and drag him off video into the bookshop.

These fucking savages!

Oleg looked into the leather satchel he had set next to him in the café, the dark steel of the AK waiting to be unleashed.

He thought of landing in Bagram, his Spetsnaz training, his multiple tours in a losing war. He thought of the years that followed and all he had done for his homeland. He thought of his new life, his wife, and stepchildren in their home by the sea.

There is no choice.

The Russian left five euros on the table, stood up, and slung his satchel over his shoulder, feeling the familiar weight of the fully loaded Kalashnikov next to his body. Keeping his cell phone in his left hand to continue monitoring the front and back of the bookshop, he exited into the street.

CHAPTER 61

"IT'S ME!" REECE SHOUTED as he dragged the terrorist up the ramp and into what was left of the bookshop.

Abelard lowered the P7, which he had recovered from amid the rubble.

The boy who had carried the backpack was propped against the far wall and Abelard was positioned next to him.

"He's still in shock. I found your leather jacket and covered him. That's the best I could do for now. Emergency services should be here any minute."

"Which means we need to work fast," Reece said, performing a press check to ensure there was a round chambered. He then ejected the magazine and pressed down on the top bullet. His fingers pushed down about two inches. At least there were a few rounds to work with. "Ask this fucker about the white man, and ask him if there are any more in the hit team."

"How many did you kill out there?"

"Six, plus this asshole who won't be with us much longer," Reece said, looking to the front of the shop.

"I take back what I said about Americans and poker," Abelard said.

"Ask him, quick!"

Reece listened as he continued to watch the front. Abelard fired off questions in rapid Arabic. Gone were the soothing tones he used to talk with the boy.

Inna lillahi wa inna ilayhi raji'un.

Upon them will be the blessings and mercy of their Lord, and it is they who are rightly guided.

"He just keeps reciting the Istirja," Abelard said.

"What's that?"

"A Quranic death verse."

Reece heard a suppressed gunshot and spun.

Abelard had put a 9mm round from his H&K pistol through the terrorist's hand.

"I can't do much from this chair in a fight, but I can do this," he said. He continued to talk to the man in Arabic.

"He said he's the last one. They are from Syria."

Syria?

"Do you think he's telling the truth?" Reece asked.

"I have no idea."

"Ask him about the white man. Was he French?"

Abelard exchanged words with their wounded prisoner yet again.

"He says, no. Not French. Russian."

"Russian?"

"What have you done to upset the Bear?" Abelard asked.

"I'm sure plenty, but nothing to warrant this."

The prisoner's eyes rolled back in his head as he bled out. Death had found him on the floor of a bombed-out bookstore in Turin.

"We need to get out of here, Mr. Donovan. Those sirens are almost here."

"Do you have binos?"

"Binos?"

"You know, binoculars."

"I do."

"Where?"

"Bottom left desk drawer," Abelard replied.

Reece took one more look through the blown-out front windows and moved to the overturned desk. He bent down to turn it over.

"What do you keep in this thing?" Reece asked as he strained to lift it. The numbness in his left shoulder was wearing off and giving way to sharp pain.

"You're bleeding," Abelard said.

Reece lifted the desk using the right side of his body. After it fell back upright, he went around it and yanked open the lower left side drawer. He dug around until he came up with an old pair of Leica binoculars. He then moved back toward Abelard to get a better angle on the far end of the alley. People had started to inch closer to the commotion now that the explosions and automatic weapons fire had subsided. Most were looking at the devastation and dead bodies that littered the street. Some had phones to their ears. Others had their phones out in front of them, taking video of the carnage.

One was doing none of those things. A single man, short, stocky, with a leather messenger bag slung cross-body over his shoulder, had his head down toward his phone. He didn't look to be the type of man who would be lost scrolling a social media app while the world burned. When he picked his head up, Reece adjusted the focus. Early sixties. Square jaw. Cauliflower ears. White.

CHAPTER 62

OLEG MANEUVERED THROUGH THE crowd, watching the video feed on his phone, working out contingencies and possibilities.

Not much time, Oleg. Authorities will be here soon. No Russian fingerprints.

No mission failure, either. Moscow does not deal kindly with those who failed the state.

He was up against a man who had just killed six and now quite possibly seven armed men in the streets of Italy.

James Reece.

No one had come or gone from the bookshop since the American had dragged the last Syrian inside.

He has got to want to get out of there as much as you want him to come out. He just killed six or seven people with what was sure to be an illegal weapon on foreign soil. CIA man or not, that was bound to cause a host of diplomatic and legal issues.

Bring him to you, Oleg.

Why run when you can stand and fight?

Oleg continued to walk down the narrow street, still in the crowd but well aware that he was standing out. He thought of ambushes, of downed Hind helicopters, Stinger missiles, dead and disfigured comrades.

When he reached the halal butcher shop that was catty-corner from Abelard's, he broke with the crowd and hustled inside.

• • •

"Is that the man?" Reece asked the child whom he now held in his right arm.

The young courier had recovered enough to be able to nod. The life had returned to his eyes.

Abelard translated into Arabic.

The boy had the Leica binoculars to his eyes, following the white man with the satchel down the street.

He dropped the binoculars and spoke in Arabic to the bookseller.

"That's him," Abelard said. "Now let's get out of here."

"Please tell him 'thank you' and let him know that he is very brave," Reece said.

Abelard said something in Arabic. The boy smiled and went back to his corner, pulling the leather jacket over his shoulders.

"And us?" Abelard asked.

"What did Tel Aviv mean when they said to assist me in any way you could?"

"I am not sure they had this in mind," Abelard said, indicating the destruction around them. "This might be the end of my information-brokering days. Might have to make an honest living restoring books."

"In the meantime, does that butcher shop across the street have a back exit?"

"It does."

"What's there?" Reece asked,

"An alley."

"Good."

"He's drawing you in, Mr. Donovan."

"I know," Reece said.

Moving to the door, he reached down and took the magazine from the weapon of the first man he had killed, the man who was now missing the right side of his head and never got a shot off. Reece removed the magazine from his AK and stowed it in his back pocket. He then pressed down on the top round to ensure the newly pilfered magazine was fully loaded, before rocking it into place. Performing a press check to ensure there was a round in the chamber, Reece sprinted across the street in pursuit of the Russian.

CHAPTER 63

IT'S AN ODD FEELING to know you are walking into an ambush. It was also one Reece knew well. Every time he had led a sniper team into Ramadi at the height of the war, he had this same sensation. They would drop over the walls of the American compound and into Ramadi in the dark of night to avoid the base gates. Reece and his team would then be enveloped by a city where every step could trigger an IED, and every angle could put you in the enemy's crosshairs.

He felt the same way now.

The sirens were close.

Reece entered the butcher shop.

The difference between now and Ramadi was that in Ramadi, when Reece's platoon came under fire they responded with overwhelming firepower and violence of action. Today, if Reece killed the Russian, his secrets died with him.

Reece entered and immediately cleared his corner and then pivoted back to his right to clear the rest of the room. It was not a good technique for clearing rooms or structures alone. A slow, deliberate combat clearance was much more effective, unless there were hostages. Then the game changed. Or if the Italian police were inbound. Reece did not want to get caught up in an Italian legal quandary. He needed to find out why someone in Russia wanted him dead and he needed to kill Nizar Kattan.

The butcher shop was seemingly empty, everyone having fled as the building across from them exploded. HALAL MEAT stood out in prominent bold letters above a refrigerated, glassed-in display filled with various meats, including a series of lamb's heads, their lifeless eyes taking in the room. Chalkboards behind the counter gave prices of the various cuts, primarily lamb and goat. Sodas were stacked against the base of the display and there were five short aisles of foodstuffs, as in any small market the world over.

Was the Russian running out the back or was he lying in wait?

Reece got his answer in gunfire.

The distinctive sound of an AK exploded from a hallway at the back of the store, followed by smaller-caliber shots. *Pistols.* Reece made his decision. *Run to the sound of the guns.*

Reece moved toward the fight, Kalashnikov up and off safe, finger on the trigger.

More rifle and pistol gunfire.

What the hell is going on?

Then Reece saw movement. *Polizia di Stato.* Italian police. A uniformed patrolman was rushing to a downed man in the hallway. As he reached down to grab him, a burst of AK fire took him in the upper chest, his body contorting around the impacts to what Reece deduced was body armor under his uniform. Reece briefly made eye contact before another burst tore through the policeman's head, his body going straight to the ground atop the man he was trying to save.

Two more men entered the hallway, firing 9mm Beretta 92FS pistols.

"No!" Reece shouted but they never heard him, the 7.62x39 rounds from an AK taking one through the throat and the other in the face.

More movement. A man entered the hallway, reaching down for one of the fallen officers' handguns. The man was not in the uniform of an Italian police officer. He was the Russian the boy had pointed out to

Reece moments earlier. Reece raised his rifle and pressed the trigger, but the Russian had seen the upward swing of Reece's weapon and thrown himself back into the room across the hall.

He was going for a battlefield pickup and he didn't have his AK in hand. He's out of ammo.

Rifle up and off safe, finger on the trigger, Reece moved down the hallway.

Closed door long, he thought to himself.

Open door right.

He angled in on the corner. *Combat clearance. Don't rush to your death.*

Reece cleared as much of the room as he could, well aware that additional Italian police officers would be converging on the site at any moment.

He needed to find the Russian and interrogate him before the police arrived and arrested or killed them both.

Reece committed to the room, clearing the unknown spaces he could not see from outside before entering. Stainless-steel tables covered in dead chickens and knives were set up around a large, grated drain in the center of the floor; a hose with a high-pressure nozzle attached lay abandoned nearby. An AK and a magazine were next to it.

The Russian had run out of ammo, ejected the magazine to check, and then dropped them both to go for a police officer's Beretta.

But where did he go?

He couldn't have just disappeared.

The walk-in freezer.

Cops will be here any minute, Reece. You lose this guy, you lose any chance of finding out why someone in the Russian government wants you dead. You will never know peace. Katie will always be at risk.

Reece moved to the side of the freezer.

Should he fire through the door? Would the rounds penetrate?

Probably. What if some kid or the shopkeepers or butchers had taken refuge in there?

Damn it!

Reece's hand went to the handle, and he pulled the heavy door open.

Combat clearance, Reece.

As he angled on the space, he was met by row upon row of beef carcasses hanging from hooks on rails.

Enter or get out of here. Time is running out.

Reece entered and cleared his left corner.

He was hit from the right side immediately. The door swung shut, leaving him and his opponent in the meat locker in complete darkness.

CHAPTER 64

REECE FELT LIKE HE had been hit by a freight train. The two bodies crashed though one carcass and then another, before landing on the frozen floor of the meat locker. Reece felt a jolt of pain shoot through his injured back. The AK did not have a sling and Reece lost his grip on it in the dark as his breath was knocked out, his diaphragm contracting in a spasm.

Find the rifle!

Reece had pushed himself to his knees and was struggling for breath, when he felt a hand on his leg. Someone else was also pushing himself to his feet in the darkness.

The blow to the side of Reece's head landed a second later.

They were fighting using senses other than sight, so the strike that might have killed him glanced off the side of his head.

He's going to follow up. Don't be in the same place when he does.

Reece stood and attempted to get his bearings.

Which way is the door?

Complete disorientation.

He didn't have much time to consider his situation as a beef carcass swung into his back, knocking him against the wall.

The Russian heard the impact and was on him.

Oleg's iron fist smashed into Reece's ribs as the Russian landed a hook, then pivoted and landed another on the side of Reece's head. Had Reece not had his left hand covering his jaw it would have been lights-out. He dropped his hip and shot an uppercut with his right to his aggressor's midsection, which the Russian absorbed like it was nothing. He felt Oleg's hand slip down and latch on to his throat, squeezing the life from him and pinning him to the wall.

This guy is a monster.

Reece grabbed the top of Oleg's hand with his right in the dark while raising his left arm and slamming his elbow down onto the crook of the Russian's arm, breaking the grip from his throat. Reece wrapped his left arm around his opponent's right, his hand on the back of the Russian's shoulder, bringing the body down, where Reece delivered a strike with his fist and then a forearm to the side of the Russian's massive head. Reece then slid his right hand to the Russian's back under his own left hand, which was still trapping the Russian's shoulder. He drove his right knee into his aggressor's solar plexus and then twisted his body, sending the Russian's head into the wall behind him.

Reece lost physical contact with his opponent in the darkness.

Where are you?

Reece felt the jab connect with his cheek.

There you are.

He knew the likelihood of a follow-up cross was high. Bobbing his head back and to the left, he felt the energy of the Russian's punch just miss him in the darkness. He felt a cold carcass on his left shoulder and swung it toward where he thought the Russian was standing. He could hear it hit something but didn't know if it was his adversary or another side of beef.

Something brushed against him to his right, something that was warmer than the beef. Covering his jaw with his left hand, Reece pivoted right and drove an uppercut into the body. It was a solid connection and the Russian grunted in response before sending a left hook glancing off

Reece's shoulder. He quickly recocked to send another to the side of the American's head.

Stars filled Reece's vision and he careened into a slab of cold beef.

Stay in it, Reece. You go down. You die.

Reece could feel the Russian coming toward him in the pitch-black confines of the meat locker and threw a jab, feeling nose cartilage breaking beneath his knuckles. The Russian kept coming. Reece followed it with a cross, his opponent slipping it in the darkness, dropping his weight and firing a cross of his own into Reece's solar plexus. Reece covered with an elbow, keeping them tight to his body. The two warriors traded punches in the dark.

This guy is a boxer. He's a better boxer than you. Don't fight his fight. Close the distance.

Knowing what to do and then attempting to do it without the sense of sight, while heavy meat carcasses are swinging to knock you off balance and a trained fighter is moving in for the kill, is another matter entirely.

Reece felt a solid jab to his jaw and knew the cross was coming. This time, instead of covering and countering, Reece changed levels and ducked his chin to his chest, launching the top part of his head forward and into the incoming fist of the Russian boxer in a Filipino destruction technique.

The Russian grunted in pain, clearly hurt, but instead of grabbing what may have been a broken hand, he sent Reece to the ground with a shot to the liver with his good fist.

Reece felt a cold sensation flow through his body. As he fought to stand, his head was viciously yanked back by his hair. Three devastating punches connected with his face and dropped him to the deck.

But the Russian had made a mistake. He had closed the distance.

Reece grabbed for the Russian's foot and found it in the darkness, moving his hand to the ankle and scooping it while driving forward in an ankle pick, taking his opponent to the floor.

It was now all about feel. It was Reece's game now.

Pulling himself atop the downed Russian, Reece found the mount and rained down a flurry of punches into the man's face before switching to more devastating elbows, causing the Russian to lock up Reece's body.

This guy is a beast.

Pushed up and out of the mount, Reece found himself on his butt. With the sense of sight out of play, Reece's other senses were heightened. Touch, sound, and the sense of spatial awareness took over as the Russian drove himself toward Reece, who wrapped his arm around his enemy's thick neck in a right-side guillotine choke. Reece planted his left arm on the floor and threw his right hip up and then sat back, cutting the angle toward his right hip while wrapping his legs around the Russian. He pulled his elbow back. Feeling his opponent's head twisting, he switched from a wrist grip to a Gable grip. The Russian fired two short punches into Reece's ribs and wrapped his arms around Reece's body, his fingers finding the bullet wound in Reece's upper back and digging inside. Reece pushed through the pain as the Russian clawed deeper into Reece's back, pushing his head free.

Reece adjusted, pulling the Russian into his guard. He took another punch to the face, but caught it before his adversary could retract it and locked it to his body. Reece quickly pivoted his hips and spun toward the Russian's left knee, throwing his left leg over the Russian's neck in and outward right arm bar and driving his hips to the opposite wall with all the power he could muster. Reece's violent effort was rewarded with a loud snap as the ligaments ruptured and tendons tore, dislocating the elbow.

Reece kicked the heavy Russian back into a hanging side of beef and frantically felt along the floor for the AK. The Russian was doing the same thing. Unfortunately for Reece, the GRU man found it first.

Reece heard the metal of the Kalashnikov's receiver scraping along the floor.

He's hurt. The first shots are not going to be accurate.

All he needs to do is get lucky once.

You have seconds.

Reece stood and began shoving beef carcasses in the direction of the Russian. Swinging right and left as they slid along their rails, they began impacting the assassin just as he cradled the rifle in his broken arm and pressed the trigger with his left index finger.

The noise of the unsuppressed AK firing fully automatic in a confined space was deafening. Bullets tore through the hanging carcasses, the muzzle flash igniting the darkness like a strobe light. That strobe illuminated the door to the meat locker. It was directly behind Reece.

The frogman turned and bailed out of the locker, slamming the door shut behind him to buy a few more seconds.

He assessed his injuries as he ran. Nothing seemed to be broken but he was having trouble moving his left arm.

As he passed one of the metal tables covered in dead chickens, Reece grabbed a cleaver.

CHAPTER 65

REECE BURST INTO THE hallway and leapt over the dead police officers as he heard the door to the meat locker open. Turning to his right, he saw the back exit, sprinted to it, and, with his left side not working well and his right hand holding the large meat cleaver, he kicked it open and exited into a back alley.

Two unoccupied police cars were parked haphazardly at one end of the narrow street.

Reece positioned himself to the left of the door.

Stand and fight. AK versus meat cleaver. American versus Russian. SEAL versus some sort of Russian special operator; Reece was sure of it.

As the door flew open, Reece took advantage of the Russian's mind being in another type of fight, a gunfight. Reece was prepared for a different kind of battle. Pinning the AK to the Russian's body, he brought the rectangular cleaver down toward the Russian's head, but instead connected with the left-side clavicle, which snapped under the heft and downward pressure of the sharp blade.

The Russian screamed in pain and launched himself into Reece with a fury known only to a cornered animal, knocking the SEAL into the wall. With both sides of his upper body devastated by Reece's attacks, he pivoted his hips and threw a Thai kick that connected with Reece's sciatic nerve and dropped him to the cobblestone alley.

As Reece pushed himself up, he saw the Russian positioning the AK from his hip.

Reece saw Lauren and Lucy holding hands in Coronado and he saw Katie by the lake in Montana, a light breeze blowing through her hair.

A gunshot brought him back to reality, but it wasn't the sound of a Kalashnikov. It was a pistol.

The bullet hit the Russian in the right shoulder from behind. A second gunshot took him closer to the spine, spinning him back toward the door and dropping him to the ground.

Reece looked over his left shoulder and saw Abelard behind the wheel of a dark vintage Mini Cooper. One hand was on the wheel, and one held the Heckler & Koch P7.

"Did you have to shoot him?" Reece asked.

"You're welcome. And what would you have me do? Allow him to riddle you with bullets or perhaps pummel you to death? Maybe I should have asked him nicely to stop?"

"Okay, now what?" Reece asked, pushing himself to his feet.

"Get him up. And in the car."

"In this clown car? I don't think we are going to fit."

"Well, I know where we will *all* fit: in the back of a police car. Get him in here and let's go!"

Reece looked at the large Russian. He was breathing but he was dead weight.

Commit to it.

Reece positioned himself on his back on the Russian's chest. Keeping his hips off the ground, he reached back and grabbed the Russian's far leg, throwing the thigh over his left shoulder. He then raised his right leg up and back and threw it forward, rolling the Russian up and onto his shoulder in a fireman's carry.

"Impressive. Put him in the backseat," Abelard said. "We will stop just outside of the city and see if we can patch him, *and you,* up. I have some tape and rope in the trunk."

"Backseat?"

"Just get him in."

Moments after the heavy Russian was stuffed in the back of the Mini Cooper, Reece climbed in the passenger seat and Abelard sped out of the city.

CHAPTER 66

Road from Turin, Italy, to Cortina d'Ampezzo, Italy

CORTINA D'AMPEZZO IS A resort town nestled in a valley in the province of Belluno, in the Dolomites of northern Italy. Best known for the canceled 1944 Winter Olympics, due to World War II, it would host the 1956 Games and become a jet-set destination for European aristocrats, models, and the occasional Hollywood star before they opted for the warmer climes of Ibiza, Spain.

Reece and Abelard had exited the A4 about halfway to Milan and pulled into a barn on a dairy farm well off the main road. There they switched out the Mini Cooper for a black Audi RS 5 with all the proper paperwork. The *Sayan* network was strong in Europe. Israel was not about to allow their people to fall victim to another Holocaust.

After Abelard checked Reece's back, noting that the wound was probably the result of a ricochet, he stuffed it with gauze from the small first-aid kit in the Mini. While Abelard disconnected his mechanical hand controls from the old Mini and reattached them to the Audi, Reece pulled their passenger from the backseat and onto the dirt. Thank God they had not been pulled over. Explaining why there was a man bound with duct tape bleeding all over the backseat would have raised a question or two. They needed a trunk and the Audi gave them one.

"Is he alive?" Abelard had asked.

"Barely," Reece replied. "Isn't there anyone closer?"

"This is my closest. Usually he's in Milan but he's fly-fishing Lake Misurina and stays at his chateau in the Dolomites this time of year."

"Terrific," Reece said. "Is he a *Sayan*?"

"No, he's part of a different network not associated with my former agency."

"I see. And you trust him?"

"We would not be driving all this way if I didn't."

Their Russian prisoner had a pulse and seemed to be breathing, but he was drifting in and out of consciousness. Reece patched and stuffed what he could.

"I think he's bleeding internally."

"Will he make the trip?" the old Mossad man asked.

"Not sure. How long from here?"

"About five and a half hours, and I have to drive the speed limit with him back there."

"Let's get moving," Reece said, removing the spare tire jack and tossing it in the backseat. He then hoisted the Russian into the trunk and slammed it shut.

Their journey took them east, passing just south of Lago di Garda. They cut north above Venice and began their trek into the Dolomites. Even in the fading light Reece could tell how beautiful it was. Lush green valleys patched with grapevine-covered hillsides gave way to the sheer walls of the Dolomite Alps. They crossed rivers and streams and passed through small mountain villages as the Audi made short work of the winding mountain roads.

I'd love to come back here with Katie.

After it's over.

"Tell me what I'm in for here, Mr. Abelard."

"Let's go with Saul. I feel like we are at that stage. James?"

"James is fine."

"Good. We are going to see a doctor who takes care of patients who can't risk a stay at a normal hospital. He's an orthopedic surgeon, specializes in knees. There are a lot of those types of injuries in a ski town."

"If business is good, why does he see people like us?" Reece asked.

"Ah, good question. Because he was one of us. Not exactly, but close."

"What do you mean?"

"He was a doctor in the Italian military, a *maggiure*."

"A major?"

"That's right. First a major, as are all the doctors, and then a lieutenant colonel. He was part of SISMI. Do you know what that is?"

"The Italian Military Intelligence and Security Service. Wasn't it called the AISE?"

"They had to change the name after the reforms in 2007," Abelard confirmed. "The government wanted to bring it under civilian control after a series of scandals."

"The Imam Rapito Affair?"

"The very one. He was the SISMI doctor assigned to the operation."

"An extraordinary rendition of Abu Omar in 2003 in Milan by SISMI and the CIA," Reece said. "I was in Afghanistan at the time, but I remember the headlines. It brought the Agency's rendition program into the light."

"Our doctor, Alessandro Catania, was lead medical on the operation and was on the flight with Omar to Egypt."

"I don't remember seeing his name in any of the articles I read about it."

"That's because his involvement was swept under the rug."

"Why's that? A lot of CIA and SISMI names saw the light of day, including the CIA Milan chief of base."

"Doctor Catania had another connection to the CIA that no one in either government wanted to see revealed."

"What was that?" Reece asked.

"What do you know of Sidney Gottlieb?"

"Rings a bell. Isn't he the mind-control LSD guy from the CIA in the fifties and sixties?"

"That's him. He was known as the chief poisoner for the CIA. Ran a program called MKUltra for twenty years at the CIA, illegal as it turns out."

"The Church Hearings uncovered it, right?" Reece asked. "The Agency was running tests on citizens without their consent: college students, hospital patients, prisoners, mental patients. I learned a little about this a few years ago."

"The Church Hearings only skimmed the surface, James. It was nasty stuff. It wasn't just about using unwitting test subjects to chronicle the effects of LSD. It was *much* more."

"How do you know so much about this?" Reece asked.

Abelard smoothly accelerated out of a turn. He looked at his mechanical hand controls and said, "I've had a lot of time to read."

"What else was MKUltra experimenting with?" Reece asked.

"It was really about torture, psychological torture to be more precise, though the physical torture certainly played a part. Gottlieb ran it under the auspices of the CIA's Office of Scientific Intelligence."

"I'm already skeptical."

"As you should be. They worked with the Army's Biowarfare Lab to develop a truth serum of sorts. That's what they were looking for, anyway. One could get away with a lot in the early days of the Cold War, James."

"Similar to the days after 9/11," Reece said, continuing the thought.

"That's right. MKUltra continued the experiments of Imperial Japan and the Nazis. Dachau was a hub of human experimentation. *Bastards.* There is even evidence that the CIA recruited Nazi doctors after the war, gave them safe passage and new identities to continue the work they had begun on the Jews of Europe and build on it, all in the name of national security."

Reece shook his head, thinking back to his SEAL Troop ambushed in the mountains of Afghanistan to cover up experiments that had given his men brain tumors.

"These doctors and vivisectionists . . ."

"What's that?" Reece asked.

Abelard paused and cleared his throat.

"It's operating or cutting an animal, in this case Jews, while they are alive for physiological or pathological *research*. My grandparents never made it out of Dachau, James. Were they part of these experiments? I'll never know."

"I'm so sorry."

"It really wasn't that long ago. And neither was 9/11."

"What does this have to do with our orthopedic surgeon?"

"Those projects from the forties, fifties, and sixties, the manipulation of mental states and brain function in pursuit of an elusive truth serum using LSD, cocaine, heroin, THC, or mescaline, in conjunction with electroshock treatment, sleep deprivation, extreme heat and cold, hypnosis, sensory deprivation, solitary confinement, even sexual abuse—those gave your agency a foundation upon which to build in the post-9/11 world. They even had the black sites of their day in Fort Clayton, Panama, and Villa Schuster and Camp King in Germany. After September eleventh there was a renewed interest in interrogation and torture, as I am sure you are aware."

"So I've heard," Reece said.

"All Gottlieb's experiments and Project MKUltra, all based on the Japanese and German human experiments, informed what would happen to enemy combatants in the early days of the War on Terror."

"What happened to Gottlieb?"

"He lost the faith. Retired in 1973. Went 'off the grid,' as I understand you Americans are fond of saying. Became a peace activist. Even took over the operation of a leper colony in India."

"Maybe he was atoning for something."

"We've all got to face atonement, James. In this life or the next."

Reece looked at his driver.

"Like I said, I've had a lot of time to read."

"Didn't he testify at the Church Hearings?" Reece asked.

"He did. Under an alias. Said he destroyed most of his records. They let him walk free."

"Maybe he kept a few records as insurance."

"Perhaps. Whatever he did, he took most of his secrets with him to the grave. He died in 1999."

"Of what?"

"No one knows. No cause of death was listed."

"Creepy."

"That it is. Those experiments and the Church Hearings informed a 1994 definition of torture as, and I'm paraphrasing, 'inflicting pain similar to organ failure or death.' After 9/11 that definition was broadly interpreted; if an enemy combatant didn't die or experience organ failure, then it wasn't torture."

"You *really* have had a lot of time to read."

"What do you know of Cat's Eye in Thailand?"

"Black site. One of those top-secret rendition locations that still ended up making the news."

"It was one of Abu Zubaydah's first stops after being captured in Pakistan in 2002. They called it Detention Site Green, a CIA prison on the Laotian border about three hundred miles northeast of Bangkok. Fell under the jurisdiction of a chief of base who would go on to become the director of the Central Intelligence Agency. Most people came to know it as Cat's Eye. It was an old Royal Thai Air Force base in Udon Thani Province that last saw extensive use in your Vietnam War. The jungle had reclaimed it by the time the CIA resurrected it. It was the ideal location for a black site."

"And somehow Alessandro Catania was involved."

"He was. The Americans captured another al-Qaeda operative along with Abu Zubaydah, an Italian citizen, though jihadi to the core. The Italian government was informed and insisted on SISMI involvement in the interrogations. Cat's Eye solved the problem for Italy. The Italian government certainly did not want the circus of a trial on Italian soil or want to draw Islamic extremist attention to Italy, so they were more than happy to let him rot in Thailand."

"And the doctor they sent in was Major Alessandro Catania."

"One and the same. Whatever he *did* there, whatever he *saw* there, protected him when the Imam Rapito Affair in Milan ripped the intelligence services apart. He escaped unscathed, though he did have to resign."

"And now he operates on ACLs at the base of the slopes in the Olympic Village."

"Yes, though he supplements his income doing the occasional job for me and others like me, even a case or two for the Italian government, or so it is rumored."

"I want to know who sent 'Ivan' back there to kill us and I want to know if he has any connection to Nizar Kattan."

"Well, if anyone can find out, it's Doctor Catania. He is the best I've ever seen when it comes to extracting secrets."

They drove into the resort town just before midnight and found the Cortina d'Ampezzo Orthopedic Center without issue. Abelard pulled around to the back, where a metallic-blue Porsche 911 Targa 4 GTS waited.

"I see you've done this before," Reece said.

"I try not to make it a habit."

Abelard turned off the car.

"Wait here," he said, reaching into the back to pull his wheelchair between the seats.

"Need any help?" Reece asked.

"I've done it a million times," the bookseller said as he opened the door, unfolded the chair, and set it at an angle wedged against the door frame of the German coupe. He then hoisted himself out of the driver's seat and into the wheelchair. He shut the door and was wheeling toward the back entrance before Reece could say another word.

Reece was in awe of how Abelard functioned. Other than asking Reece to find his pistol in the mayhem of the explosion, he had not asked him for help with anything. Reece found himself forgetting that the man was even *in* a wheelchair.

He adjusted the rearview mirror and watched as the back door opened. Abelard exchanged words with someone and then wheeled back to the Audi.

Opening the door he said, "Cameras are off. Facility is clear except for the doctor. Let's bring him in."

Reece exited the vehicle and opened the trunk. The Russian was still unconscious but had a pulse. Reece struggled to get the body in a position where he could get him up and onto his good shoulder, but he eventually managed. He shut the trunk and walked across the dark parking lot and into the medical facility. A wheeled stretcher awaited.

"Set him down here," a heavily accented Italian voice said.

Reece dropped his cargo onto the stretcher and identified the source of the new voice.

He had a runner's build and was an inch taller than Reece. By his thick salt-and-pepper hair, Reece judged him to be in his late fifties. He wore a white lab coat over dark blue scrubs. Crocs with socks were on his feet.

As Reece extended his hand, the doctor cautioned, "No names. I want to know as little about you as possible."

"Understood," Reece said.

"You obviously know *my* name. It's on the surgery center door and on my coat. Saul has given you my background, I assume."

"He did," Reece answered.

"My job here is to save this man's life and then use that background to elicit information. Saul is taking care of payment."

Reece looked back at Abelard and then at the doctor.

"Someone has to pay for my two ex-wives and make the payments on the Targa outside." He smiled. "Wheel him back and I'll see what I can do."

CHAPTER 67

ONCE IN THE EXAMINATION room, Reece stepped back to let Dr. Catania examine the patient.

It was obvious even to Reece that the Russian did not have much time. He was pale, his breathing was shallow, and he was already beginning to smell of the dead.

Reece and Abelard watched as the doctor cut away the Russian's clothing with practiced precision, leaving him naked on the examination table.

"Left upper abdomen, probably a nick to the spleen, slow trickle, unstoppable bleed," he said. "I'd advise you to just ask him when I wake him up, but if he doesn't answer then you are out of luck.' "

"What do you mean?" Reece asked.

"What I mean, is that if he had more time, we would be able to exercise patience, but he's got minutes, not hours, left. We need to bring him back and be prepared for him to stall."

"Okay, Doc, let's do it," Reece said.

"Stand back."

Dr. Catania removed a long eighteen-gauge needle from a drawer and with one quick pass slid it under the clavicle of the left shoulder at the base of the neck. Reece saw dark purple blood flush back into the hub.

"That's the subclavian vein," the doctor explained. "An easy hit. It supplies blood to the head, neck, shoulders, and arms."

Catania strapped the Russian's hands and feet to the examination table with leather cuff restraints and added a chest strap.

"Now I'm going to put him in a near coma."

Reece looked at Abelard and then the doctor.

"If he's in a coma, how can I ask him questions?" Reece asked.

"The coma is just step one. Trust me."

Reece watched as the surgeon opened a cabinet.

"I'm giving him a bolus of two hundred milligrams ketamine."

"What's a bolus?"

"A medical term for a single large use of a drug, in this case ketamine. It's a widely used international sedative for inducing anesthesia. It's also an NMDA receptor antagonist that effects a psychological out-of-body response at lower doses."

"Do all doctors have these things lying around?" Reece asked.

"Not all doctors," Catania responded. "This is a bolus of PCP; you might know it as angel dust. This results in a similar reaction, but the combo induces more of a 'bad trip' as you might say."

"Is that intel from the Gottlieb experiments?" Reece asked.

Catania looked at Reece, impressed.

"As you are familiar with Gottlieb and the history of the MKUltra project, this should not come as a surprise."

Catania opened another drawer and removed two long, plastic-coated needles. He inserted them under the skin against the Russian's pelvis bone.

"These are normally used against the spine to create heat lesions for pain relief."

"Like a rhizotomy?" Reece asked.

"Exactly. They burn the nerve fibers, sending pain signals to the brain. We can kill them with a chemical or with an electrical current.

Even under full anesthesia it creates a pain response that causes the blood pressure and heart rate to spike. I'm about to wake him up. Are you ready with your questions? You won't have much time."

"I'm ready."

"Okay, this is one hundred milligrams of methamphetamine," the former SISMI doctor said. "It's about three times the normal drug-addicted dose. If his heart holds, we may push more. The sudden jolt to his system in the transition out of the coma will leave him in a completely dissociative state. With the pain from his internal wounds, along with jolts of electricity from the rhizotomy needles, we will manipulate his mental state and send him on the worst psychedelic trip you can imagine."

As Dr. Catania shot the amphetamine directly into the Russian's subclavian vein, Reece watched the heart monitor shoot from 60 to 160 instantly, his blood pressure increasing to 180/100.

"He tolerated that well," said the doctor, drawing fifty additional milligrams of methamphetamine. "I'm going to hit him a little harder."

Catania injected the drug into the Russian and their patient's bloodshot eyes opened wide with horror. He pulled at the restraints, arching his back and twisting in an attempt to break free, unaware that the agony was an artificially altered brain state and there was nothing he could do to stop it. Foam formed around his mouth as he tried to cry out, the fire in his brain inhibiting an intelligible audible response.

"Ask him now. You only have a few minutes before his brain or body gives out."

Reece moved to the opposite side of the examination table across from the doctor.

"Do I look familiar?" Reece asked.

The Russian nodded.

"Let's start with your name."

The man strapped to the table remained silent.

It was never a good idea to start an interrogation with questions to which the inquisitor did not know the answers. Reece knew it. The Russian knew it, too.

"Hit him, Doc," Reece said.

Catania pressed the hot button on the rhizotomy probe, sending the Russian's body into convulsions, his heart rate hitting 170 beats per minute and blood pressure rising instantly to 220/120. After forty-five seconds the doctor took his finger off the button and shoved the needles in farther.

"I need to create a new burn area with each shot," he said.

"Let's try this again. What's your name?"

It was apparent that in his altered state, the Russian could barely function.

"I am Oleg Berzin, but I have gone by many names," he whispered in a Russian accent as thick as his chest, the foam bubbling from his mouth.

"Are you SVR?"

Even with his brain barely functioning, Oleg found the question funny.

"No. SVR are former KGB pricks. I was GRU. Spetsnaz."

Reece looked at Abelard.

"And why do you want me and my friend here dead?"

Oleg tilted his head ever so slightly and saw the man in the wheelchair staring up at him.

"I'm dying," he said.

"Yes, you are," Reece said. "I'm sorry, there is nothing I can do about that. You get to control how you go out from here. You choose how painful your last moments on earth are going to be. Help me and I'll end you quick."

"I didn't want to kill the boy, you know."

"You almost did."

"I wouldn't have thought twice in the old days. At least I thought twice."

"Progress," Reece said.

"Those Syrian savages don't care who they kill."

Syrians.

"Let's try again. Who hired you to kill me and my friend and why use Syrians?"

Oleg strained, attempted to say something, and then clammed up.

"Hit him again," Reece commanded.

The doctor pushed the remaining amphetamine into Oleg's bloodstream and pressed the rhizotomy probe button, sending another forty-five seconds of excruciating agony into the GRU man's body and brain.

The eyes that had once been bloodshot were now completely filled with blood. They darted back and forth, desperately looking for an escape where one did not exist; the cornered animal knew it was going to die.

"Tell me or we will keep you alive all night like this!"

"Do me a favor and I will tell you everything."

"You are not exactly in a position to be asking for favors," Reece said.

"I know you. You are James Reece. I researched you when I got the assignment. I know you lost your family. I have a family now. They did not know the old me. They know me now. They know the man who did not want to blow up the boy, do you understand?"

"I understand," Reece said.

"You promise me that you will find my bank accounts. I have many. They are hidden but *you* can find them. Get that money to my wife and stepchildren. They are good kids. Not like me. They deserved better."

"I can do that," Reece said. "Now tell me."

Oleg struggled to breathe through the saliva and foam accumulating in his mouth and threatening to block his airway.

"The SVR wants you dead, Mr. Reece. The Jew was just cover. They wanted it to look like another act of violent Islamic extremism with the Jewish bookstore, but it's you they want."

"Who? Exactly."

"It's one of three people—no, not one, it could be two or all three."

"Who?"

"Mikhail Gromyko, director of the SVR, or Pavel Dashkov, director of the FSB. One or both, I do not know."

"And the third?"

"The third. The third is the Russian president."

That confirms what Katz told you, Reece.

"And the why?"

"Always the why. That is above my pay grade. Rarely did I ever know the why."

"How about, why did they pick you?"

"Ah, I am as retired as one can get from the Spetsnaz of the GRU. I was living in Italy and I've handled these types of operations before."

Reece noted the heart rate and blood pressure continuing to rise. He looked at the doctor, who shook his head.

"What types of operations?"

"Nonattributable, using PLO, Black September, Hezbollah, Hamas, al-Qaeda, ISIS."

"But at the behest of Russia."

"First the Soviet Union and then Russia, but yes."

"And Nizar Kattan?"

"Who?"

"Nizar Kattan. He's a sniper."

"The one who killed the former Russian president?"

"That's him."

"That was a good shot." Oleg coughed. Blood was beginning to mix with the yellow phlegm and drip down his chin.

"Hit him, Doc," Reece said.

"No. We made our deal. I am telling you the truth. I know nothing about this Kattan."

"And Jean-Pierre Le Drian?"

"Never heard of this man."

"And the hit in Israel?"

"Not my department. Seems a lot of people want you dead. Maybe you will be joining me soon."

"You worked with the PLO?" Abelard asked, rolling closer to the examination table.

"The man in the wheelchair speaks."

"Answer him," Reece ordered.

"I did. Many times. Had I written a book about it, I might be on the speaking circuit like all the American SEALs rather than strapped to this table."

"Were you in Berlin in 1986?" Abelard asked.

"Answer him or we hit you again," Reece said.

"I was not. I was still in Afghanistan. But I know what you are asking. You are asking if I was the one who put you in that chair." He paused to cough. "I was not. But you have something in common with your friend."

"Oh? What's that?" Abelard asked.

"Mikhail Gromyko."

"The director of the SVR?"

"He was in Berlin in 1986. It might be the last time the KGB got their hands dirty."

He coughed again. There was more blood than yellow foam dripping from his mouth to his chest now.

Reece looked at Abelard. After more than thirty years of waiting, the bookseller had his answer.

"Hey, America," Oleg said to Reece. "I got to land a few blows."

"You did," Reece said. "More than a few."

"I should have gotten out earlier. I should have left this life behind when I saw what was happening to your country in Afghanistan. I should have disappeared. Instead, I waited until I watched that last American plane leave on the news. Just like our tanks crossing the Amu Darya River in 1989. I waited too long." The Russian coughed. "It was a good bout."

Oleg's vitals flatlined. The old warrior had fought his last battle.

Dr. Catania reached up and turned off the machine.

"Did you get what you needed?" he asked.

"I still have questions," Reece said. "I'm beginning to think I'll never have the answers."

"I'll give you the room," Catania said. "But before you go, let me dig that bullet out of your shoulder and sew you up."

When he was done, he left Reece and Abelard to talk in private.

Abelard pushed himself back from the table and spun around to face Reece.

"He didn't know about Kattan and Le Drian. The hits might be connected but they are different cells, so if one is destroyed or compromised it does not disrupt the operation of the others. You have something on someone high up in the Russian hierarchy."

"I don't even know what it could be," Reece said.

"If that's the case, they want to kill you before you figure it out."

"It appears so," Reece said, once again thinking of Katie and wondering if a life with him would forever put her at risk.

Maybe she would be better off without you.

Figure that out later, Reece. You still have work to do.

"It also appears we have a common enemy."

"Gromyko."

"Yes."

"I have a thought," the man in the wheelchair said.

"As do I," Reece responded. "Before we discuss yours, you said you met Kattan in person in Dubrovnik, is that right?"

"Yes, but I suspect he wanted to meet there not because Croatia is his base of operations, but because it is close enough that he can travel there without much trouble."

"So, he's in a neighboring country."

"That would be my suspicion. I just don't know which one."

"I have someone who can help us," Reece said, thinking of the golden wires and circuitry suspended under Lackland Air Force Base.

"And if you can locate him?"

"Then I'll need a contact who can get me a sniper rifle in the Balkans."

"Lucky for you, that's just my game."

PART FOUR

NIZAR

THE ASSASSIN

EVERYTHING COMES IN TIME TO HIM
WHO KNOWS HOW TO WAIT.
—LEO TOLSTOY, *WAR AND PEACE*

CHAPTER 68

SVR Headquarters, Moscow

PERCHED IN HIS OFFICE overlooking a wooded section of Moscow just south of the Yasenevo District, Mikhail Gromyko gazed upon the forest below. It was a beautiful view, but the location was not chosen for its aesthetics. Rather it was selected for standoff distance; for security.

The Yasenevo District was one of Moscow's administrative hubs and the Foreign Intelligence Service was situated past the outer edge of the capital's Ring Road, adding to the mystery of its already ominous reputation. Much as its Western counterpart was nestled into the wooded hills of Langley, so too was its Russian nemesis set apart as different and superior to other government services crammed into more pedestrian locales.

A large ballistic glass window dominated the outer wall of the office inside a facility surrounded by fences, sensors, drones, dogs, and roving guards. Layers of security on the vast property ensured that no one inadvertently or intentionally set foot on the grounds of Russia's premier intelligence agency.

But Gromyko was not thinking about the inherent beauty of the landscape, nor the security precautions that kept the campus free from prying eyes; he was thinking about next steps. He was feeling weaker and had increased his nicotine intake to compensate. Something about the cigarettes centered him, steadied him, brought him back to the old days, when he was young and full of life, with a discernable enemy to combat in the shadows. Then the world shifted. The Soviet Army departed Afghanistan, the Berlin Wall came down, and on December 25, 1991, at 7:32 p.m., the red Soviet flag with its distinctive gold hammer-and-sickle, representing the strength of workers and peasants, was lowered over the Kremlin. It would never be raised again. That fool Gorbachev had led the Soviet Union to its dissolution with his radical reforms. *Glasnost and perestroika*. The West had applauded him with *Time* magazine covers first "Man of the Year" and then "Man of the Decade." Even the committee in Oslo got in on the act, honoring the Soviet leader with a Nobel Peace Prize. The following year the Soviet Union would cease to exist. It was as if the Bolshevik Revolution had never happened. After abandoning his nation, Gorbachev continued to insult Mother Russia by accepting the Ronald Reagan Freedom Award, an award of surrender. The bald, fat man had even received a Grammy. He received no such awards from the state he led into ruin. The man who destroyed an empire continued to criticize the current president from a dacha outside of Moscow, but the old reformer did not have long. Age had caught up to him.

Age will catch up to us all.

That is why we must act when we can.

A large flat-screen television was set to CNN. It was on mute. The SVR director had listened to the commentary coming out of northern Italy most of the morning.

The attack in Turin had failed. The boxer had failed. Perhaps Oleg Berzin had lost his edge in his later years?

Perhaps we all have.

Italian authorities were blaming the attack on Syrian refugees targeting a Jewish-owned business. The bookseller had not been seen since the explosion. News reports suspected that he had not returned to his store for fear of reprisals by Islamic militants. According to CNN, he had not answered the door to his flat above his store. Local and international news organizations were camped out at his building, just beyond the police tape that cordoned off the crime scene. Some commentators speculated he was seeking refuge in Israel after the traumatic event. Italy did share a border with France, and the images of Paris and Nice, the Theo van Gogh murder, *Charlie Hebdo,* and a headless schoolteacher were more than enough to push the bookseller into hiding.

Italian politicians quickly maneuvered to use the attack as further justification for their deportation policy, put in place by the Interior Ministry in the wake of the July 7, 2005, bombings in London. The policy was broad by design and allowed Italy to expel anyone with suspected terrorist ties. Neither a valid accusation nor a conviction was necessary. One could appeal, but they would be doing so from Syria or Tunisia, not Italian soil. That policy, along with their 300,000-person police force, which was the largest in Europe and double that of the United Kingdom, had been credited with keeping terrorist attacks in Italy to a minimum. That those responsible for the bombing of the bookstore were from Syria only strengthened Italy's resolve. The Italians had largely given the middle finger to the European Court of Human Rights, an organization that had attempted to curtail Italy's deportation of Muslims with minimal success. This latest incident reinforced to Italy's political elite that they were on the right side of history.

There were no indications that Italy suspected Russian involvement: dead Syrian immigrants in the streets, a crude bomb similar to what would be used by Hezbollah or Hamas, the target a Jewish-owned business, four dead Italian police officers who sacrificed themselves to protect Italian citizens. Any logical analysis pointed to Islamic extremists as the responsible party.

How did all seven Syrians die? Did those four police officers kill them? The Italian authorities had been unusually tight-lipped about that. Gromyko could understand one dying in the explosion, but all seven being killed by the police? And what of Oleg Berzin? There had been no contact through any of the clandestine reporting channels and no chatter picked up by Russian electronic collections. No sign. No Russian body. The former GRU man had vanished.

Gromyko extinguished his cigarette and settled into the high-backed black leather chair at his desk. He picked up a hardwired phone and pressed a button. The secure line was established to reach a half-dozen officials in the Russian government, including Pavel Dashkov at FSB headquarters in Lubyanka Square.

"Da?"

"Are you watching?"

"Of course. Are you smoking?"

Gromyko ignored the comment.

"Anything from signals collection?" the FSB director asked.

"Yes," Dashkov said.

"Well?"

There was a pause and Gromyko could tell that his comrade was taking the time to light his pipe. Whether it was because he needed a smoke or just wanted to aggravate his old friend, Mikhail could not be sure.

"Mikhail, old friend, you continue to worry too much. This exact contingency is why we activated Kattan in the first place. The data mining by our electronic collections and help from our friends in Silicon Valley gave us a weakness to exploit."

"Yes, the woman. The Israeli."

"That's right. Blowing her out of the sky may have been excessive, but when you give a man like Nizar Kattan an order and then allow him the freedom to do it without oversight, there are bound to be second- and third-order effects of his actions."

"And those second- and third-order effects have consequences."

"*Da,* oftentimes *unintended* consequences," Dashkov conceded. "Remember, Mikhail, we green-lit these operations to prevent us from having to exercise the final option."

"I remember," Gromyko said. That final option would result in irreversible changes to the U.S.-Russia relationship. He was not sure he was ready yet to take that step.

"Kattan had already accepted the contract to liquidate Reece from another source, from the American private military company man who died in some sort of accident on the island of Mustique last year. Kattan just needed some technical help and another five million dollars from us."

"I am aware."

"And it's working. It pulled Commander Reece from his home country, exposing his flanks and giving us opportunity to eliminate him with no Russian fingerprints. We have his cell phone IMEI and are tracking him right now using assets from our electronic collection apparatus and the Internet Research Agency."

"Where is he?"

"He is in the middle of the Adriatic; on a ferry it appears."

"Headed for Ulcinj?"

"Yes."

"Good. Kattan has it from here."

"We will continue to monitor him and relay his location to the Frenchman every step of the way."

"This time it shouldn't make the news. Commander Reece needs to take a bullet to the head."

"Kattan and Le Drian will be waiting and ready. You worry me, Mikhail. This constant fretting about James Reece is unlike you. Are you sure you feel well? Up to the task?"

Dashkov, he loves his games. Did he found out about the cancer or is he just probing, looking for a reaction?

"You should worry, too, Pavel."

"I have outsourced that worry to my security detail. You should do the same."

Gromyko grunted and opened a desk drawer for his pack of Marlboros.

"And while we are on the subject of worrying: Any future discussions on this matter should be done in person, especially if we need to take the next step, the one for which we will need presidential concurrence."

"*Da.* Agreed," Gromyko said. "That's the most sensible thing you have suggested in a long time, comrade."

"I suspect that will not be necessary, though. In the coming days we will track James Reece right into Kattan's crosshairs."

CHAPTER 69

Adriatic Sea between Italy and Montenegro

EARLY ON IN THE wars in Afghanistan and Iraq, it had become apparent that some viewed the Western incursion as an opportunity to settle century-old scores. The family that killed your great-grandfather's goat a hundred years ago was now an "al-Qaeda facilitator" in your reports to the Americans, who were all too eager to find and kill or capture and question anyone who fell into the category of "terrorist" or "insurgent." Reece had learned the lesson well. It was necessary to corroborate information through disassociated HUMINT networks and more technical collection means from cell phones, emails, or intercepted satellite or Thuraya calls before launching a mission. One had to confirm that the targeted individual was, in fact, a threat to allied forces and not just someone who had slighted a relative in a generation past.

Three years earlier, Reece had made a deal. He had spared the life of Ivan Zharkov, a Bratva *Pakhan,* in the barrens of Siberia in exchange for an open line of communication to the Russian underworld. The Bratva was Russian mafia. Their leaders had consolidated such power in the new Russia that the lines between their activities, the Russian intelligence services and the politicians who were, more often than not, bought and paid for, were more than blurred; they were often nonexistent. Ivan's son, Aleksandr, had been the deputy director in Directorate S of Russia's Foreign Intelligence Service and could produce legitimate passports to match false identities for the crime family. He was valuable. Aleksandr had also developed an addiction to hunting the most dangerous of game, game that could reason. He had hunted and killed Jonathan and Caroline Hastings's youngest daughter on Medny Island, in Kamchatka. He had almost succeeded in killing Raife as well. He was about to press the trigger on a crossbow and send a bolt through Raife's heart when first one, then two arrow shafts had pierced his chest and sent him toppling into the Bering Sea. Reece had taken care of a problem for Ivan Zharkov; even in the Bratva it is difficult to kill one's own flesh and blood, regardless of how demented they may be. Reece had made that problem go away and had let the elder patron live. It was time to cash in a favor.

Reece had placed the call before boarding the ferry in Italy and made his request. Ivan called back when Reece was in the middle of the Adriatic.

"It is confirmed. My counterparts in the Škaljari Clan verify he moves between a flat in Ulcinj and a cabin in the north, outside of Žabljak. The *Crnogorska mafija* provided both through front companies. They have used him for almost three years, providing protection, employment, and female companionship. Apparently he slit one girl's throat a year ago. He paid for her in cash, though."

Montenegro had been a way station for all manner of illicit trade for millennia: guns, drugs, gems, precious metals, wildlife, and humans. The appetite for young girls and boys both to the east and the west was almost insatiable. The Montenegrin mafia did not want for demand.

"Grid?"

"I have a lat-long for you," Ivan replied, referring to latitude-longitude.

"Send it," Reece replied.

"Before I do, I would be remiss if I did not tell you that this is obviously a trap. Nizar knows you are coming."

I'm counting on it, Reece thought.

"Just pass it."

"After I give you this information, it may be best to terminate our relationship."

"Pass me the location."

Reece scribbled the numbers down and ended the call.

Just like in the wars, Reece's single-source intelligence needed to be confirmed. Instead of working strategic or tactical-level SIGINT channels, as he would have in the SEAL Teams, Reece had another point of contact; he had Alice.

When Reece exited the ferry six hours later in Bar, Montenegro, he had his answer. His target was in the mountains outside of Žabljak, 125 miles north of Ulcinj. His HUMINT had passed him a lat-long. His technical collections platform had confirmed a voice match to Jean-Pierre Le Drian at the same location. Switching phones, burner phones, spoofing IMEI numbers, and closed-node networks were no match for a quantum computer when that technology was tasked to find you.

Reece knew the location of his target.

It was time to see a man about a rifle.

CHAPTER 70

Žabljak, Montenegro

JEAN-PIERRE LE DRIAN HIT End on his new phone.

"He's in Ulcinj. Took the ferry over from Bari and then a cab south. His phone is geolocated at Hotel Palata Venezia."

"Good," Nizar said. "One step closer."

They were seated at a rickety wooden kitchen table in a rustic cabin. It was a simple one-floor structure consisting of a small kitchen and living area with a wood-burning stove that kept the small space warm, making it livable in the colder months. There was a cot against one corner, where the Frenchman had been sleeping, and a separate room with a slightly larger bed covered in wool blankets, where Nizar slept. An outhouse with a bucket of lime next to the toilet seat provided the only bathroom. Without plumbing, water for drinking, cooking, and cleaning had to be hauled up to the cabin in buckets from a nearby stream.

Le Drian was looking forward to getting back to Africa.

"Do you think he's tracking us?" the Frenchman asked, pointing to an older mobile phone on the table.

"I know he is," Nizar answered.

"How?"

"A man like James Reece is not going to come all this way just hoping to run into me in Montenegro. That is the only electronic device in the area. He's tracking us. Be certain of it."

"And now we use the phone to lure him in?"

"We do, but as with any plan, we need to assume our enemy is thinking a step or two ahead. Remember, James Reece is growing older in a profession where most die young."

"Contingencies."

"That's right," Nizar said.

"What do you need from me?"

Nizar shifted his gaze from the mercenary to weapons on the table before them. Le Drian's eyes followed, sweeping over two Yugoslavian M70 Kalashnikov variants with the distinctive Bosnian fleur-de-lis at the base of their magazines, an SVD-S Dragunov with black composite furniture and folding stock, and one Orsis T-5000 Tochnost chambered in .375 CheyTac with a Nightforce ATACR 7-35x56mm F1 long-range riflescope.

"I know the T-5000, AKs, and Dragunov, but what is this?" Le Drian asked, pointing at an odd-looking rifle with a wood, skeletonized thumbhole stock and optic similar to the Dragunov, but with an integrally suppressed barrel.

"That is an old Soviet VSS Vintorez in 9x39mm. It's a subsonic optimized rifle cartridge."

Le Drian nodded in approval as he shifted focus and picked up the M70. This AK-type rifle with three distinctive cooling slots cut into its beechwood handguard was fitted with folding front and rear night sights and a flip-up grenade sight. The Yugoslavian military required all their domestically produced AK variants to be fitted with grenade sights that also acted as gas cutoff levers, so that every rifleman could double as a grenadier. A special blank cartridge could propel a variety of grenades when the rifle was fitted with a launching spigot. Le Drian was happy to note that these rifles did not have spigots attached, as they would have extended the overall length of the weapon by five inches. He brought the thin rubber recoil pad to his shoulder and dropped his cheek to the distinctive high comb of the buttstock lining up the sights.

"I never liked the high combs on these fixed-stocked AKs," he said.

"They were built for a Yugoslav, not a Frenchman," Nizar replied.

Le Drian grunted.

"They didn't even chrome-line their barrels. This one better not look like a sewer pipe."

"There is some corrosion but it's still a shooter. We will confirm zero before you take it into the mountains."

Le Drian lowered the rifle.

"Have you wondered why so many people want Commander Reece dead?" the former French Foreign Legion soldier asked.

"He is a man with many enemies."

"Like you?"

"I am not his enemy."

"Then what are you?"

"I am just an instrument."

"Of death?"

"Like you, that has been my path."

"And after this?"

"Right now, there is only this. If we are unsuccessful in eliminating our mark, we can expect him to come for us. No matter where we go in the world, he will find us. James Reece is not one to forgive transgressions."

"Then let's be sure he does not leave these mountains alive."

"That is why we have all of these," Nizar said, sweeping his hand over the weapons on the table.

"And if he believes we know he is tracking the phone?"

"I have someone in Ulcinj who has instructions to prod him along. He will be calling you to let us know when it is done."

"Why not have this person kill him?"

"It is not that type of asset."

"And if Reece kills him?"

"Then that's one less loose end to clean up. Now, let's go over the plan."

As the sniper spoke, working through the concept of the operation and actions on the objective, Le Drian couldn't help but wonder if he was one of those loose ends.

CHAPTER 71

Ulcinj, Montenegro

REECE SPOTTED HIS TAIL almost immediately.

It wasn't a professional team, as far as he could tell. In fact, it wasn't a team at all. It was one man in a silver Peugeot who attempted to change his appearance with different hats and shirts.

The SEAL rented a Kawasaki KLR 650 and spent almost a week in the southern coastal city playing tourist and getting the lay of the land, which allowed him time to plan and conduct SDRs to identify any other surveillance aside from the man in the Peugeot. He walked the narrow stone streets of the ancient seaport, visiting its various shops and cafés. When he ventured farther outside of town he would take the rented dual-sport bike, its knobby tires perfect for the dirt roads south of the city. He made time to explore Ulcinj Castle and its surrounding neighborhood. Built more than 2,500 years ago, it was a testament to the resiliency of a country often at the crossroads of illicit trade and the violence that accompanied it. He visited the Tower of the Balšić—not in the Palace and Court, its various fountains, the Church-Mosque, and its slave market, where pirates auctioned off or ransomed men, women, and children abducted in raids on villas in Sicily and the southern coast of Italy.

Each time he thought he had surreptitiously lost his tail, the silver

Peugeot would reappear. Were they tracking him physically or electronically?

To find out, Reece left his personal phone in his room one night, made his way to the roof of his hotel, and dropped off the back side, working his way down the balconies as he descended to a cobblestone back alley. He made his way to the beach and then doubled back. His tail was still where he had left him six hours earlier. The next night he did the same thing carrying his personal phone. And sure enough, the Peugeot was parked on the side of the road above "Miami Beach" waiting for him.

The phone was hot. That was information Reece could use.

But, if they had the phone, why use such inept surveillance?

Did someone want him to know that he was being followed?

Was it the Russians? Kattan?

After a week on the ground, Reece went to meet a contact of Abelard's; a man who dealt in weapons.

Reece rode the dual-sport ten miles southeast on Route 17, paralleling the coast toward the Buna River, which marked the border with Albania. He took a dirt road inland as instructed and veered off just shy of the Shenkolli Church, where he maneuvered his bike down to a dirt parking lot at the river's edge.

The Peugeot stayed with him but when he turned off the bike and swung his leg over the saddle, Reece could see a trail of dust keep moving and then come to a stop about a thousand yards down the main road.

The area was secluded and, not wanting to end up in a sniper's scope while he waited, Reece hid his personal phone under a thick green bush near his bike and quickly circled around and up the slope to where he had seen the cloud of dust come to a halt. He stopped well back in the shadows and observed the man in the silver car looking intently at a phone.

Who is this guy?

As confident as he could be that the tail was keeping tabs on him via his cell phone, Reece made his way back to his bike and collected his phone.

An hour later a 1970s-era Datsun 120Y took a left off the coastal road and coasted down into the dirt lot.

The four-door Japanese import would have been considered an economy car when it first rolled off the line. Today, in certain circles, it was a classic. Its side-view mirrors were located halfway down the hood for some reason and its whitewall tires stood out in contrast to the chocolate-brown paint.

The car came to a stop next to Reece, the dust blowing past him and then dissipating as the winds from the sea swirled in defense.

The right-side-drive vehicle's door opened and a short man stepped from a car no one in 1973 would ever have thought would one day increase in value. He hiked his pants over a robust belly and ran his hands through thinning black hair arranged in a comb-over that was not cooperating with the coastal winds. He stretched, yawned, and farted before extending his hand.

"You Donovan?" he asked. "I get call that say you need delivery."

Reece reluctantly took the offered cold, weak, and clammy hand.

"I Luka," the man said in broken English. "You like my car?"

"I do," Reece replied. "Datsun?"

"Yeah, man. Chicks dig it. Just don't tell wife." He laughed.

"Good tip," Reece said.

"What happen?" he asked, pointing at the cuts and bruises on his new acquaintance's face.

"It's why I need your delivery," Reece said.

"I like this guy," Luka said, pointing at Reece. "You funny."

"Only around Datsuns. What do you have for me?"

"I told you need bang-bang. Quick. Long distance," Luka said, mimicking a rifle shot toward the ocean. "And pistol. A quiet one."

"That's right."

"Come," Luka said, motioning toward the rear of the vehicle with his head. "Luka find you good deal."

Reece followed the arms dealer to the trunk of the car, looking up at the hill above them.

Should have done this from high ground.

Luka popped the trunk and pulled back a blanket to reveal two rifles and a pistol.

"What you think?"

Reece looked at the three weapons. Each one was older than the vehicle in which they had arrived.

"Is this thing a time machine?" Reece asked.

"What you mean?"

"May I?" Reece asked.

"Yes. Yes."

Reece reached in and pulled out a 7.62x54R M1891 (M91) Mosin-Nagant.

"Who am I? Simo Häyhä?" Reece whispered.

"What?" Luka asked.

"Never mind."

Reece pulled back the bolt on a rifle built around 1900. A round did not eject from the chamber and the five-round internal magazine was empty. He examined the iron sights and noted the Russian Imperial Crest and Finnish markings.

Battlefield pickup, Reece thought, wondering who in the Russian and Finnish armies had pressed the trigger over its lifetime.

"You like?" Luka asked.

Without answering, Reece returned it to the trunk and picked up a rifle with which he was intimately familiar, the Dragunov.

Officially the SVD-63, denoting the year it was accepted for use in the Soviet military, it was a unique blend of dark machined metal with wood furniture and skeletonized stock topped with a PSO-1M2 4x24 optic with an illuminated reticle. The semiautomatic gas-operated rifle used the 7.62x54R round fed from a ten-round magazine. Reece had studied the rifle in depth when he had been part of a training element sent to Uzbekistan to teach a sniper course to their Spetsnaz. He remembered thinking it would be a good idea not to teach them too well, lest he or any of his Teammates end up in their sights on a future battlefield. The "snipers" he ended up teaching were actually "designated marksmen." Reece found that the SVD only ended up extending the range of the more common AK by a couple of hundred yards once he put one through the paces.

Almost seventy years old.

"Ah, sexy, yes?" Luka said, undulating his hips with a huge smile on his face.

Reece pushed the safety lever down and pulled the charging handle to the rear, locking it back on its empty magazine.

"Got rounds for these?" Reece asked.

"Rounds?"

"Cartridges."

"Cartridges? Bullets? Oh yeah, I got bullets," Luka said, reaching into the trunk and pulling out a cardboard box. He shook it. Reece could hear rounds rattling around.

Reece took the box, opened it, and inspected the cartridges. They were certainly not all from the same lot, but they appeared to be the correct caliber.

"They will work, yes?" Luka asked.

"They will," Reece said. He returned it to the trunk and removed a revolver from a worn leather holster.

"You like, yes?" Luka said.

Reece had handled and fired a Nagant M1895 revolver, but it had been a long time. Thomas Reece had taken one off a Soviet military advisor that his MACV-SOG reconnaissance team had killed in an ambush in Laos in 1971. He wasn't supposed to take it home. His team wasn't officially supposed to be in Laos either.

Most revolvers are designed with a gap between the cylinder holding the cartridges and the barrel, which allows high-pressure gases to escape after the shot is fired, resulting in noise from what is essentially a small explosion. This also makes them impossible to suppress. The seven-shot Nagant revolver was different in that it incorporated a gas seal, moving the cylinder forward and creating a seal that trapped the gases in the chamber when the shot was fired. This allowed the Nagant to be effectively used with a suppressor. A crude homemade version was screwed onto the end of the barrel.

A star with what looked like an arrow was engraved on the left side of the frame just above the wood grip. "1941" was engraved underneath it, which meant it was the double-action model, the single-action-only model having been discontinued in 1918. This particular revolver did not have a swing-out cylinder, so he swiveled the loading gate down, twisted the end of the ejection rod, rotated it toward him, and pushed it back to remove a cartridge. He turned it over to examine it. The 7.62x38R was distinctive in that the bullet was seated below the mouth of the casing, which appeared to be made of brass or copper-washed steel, indicating they were probably of Soviet origin. When fired the brass would expand, blocking any gases that might escape back toward the cylinder.

The former frogman remembered his father teaching him about the pistol's history before they shot it together for the first time, when Reece was in high school. What had stood out to the younger Reece was that Czar Nicholas II was a proponent of the Léon Nagant–designed pistol because it held more rounds than other revolvers, which he equated to an advantage on the field of battle. That the gas-seal design increased muzzle velocity was also appealing to the Russian Imperial Court. It was approved as the issued sidearm of the Russian Army. In an ironic twist of fate, the same pistol that the last emperor of Russia championed was also used to execute him, his wife, and their children after the Bolsheviks took power.

Reece reinserted the cartridge into the revolver and pushed the loading gate back into place.

"Is this ammo subsonic?"

"What do you mean?"

"Is it quiet?"

"Ah, yes, subsonic. Very quiet."

"Is there a place we can go confirm that and sight these in?" Reece asked.

"This is Montenegro. Of course, but it will cost you."

"Add it to my tab. There is something else."

"Oh?"

"How would you like to stay in Hotel Palata Venezia for a few days?"

"What?"

"Enjoy yourself. Stay in my room."

"What do you want me to do?"

"Stay at the hotel. Explore your city. But carry this phone with you everywhere you go," Reece said, handing his personal phone to the arms dealer. "Keep it on. Keep it charged."

"You want someone to think I am you?"

"That's right."

"And what if there is physical surveillance?" Luka asked, his English making a sudden improvement. "If you failed to notice, I may have an extra layer or two." Luka grabbed the considerable girth around his midsection to accentuate his point.

"Oh, there is physical surveillance, but we are going to take care of that in a few minutes."

"So that's it? Just drive around town and stay at the hotel?"

"There is one other thing."

"And what is that?"

"In four days, I want you to drive to the village of Provalija. Do you know where that is?"

"I know it. Almost a four-hour drive."

"When you get there, pull over and text this number," Reece said, handing him a piece of scrap paper with a U.S. cell phone number on it. "Text: 'I'm going in. I'll call you when it's over.' Then I want you to take a hammer or a rock and smash the phone until it's unrecognizable."

"And then?"

"Then drive home. Take the pieces with you and throw them in the garbage somewhere along the route."

"That's it?" Luka asked again.

"That's it."

"And what do I get for this service?"

"A few days at the Palata Venezia. Enjoy it. Bring your girlfriend, your wife, maybe both."

Luka laughed.

"I'll do it," he said, already thinking of the days in bed with one of his girlfriends and figuring out what he would tell his wife. "But it is going to cost you."

"How much?"

"My time is valuable. It's going to cost you twenty thousand euros."

"Done," Reece said.

Quickly backpedaling, knowing he should have asked for more, the man looked at Reece's wrist. "And that watch."

Reece looked down at his father's stainless-steel Rolex Submariner.

"Sorry."

"We get the knockoffs here," the man said. "All the girls know how to spot a fake."

"I see," Reece said.

"Watch and twenty thousand euros or no deal."

"How about this?" Reece offered. "Twenty-five thousand euros and when I get back to the States, I'll send you a Submariner."

The arms dealer eyed the man before him.

"There is no risk to you," Reece continued. "Walk and drive around town. In four days, drive to Provalija. Text the number I gave you and destroy the phone. Then get back to your girlfriend. Easy money."

"Usually I'm the one saying 'easy money' and it never is. That makes me question."

"Good point," Reece conceded. "Thirty thousand and a watch."

"You have yourself a deal," Luka said, sticking out his hand.

"And Luka, if I find out you don't send that text, I'll remove you from the face of the earth."

Luka swallowed.

"That won't be necessary."

"Just want us to understand one another," Reece said. "Oh, I'm also going to need a car, preferably an old one."

Reece looked at the Datsun.

Luka's frown turned to a smile.

"Have I got a deal for you, American."

"I'm sure you do. Now, let's go deal with my surveillance."

CHAPTER 72

JOVAN KUJOVIĆ LOOKED DOWN at his Samsung Galaxy. He loved playing Starblind but he needed to ensure his target had not moved, so he swiped it away and checked the map. A red dot marked the position of the man he had been hired to tail.

What is he doing down there? Maybe he's swimming?

He looked to be in good shape, so that was a possibility.

Kujović had parked his car just off the road and was alternating between his video game and the job he had been hired to do.

As a courier for the Nikšić Mob, he assisted the more senior members of the gang with smuggling drugs from Albania into Montenegro. They also dabbled in moving weapons and stolen luxury vehicles into Albania, in partnership with the Albanian Mafia, but it was the drugs that were the most profitable, especially heroin and cocaine. As a low-level courier, he had supplied a mysterious Syrian man with blond Russian girls and would occasionally run an errand for him. He always requested girls who could speak English. The Syrian paid well and sometimes Kujović could get a piece of the action when returning the girls to one of the brothels the Nikšić Mob ran in the city. It wasn't a bad arrangement.

When the Syrian had tasked him with this mission, he was not in a position to say no. The cash was good but more than that, the Syrian made him nervous. He was afraid to say no.

Soon he would complete his task and deliver the message.

The American made him nervous, too. He looked forward to the day when he would be rid of them both and could get back to moving the drugs that he would occasionally sample. They had enough police and government officials on the payroll to make the threat from law enforcement almost nonexistent. Rival gangs and syndicates were another story.

How long is he going to stay there? Kujović wondered.

He flipped back to the app.

Still by the river.

Even if Kujović's pistol had been in hand and not in the glove box, he still would not have had time to adjust and move it in the direction of the figure who opened the door and sat down in the passenger seat, a strange-looking revolver with a massive suppressor pointing at his chest.

The American.

"Hands on the wheel. You speak English?"

Kujović quickly put his hands on the wheel, perspiration starting to soak his shirt even in the cooler weather.

"Y-yes," he stammered.

"Keep your movements slow, Mr. Peugeot."

Kujović swallowed.

"In case you are familiar with this pistol, you will see the hammer is back in single-action mode, so I don't have the heavy trigger pull to contend with if I decide to put a bullet through your heart. Understand?"

Kujović nodded enthusiastically.

"Good. Now, tell me why you've been following me."

The Syrian had told him he would end up in this position and that his only job was to relay a message.

He started to speak in Serbo-Croatian.

"English," Reece said firmly.

"I am just to give you message."

"What message?"

"From the Syrian man."

"Tell me."

"It's in my pocket. Can I reach?"

"Slowly," Reece said.

Kujović very deliberately reached into his pocket and pulled out a piece of paper and handed it across the center console.

Reece took it and, without taking his eyes from the man across from him, asked, "What is it?"

"It's a map. To the Syrian's cabin in Žabljak. He wants to meet you there."

"When?"

"Five days."

Reece slid the note into his pocket.

"Anything else?"

"That is it, I swear! Please, don't kill me. I have a wife, daughters," the gangster lied.

Reece considered the man next to him. There were very practical reasons to kill him, just as there were practical reasons to let him live. Entanglements with local law enforcement would only hinder his mission to hunt down and put Nizar Kattan in the dirt.

"You caught me on a good day. I'm going to let you live."

Kujović felt his bladder loosen as his body involuntarily relaxed, his reptilian brain registering that he would live another day.

"Thank you. Thank you, American."

"Don't mistake this decision for weakness. If I see you on the battlefield again, I'll kill you."

As quickly as he had appeared, the American was gone.

Kujović waited another three hours in his Peugeot before he got the nerve to start the car and drive back to Ulcinj. During that time, he never once looked at his phone.

• • •

Twenty-five miles to the northwest, the weekly ferry from Bari, Italy, was docking in Bar, Montenegro. It made the eleven-hour journey once a week, weather permitting, one of only a few ferry routes to connect Italy with its Balkan neighbors across the Adriatic.

Thick lines were thrown over pylons and the ferry came to rest against the pier. Among the throngs of people disembarking was a man in a wheelchair. He rolled down the gangplank, a small bag in his lap. He waited in line to show his Italian ID card to the customs agent, who entered his information into a database. It came back clean, just as Reece said it would, and he was allowed entry. Without asking for any assistance, he wheeled through the ferry terminal and got into line to catch a taxi.

CHAPTER 73

Dinaric Alps, Montenegro

NIZAR HIT END ON Le Drian's phone and handed it back. They were sitting in an old Series I Land Rover off a dirt road, surrounded by rocks and trees in the Durmitor mountains.

He had been receiving updates on Reece's geolocational data in his phone through the Russian Internet Research Agency. The former SEAL had spent the past four days in the Hotel Palata Venezia, hardly leaving his room. Earlier that morning they had received notice that Reece was moving north.

"It is time to get in position. He sent a text to the United States from Provalija and then they lost the signal."

"He's close," Le Drian commented.

"He is, but our decoy is in place with your old phone. He won't go to the cabin. He will come here. More specifically, he will find a shooting position just below that ridgeline I showed you on your map. He is getting updates on that phone, just as we have been on his. He will find his position, glass until he finds our decoy, and then take his shots. That is where you intercept him."

"And if I don't?"

"If you don't then I am across the canyon and will finish the job, sniper to sniper, as it should be. If I don't find him as he gets into position, I'll find him when he shoots. If you have not taken him out by then, you will hear the shot and can move to intercept. James Reece is not leaving these mountains alive."

They exited the vehicle and shouldered their packs. Kattan's sniper rifle was strapped to the outside, the suppressed VSS Vintorez in his hands. Le Drian held the Yugoslavian Kalashnikov.

"Meet you back here when it's done," Le Drian said.

"*Bonne chance,*" Kattan said.

Good luck in French.

The Syrian continued to surprise the Foreign Legion sergeant.

Le Drian watched as the sniper moved across the dirt road and up a game trail. Before he disappeared into the bush, the Frenchman wondered if there might be another reason he was on the same mountainside as their target.

• • •

Reece studied his map, adjusted his compass, and took a bearing. No GPS on this one. He knew where he was going.

He had been in the mountains for four days, getting to know them, making them his home. The sights, sounds, smells, and tastes of the region were now a part of him. The old Dragunov felt natural to him as well. He knew its capabilities and, more importantly, he knew its limitations, essential factors to understand in your rifle, in yourself, and in your enemy.

Alone in the mountains with a rifle, he was at home.

He looked down at the KryptAll. Alice had geolocated the target phone in a stationary position across the canyon. It had moved into place earlier that morning and had not stirred since.

Reece was focused. He knew his capabilities and he knew his limitations. The question was, did his enemy?

• • •

For Nizar, it wasn't the waiting that wore on him. He had the hunter's patience. It was the thinking, the maneuvering, the double guessing. It was knowing and studying his prey, his target, and attempting to anticipate how much his adversary had studied him in the deadliest game of all.

Nizar had laid the trap and drawn in his prey. Americans may be good on the gun, but they were lazy. They had become too comfortable. He had read that it was oftentimes called imperial hubris. How else could the country with the most technologically advanced guns, bombs, aircraft, ships, submarines, and satellites have been sent running by men with AKs and IEDs from the mountains of Afghanistan and the cities and deserts of Iraq? That same affliction would be the end of James Reece as well. The American technology that was guiding Reece to his final shooting position would put him directly in the Syrian's crosshairs.

Nizar knew the terrain. He knew the weather patterns in and out of the valley. He knew the birds, the red and roe deer, the Balkan chamois, brown bears, lynxes, wolves, golden jackals, the shifting winds, and the smells. Reece was an outsider, an alien, an intruder on foreign land. He had been tricked into entering unfamiliar territory, hunting a quarry whose skills he underestimated and whose motivations he could not fathom. America and those who fought for her were in decline. They had been lured into a strategic ambush, wasted twenty years of blood and fortune, only to retreat in an embarrassing defeat, leaving their enemy better armed and with a standing on the world stage they could only have dreamt about prior to 9/11. The great Osama had won, even in death. Nizar scoffed at the word *great.* Osama had fallen victim to the same hubris as the Americans and it had led to his execution. The "Manhattan attack," as he had heard it called, was intended to push the United States from the Middle East, to topple apostate regimes propped up by *infidels* on holy land. The exact opposite had happened, with

American influence only intensifying in the region. Of course, bin Laden had spun it years later in a statement claiming that "bleeding America to the point of bankruptcy" had been his goal from the beginning. *Lies.* He had died not bravely waging his jihad. He had been assassinated, hiding in a suburban compound, putting up no resistance even though he had a rifle in the room in which he was killed. The man who changed the course of history was a fraud. Nizar would no longer serve the likes of zealots who turned out to be nothing more than hypocrites. But Osama had inadvertently drawn the United States into the Great Game, and the mujahideen along with the mountain tribesmen of the Hindu Kush had a history of sending those weak of mind and spirit back to from whence they came.

James Reece was no different. He had made the same mistake. And he was about to pay with his life.

CHAPTER 74

REECE MOVED METHODICALLY THROUGH the mountains. He was in his element. One game trail would intersect with another as he worked his way upward. High ground. The message had been delivered. The challenge accepted. Only one of them would leave this valley alive. Reece was on unfamiliar terrain, but that was not a new experience for the former SEAL. He was a warrior, a hunter, a sniper, a killer of men. He was comfortable being uncomfortable.

His legs burned with the exertion at altitude. He was alive and on the hunt.

But there was another sniper in these mountains, another killer of men, a triggerman who was also calculating distances, winds, altitude, and barometric pressures. A man who was focused on outthinking his prey.

Reece briefly thought of George Patton reading Erwin Rommel's *Infantry Attacks* prior to defeating the German general in the North African desert.

Nizar had not written a book for Reece to read, but Reece knew him just as if he had.

Alice had pinpointed the location of Le Drian's cell phone and passed it to Reece via the KryptAll device she had sent him in Israel. The Legionnaire's phone was now stationary across the valley. Was the

Frenchman acting as Kattan's spotter? Or was the Syrian angling for an advantage?

Nizar Kattan was a hunter of men as well.

They were snipers. And one of them was going to die.

• • •

Nizar was on his optics. He understood the importance of what he knew the Americans called "good glass" and the Nightforce scope with its Horus TREMOR3 illuminated reticle certainly qualified.

The Syrian knew that Reece would do a map study of the area, using topographic maps and Google Earth. He would pinpoint multiple locations and prioritize them as Nizar's probable sniper hide site. He would set up using natural vegetation and do exactly what Nizar was now doing, burning through the foliage, trees, and shrubs, looking for anything unnatural that would give away the position of the man he wanted to kill.

What Reece didn't know was that Nizar had done the same thing. He had put himself in the American's shoes and plotted those same points, using the same maps and technology. Nizar had then intentionally chosen what would seemingly be a tactically disadvantageous position.

He had also set up a dummy location. Hidden deep in the trees was a rifle obscured by natural vegetation, a human shape behind it, a crazy old man who lived in the mountains and whom no one would miss for months. As an added benefit, the old man was light and frail. Packing the body in had been difficult but not impossible, though it had been harder than Nizar had anticipated to position it behind the rifle with rigor mortis setting in. He had gotten as close as he could in the old Land Rover, put the old man on a sled normally reserved for hauling firewood in winter, and dragged him into the mountains. Even with Le Drian's help it had been taxing. The lime with which they had doused the body would keep the jackals away, at least for as long as it took to play its part. He could see it from his position if he strained his neck to look northwest. The crown, the muzzle end of the barrel, was just visible if one knew what to look for, if one was a sniper. It could not look too obvious. Nizar had been conflicted about leaving the phone there as part of the decoy. Was it too obvious? Or would Reece conclude that Nizar was with Le Drian, with the Frenchman acting as security or as a spotter? A professional like Reece might have predicted a move like this. But as with any good plan, Nizar had contingencies. In this case, he had two.

The odds were stacked against the foreigner. If Nizar's bullet didn't take Reece down, there were two other options the SEAL would not anticipate. The time was close. Soon Reece would be dead, and Nizar would have another eight million dollars with which to disappear and start a new life.

CHAPTER 75

REECE DROPPED INTO THE prone about a hundred yards off from what was to be his final shooting position. He pressed his face into the cold but not yet frozen soil, breathing in the essence of the earth. He closed his eyes and listened, heightening his other senses. Opening his eyes, he remained still for another hour, just listening, smelling, slowly scanning the area, becoming a part of it.

He then rolled to his side and removed the classic Soviet-era rifle from his pack. He moved the selector to fire and pulled back on the charging handle to confirm that a round was chambered, before putting the rifle back on safe. He studied the area ahead through binoculars, examining the position from which he would take his shot, taking note of the surroundings. He then carefully dug into his pack and tied in the natural vegetation he had collected over the last two hours of movement. With rubber bands and thin zip-ties he attached the "veg" to his bipod, along the sides of his scope and into his sniper veil to give the camouflage depth. When he was satisfied, he left his pack behind and began to crawl toward his perch.

• • •

Nizar burned through the vegetation in the areas he had determined would be Reece's probable shooting positions. Knowing his enemy's last known location, and that he was tracking the phone with the decoy, was a distinct advantage. Nizar also knew the mountains. *Home field advantage,* one of the prostitutes who helped him improve his English had once said.

Each of the areas he studied looked the same. No changes. That would be the tell. *Changes.* Variations in color, fading leaves that should be green, symmetrical shapes foreign to the natural world. He had learned a lot from the *Shishani* before he had killed him, after he had pressed the trigger on his CheyTac M200 and sent a 350-grain bullet on just over a three-second flight into the man James Reece had come to avenge. Life was mysterious that way. The rifleman he now knew as Fredrick Strain had brought his life and Reece's to a crossroads. That copper projectile had given Nizar a chance at a life he never believed could be within his reach as a boy soldier in his native Syria. It was not *qadar,* the Islamic concept of fate he had learned as part of *aqidah* in his youth. He had not believed in the final of Islam's Six Articles of Faith then, and the intervening years had done nothing to change his opinion. Fate was not the will of Allah. That ancient religion, like all religions, was only intended to keep the people in line. To keep them obedient. *The Five Pillars.* All they did was relegate the masses to poverty and misery. There was no God. There was only man and rifle.

CHAPTER 76

JEAN-PIERRE LE DRIAN WAS also in his element, though it had been a long time since he had tracked someone not on African soil. The payment from Nizar was generous, as was the bonus if he was the one to take the life of James Reece. He wanted to get it done. To get out of the cold and back to the Africa that now felt more like home than his native France.

He had learned the basics of tracking in his training with the Legion, but it was in Africa where he had truly developed the skill, learning from those who put food on the table through their ability to track plains game, and then transitioned those skills to the tracking of man in the waning days of the bush wars. Le Drian envied those who got to experience Africa in the heyday, in the 1960s and 1970s when it was what he knew the Americans liked to call the "Wild West." What he would have given to have lived back then. No rules. Living, fighting, killing in its purest form.

The feeling he had now was close. He was man tracking. Like the Selous Scouts or Grey's Scouts of old, he was on the track. *Spoor.* But not spoor of an animal. This one could think. He could reason. What he didn't know was that Le Drian was on his trail. The Frenchman could take his time. Don't rush. Find the spoor, stop, look, listen, smell, feel. Where would you go next if you were James Reece? Move forward, slowly, cautiously, Kalashnikov at the ready.

• • •

James Reece settled in behind the rifle, "building his house" as he had learned to do all those years ago. He was in the kill zone. He wished Freddy was with him, spotting, providing security. He thought of his men, slaughtered in the mountains of Afghanistan, his brothers in arms lying dead in the darkness. He had avenged them, just as he was avenging Freddy. He remembered his old sniper school partner, talking him through the shot: *slow and steady, brother, slow and steady.* Reece had always been the better shot, but when it came to the art and science of sniping, the spotter was the most valuable member of the team. Freddy was the spotter. That was where he excelled.

Talk to me, brother.

Freddy beside him on a spotting scope, a building in Iraq.

You know what to do, brother. Build that house. Solid. Trust the acceptable reticle movement. Breathing. It's all about that breathing and that slow trigger press to the rear. When the time is right. When you have your target.

I'm on it, Freddy.

I don't need to tell you, but just in case: Press the trigger, don't forget to follow through, ride the bull, call your shot, and get ready to reengage.

Reece gave an imperceptible nod.

You are the best I've ever worked with, Freddy said. *No one better behind the glass. Make sure you are doing this for the right reason.*

Reece closed his eyes. *What?*

The right reason.

Breathe. It's time to work.

I'm gone, Reece. Your Team is gone. I know what you did for Sam. He's going to be taken care of because of you. Who knows if I could have done that had I lived? You did it, brother. Joanie doesn't know who deposited that money, but I do.

Not now, Freddy.

Reece, if you get this done, do me a favor.

What?

Live.

What?

Live. Not in the past. Not on that rooftop in Odessa. Not on a mountain in Afghanistan. Not in the house where your family was murdered. Live in the moment. Be present. Do it for me and all those who love you. Do it for Katie.

I need to focus. Find my target.

Forgive.

What are you talking about? Forgive what?

Forgive Nizar. Forgive yourself. Live.

Reece turned his head.

Freddy was gone. Reece was not in Ramadi. He was back in Montenegro. All that was left were the rocks and trees of the Montenegrin mountains. The rotting wood, the birds, the breeze. His friend had vanished. Reece was back on mission. Back where he belonged. Behind the rifle.

CHAPTER 77

LE DRIAN PUSHED HIMSELF forward, driven not just by the money, though as a mercenary that was a large part of it. He was also driven by the challenge. James Reece. *Motherfuckin' James Reece.*

If you put this guy down you will get a payday and you will be the man who did what even the U.S. government couldn't pull off and, if rumors were true, what the Russians couldn't do, either.

Le Drian might even find his name in a book. Maybe he would write his own, from exile. Shit, maybe he'd write a few like Mad Mike Hoare had done back in the day.

Later. First kill this son of a bitch.

Le Drian stopped short. What was that?

Up ahead, an unnatural shape. A pack.

The Frenchman brought up the AK and slowly went to a knee. Had he the indigenous man-trackers from Africa with him, he would have flankers to signal. He was on his own now. Well, not exactly. There was another man on the mountain with a rifle hunting the former SEAL. But it was Le Drian who had found him. The Frenchman's eyes scanned ahead.

Do not rush. Reece is a sniper. He will be taking his time. He knows we are out here, but he does not know he is being tracked. He is focused on another threat and he thinks that my phone in the decoy is his target.

The French Foreign Legion sniper training took over, as he scanned slowly for the target for the first five meters, then to ten meters, his eyes shifting back and forth in concert with the barrel of the Kalashnikov. Reece's tracks had changed. Even from a distance Le Drian could tell that Reece had dropped his pack and crawled forward into a shooting position with just his rifle. Le Drian's heart rate increased, a cold sweat seeping through his skin. The kill was close. Just a few more yards and James Reece would be in his sights.

The fool. That's what happened when you got emotional in this business. You ended up dead.

Should I shoot him from here? Or get closer?

Don't be an idiot. Use the AK. Shoot as soon as you—

There!

A rifle, vegetation . . .

But no Reece.

In the instant that Le Drian realized what was happening he began to spin to his six o'clock but froze when a hushed voice pierced the still, cold air.

"Drop it."

"Fuck!"

"Put the rifle on the ground and turn around."

Action being faster than reaction, had Le Drian been facing the other direction he would have made a move, knowing he had a better than average chance of getting a shot off before his adversary. But he was not facing the sniper. He had walked right into the trap.

What did he have to work with?

He had information. That information was now his weapon. He owed no loyalty to Nizar. Le Drian was a mercenary. Mercenaries worked for money and, in this situation, he had something of value to sell.

"Okay, Mr. Reece, I am putting it down."

He was already in the kneeling position, so the rifle did not have far to go.

When it was on the ground, Le Drian slowly raised his hands above his head.

"May I turn?"

"You may." The voice was devoid of emotion. It was coarse. Rough. Resolved.

Le Drian swallowed and rotated around, still on his knees.

Merde.

What he saw made his eyes go wide with terror.

The man before him looked like he was a part of the land, an animal, a savage. Even more disconcerting was that he appeared at peace.

"Mr. Reece, I am Jean-Pierre Le Drian. I am a soldier, like you."

"I know who you are. You're a merc. You shot a friend of mine out of the sky. Killed her along with a hundred and twenty-eight innocent people. You're no soldier."

"And you? What are you?"

"You won't be of this earth long enough to find out."

Le Drian's eyes moved to Reece's hands. Both were at his sides. One held a menacing-looking tomahawk with a protruding front spike the likes of which Le Drian had never seen before. In the other he held a small pistol that Le Drian recognized as an old Nagant with a suppressor.

"Mr. Reece, we can make a deal, yes? I know where Nizar is. I know his plan. I can help you."

There was no flash of consideration, no moment of reflection. Reece's eyes remained cold, calculated. There was but one thing on his mind. Death.

"If you kill me, Mr. Reece, your odds of taking Nizar go down dramatically."

"They don't."

Le Drian took a breath, coming to terms with what was going to happen.

Already on his knees, he brought his hands together and began to recite the Lord's Prayer.

". . . and lead us not into temptation, but deliver us from evil. For thine is the kingdom, the power, and the glory. For ever and ever."

The mercenary paused.

"Amen."

When he opened his eyes, Reece was still standing there. His executioner had not moved.

"Blade or bullet?"

"Are you really going to let me choose?"

"No."

Reece raised his pistol and put one suppressed 7.62x38R round into the legionnaire's face.

CHAPTER 78

THE SNIPER CONTINUED TO scan. Smoothly. Methodically. This part of the game was all about patience. If he heard the report of a 7.62x39, he would know that the Frenchman had found his mark. Nizar thought about killing Le Drian rather than paying him, just as he had with his mentor, the master sniper known as the *Shishani*. It's possible the Frenchman would anticipate that move and disappear, only to reemerge and hunt down Nizar if the payment didn't come through.

If I have him in my scope after I kill Reece, I'll take him down. If he's smart enough to disappear, he'll get his payment.

Nizar wondered if he would kill twice this day.

He froze.

A change.

Subtle, but a change nonetheless.

Green against a rock where there had not been green an hour ago.

Nizar slowly adjusted the focus in and out to burn through the vegetation with his binoculars. Hard to tell but something was different.

An elbow.

The crown of a barrel.

It was pointing across the valley but not at Nizar. It was aiming directly at the dummy position Nizar had set up.

Move fast, but not too fast, Nizar, he heard the *Shishani* caution him.

At any moment Reece could figure out that the man in his sights was a decoy. Time became of the essence.

Would Reece rush the shot?

No. He was a sniper like Nizar; a master of his craft.

Only control what you can control, Nizar, he heard the *Shishani* advise.

He pushed thoughts of the old sniper out of his mind.

Master Sniper? I outwitted you and I've outwitted James Reece.

He thought of the millions that would soon be transferred into his account through the Montenegrin construction corporation and he thought of where he would go. Argentina? Thailand? Probably Thailand. If he ever got tired of Thai girls, he could make a base in Argentina. Besides, both Thai and Russian hookers were a commodity the world over.

Not now, Nizar, make this shot and end it.

Behind the scope, he made his elevation adjustment and a micro-adjustment to his focus knob and parallax, slowly zooming in on the barrel and then following it back to the elbow. Reece was still pointing at the decoy.

Yes, adjust from here. Barrel, elbow, that means the head is right about... there... and the body...

The shot took Nizar by surprise even though the dummy location was set up for just this purpose. The bullet flew harmlessly across the valley and quite probably into the already dead man that Nizar had camouflaged behind the rifle.

Nizar made a final analysis of the constantly changing environmental factors, lastly evaluating the swirling winds. He noted the leaves next to his target's position, which indicated the wind was moving left to right closest to Reece, where it was most likely to affect the bullet. Holding to the left for wind, Nizar took a deliberate breath, evenly exhaling until he hit the bottom of his natural respiratory pause. Then he pressed back on the trigger.

CHAPTER 79

THE SHOT EXPLODED ACROSS the valley. 1,180 meters. Nizar called his impact. *Center.* He racked the bolt on his rifle, settled back on the target, and sent a second round. *Center.* He racked the action again, adjusted to where Reece's head would be, went through his shot sequence, and pressed the trigger again. He moved the reticle back to Reece's center mass, cheating a bit toward the head to put his bullet into his target's upper thorax, the heart and lungs. *Center.* Opening the bolt, he smoothly reloaded with the four bullets he had neatly arranged to his right, and prepared to reengage.

No movement.

Nizar reached up to the focus dial on his scope and moved it ever so slightly back and forth in an attempt to confirm his hits.

What's that?

He moved back to the elbow that had now fallen away from the body, exposing a silver watch. Reece wore a stainless-steel Rolex. His target package had been specific.

He stayed focused on the wrist and watch for ten minutes.

No movement.

He moved his scope around the target area.

A symmetrical shape. A shoe?

Yes.

Nizar focused in.

A Salomon shoe so popular with American special operators.

He focused on the shoe for what must have been fifteen minutes.

Still no movement.

Nizar almost couldn't believe it.

Fighting the urge a hunter has to confirm his kill, he stayed in position, switching from his scope to binoculars.

Watch and boot in the same positions.

He fought to control his breathing.

James Reece dead.

Money in the account.

One loose end with Le Drian. Pay or kill: The choice was the Frenchman's.

The sniper waited another forty-five minutes. No sign of moment. No sign of life.

It was time to disappear.

Nizar checked that his rifle was on safe, stuffed his binoculars beneath his shirt, and pushed himself backward out of his hide site in the side of the mountain, maneuvering into a position behind a large rock, in the "dead space" out of sight from anyone observing him from afar. He stretched his legs and forced blood back into extremities, which had cramped up from holding position for so long.

He collected himself faster than he would have thought. The implications of killing James Reece and becoming wealthy beyond his expectations warmed his chilled bones.

Confirm the kill, get off the mountain, and then leave this life behind.

Nizar secured the Orsis T-5000 in his pack, the barrel protruding above his head. He stood, slung, and adjusted the pack, then picked up the integrally suppressed Soviet Vintorez rifle and began to make his way toward the dirt road where he had parked the old Land Rover.

Thailand awaits.

CHAPTER 80

NIZAR FORCED HIMSELF TO work his way deliberately down the mountain toward his vehicle. No trails existed in this corner of Montenegro and the sniper was careful to take a circuitous route instead of following the tracks he had left on his way in, just in case the French mercenary had designs on taking him out. That was not likely; it was much more likely the other way around, which Nizar was sure the Frenchman recognized. To get paid, Nizar needed to live. The Frenchman would probably disappear, stay out of Nizar's sights, accept payment, and return to his beloved Africa. But this was a thinking man's game. Those who believed it was only about triggers and optics didn't last long. Just in case Le Drian had any ideas, Nizar had a contingency plan in place.

The Syrian caught sight of the road about two kilometers from where he had parked his truck. Even though his old 1966 Series I Land Rover was always breaking down, the engine was still simple enough that Nizar could diagnose the issue and fix it himself. It got him where he needed to go on the rutted-out roads of the Durmitor mountain region.

He paralleled the dirt road until he was almost opposite the vehicle. Once again, he exercised a sniper's patience and nestled into the brush, putting the Vintorez on the ground and bringing the old Leica binoculars to his eyes. He observed the vehicle for any signs that it had been tampered with. He always left it dirty for just this purpose; easier to see handprints that didn't belong. The ground around it was absent of tracks that were not there when he left and the surrounding hillsides were clear of any signs that there was a person or team lying in wait.

This was his territory. The Montenegrin mafia saw to it that he was protected here. They were the de facto government of Montenegro, but Nizar had not lived this long by trusting those within his sphere. He continued to watch the truck and surrounding area for another hour. Satisfied all was as it should be, he worked his way down to the vehicle.

He had called it; the Frenchman was nowhere to be seen. The mercenary was smarter than he looked. Nizar would not need to exercise his contingency plan after all.

He opened the passenger-side door of the right-side-drive Land Rover and unslung his pack with the T-5000 rifle. He set it upright on the floorboards, and closed the door. Looking back up at the surrounding hillsides, Vintorez in hand, he walked around the front of the vehicle and opened the door. He slid the Soviet-era rifle next to his seat and was about to step in when he sensed he was not alone.

He turned to his left.

There in the road was a *jinn*—a supernatural creature he had long ago relegated to the trash with the rest of the Quranic teachings of his youth. Those teachings came back to him now.

Standing in front of him was a ghost, an apparition holding a Kalashnikov.

CHAPTER 81

NIZAR'S DISBELIEF QUICKLY SWITCHED gears to calculations of time, speed, and accuracy. Sniper rifle in the passenger seat, VSS Vintorez muzzle down against the far side of the driver's seat. Reece was about ten meters away. He held the Kalashnikov, Le Drian's Kalashnikov, by its pistol grip. The rifle was slung and pointed at the ground.

Maybe there is time to go for the weapon?

Is Reece a vision?

How could this be?

Leaving the door open, Nizar turned to face the man he thought he had sent to the grave, a grudging sense of wonder replacing the disbelief.

"You continue to prove harder to kill than one would expect," Nizar said.

Keep him standing there. There is one last option.

"Who did I kill on the mountain?" Nizar asked. "I didn't miss."

Reece let a small pack slide from his shoulder

Nizar thought of his plan, an understanding coming to him as he studied his adversary, moving from his weapon to his face and then to Reece's clothes. The clothes he had last seen on Jean-Pierre Le Drian. Reece reached in the pack and pulled out the mercenary's head, tossing it to the dirt at Nizar's feet.

The Syrian stared into the one upturned eye of the man he had hired to track down and kill the SEAL who now stood before him, seemingly holding the upper hand. One of the mercenary's eyes was gone, replaced by an entry wound. The low-velocity bullet had entered through the left eye, expanded, torn through Le Drian's brain, and taken a large section of the back skull with it as it exited, giving the head a lopsided shape where it had caved in. Nizar looked back to the American.

Stall. There is one last contingency.

"I warned him not to, what is the American word, *underestimate* you. It appears I should have taken my own advice."

"Perhaps," Reece said.

"How did you fire that shot? Had you not fired, I might have given it a bit more time to confirm you were behind that Dragunov."

Reece reached into his pocket and pulled out a knotted ball of twine.

Nizar shook his head.

"And the watch?"

"It's on Le Drian's other arm, which is still next to my rifle. Don't worry, I'll be going back to collect it."

"That Rolex was a nice touch. You got me with the watch trick. It's not personal, you know. It's business," Nizar said, changing the direction of the conversation.

"It's personal to me."

"Ah yes, your friend. The SEAL. Fredrick. I read his name in the target package."

"That's right, Senior Chief Fredrick Strain. Freddy. This is his tomahawk," Reece said, reaching behind his belt and unsheathing the ancient weapon.

"I thought a fellow sniper would want to take me the same way I took your friend."

"You thought wrong." Reece pushed the Kalashnikov to his left side and dropped the Winkler into his right hand.

"Is this how you killed Le Drian?"

"No. He got a bullet to the face. This is for you," Reece said, stepping forward to snatch the soul of the man who had killed his friend and Teammate.

Nizar held up his hand, but not toward Reece; instead it was toward the tree line to the east.

"Before you kill me, you should remember. I too am a sniper, and I too can plan for contingencies." Nizar turned his head to the left and into the thicket just off the road.

Reece's eyes followed, right into the barrel of an AK.

The man holding it knew enough to stay behind the cover of a thick tree, just the rifle and the side of his head against the stock, his right eye sighting down the irons. Even slightly obscured, Reece recognized the face of the man from the silver Peugeot, the man Reece had let live.

CHAPTER 82

"IT SEEMS AS THOUGH I have outplayed you, Commander Reece," Nizar said, his left hand up, holding off his shooter for the time being. "You will soon join your friend, Freddy. What was he doing on that roof in Odessa? It was supposed to be someone else; a Georgian, if memory serves."

"He was doing his job."

"Ah yes, you Americans and your sense of duty. I've studied it. Commendable in some regards. It did make this next phase of my life possible, so perhaps I should thank you."

"What part?"

"The part where I leave this." Nizar moved his hands, gesturing to all around him. "Where this life becomes my past."

Reece's face had not changed since their eyes had first met.

He has to know he's about to die, Nizar thought. *Where is the fear?*

"Was your plan to do this forever?" Nizar asked.

"No. Just until I killed you."

"Well, I do hate to disappoint. It seems like imperial hubris is not just an ailment of your ruling class. We are more alike than you think, Mr. Reece."

Nizar saw the change. A flicker of recognition in Reece's eyes. *We are the same.*

"Good-bye, Mr. Reece. *Ma'a salama.* Or as my former Russian employers would say, *Da svidania.*"

"Nizar."

"Yes?"

"Remember what you said about contingencies?"

Instant fear, recognition, anger, and surprise flashed across Nizar's face as he dropped his hand and yelled, "*Qutil!*"—"shoot"—to the man behind the tree.

The snap of a bullet breaking the sound barrier registered before the reverberations of the shot echoed off the canyon walls, but not before the side of Jovan Kujović's head caved in, a pink and gray mist left hanging momentarily in the cold air as his body dropped straight to the earth.

CHAPTER 83

NIZAR JUMPED AS THE bullet snapped across the road and put his last contingency in the ground. Reece did not flinch. His eyes were on Nizar, ensuring he didn't go for the weapon in the Land Rover, ready to raise and fire the Kalashnikov if he made a move.

Nizar turned from his dead asset back to Reece. A fear he had not known since his first firefights in Syria as a boy began to take hold.

Where did that bullet come from?

Slowly raising his hands, he fought for the words that might spare his life even as he resigned himself to his fate.

"I can be valuable to you, to your intelligence services."

Reece didn't acknowledge the offer, walking toward the man he had hunted across the globe.

Think, Nizar.

"I am not the only one who wants you dead, Mr. Reece. I was on the helicopter with you in Africa. That local security man was aiming for you, not me."

Undeterred, Reece continued his approach.

"Why does everyone want you dead, Mr. Reece? The Russians! Why do they want you dead?"

Reece pressed forward. All that mattered was putting Nizar in the ground.

"This was Freddy's Team axe. He gave it to me right before you killed him."

"I will not beg for my life, Mr. Reece. You know I can offer your government information on organized crime syndicates in Montenegro, Russia, Europe, and the United States. Terrorist organizations, drug cartels, human trafficking syndicates."

There is power in forgiveness. Reece heard Caroline Hastings's admonition in his head as he walked toward his target.

"What?" Nizar said, puzzled.

Reece paused for a moment. Freddy's words to him on the mountain were coming back to him.

Forgive. Forgive Nizar. Forgive yourself. Live.

Nizar's eyes went to the Vintorez. He lunged, catching a blur of movement as Reece closed the distance.

Nizar felt the blade impact his shoulder, sending him stumbling partway into the driver's seat, and pain of flesh and bone giving way to Reece's wrath sent his body into instant shock. That recognition was followed by an unfamiliar heavy pressure across his stomach as the front spike of the tomahawk ripped across his abdomen.

He was being disemboweled.

I can reach it.

His dive for the rifle was stopped short as Reece adjusted levels and tore the primal weapon across Nizar's upper right leg, slicing through the femoral artery and dropping the Syrian to his knees against the truck.

Nizar slumped to the dirt, leaning against the faded green vehicle and watching the blood spurt from his leg, knowing that without a tourniquet he would be dead in minutes. He felt an odd sensation as he watched his intestines sliding from his stomach and mixing with the soil of his adopted land, into the dark blood that was now pooling around him. He felt cold. It took all his effort to raise his head and look into the eyes of the specter of death who had come for him in the form of a sniper, a sniper who had outthought him by not playing the same game.

As his strength waned, the evening clouds cast his executioner in deep shadow. Nizar watched as Reece hit the pommel of his axe against his thigh, moving the weapon into a hammer grip. His breath coming in short gasps, he saw the American's lips move.

"What?" Nizar whispered.

"I forgive you," Reece said.

Confused, Nizar looked up in time to see the leading edge of the Sayoc 'hawk slice through the cold mountain air.

No soul may die except with God's permission at a predestined time . . .

His final thought was of this Quranic teaching from his youth. The nonbeliever wondering if he was destined for *Jannah* or *Jahannam.* Heaven or Hell.

The forward edge of the tomahawk impacted the center of Nizar's head and split his skull in two. He was dead before the blade came to rest, catching in the meat, sinew, and bone of his throat and spine.

Reece paused for a moment, thinking of Joanie and his words when she had met him on the tarmac at Andrews.

I'll find who did this, Joanie. I'll find everyone responsible. I promise.

As Reece picked up his foot, placed it on Nizar's chest, and violently twisted the 'hawk to remove it from the bone and brain matter that held it fast, he heard Joanie's response echo through his soul.

I know, she had said.

Reece wiped the blade on Nizar's body and sheathed it.

It was done.

The man who ensured that Freddy would never walk through the door to hold his wife and kids again, who left his widow to care for their special needs child, was dead.

First dig two graves . . .

Reece took the Vintorez from the driver's seat, rocked the magazine out, and pressed down on the top round before reinserting it and performing a press check. He then walked to the dead body by the tree, took the AK, checked its status, removed the magazine, and put it in his pocket. He ejected the round from the chamber and pushed it into the magazine before flinging the weapon into the forest. Returning to the vehicle, he dragged Nizar's body into the tree line.

Only then did he look to the hillside hide site five hundred yards away and start his hike to where he had placed the man in the wheelchair with the Mosin-Nagant rifle four days earlier.

CHAPTER 84

Gorky Park, Moscow, Russia

MIKHAIL GROMYKO KEPT THE Moskva River on his right as he worked his way deeper into Gorky Park, hands in his pockets to ward off the chill. The cold had not used to bother him this much. Maybe it was his aging bones?

Maybe it's the cancer.

The director of the SVR shook off thoughts of his mortality and turned up his collar. He had crossed the river from which the city took its name over the Pushkinsky Pedestrian Bridge, using its open-air walkway, noting that the water that flowed through Moscow would eventually connect to the Volga and make its way to the Caspian Sea. He had been getting his exercise while practicing the tradecraft of his youth. The discipline to always plan and utilize surveillance detection routes was his responsibility as a professional. Never failing himself or a foreign asset by getting lazy is what had kept him alive.

Perhaps Dashkov was right; maybe it was time for him to get a protection detail, enjoy the time he had left. The doctor was confident that he had years to live with the proper treatments. Receiving them in Moscow in secret was another matter. It might be time to leave the Russian capital for Switzerland and get his treatments on the shores of Lake Zurich. But he couldn't leave Moscow, could he? He had devoted his life to

Mother Russia. Or had he devoted that life to power? Ah, Kissinger, he was right. *Power is the ultimate aphrodisiac.* Would he even be allowed to leave? He still had secrets locked away in his head, secrets that would make some, including Dashkov and the president, nervous.

Gromyko peered across the path to a large amphitheater. Empty tonight. His oval lenses had slid down the bridge of his nose and he adjusted his glasses for what seemed like the hundredth time that evening. He would have to get a new set that would stay on his ever-thinning face.

The park had another thirty minutes until it shut down for the night. The old spy knew its paths by heart. Nothing appeared out of place. Even though it had been cleaned up and modernized in recent years, with the prostitutes, carnival rides, decrepit structures, and drug dealers replaced by skateboarders, cafés, playgrounds, and museums, there remained dark corners where one could meet in private. The hunting lodge of Count Orlov, Trinity Church, and the Belaya Ladya chess club still graced its grounds but so did trendy restaurants, a movie theater, and an ice rink. He did miss the days before the Internet and algorithms, days when a clever intellect and gut instinct were what separated the great from the good, and oftentimes the great from the dead.

They had not heard back from Nizar Kattan. That was not entirely unusual or unexpected. The sniper had a reputation for strict adherence to operational security protocols, but Gromyko *had* expected to hear from the Frenchman. They had both gone dark. James Reece had not appeared on any facial recognition databases monitored by the Internet Research Agency, which was constantly scanning airports, train stations, and ports and traffic and security cameras. Reece's phone had been active in Ulcinj for a few days after his arrival. Geolocational tracking data collected by the Federal Protective Service's Special Communications and Information Service, better known as Spetssviaz, indicated that Reece had stayed at the Hotel Palata Venezia for four days before driving north. He sent a text message to Victor Rodriguez at the CIA from just outside the village of Provalija, at which point the signal had gone dark. Kattan and Le Drian were already in position, waiting for their prey to enter the kill zone. Spetssviaz was tasked with the collection and analysis of foreign communications and signals intelligence. It had once fallen under Dashkov's Federal Security Service, the FSB, and though it was now the purview of the FSO, the Federal Protective Service, the FSB director still maintained official and unofficial ties to what was the Russian version of the NSA.

Gromyko veered off the Pushkinskaya Embankment and took a trail into the heart of Gorky Park. There were sections that made one forget for a moment that they were in the middle of one of the largest and most populous cities on earth.

Dashkov had requested the meeting. He had beaten Gromyko to it. An in-person meeting away from the prying ears and ears of their offices was in order. There may have been a development through the long electronic reach of Spetssviaz. Was Reece alive or dead? If the SEAL had escaped Nizar's ambush in Montenegro, they would need to take more drastic measures, measures upon which Dashkov and the president would need to concur.

Gromyko passed a semiclothed statue of a ballerina and took a seat on a bench. Andreyevsky Pond was visible through the trees. A light breeze cut the stillness of the night.

No sign of Dashkov or his goons.

Dashkov, always with the games.

Apparently, this time he had decided to make his old friend wait in the cold.

No matter. Spying was a game of patience; patience, trust, and creative problem solving.

Dashkov must have information that would shed light on what had happened in Montenegro. That information would dictate their next move.

Dashkov, where are you?

The SVR director reached into the pocket of his dark wool jacket and removed his pack of Marlboros and a plastic lighter.

This should warm these old bones.

In a long-practiced motion taught to him by his KGB instructors not far outside of Moscow, he tapped the pack and removed a cigarette, returning the pack to his pocket and striking the lighter with his thumb. The warm smoke filled his lungs as the nicotine was quickly absorbed by his blood and went to work stimulating neuron receptors and releasing the dopamine that activated the reward circuits in his brain.

As the dopamine and endorphins hit, the spymaster leaned back on the bench. Gromyko was so absorbed in thought that he was not aware death had come for him until the long, plastic zip-tie was already over his head and around his neck.

He heard the clicks of the teeth and shank engaging in the plastic head as the cable was pulled tight against his windpipe.

He dropped his cigarette, and his hands went to his throat, clawing at the thick plastic band that stopped just short of cutting off the supply of oxygen and blood to his brain.

There is nothing quite so terrifying as suffocation. Even more terrifying is when that suffocation appears in the form of a ghost out of the night.

Gromyko tried to twist away but a powerful arm pushed him down and anchored his thin frame to the bench.

"Relax."

English.

"Relax or I will pull back, the zip-tie will cut off blood and oxygen to your brain, and you will die."

American English. James Reece.

The SVR director stopped struggling and forced himself to take short breaths, barely enough oxygen making its way to his brain to keep him alive.

The hand that anchored him to the bench left his shoulder and pointed down the trail. Gromyko caught it in his peripheral, then shifted his eyes before slightly canting his head.

Movement?

What is that?

Between short gasps he watched as a wheelchair emerged from the darkness.

Gromyko watched in horror as the man he had put in the chair wheeled up to him, trapping the Russian's legs between the right wheel and the bench.

The American's hand returned to his shoulder, his other still grasping the cable of the zip-tie. One more pull and the plastic tie would cut all oxygen and blood from Gromyko's brain.

"I've wanted to look you in the eye for thirty-five years, comrade."

Unable to speak, the Russian could only stare at Abelard.

"I see the fear in your eyes, old man. Did you mean to kill me all those years ago?"

Gromyko nodded, his eyes darting about, searching.

"Tonight, I return the favor. Though I am going to succeed where you failed."

Maybe Dashkov's security men will round the corner at any moment? Maybe there is still hope?

"What are you searching for, Comrade Gromyko? For your friend Dashkov? Did you think you were meeting him here? No. That was us. We set up this meeting."

Confusion flashed across the SVR man's face.

What? How?

"Your Spetssviaz and your Internet Research Agency are easily fooled. Just as in the Cold War, the Americans have outplayed you. No one is coming."

Gromyko's hand went back to the plastic at his throat.

"It's futile, Mikhail. Use these precious seconds you have left wisely. Are you wondering what happened to Oleg Berzin?"

How do they know so much?

"No need to worry. You will see him soon. He no longer draws breath, but he told us something interesting before he died. He needed a favor, so in exchange he told me who put me here," Abelard said, gesturing to the wheelchair. "Which leads us to the question at hand: Why do you want James Reece dead?"

Reece's left hand twisted the plastic tie just enough to let a little more air pass through, allowing Gromyko to answer the question.

"I don't," the Russian managed to rasp out.

"It's no use lying, comrade. We know you have been trying to kill the man behind you for quite some time. I must say you have not done a particularly good job, as you can tell from your current predicament."

Think, Mikhail.

"Now, why do you want him dead?"

Gromyko thought of all the men he had seen die, all those he had ordered to their deaths. He thought of his training, his assignments, his ascension to the top of the Russian intelligence hierarchy. He thought of the long-term agents inserted deep into the heart of the West, the ones who had families, who had ushered in a second generation of deep-penetration assets. Behind enemy lines. Infiltrating an entire society. Poisoning it from within. He thought of the multigenerational plan to destroy the United States. And he thought of the man who had almost stopped it: Thomas Reece.

There was nothing these two men could do.

"Because of the list," he whispered.

"The list?" Abelard asked. "Explain."

Abelard lifted his eyes to look at Reece, who gave an almost imperceptible nod.

"Ask him," Gromyko said.

Abelard looked back to the big man.

"This is about the letter?" Reece asked.

"Not a letter. A list."

"What's on it?" Reece asked.

Gromyko shook his head.

"Air," the old man said.

"No," Reece said. "You have enough to speak. Where's the list?"

"Smoke?"

"What?" Reece asked.

"Cigarette?"

Reece looked at Abelard, who nodded.

Keeping a hand on the back of the zip-tie, Reece reached down from behind the bench into the Russian's coat pocket. He fished out a pack of cigarettes and small lighter. He handed them to the old spy.

Gromyko slowly tapped the pack against his shaking palm as he had done thousands of times over the preceding decades, but this time, just as he had been taught by his KGB instructors, he maneuvered a special cigarette into the rotation and pulled it out with cold, shaky fingers. He remembered his KGB cadre briefing his class on potassium cyanide. It had been exciting back in 1983. It was not so exciting now. As he pulled the Marlboro from the pack, he felt the filter to ensure it was the correct one. It was.

"The list," Reece said, getting impatient.

"The list," Gromyko repeated. "Your father made it. He didn't tell you where it was?"

Reece stood silent at the mention of Thomas Reece.

"No answer? I see he did not. At least I can go to my grave knowing those secrets died with him."

The Russian slowly inserted the cigarette between his lips, then shoved it into the back of his mouth and bit down.

The "L-pill" embedded in the cigarette's filter broke apart before Abelard or Reece could stop it.

Reece let go of the zip-tie and pulled Gromyko's head back, trying to force his fingers into the man's mouth to dislodge the pill. The spy clamped his jaw shut and twisted his head back and forth in an effort to defend against the SEAL's attack.

"How much time do we have?" Reece asked, looking at Abelard.

"Probably cyanide. Not long. Minutes. It's over, James," Abelard said. "Let him die."

Reece looked into the eyes of the man who held the secrets. They were already glazing over as the old man struggled to breathe, the cyanide blocking his frail body's ability to perform basic functions, the muscles of his diaphragm and heart losing their ability to circulate oxygen and blood. What his instructors outside of Moscow had failed to mention was that death by potassium cyanide poisoning is one of the most painful ways to leave the earth.

As the old spy thrashed about in agony, Reece eyed the man in the wheelchair, who looked on without a hint of remorse. Reece reached back to the zip-tie, placed his hand at the head where the band passed though the claws, and gave a powerful tug, tightening the garotte and putting the old man out of his misery.

Reece glanced at the stainless-steel watch on his wrist. The park would be closing soon.

He then looked into the upturned eyes of the Russian spymaster.

What secrets did you take to the grave?

Reece then hauled the smaller man over the back of the bench and carried him across a patch of grass and into the wood line.

As the cerebral hypoxia shut down Mikhail Gromyko's brain, he had the vague sensation of floating. He realized he was being carried.

His last thought before he drifted away was that James Reece looked a lot like his father.

Reece threw the dead man unceremoniously into the shrubbery of the park that Gromyko had known so well, then returned to the man in the wheelchair.

Reece walked next to him back toward one of the main paths that paralleled the Moscow River.

"Facial recognition, identification, that should all be good. The technology department at the Agency will take care of it," Reece said, knowing full well that it wasn't the CIA or NSA, but an entity trapped in a maze of golden wires beneath Lackland Air Force Base. "Once we get home, I can't say. We are in uncharted territory."

"I'll take it from there," Abelard said.

"What are you going to do?" Reece asked.

"I'll do what I always do," he said, gesturing to the wheelchair. "I'll adapt. But this time, I might adapt back home."

"Home?"

"Israel."

Reece smiled.

"And you?" Abelard asked. "What will you do?"

Reece paused. They had reached a fork in the trail.

"I'm going to do the same."

To Abelard's questioning look Reece offered, "I'm going to adapt."

"Good-bye, Reece," Abelard said, reaching up to shake the SEAL's hand before pushing off into the night.

"Good-bye," Reece whispered after the bookseller had disappeared.

He stood there a moment longer, allowing himself a brief moment to reflect.

What of the list and his father's connection to Russian intelligence? Some things were best left to die in darkness.

He thought of Katie and the mountains of Montana. It was time to go home.

Their routes out of Moscow were cleared, their faces and identities electronically altered. No facial recognition technology would identify them at any point along their journey; their passport aliases would be approved as valid. They were clean.

As Reece worked his way to the park exit, he looked up at a statue of a partially clad woman. She appeared to be dancing. He thought of the new woman in his life. The woman who had made the assassination of the director of Russia's Foreign Intelligence Service possible. A woman named Alice.

EPILOGUE

Upon this, one has to remark that men ought either to be well treated or crushed, because they can avenge themselves of lighter injuries, of more serious ones they cannot; therefore the injury that is to be done to a man ought to be of such a kind that one does not stand in fear of revenge.

—Niccolò Machiavelli, The Prince

Kumba Ranch, Flathead Valley, Montana

Reece ran his fingers around the ring in the pocket of his jeans for around the thousandth time that evening.

Just ask her.

No, wait for the right time.

Time.

I'm so bad at this.

Reece's mind wandered to all that had come to light since his return from Russia.

A senior Russian intelligence official with ties to the president had been found dead in Gorky Park a month earlier. According to Russian authorities, he had died of natural causes. He had been battling cancer for quite some time. Western news outlets noted that unusual numbers of both friends and enemies of the Russian president died of "natural causes."

A man with a beard had been captured on multiple cell phone videos running across a street in Turin, Italy, with an AK-type rifle. The videos were of varying quality and seemed to show him sprinting into a building across the street from a bookshop that had just been destroyed by a terrorist bomb. The explosive device had the hallmarks of an Islamic terror cell. It was the same type of IED that had been used in the July 7, 2005, attacks in London. It had been widely reported that a terror cell of Syrian refugees had targeted the rare book restoration business because its owner was Jewish. The beloved man in the wheelchair had not been seen since the attack. Speculation was that he had gone into hiding following the traumatic event. Some ventured that he might be in Israel.

The bearded man had not been seen since the attack. The response to requests for information by news agencies to the CIA, FBI, INTERPOL, and the Italian intelligence services was that their investigations were ongoing and that anyone with information on the bearded man should contact their public tip hotlines. He remained a person of interest.

A woman in Brindisi, Italy, had held out hope for her husband's return. She did not want to lose a second husband, especially one who was so kind to her and her children. That hope faded when 1.4 million euros appeared in her bank account. It came from a multinational investment fund that was financing small businesses across the globe. In this case it was an investment in Italy's youth through a boxing gym. It was all perfectly legitimate; at least it appeared so in the event anyone came looking. That the money was withdrawn from multiple offshore accounts in Panama, Singapore, and Switzerland by a quantum computer beneath the runways of Lackland Air Force Base was known only to Reece and Alice.

He flipped the ring around in his right pocket and looked at Katie. She was the one.

I've seen you run, but even you can't outrun time.

Reece dug into his left pocket and felt the safe-deposit box key, a final gift, or perhaps a curse, left to him by his father. He remembered finding the long-term storage facility that Tom Reece had arranged to receive recurring payments even after his death. In the back of the old Wagoneer parked in the storage bay was a case with an Ithaca Model 37 shotgun inside, the same weapon Tom Reece had used in the jungles of Vietnam. Behind the foam of the aluminum case were a key and letter addressed to James. The key had no markings to indicate its origin, and the letter offered no clues as to the location of the safe-deposit box to which it belonged. Not a day had passed since their discovery that Reece had not contemplated his father's words. Perhaps some secrets were best lost to history.

I think it's time to let you go.

"James . . . James!"

"Huh?"

"What are you thinking about?" Katie asked, a prying yet playful tone in her voice.

"Uh, time. I mean, nothing. I mean, the back straps. Need to stay on it when they are on the Burch Barrel."

"James Reece, you are and have always been a horrible liar."

Katie smiled. She came around the island, locking her fingers behind Reece's head and pulling him to her lips. "It's one of the things I love about you."

"Now I'm thinking we should just let dinner burn," Reece said, his eyes indicating the open door to the bedroom.

"You are going to have to wait. I'm famished," she teased. "Wine, dinner, then . . ." Now it was Katie's turn to look to the bedroom.

"Well, I'm going to raise the coals out there and speed this process up," Reece said, his eyes taking in the woman before him.

"Deal," Katie replied.

"You are so beautiful."

"Flattery will get you everywhere," Katie said. "What can I open?"

"Anything you'd like," Reece said, looking out past the deck to the expansive lake, smoke billowing from the grill.

"Let's start with white and then switch to a nice Cab with dinner."

"That works," Reece said. "I liberated a couple bottles of Kistler from Jonathan's cellar a few days ago."

"They make an exquisite Chardonnay."

"That they do," Reece said, moving toward the sliding glass door that opened onto the deck.

Just ask her.

No, wait until after dinner.

That's it. After dinner.

Katie walked to the attached garage, where Reece had installed the large stand-alone wine fridge that Jonathan had ordered.

If you are going to steal my wine, you bloody well better store it at the correct temperature, Jonathan had teased when it was delivered. Katie knew he looked at Reece like a son. With one daughter gone, it had been Reece who had taken the life of her killer while at the same time saving Raife's. Reece was family.

Katie poured two glasses of Kistler's finest and joined Reece on the deck.

"Cheers," Katie said.

"To new beginnings?" Reece tried.

"You really are bad at toasts, but you make up for it in other ways." Katie smiled.

"To us?"

"Getting slightly better. To us," Katie repeated.

She turned to take in the view. A light breeze off the lake hit her face and she closed her eyes. "I could live here."

"You could? What about D.C.? Work? Your own show?"

"It might be time for a change."

Reece swallowed.

Should I ask her now? By the grill?

"Ugh, Katie, I um . . ."

"James."

"What?"

"I think dinner is burning."

"Dang it!"

Reece raised the lid of the grill and quickly transferred the steaks to a waiting cutting board.

"I raised the coals too high. I guess I was a bit distracted."

"Get your head out of the gutter, mister."

"That's a losing battle. Let's eat!"

Katie held the door as Reece passed into the kitchen and set the board on the counter.

"I think we got to them just in time," he said, gently probing the meat with his thumb.

"Ah, disaster averted," Katie concurred. "I took the liberty of decanting a bottle of Tuck Beckstoffer Mockingbird Blue. I thought this would be a good night for it. We also received a box from War Paw Wines in Napa. I think it's a two-bottle night, so I went ahead and opened that, too."

"Perfect," Reece said, turning his attention to the salad. "Potatoes have another ten minutes in the oven and then we'll be good to go."

He turned back to Katie. She was staring at him, her deep blue eyes probing, curious, with a hint of mystery.

"James, are you really done with the CIA?"

Reece turned on the faucet, the warm water seeping between his fingers. He dried his hands on a dish towel and tossed it to the side before answering. He thought of the letter from his father; a letter and a key.

Perhaps some things are better left buried.

"I'm done, Katie. Freddy's killer is dead. The same guy who killed

Aliya. All those who killed Lauren and Lucy, my SEAL Troop, the man who ordered the assassination of my father, all dead. It's time to move on. Time for a new chapter. It's time to live, here in the present. Nothing has ever been more clear to me."

"And what did Vic and the president say when you told them you'd be officially retiring?"

"The president was all for it. He thanked me for my service and told me to call him if I ever needed anything."

"That's a good favor to have in the bank. You did save him from having to wipe two U.S. cities off the map a year ago, after all."

"There is that," Reece said as he remembered leveling the Tabuk Kalashnikov at Iranian General Ja'far al-Sadiq's head, pressing the trigger and then leaving the president's fiancée's ring in the dead general's hand.

"Though you are going to have a hard time getting in touch with him without a cell phone or a computer."

"Maybe that's the point?" Reece ventured, taking another sip of the chilled Chardonnay. "This is great, by the way."

"That it is," Katie confirmed. "And Vic?"

"Vic just said 'we'll see.'"

"Ah, he knows you too well."

"Not well enough," Reece said, putting down his wineglass. He took Katie's from her hand and set it on the counter. Then, without another word, he swept her off her feet and carried her to the bedroom.

• • •

The snipers had been dropped off on an adjoining property and had double-timed it to their positions above the cabin at the edge of the lake. National-level intelligence well beyond their pay grade had confirmed that the robust security measures employed on the property had been disabled. A satellite and drone provided real-time imagery to their Getac tactical tablets. They took up positions on the hillside, one team covering the driveway and entrance and the other covering the back porch and dock.

"ALPHA ONE FOUR has eyes on."

"Roger that, Alpha Team."

"CHARLIE ONE SIX is in position."

"Good copy, Charlie Team."

The spotter from Alpha Team typed a SALUTE report into his tablet and pressed Send.

• • •

Katie had never seen him so at peace. Though he was still never out of arm's reach of a pistol, she had noticed a shift as they hiked and talked. The eyes that had always scanned seemed more focused on her rather than on threats from the unknown. For the first time, she felt that he was not a thousand miles away on a distant battlefield or fighting the internal demons that were a consequence of a life at war; he was present. He was with her, in the moment. She sensed that he was feeling a freedom he had never known.

"Well, Mr. Reece," Katie said, putting on her reporter's hat as they sat down to enjoy the now-cold sliced venison back straps, "now I really am starving."

"That was all part of my plan," Reece said. "I needed you to be hungry enough that you wouldn't notice how much I overcooked these."

"Mission success," Katie confirmed. "What are you thinking?"

"I'm thinking I need to work on my flexibility," he said mischievously.

"Mr. Reece," Katie said, pointing her steak knife in his direction across the table, a gleam in her eye.

"Just kidding, though that may be true. I'm thinking about us."

"Oh, do tell. What about us?" Katie probed.

Does she know?

"Uh, I don't know. Just about life. The future," Reece said, slicing off a bite of venison.

I am not the only one who wants you dead, Mr. Reece. I was on the helicopter with you in Africa. That local security man was aiming for you, not me.

Not now, Reece. Be present.

"Well, let's start there," Katie said, guiding him along and pouring more deep red liquid into his glass. "Without the CIA or running around the world at the behest of the president, what do you want to do with this next chapter?"

"I don't know."

"That I am not buying for a second."

"Okay, I have a thought or two."

"Well . . . ?"

"Well, I was thinking of sticking around for a while."

"Oh, you were, were you? Not zipping off to parts unknown to battle the forces of evil?"

"I'm thinking it's time to pass the torch."

"Your beard isn't getting any less gray," Katie teased again.

"Besides," Reece continued, "we've hardly put a dent in Jonathan's wine cellar. And I get the sneaking suspicion that Raife has taken to hiding some of the more interesting and expensive bottles, which poses a challenge."

"You are not one to back down from a challenge."

"This is true. Besides, I'm just getting started luring Raife into competitions for which I've spent months preparing and setting the conditions. I'm thinking a lever-action rifle and revolver challenge next. Just need to walk him into it. Make it his idea."

Katie rolled her eyes.

"And for employment?"

"Well, as part of the deal in tracking down Mo a few years back, the Navy included a retirement package."

"Ah, the big bucks," Katie said, taking a sip of wine.

"Yeah, it's not much but it's something. And I . . ."

"What, James?"

"Well, I thought I could guide some hunts with Raife. You could help me improve my fly fishing."

"You do need all the help you can get on that front."

"And . . ."

Should I ask her now?

"And what?"

"I thought of starting a business."

"Oh, James, an entrepreneur. That's kind of a turn-on."

"I was hoping you'd say that."

"Continue . . ."

"Well, a couple things, actually. The owner of Glacier Archery is getting ready to retire. He's mentioned it to me a few times now. I think he's testing the waters. Raife and I might buy it."

Katie put down her fork.

"James, I kind of thought you were kidding. Are you sure? A new chapter?"

"A new chapter. I've always loved local archery shops. Archery is so beneficial for veterans. I think we hire prior military, train them up, connect it with Raife's hunting program. A one-stop shop to get people in the right bow, putting in the reps, and then get them out in these mountains after elk and mulies."

"Raife with customer service?"

"I'd keep him as an investor. Not sure I'd even allow him in the store."

"That's a wise first decision. You might just have a knack for this."

"And . . ."

Ask her.

"And?" Katie asked.

"And, I thought of opening a coffee shop and bookstore in Whitefish. Locally roasted coffee. Old, hard-to-find, and restored books."

"Reece, really?" The hope was evident in her voice.

"I'm thinking about it. Maybe spice it up a bit with archery, a bookstore, coffeehouse, and whiskey bar highlighting veteran-owned whiskeys—there are quite a few out there these days."

Katie took Reece's hand across the table. Was there hope for them? Hope for a future with Reece, devoid of the killing that had permeated their lives since they had first met?

"I love it. What would you call it? Reece's Relics?"

Reece shook his head.

"That sounds like an antiques store or salvage yard."

"I can tell you have an idea."

"I was thinking about Abelard's."

"Abelard's?" Katie asked.

"Yep."

"I think I've heard that name in the news recently."

"It was the name of a guy I knew once. He helped me when I needed it."

"Abelard's," Katie said, contemplating the name.

"Yep. Abelard's Books, Coffee, and Whiskey."

"That's quite a combination. I love it."

"All my favorite things in one place."

"All your favorite things?" Katie said, smiling.

"Well, most of them. And, I, uh . . ."

Do it!

"You what?"

"I, uh, thought it might be a good place for our kids to work in high school."

Katie's eyes misted over. She bit her quivering lip, and in a voice tinged with emotion, asked, "James, are you serious?"

Do it!

Reece took Katie's hands in his.

"Katie, I've never been more serious or sure about anything. I'm done with the Agency. I'm done with the government. If you'll have me, I want to spend the rest of my life making you the happiest woman on earth."

Katie was in a state of shock. There was nowhere she would have rather been.

Reece stood up, reached into his pocket, and then took a knee.

"Katie Buranek . . ."

Reece swallowed.

A sound disturbed the moment. At first it didn't register.

It was Katie's ringtone.

They didn't have cell service at the cabin.

An alarm?

Katie's purse was on the couch.

"Oh my God! I am so sorry. I swear I'm going to throw that thing in the lake."

"You'll have to beat me to it," Reece said.

The ringtone was louder than Reece remembered. Katie stood and went to the couch, fishing out her phone thinking she would just turn off the alarm, but it wasn't an alarm. It was a phone call.

"That's weird."

"What is it?" Reece asked.

"It's a phone call. From Alice? I don't think I know an Alice."

Reece stood, turning all business in less than a second. He walked to Katie.

"Let me see it."

It now read: MISSED CALL.

"James, I don't have cell service here and you dismantled the Internet."

Reece was about to press on the missed call when the phone chirped again with a message received.

Reece hit the text message icon.

`Turn on the radio.`

Reece's head rotated to the radio they used to communicate on the ranch. Repeaters were set up at high points so that Jonathan could connect with them at remote locations around the property.

"James?"

He handed Katie her phone, walked to the radio, and turned it on. He had turned it off before dinner, wanting nothing to disturb them.

Reece twisted the dial to turn up the volume.

What he heard over the speaker turned his blood to ice. It was Raife and he said only one word.

"Avalanche."

Reece's head snapped toward the door and then to the rifle in the corner next to his body armor.

It wasn't Raife's voice he heard next. It was Jonathan Hastings. The Rhodesian accent was level and unmistakable. Reece had not heard that tone since they had linked up in Kamchatka, Russia, where Reece had delivered the news that Jonathan's daughter was dead.

"Son, I want you to listen to me. If you never listen to another *bloody* thing I say. Stand down. The sheriff is here along with some serious boys from HRT. They don't want a fight, but by God, they are ready for one. I told them I could talk you out. I promised them you would come out without a fight. I am not going to lose you, son."

The radio was set up on a desk near a window facing the driveway. Reece pushed aside the curtain, seeing a caravan of headlights headed toward the cabin.

"Come out, lad. No weapons. Hands high. Just do what they say. This is *not* the time to fight. Trust me. You know I'd shoot straight with you and you know I'd pick up a rifle if I thought that was the call. It's not."

Reece said nothing. He was counting the vehicles.

"Reece, confirm you received this and that you are standing down. I promise you we will get you the best lawyers."

"James, what's happening?" Katie asked, panic creeping into her voice.

"It's all over the news, Reece," Jonathan said. "Turn on the TV, son."

Reece set the handset down and instead of turning on the television, he went to the AR by the door, and confirmed there was a round chambered and that it had a full magazine.

"Katie, put on your body armor and go lie down in the bedroom," he said, sliding an arm through his plate carrier and pulling it into place over his head.

"I'll do no such thing! Not until you tell me what's happening!"

"Reece." It was Jonathan's voice on the radio. "Are you there? *Reece!*"

Reece looked at the radio and then picked up a remote control and hit the power button. The TV was already set to a cable news channel.

The banner read: CHAOS IN THE CAPITOL.-PRESIDENT ASSASSINATED.

"Just thirty-five minutes ago, shots were fired at President Alex Christensen by a member of the armed forces during a Veterans Day parade in the nation's capital."

The video went to troops in formation marching down Pennsylvania Avenue, the president standing with his vice president and cabinet on a platform to observe the parade. A soldier stepped from the line, raised his rifle at the president, and pressed the trigger. The bullets impacted the glass barrier protecting the commander in chief, the thick plastic absorbing the bullets. The president's and vice president's protection details throwing them to the deck as the shooter took a round to the chest from what Reece knew was a sniper, just seconds before his head exploded from a shot that was probably fired by an undercover Secret Service agent in the crowd. Chaos. The troops, police, Secret Service, the crowd all descending into turmoil as the president and vice president were rushed to waiting vehicles to usher them to safety.

Reece and Katie watched in disbelief as the camera switched to more grainy footage from a street surveillance camera. The president's limo and Secret Service Suburbans rocketed through Washington for a secure location. Then the screen turned to dust.

"Our security analysts confirm that the president's motorcade was hit with what we are being told were chain-linked EFPs—explosively formed penetrators—improvised explosive devices that came to prominence during the war in Iraq. The president was rushed to George Washington University Hospital, where he was pronounced dead. The vice president has taken the oath of office and will address the nation at the top of the hour, some eight minutes from now."

"James," Katie said, looking up at him, the horror apparent in her eyes.

Reece shifted his focus from the screen to Katie and then to the rifle in his hands. The line of black Suburbans were close now. He heard a helo overhead, then a second off the dock at the back of the cabin, hovering over the moonlit water.

"JAMES REECE. YOU ARE SURROUNDED BY FEDERAL AND LOCAL LAW ENFORCEMENT," came a voice from one of the Suburbans. "COME TO THE FRONT OF THE HOUSE, UNARMED. IF YOU SURRENDER PEACEFULLY, YOU WILL NOT BE HARMED."

Reece knew there would be snipers in the woods in elevated positions and snipers on each helicopter.

He looked at the rifle again. Then to Katie.

"I love you, Katie."

"James . . ."

He set the rifle on the ground, then drew his pistol from its holster on his belt, then putting it on the table. He then removed his plate carrier.

He leaned down, looked Katie in the eyes, and kissed her.

"Hold on to this for me," he said, pressing a diamond engagement ring into her hand. "And this."

Katie looked down and saw a safe-deposit box key.

Before she could utter a word, Reece pulled off his shirt and went to the door.

"I'm coming out. I'm unarmed!" he shouted.

"OPEN THE DOOR—SLOWLY—AND SHOW US YOUR HANDS."

"Opening the door!" he shouted through the crack.

Reece stepped to the porch.

"KEEP YOUR HANDS HIGH, COMMANDER. SLOWLY TURN AROUND."

Reece did as he was told, turning in a slow 360 to confirm that he had no weapons and was not strapped with a suicide vest.

"WALK DOWN THE STEPS AND GO PRONE."

Reece obeyed, taking in the army of heavily armed federal agents who had him in their sights.

"CROSS YOUR LEGS, ARMS OUT TO YOUR SIDES. TURN YOUR HEAD."

Reece did as he was instructed. He heard the rush of feet in the gravel driveway as agents converged. A team blew past and up the steps into the cabin and he could hear Katie demanding to see a warrant. He felt his right arm and then his left wrenched behind his back, plastic zip-ties securing his wrists. An agent frisked his ankles up to his crotch and then belt line, removing his belt in the process. He was ordered to roll to his left and get to his feet as they assisted him.

Barefoot, in jeans and no shirt, Reece scanned the front driveway. It looked like every law enforcement agent in the western United States was in his front yard.

Jonathan and Caroline stood by a Suburban with Raife by their side. Raife had the look of a predator ready to start ripping heads from bodies. It didn't escape notice that he had four agents on him, just in case.

A man and a woman approached, both wearing jeans and dark blue FBI windbreakers.

Reece knew what they were going to say before they opened their mouths.

"James Reece, I'm Special Agent in Charge Jim Klein, and this is Special Agent Kathryn Edwards from the Salt Lake Field Office. You are under arrest for conspiracy to assassinate the president of the United States."

Flanked by heavily armed agents, two of the larger ones grabbed his arms and ushered him toward a vehicle waiting with the rear passenger door open, an agent already in the far seat. Reece locked eyes with Caroline, Jonathan, and then Raife, holding their gaze as long as he could, before his head was pushed down and he was moved into the center seat, one of his escorts sliding in next to him while the other closed the door.

Reece's thoughts were not on the agents to his right and left, not on the president or the country, not on Katie, the Hastings family, or a future that had just been ripped away from him.

His thoughts were on a letter. A letter from the grave.

AUTHOR'S NOTE

IT TAKES SKILL TO kill with a rifle. It takes something else to outmaneuver and outthink your adversary. To do that, you must know your capabilities and limitations and those of your enemy. That means study and immersion. As Sun Tzu wrote in chapter three, Attack Stratagems, of *The Art of War*, "If you know the enemy and know yourself, you need not fear the result of a hundred battles." The mind remains the most capable and lethal of weapons.

As with my previous novels, *In the Blood* is a work of fiction. That fiction is informed by whispers of truth.

The HVT Bar in Baghdad's Green Zone did exist and did play a role in building trust among a CIA-led team of intelligence officers, paramilitary contractors, and a select few active-duty military special operators. I still have my shot glass. It was an honor.

Those familiar with Kibbutz Merom Golan will know I took some artistic license. For security reasons, I did not describe the actual level of preparedness in that community. What I will say is that if a team of terrorists were to infiltrate Merom Golan the way I portray, they would not be long for this world.

The Soviet Mi-24 "Hind" helicopters did indeed dominate the skies over Afghanistan up until September 26, 1986, when three were shot down in a single afternoon with American Stinger missiles.

The Borgo Dora enclave of the Aurora District of Turin is as depicted, save for the royal green awning with *Abelard's Libri Rari e Restauro* inscribed on its valance. If such a business did exist, the owner may very well have a curriculum vitae that included the Central Institute for the Conservation and Restoration of Damaged Books in Rome, an internship at Giulio Giannini e Figlio in Florence, and time with Conti Borbone in Milan. It is unknown whether the purveyor of said fictious establishment would have a hidden safe stocked with weapons and history as an assassin for the Mossad.

The bombs used by the Syrian terrorists do bear the hallmarks of the homemade explosive devices used in the July 7, 2005, bombings in London. Though more-specific instructions are readily available online, I chose to leave some of the particulars out of this manuscript.

The history of the CIA's MKUltra project and Sidney Gottlieb's involvement is accurate, based on sworn testimony before the Church Committee in 1975 and declassified records that survived destruction ordered by the CIA director in 1973.

As with the biomedical research I did while writing *The Devil's Hand,* I had no touchpoint with quantum computing, cyber warfare, Internet levels, artificial intelligence, mass data storage, or NSA surveillance of American citizens during my time in the military. That meant I needed to dig. Much as with the bioweapons research, officially called "biodefense" research by the United States government, which I did for my previous novel, I went deep "down the rabbit hole" into the world of cyber warfare and quantum computing for *In the Blood.* Through books, journal articles, and personal interviews I was able to piece together the facility and capabilities described in these pages. Those capabilities were toned down to keep this book out of the science fiction section.

Is Alice real? The best way to answer that is to wish her a good day; there is no doubt she is watching me as I type this right now.

GLOSSARY

160th Special Operations Aviation Regiment: The Army's premier helicopter unit that provides aviation support to special forces. Known as the "Night Stalkers," they are widely regarded as the best helicopter pilots and crews in the world.

.260: .260 Remington; .264"/6.5mm rifle cartridge that is essentially a .308 Winchester necked down to accept a smaller-diameter bullet. The .260 provides superior external ballistics to the .308 with less felt recoil and can often be fired from the same magazines.

.300 Norma: .300 Norma Magnum; a cartridge designed for long-range precision shooting that has been adopted by USSOCOM for sniper use.

.375 CheyTac: Long-range cartridge, adapted from the .408 Chey- Tac, that can fire a 350-grain bullet at 2,970 feet per second. A favorite of extreme long-range match competitors who use it on targets beyond 3,000 yards.

.375 H&H Magnum: An extremely common and versatile big-game rifle cartridge, found throughout Africa. The cartridge was developed by Holland & Holland in 1912 and traditionally fires a 300-grain bullet.

.404 Jeffery: A rifle cartridge designed for large game animals, developed by W. J. Jeffery & Company in 1905.

.408 CheyTac: Long-range cartridge adapted from the .505 Gibbs, capable of firing a 419-grain bullet at 2,850 feet per second.

.500 Nitro: A .510-caliber cartridge designed for use against heavy dangerous game, often chambered in double rifles. The cartridge fires a 570-grain bullet at 2,150 feet per second.

75th Ranger Regiment: A large-scale Army special operations unit that conducts direct-action missions including raids and airfield seizures. These elite troops often work in conjunction with other special operations units.

AC-130 Spectre: A ground-support aircraft used by the U.S. military, based on the ubiquitous C-130 cargo plane. AC-130s are armed with a 105mm howitzer, 40mm cannons, and 7.62mm miniguns, and are considered the premier close-air-support weapon of the U.S. arsenal.

Accuracy International: A British company producing high-quality precision rifles, often used for military sniper applications.

ACOG: Advanced Combat Optical Gunsight. A magnified optical sight designed for use on rifles and carbines, made by Trijicon. The ACOG is popular among U.S. forces as it provides both magnification and an illuminated reticle that provides aiming points for various target ranges.

AFIS: Automated Fingerprint Identification System; electronic fingerprint database maintained by the FBI.

Aimpoint Micro: Aimpoint Micro T-2; high-quality unmagnified red-dot combat optic produced in Sweden that can be used on a variety of weapons platforms. This durable sight weighs only three ounces and has a five-year battery life.

AISI: The latest name for Italy's domestic intelligence agency. Their motto, *scientia rerum republicae salus*, means "knowledge of issues is the salvation of the Republic."

AK-9: Russian 9x39mm assault rifle favored by Spetsnaz (special purpose) forces.

Al-Jaleel: Iraqi-made 82mm mortar that is a clone of the Yugoslavian-made M69A. This indirect-fire weapon has a maximum range of 6,000 meters.

Alpha Group: More accurately called Spetsgruppa "A," Alpha Group is the FSB's counterterrorist unit. You don't want them to "rescue" you. See Moscow Theater Hostage Crisis and the Beslan School Massacre.

AMAN: Israeli military intelligence.

Amphib: Shorthand for Amphibious Assault Ship. A gray ship holding helicopters, Harriers, and hovercraft. Usually home to a large number of pissed-off Marines.

AN/PAS-13G(v)L3/LWTS: Weapon-mounted thermal optic that can be used to identify warm-blooded targets day or night. Can be mounted in front of and used in conjunction with a traditional "day" scope mounted on a sniper weapons system.

AN/PRC-163: Falcon III communications system made by Harris Corporation that integrates voice, text, and video capabilities.

AQ: al-Qaeda. Meaning "the Base" in Arabic. A radical Islamic terrorist organization once led by the late Osama bin Laden.

AQI: al-Qaeda in Iraq. An al-Qaeda–affiliated Sunni insurgent group that was active against U.S. forces. Elements of AQI eventually evolved into ISIS.

AR-10: The 7.62x51mm brainchild of Eugene Stoner that was later adapted to create the M16/M4/AR-15.

Asherman Chest Seal: A specialized emergency medical device used to treat open chest wounds. If you're wearing one, you are having a bad day.

AT-4: Tube-launched 84mm anti-armor rocket produced in Sweden and used by U.S. forces since the 1980s. The AT-4 is a throwaway weapon: after it is fired, the tube is discarded.

ATF/BATFE: Bureau of Alcohol, Tobacco, Firearms and Explosives. A federal law enforcement agency formally part of the U.S. Department of the Treasury, which doesn't seem overly concerned with alcohol or tobacco.

ATPIAL/PEQ-15: Advanced Target Pointer/Illuminator Aiming Laser. A weapon-mounted device that emits both visible and infrared target designators for use with or without night observation devices. Essentially, an advanced military-grade version of the "laser sights" seen in popular culture.

***Avtoritet*:** The highest caste of the incarcerated criminal hierarchy. Today used in association with a new generation of crime bosses.

Azores: Atlantic archipelago consisting of nine major islands that is an independent autonomous region of the European nation of Portugal.

Barrett 250 Lightweight: A lightweight variant of the M240 7.62mm light machine gun, developed by Barrett Firearms.

Barrett M107: .50 BMG caliber semiautomatic rifle designed by Ronnie Barrett in the early 1980s. This thirty-pound rifle can be carried by a single individual and can be used to engage human or vehicular targets at extreme ranges.

BATS: Biometrics Automated Toolset System; a fingerprint database often used to identify insurgent forces.

Bay of Pigs: Site of a failed invasion of Cuba by paramilitary exiles trained and equipped by the CIA.

BDU: Battle-dress uniform; an oxymoron if there ever was one.

Benelli M1 Super 90: An auto-loading shotgun.

Beneteau Oceanis: A forty-eight-foot cruising sailboat, designed and built in France. An ideal craft for eluding international manhunts.

Black Hills Ammunition: High-quality ammunition made for military and civilian use by a family-owned and South Dakota–based company. Their MK 262 MOD 1 5.56mm load saw significant operational use in the GWOT.

Blue-badger: Often used to denote a "staff" CIA paramilitary operations officer. Why? Because their badges are blue.

***Bratok*:** Member of the Bratva.

Bratva: The Brotherhood. An umbrella term for Russian organized crime, more technically referring to members of the Russian mafia who have served time in prison.

***Brigadir*:** Lieutenant of a Bratva gang boss.

Browning Hi-Power: A single-action 9mm semiautomatic handgun that feeds from a thirteen-round box magazine. Also known as the P-35, this Belgian-designed handgun was the most widely issued military sidearm in the world for much of the twentieth century and was used by both Axis and Allied forces during World War II.

BUD/S: Basic Underwater Demolition/SEAL training. The six-month selection and training course required for entry into the SEAL Teams, held in Coronado, California. Widely considered one of the most brutal military selection courses in the world, with an average 80 percent attrition rate.

C-17: Large military cargo aircraft used to transport troops and supplies. Also used by the Secret Service to transport the president's motorcade vehicles.

C-4: Composition 4. A plastic-explosive compound known for its stability and malleability.

Caesarea: A department of the Mossad. It is wise to stay off their list.

CAG: Combat Applications Group. See redacted portion of glossary in the "D" section.

CAT: Counter-Assault Team; heavily armed ground element of the Secret Service trained to respond to threats such as ambushes.

CCA: According to *Seapower Magazine*, the Combatant Craft, Assault, is a 41-foot high-speed boat used by Naval Special Warfare units. Essentially, an armed "Cigarette" boat.

CDC: Centers for Disease Control and Prevention. An agency of the Department of Health and Human Services, its mission is to protect the United States from health threats to include natural and weaponized infectious diseases.

Cessna 208 Caravan: Single-engine turboprop aircraft that can ferry passengers and cargo, often to remote locations. These workhorses are staples in remote wilderness areas throughout the world.

CIA: Central Intelligence Agency

CIF/CRF: Commanders In-Extremis Force/Crisis Response Force; a United States Army special forces team specifically tasked with conducting direct-action missions. These are the guys who should have been sent to Benghazi.

CISA: Cybersecurity and Infrastructure Security Agency. It's official Web page states: "CISA is the Nation's risk advisor, working with partners to defend against today's threats and collaborating to build more secure and resilient infrastructure for the future." For an agency with such an innocuous Dunder Mifflinesque mission statement, in times of crisis they assume an inordinate amount of control.

CJSOTF: Combined Joint Special Operations Task Force. A regional command that controls special operations forces from various services and friendly nations.

CMC: Command Master Chief, a senior enlisted rating in the United States Navy.

CQC: Close-quarter combat

CrossFit: A fitness-centric worldwide cult that provides a steady stream of cases to orthopedic surgery clinics. No need to identify their members; they will tell you who they are.

CRRC: Combat Rubber Raiding Craft. Inflatable Zodiac-style boats used by SEALs and other maritime troops.

CTC: The CIA's Counterterrorism Center. Established out of the rise of international terrorism in the 1980s, it became the nucleus of the U.S. counterterrorism mission.

CZ-75: 9mm handgun designed in 1975 and produced in the Czech Republic.

DA: District attorney; local prosecutor in many jurisdictions.

Dam Neck: An annex to Naval Air Station Oceana near Virginia Beach, Virginia, where nothing interesting whatsoever happens.

DCIS: Defense Criminal Investigation Service

DEA: Drug Enforcement Administration

Delta Force: A classic 1986 action film starring Chuck Norris, title of the 1983 autobiography by the unit's first commanding officer and, according to thousands of print and online articles, books, and video interviews across new and legacy media, the popular name for the Army's 1st Special Forces Operational Detachment—Delta. I wouldn't know.

Democratic Federation of Northern Syria: Aka Rojava, an autonomous, polyethnic, and secular region of northern Syria.

Det Cord: Flexible detonation cord used to initiate charges of high explosive. The cord's interior is filled with PETN explosive; you don't want it wrapped around your neck.

DIA: Defense Intelligence Agency

Directorate I: The division of the SVR responsible for electronic information and disinformation.

Directorate S: The division of the SVR responsible for their illegals program. When you read about a Russian dissident or former spy poisoned by Novichok nerve agent or a political rival of the Russian president murdered in a random act of violence, Directorate S is probably responsible.

DO: The CIA's Directorate of Operations, formerly known by the much more appropriate name: the Clandestine Service.

DOD: Department of Defense

DOJ: Department of Justice

DShkM: Russian-made 12.7x108mm heavy machine gun that has been used in virtually every armed conflict since and including World War II.

DST: General Directorate for Territorial Surveillance. Morocco's domestic intelligence and security agency. Probably not afraid to use "enhanced interrogation techniques." DST was originally redacted by government censors for the hardcover edition of *True Believer*. After a five-month appeal process, that decision was withdrawn.

EFP: Explosively Formed Penetrator/Projectile. A shaped explosive charge that forms a molten projectile used to penetrate armor. Such munitions were widely used by insurgents against coalition forces in Iraq. EKIA: Enemy Killed In Action.

Eland: Africa's largest antelope. A mature male can weigh more than a ton.

EMS: Emergency medical services. Fire, paramedic, and other emergency personnel.

ENDEX: End Exercise. Those outside "the know" will say "INDEX" and have no idea what it means.

EOD: Explosive Ordnance Disposal. The military's explosives experts who are trained to, among other things, disarm or destroy improvised explosive devices or other munitions.

EOTECH: An unmagnified holographic gun sight for use on rifles and carbines, including the M4. The sight is designed for rapid target acquisition, which makes it an excellent choice for close-quarters battle. Can be fitted with a detachable 3x magnifier for use at extended ranges.

FAL: Fusil Automatique Léger: gas-operated, select-fire 7.62x51mm battle rifle developed by FN Herstal in the late 1940s and used by the militaries of more than ninety nations. Sometimes referred to as "the right arm of the free world" due to its use against communist forces in various Cold War–era insurgencies.

FBI: Federal Bureau of Investigation; a federal law enforcement agency that is not known for its sense of humor.

FDA: Food and Drug Administration

FLIR: Forward-Looking InfraRed. An observation device that uses thermographic radiation, that is, heat, to develop an image.

Floppies: Derogatory term used to describe communist insurgents during the Rhodesian Bush War.

FOB: Forward Operating Base. A secured forward military position used to support tactical operations. Can vary from small and remote outposts to sprawling complexes.

Fobbit: A service member serving in a noncombat role who rarely, if ever, leaves the safety of the Forward Operating Base.

FSB: Russia's federal security service responsible for internal state security and headquartered in the same building in Lubyanka Square that once housed the KGB. Its convenient in-house prison is not a place one wants to spend an extended period.

FSO: Federal Protective Service. Russia's version of the Secret Service.

FTX: Field Training Exercise

G550: A business jet manufactured by Gulfstream Aerospace. Prices for a new example start above $40 million but, as they say, it's better to rent.

Galil: An iconic Israeli-made rifle incorporating elements of the Kalashnikov and Finnish RK 62.

Game Scout: A wildlife enforcement officer in Africa. These individuals are often paired with hunting outfitters to ensure that regulations are adhered to.

Glock: An Austrian-designed, polymer-framed handgun popular with police forces, militaries, and civilians throughout the world. Glocks are made in various sizes and chambered in several different cartridges.

GPNVG-18: Ground Panoramic Night Vision Goggles. Forty-three-thousand-dollar NODs used by the most highly funded special operations units due to their superior image quality and peripheral vision. See Rich Kid Shit.

GPS: Global Positioning System. Satellite-based navigation systems that provide a precise location anywhere on earth.

Great Patriotic War: The Soviets' name for World War II; communists love propaganda.

Green-badger: Central Intelligence Agency contractor

Ground Branch: Land-focused element of the CIA's Special Activities Division, according to Wikipedia.

GRS: Global Response Staff. Protective agents employed by the Central Intelligence Agency to provide security to overseas personnel. See 13 Hours. GRS was originally redacted by government censors for the hardcover edition of *True Believer.* After a five-month appeal process, that decision was withdrawn.

GRU: Russia's main intelligence directorate. The foreign military intelligence agency of the Russian armed forces. The guys who do all the real work while the KGB gets all the credit, or so I'm told. Established by Joseph Stalin in 1942, the GRU was tasked with running human intelligence operations outside the Soviet Union. Think of them as the DIA with balls.

GS: General Schedule. Federal jobs that provide good benefits and lots of free time.

Gsh-18L: According to Forgotten Weapons, a rotating-barrel Tula pistol "designed around a 9x19mm AP cartridge."

Gukurahundi Massacres: A series of killings carried out against Ndebele tribe members in Matabeleland, Zimbabwe, by the Mugabe government during the 1980s. As many as twenty thousand civilians were killed by the North Korean–trained Fifth Brigade of the Zimbabwean army.

GWOT: Global War on Terror. The seemingly endless pursuit of bad guys, kicked off by the 9/11 attacks.

Gym Jones: Utah-based fitness company founded by alpine climbing legend Mark Twight. Famous for turning soft Hollywood actors into hard bodies, Gym Jones once enjoyed a close relationship with a certain SEAL Team.

Hell Week: The crucible of BUD/S training. Five days of constant physical and mental stress with little or no sleep.

Hilux: Pickup truck manufactured by Toyota that is a staple in third-world nations due to its reliability.

HK416: M4 clone engineered by the German firm of Heckler & Koch to operate using a short-stroke gas pistol system instead of the M4's direct-impingement gas system. Used by select special operations units in the U.S. and abroad. May or may not have been the weapon used to kill Osama bin Laden.

HK417: Select-fire 7.62x51mm rifle built by Heckler & Koch as a big brother to the HK416. Often used as Designated Marksman Rifle with a magnified optic.

HK G3: Classic 7.62x51mm battle rifle.

HK MP5: A submachine gun extremely popular with hostage rescue and counterterrorism units until it became evident that it might be wise to have a rifle, especially if you run into a fight going to or from your target.

HK P7: A favorite of Hans Gruber's.

HRT: Hostage Rescue Team. The FBI's premier continental United States focused hostage-rescue, counterterrorism, and violent criminal apprehension unit.

HUMINT: Human Intelligence. Information gleaned through traditional human-to-human methods.

HVI/HVT: High-Value Individual/High-Value Target. An individual who is important to the enemy's capabilities and is therefore specifically sought out by a military force.

IDC: Independent Duty Corpsman. Essentially a doctor.

IDF: Israel Defense Forces. One of the, if not the most, experienced militaries on the planet.

IED: Improvised Explosive Device. Homemade bombs, whether crude or complex, often used by insurgent forces overseas.

Internet Research Agency: Commonly referred to as a "Russian Troll Farm," it is a de facto arm of the Russian political-military-intelligence apparatus conducting online influence operations. Connected via ownership to the Wagner Group.

IR: Infrared. The part of the electromagnetic spectrum with a longer wavelength than light but a shorter wavelength than radio waves.

Invisible to the naked eye but visible with night observation devices. Example: an IR laser-aiming device.

Iron Curtain: The physical and ideological border that separated the opposing sides of the Cold War.

ISI: The Pakistani Inter-Service Intelligence.

ISIS: Islamic State of Iraq and the Levant. Radical Sunni terrorist group based in parts of Iraq and Afghanistan. Also referred to as ISIL. The bad guys.

ISR: Intelligence, Surveillance, and Reconnaissance

ITAR: International Traffic in Arms Regulations. Export control regulations designed to restrict the export of certain items, including weapons and optics. These regulations offer ample opportunity to inadvertently violate federal law.

JAG: Judge Advocate General. Decent television series and the military's legal department.

JMAU: Joint Medical Augmentation Unit. High-speed medicine.

JSOC: Joint Special Operations Command. According to Wikipedia, it is a component command of SOCOM, that commands and controls Special Mission Units and Advanced Force Operations.

Katsa: Mossad case officer.

Katyn Massacre: Soviet purge of Polish citizens that took place in 1940 subsequent to the Soviet invasion. Twenty-two thousand Poles were killed by members of the NKVD during this event; many of the bodies were discovered in mass graves in the Katyn Forest. Russia denied responsibility for the massacre until 1990.

KGB: The Soviet "Committee for State Security." Excelled at "suppressing internal dissent" during the Cold War. Most often referred to by kids of the eighties as "the bad guys."

KIA: Killed in Action

Kidon: "Bayonet." The unit of the Mossad's Caesarea tasked with executing "negative treatments."

Kudu: A spiral-horned antelope, roughly the size and build of an elk, that inhabits much of sub-Saharan Africa.

Langley: The Northern Virginia location where the Central Intelligence Agency is headquartered. Often used as shorthand for CIA.

LaRue OBR: Optimized Battle Rifle. Precision variant of the AR-15/AR-10 designed for use as a Designated Marksman or Sniper Rifle. Available in both 5.56x45mm and 7.62x51mm.

Law of Armed Conflict: A segment of public international law that regulates the conduct of armed hostilities.

LAW Rocket: M-72 Light Anti-armor Weapon. A disposable, tube-launched 66mm unguided rocket in use with U.S. forces since before the Vietnam War.

Leica M4: Classic 35mm rangefinder camera produced from 1966 to 1975.

Long-Range Desert Group: A specialized British military unit that operated in the North African and Mediterranean theaters during World War II. The unit was made up of soldiers from Great Britain, New Zealand, and Southern Rhodesia.

L-Pill: A "lethal pill" or suicide pill developed during World War II and later issued to high-risk agents and operatives on both sides of the Cold War.

M1911/1911A1: .45-caliber pistol used by U.S. forces since before World War I.

M3: World War II submachine gun chambered in .45 ACP. This simple but reliable weapon became a favorite of the frogmen of that time.

M4: The standard assault rifle of the majority of U.S. military forces, including the U.S. Navy SEALs. The M4 is a shortened carbine variant of the M16 rifle that fires a 5.56x45mm cartridge. The M4 is a modular design that can be adapted to numerous configurations, including different barrel lengths.

MACV-SOG: Military Assistance Command, Vietnam—Studies and Observations Group. Deceiving name for a group of brave warriors who conducted highly classified special operations missions during the Vietnam War. These operations were often conducted behind enemy lines in Laos, Cambodia, and North Vietnam.

Mahdi Militia: An insurgent Shia militia loyal to cleric Muqtada al-Sadr that opposed U.S. forces in Iraq during the height of that conflict.

Makarov: A Soviet-era pistol favored by the bad guys.

MANPADS: Man-Portable Air-Defense System. Small antiaircraft surface-to-air guided rockets such as the U.S. Stinger and the Russian SA-7.

Marine Raiders: U.S. Marine Corps special operations unit; formerly known as MARSOC.

Maritime Branch: It's best to just google it.

Mazrah Tora: A prison in Cairo, Egypt. You do not want to wake up here.

MBITR: AN/PRC-148 Multiband Inter/Intra Team Radio. A handheld multiband, tactical software–defined radio, commonly used by special operations forces to communicate during operations.

McMillan TAC-50: Bolt-action sniper rifle chambered in .50 BMG used for long-range sniping operations, used by U.S. special operations forces as well as the Canadian army.

MDMA: A psychoactive drug whose clinical name is too long to place here. Known on the street as "ecstasy." Glow sticks not included.

MH-47: Special operations variant of the Army's Chinook helicopter, usually flown by members of the 160th SOAR. This twin-rotor aircraft is used frequently in Afghanistan due to its high service ceiling and large troop- and cargo-carrying capacity. Rumor has it that, if you're careful, you can squeeze a Land Rover Defender 90 inside one.

MH-60: Special operations variant of the Army's Black Hawk helicopter, usually flown by members of the 160th SOAR.

MI5: Military Intelligence, Section 5. Britain's domestic counterintelligence and security agency. Like the FBI but with nicer suits and better accents.

MIL DOT: A reticle-based system used for range estimation and long-range shooting, based on the milliradian unit of measurement.

MIL(s): One-thousandth of a radian; an angular measurement used in rifle scopes. 0.1 MIL equals 1 centimeter at 100 meters or 0.36" at 100 yards. If you find that confusing, don't become a sniper.

MIT: Turkey's national intelligence organization and a school in Boston for smart kids.

Mk 46 MOD 1: Belt-fed 5.56x45mm light machine gun built by FN Herstal. Often used by special operations forces due to its light weight, the Mk 46 is a scaled-down version of the Mk 48 MOD 1.

Mk 48 MOD 1: Belt-fed 7.62x51mm light machine gun designed for use by special operations forces. Weighing eighteen pounds unloaded, the Mk 48 can fire 730 rounds per minute to an effective range of 800 meters and beyond.

Mosin-Nagant: Legendary Russian bolt-action service rifle found on battlefields across the globe.

Mossad: The Israeli version of the CIA but even more apt to make their enemies disappear.

MP7: Compact select-fire personal defense weapon built by Heckler & Koch and used by various special operations forces. Its 4.6x30mm cartridge is available in a subsonic load, making the weapon extremely quiet when suppressed. What the MP7 lacks in lethality it makes up for in coolness.

MQ-4C: An advanced unmanned surveillance drone developed by Northrop Grumman for use by the United States Navy.

Robert Mugabe: Chairman of ZANU who led the nation of Zimbabwe from 1980 to 2017 as both prime minister and president. Considered responsible for retaliatory attacks against his rival Ndebele tribe as well as a disastrous land redistribution scheme that was ruled illegal by Zimbabwe's High Court.

MultiCam: A proprietary camouflage pattern developed by Crye Precision. Formerly reserved for special operators and air-softers, MultiCam is now standard issue to much of the U.S. and allied militaries.

Nagant M1985: As described in the novel, this pistol was used to execute Czar Nicholas II and his family.

NATO: North Atlantic Treaty Organization. An alliance created in 1949 to counter the Soviet threat to the Western Hemisphere. Headquartered in Brussels, Belgium, the alliance is commanded by a four-star U.S. military officer known as the Supreme Allied Commander Europe (SACEUR).

Naval Special Warfare Development Group (DEVGRU): A command that appears on the biographies of numerous admirals on the Navy's website. Joe Biden publicly referred to it by a different name when he was the vice president.

NBACC: National Biodefense Analysis and Countermeasures Center. A facility on Fort Detrick in Maryland that for sure does not weaponize and test infectious diseases in the Bat Cave.

NCIS: Naval Criminal Investigative Service. A federal law enforcement agency whose jurisdiction includes the U.S. Navy and Marine Corps. Also a popular television program with at least two spin-offs.

Niassa Game Reserve: Sixteen thousand square miles of relatively untouched wilderness in northern Mozambique. The reserve is home to a wide variety of wildlife as well as a fair number of poachers looking to commoditize them.

NKVD: A federal law enforcement arm of the former Soviet Union. Best known as the action arm of Stalin's Great Purge under the guise of protecting "state security" and responsible for mass executions and imprisonments of "enemies of the people."

NODs: Night observation devices. Commonly referred to as "night vision goggles," these devices amplify ambient light, allowing the user to see in low-light environments. Special operations forces often operate at night to take full advantage of such technology.

NSA: National Security Agency. U.S. intelligence agency tasked with gathering and analyzing signals intercepts and other communications data. Also known as No Such Agency. These are the government employees who listen to our phone calls and read our emails and texts for reasons of "national security." See *Permanent Record* by Edward Snowden.

NSC: National Security Council. This body advises and assists the president of the United States on matters of national security.

NSW: Naval Special Warfare. The Navy's special operations force; includes SEAL Teams.

Officer Candidate School (OCS): Twelve-week course where civilians and enlisted sailors are taught to properly fold underwear. Upon completion, they are miraculously qualified to command men and women in combat.

OmniSTAR: Satellite-based augmentation system service provider. A really fancy GPS service that provides very precise location information.

Ops-Core Ballistic Helmet: Lightweight high-cut helmet used by special operations forces worldwide.

Orsis T-5000 Tochnost: Russian bolt-action precision rifle.

P226: 9mm handgun made by SIG Sauer, the standard-issue sidearm for SEALs.

P229: A compact handgun made by SIG Sauer, often used by federal law enforcement officers, chambered in 9mm as well as other cartridges.

P320: Striker-fired modular 9mm handgun that has recently been adopted by the U.S. armed forces as the M17/M18.

P365: Subcompact handgun made by SIG Sauer, designed for concealed carry. Despite its size, the P365 holds up to thirteen rounds of 9mm.

Pakhan: The highest-ranked *blatnoy* in prison. Now more synonymous with "senior criminal."

Pakistani Taliban: An Islamic terrorist group composed of various Sunni Islamist militant groups based in the northwestern Federally Administered Tribal Areas along the Afghan border in Pakistan.

Pamwe Chete: "All Together"; the motto of the Rhodesian Selous Scouts.

Panga: A machete-like utility blade common in Africa.

Peshmerga: Military forces of Kurdistan. Meaning "the one who faces death," they are regarded by Allied troops as some of the best fighters in the region.

PETN: PentaErythritol TetraNitrate. An explosive compound used in blasting caps to initiate larger explosive charges.

PG-32V: High-explosive antitank rocket that can be fired from the Russian-designed RPG-32 rocket-propelled grenade launcher. Its tandem charge is effective against various types of armor, including reactive armor.

PID: Protective Intelligence and Threat Assessment Division. The division of the Secret Service that monitors potential threats to its protectees.

PKM: Soviet-designed, Russian-made light machine gun chambered in 7.62x54R that can be found in conflicts throughout the globe. This weapon feeds from a non-disintegrating belt and has a rate of fire of 650 rounds per minute. You don't want one shooting at you.

PLF: Parachute Landing Fall. A technique taught to military parachutists to prevent injury when making contact with the earth. Round canopy parachutes used by airborne forces fall at faster velocities than other parachutes, and require a specific landing sequence. More often than not, it ends up as feet-ass-head.

PMC: Private Military Company. Though the profession is as old as war itself, the modern term *PMC* was made infamous in the post-9/11 era by Blackwater, aka Xe Services, and now known as Academi. POTUS: President of the United States; leader of the free world.

PPD: Presidential Protection Detail. The element of the Secret Service tasked with protecting POTUS.

President's Hundred: A badge awarded by the Civilian Marksmanship Program to the one hundred top-scoring military and civilian shooters in the President's Pistol and President's Rifle matches. Enlisted members of the U.S. military are authorized to wear the tab on their uniform.

Professional Hunter: A licensed hunting guide in Africa, often referred to as a "PH." Zimbabwe-licensed PHs are widely considered the most qualified and highly trained in Africa and make up the majority of the PH community operating in Mozambique.

***The Protocols of the Elders of Zion*:** An anti-Semitic conspiracy manifesto first published in the late 1800s by Russian sources. Though quickly established as a fraudulent text, *Protocols* has been widely circulated in numerous languages.

PSO-1: A Russian-made 4x24mm illuminated rifle optic developed for use on the SVD rifle.

PTSD: Post-traumatic stress disorder. A mental condition that develops in association with shocking or traumatic events. Commonly associated with combat veterans.

PVS-15: Binocular-style NODs used by U.S. and allied special operations forces.

QRF: Quick Reaction Force. A contingency ground force on standby to assist operations in progress.

Quantum Computing: A rapidly emerging technology that employs the laws of quantum mechanics and physics to perform computations.

Ranger Panties: Polyester PT shorts favored by members of the 75th Ranger Regiment that leave very little to the imagination, sometimes referred to as "silkies."

REMF: Rear-Echelon Motherfucker. Describes most officers taking credit for what the E-5 mafia and a few senior enlisted do on the ground if the mission goes right. These same "people" will be the first to hang you out to dry if things go south. Now that they are home safe and sound, they will let you believe that when they were "downrange" they actually left the wire.

RFID: Radio Frequency Identification. Technology commonly used to tag objects that can be scanned electronically.

RHIB/RIB: Rigid Hull Inflatable Boat/Rigid Inflatable Boat. A lightweight but high-performance boat constructed with a solid fiberglass or composite hull and flexible tubes at the gunwale (sides).

Rhodesia: A former British colony that declared its independence in 1965. After a long and brutal civil war, the nation became Zimbabwe in 1979.

Rhodesian Bush War: An insurgency battle between the Rhodesian Security Forces and Soviet-, East German–, Cuban-, and Chinese-backed guerrillas that lasted from 1964 to 1979. The war ended when the December 1979 Lancaster House Agreement put an end to white minority rule.

Rhodesian SAS: A special operations unit formed as part of the famed British Special Air Service in 1951. When Rhodesia sought independence, the unit ceased to exist as part of the British military but fought as part of the Rhodesian Security Forces until 1980. Many members of the Selous Scouts were recruited from the SAS.

Rich Kid Shit: Expensive equipment items reserved for use by the most highly funded special operations units. Google JSOC.

RLI: Rhodesian Light Infantry. An airborne and airmobile unit used to conduct "fireforce" operations during the Bush War. These missions were often launched in response to intelligence provided by Selous Scouts on the ground.

ROE: Rules of engagement. Rules or directives that determine what level of force can be applied against an enemy in a particular situation or area.

RPG-32: 105mm rocket-propelled grenade launcher that is made in both Russia and, under license, in Jordan.

SAD: The CIA's Special Activities Division. Though it is now called the Special Activities Center, it's still responsible for covert action, aka the really cool stuff.

SALUTE: A report used to transmit information on enemy forces. Size / Activity / Location / Unit / Time / Equipment.

SAP: Special Access Program. Security protocols that provide highly classified information with safeguards and access restrictions that exceed those for regular classified information. Really secret stuff.

SALUTE: A report used to transmit information on enemy forces. Size / Activity / Location / Unit / Time / Equipment.

Sayanim: Usually non-Israeli, though most often Jewish, worldwide network of Mossad facilitators.

Sayeret Matkal: The General Staff Reconnaissance Unit of the IDF responsible for hostage rescue and counterterrorism operations beyond Israel's borders. The Israeli equivalate of the British SAS, U.S. Army's Delta Force, and a certain SEAL Team between the numbers of 5 and 7.

SCAR-17: 7.62x51mm battle rifle produced by FN. Its gas mechanism can be traced to that of the FAL.

Schmidt & Bender: Privately held German optics manufacturer known for its precision rifle scopes.

SCI: Special Compartmentalized Information. Classified information concerning or derived from sensitive intelligence sources, methods, or analytical processes. Often found on private basement servers in upstate New York or bathroom closet servers in Denver.

SCIF: Sensitive Compartmented Information Facility. A secure and restricted room or structure where classified information is discussed or viewed.

SEAL: Acronym of SEa, Air, and Land. The three mediums in which SEALs operate. The U.S. Navy's special operations force.

Secret Service: The federal law enforcement agency responsible for protecting the POTUS.

Selous Scouts: An elite, if scantily clad, mixed-race unit of the Rhodesian army responsible for counterinsurgency operations. These "pseudoterrorists" led some of the most successful special operations missions in modern history.

SERE: Survival, Evasion, Resistance, Escape. A military training program that includes realistic role-playing as a prisoner of war. SERE students are subjected to highly stressful procedures, sometimes including waterboarding, as part of the course curriculum. More commonly referred to as "camp slappy."

Shin Bet / Shabak: Israel's equivalent of the FBI or MI5.

Shishani: Arabic term for Chechen fighters in Syria, probably due to "Shishani" being a common Chechen surname.

SIGINT: Signals Intelligence. Intelligence derived from electronic signals and systems used by foreign targets, such as communications systems, radars, and weapons systems.

SIPR: Secret Internet Protocol Router network. A secure version of the internet used by DOD and the State Department to transmit classified information.

SISDE: Italy's Intelligence and Democratic Security Service. Their suits are probably even nicer than MI5's.

SISMI: Italian version of the CIA. Formerly called the AISE until scandals forced a housecleaning and name change.

SOCOM: United States Special Operations Command. The Unified Combatant Command charged with overseeing the various Special Operations Component Commands of the Army, Marine Corps, Navy, and Air Force of the United States armed forces. Headquartered at MacDill Air Force Base in Tampa, Florida.

Special Boat Team-12: The West Coast unit that provides maritime mobility to SEALs using a variety of vessels. Fast boats with machine guns.

Special Reconnaissance (SR) Team: NSW Teams that conduct special activities, ISR, and provide intelligence support to the SEAL Teams.

Spetsnaz: An umbrella term for Russian special operations units and special operations units in post-Soviet states.

Spetssviaz: Officially the Special Communications and Information Service of the Federal Protective Service of the Russian Federation. The Russian version of the NSA. Yes, they have all your personal electronic data and credit card information.

SR-16: An AR-15 variant developed and manufactured by Knight Armament Corporation.

SRT: Surgical Resuscitation Team. You want these guys close by if you take a bullet.

Strela-2: Cold War era Soviet-designed shoulder-fired surface-to-air missile.

StrongFirst: Kettle-bell-focused fitness program founded by Russian fitness guru Pavel Tsatsouline that is popular with special operations forces.

SVD: Officially the SVD-63 to denote the year it was accepted for use in the Soviet military, it is known the world over as the Dragunov.

S-Vest: Suicide vest. An explosives-laden garment favored by suicide bombers. Traditionally worn only once.

SVR: The Foreign Intelligence Service of the Russian Federation, or as John le Carré describes them, "the KGB in drag."

Taliban: An Islamic fundamentalist political movement and terrorist group in Afghanistan. U.S. and coalition forces have been at war with members of the Taliban since late 2001.

Targeting Officer: The CIA's website reads that as a targeting officer you will "identify new opportunities for DO operational activity and enhance ongoing operations." Translation—they tell us whom to kill.

TATP: Triacetone triperoxide. An explosive compound nicknamed "Mother of Satan." Its chemical precursors can be found in commonly available products the world over.

TDFD: Time-delay firing device. An explosive initiator that allows for detonation at a determined period of time. A fancy version of a really long fuse.

TIC: Troops in contact. A firefight involving U.S. or friendly forces.

TOC: Tactical Operations Center. A command post for military operations. A TOC usually includes a small group of personnel who guide members of an active tactical element during a mission from the safety of a secured area.

TOR Network: A computer network designed to conceal a user's identity and location. TOR allows for anonymous communication.

TQ: Politically correct term for the timely questioning of individuals on-site once a target is secure. May involve the raising of voices.

Troop Chief: Senior enlisted SEAL on a forty-man troop, usually a master chief petty officer. The guy who makes shit happen.

TS: Top Secret. Information, the unauthorized disclosure of which reasonably could be expected to cause exceptionally grave damage to national security and that the original classification authority is able to identify or describe. Can also describe an individual's level of security clearance.

TST: Time-sensitive target. A target requiring immediate response because it is highly lucrative, is a fleeting target of opportunity, or poses (or will soon pose) a danger to friendly forces.

UAV: Unmanned Aerial Vehicle. A drone.

UCMJ: Uniform Code of Military Justice. Disciplinary and criminal code that applies to members of the U.S. military.

UDI: Unilateral Declaration of Independence. The 1965 document that established Rhodesia as an independent sovereign state. The UDI resulted in an international embargo and made Rhodesia a pariah.

V-22: Tilt-rotor aircraft that can fly like a plane and take off/land like a helicopter. Numerous examples were crashed during its extremely expensive development.

VBIED: Vehicle-Borne Improvised Explosive Device. A rolling car bomb driven by a suicidal terrorist.

VC: National Liberation Front of South Vietnam, better known as the Viet Cong. A communist insurgent group that fought against the government of South Vietnam and its allies during the Vietnam War. In the movies, these are the guys wearing the black pajamas carrying AKs.

VI: Vehicle Interdiction. Good fun, unless you are on the receiving end.

***Vor v Zakone*:** An individual at the top of the incarcerated criminal underground. Think godfather. Top authority for the Bratva. Today, each region of Russia has a *Vor v Zakone*.

***Vory*:** A hierarchy within the Bratva. Career criminals. More directly translated as "thief."

VPN: Virtual Private Network. A private network that enables users to send and receive data across shared or public networks as if their computing devices were directly connected to the private network. Considered more secure than a traditional internet network.

VSK-94: Russian-made Sniper/Designated Marksman rifle chambered in the subsonic 9x39mm cartridge. This suppressed weapon is popular with Russian special operations and law enforcement units due to its minimal sound signature and muzzle flash.

VSS Vintorez: Integrally suppressed Soviet rifle chambered in 9x39mm.

Wagner Group: A Russian private military company with close ties to the Russian government.

War Vets: Loosely organized groups of Zimbabweans who carried out many of the land seizures during the 1990s. Often armed, these individuals used threats and intimidation to remove white farmers from their homes. Despite the name, most of these individuals were too young to have participated in the Bush War. Not to be confused with ZNLWVA, a group that represents ZANU-affiliated veterans of the Bush War.

WARCOM/NAVSPECWARCOM: United States Naval Special Warfare Command. The Navy's special operations force and the maritime component of United States Special Operations Command. Headquartered in Coronado, California, WARCOM is the administrative command for subordinate NSW Groups composed of eight SEAL Teams, one SEAL Delivery Vehicle (SDV) Team, three Special Boat Teams, and two Special Reconnaissance Teams.

Westley Richards Droplock: A rifle or shotgun built by the famed Birmingham, England, gunmakers that allows the user to remove the locking mechanisms for repair or replacement in the field. Widely considered one of the finest and most iconic actions of all time.

Whiskey Tango: Military speak for "white trash."

WIA: Wounded In Action.

Yamam: An elite unit of Israeli border police that conducts high-risk hostage rescue and counterterrorism operations in Israel.

Yazidis: An insular Kurdish-speaking ethnic and religious group that primarily resides in Iraq. Effectively a subminority among the Kurds, Yazidis were heavily persecuted by ISIS.

YPG: Kurdish militia forces operating in the Democratic Federation of Northern Syria. The Turks are not fans.

ZANLA: Zimbabwe African National Liberation Army. The armed wing of the Maoist Zimbabwe African National Union and one of the major combatants of the Rhodesian Bush War. ZANLA forces often staged out of training camps located in Mozambique and were led by Robert Mugabe.

Zimbabwe: Sub-Saharan African nation that formerly existed as Southern Rhodesia and later Rhodesia. Led for three decades by Robert Mugabe, Zimbabwe ranks as one of the world's most corrupt nations on Transparency International's Corruption Perceptions Index.

ZIPRA: Zimbabwe People's Revolutionary Army. The Soviet-equipped armed wing of ZAPU and one of the two major insurgency forces that fought in the Rhodesian Bush War. ZIPRA forces fell under the leadership of Josh Nkomo, who spent much of the war in Zambia. ZIPRA members were responsible for shooting down two civilian airliners using Soviet SA-7 surface-to-air missiles in the late 1970s.

Zodiac Mk 2 GR: A 4.2-meter inflatable rubber boat capable of carrying up to six individuals. These craft are often used as dinghies for larger vessels.

ACKNOWLEDGMENTS

THIS NOVEL, AS WITH the four that preceded it, could not have been written without a foundation. I am indebted to my parents for making reading a natural part of my life. I can't recall a time that I have ever been without a good book.

To all the authors who provided my early education in the art of storytelling during my formative years: **Joseph Campbell**, **David Morrell**, **Stephen Hunter**, **Tom Clancy**, **John le Carré**, **Marc Olden**, **Ian Fleming**, **Robert Ludlum**, **Frederick Forsyth**, **Louis L'Amour**, **Nelson DeMille**, **Jack Higgins**, **Clive Cussler**, **Ken Follett**, **J.C. Pollock**, and **A.J. Quinnell**. To those who moved the genre forward while I was engaged in life's first chapter: **Vince Flynn**, **Steven Pressfield**, **Daniel Silva**, **Lee Child**, and **Mark Greaney**. And to **Brad Thor** for making this post-military chapter in life possible. Thank you, all.

To the authors whose research and books informed these pages: *The Ledger* by **David Kilcullen** and **Greg Mills**, *The Bear Went Over The Mountain* edited by **Lester W. Grau**, *Inside Spetsnaz* edited by **Maj. William H. Burgess III**, *Spetsnaz* by Viktor Suvorov, *The Soviet-Afghan War* by the **Russian General Staff**, *Charlie Wilson's War* by **George Crile**, *Soldier Spies* by **Samuel M. Katz**, *The Night Raiders* by **Samuel M. Katz**, *The Ghost Warriors* by **Samuel M. Katz**, *Six Days of War* by **Michael B. Oren**, *Rise and Kill First* by **Ronen Bergman**, *The Price of Paradise* by **Iain**

Overton, *Dying to Win* by **Robert A. Pape**, *Poisoner in Chief* by **Stephen Kinzer**, *The Kill Chain* by **Christian Brose**, *No Place to Hide* by **Glenn Greenwald**, *Permanent Record* by **Edward Snowden**, and **Jaydev Joshi**'s article in **Medium** titled "The Mysterious Side of the Internet."

To those who live "down the rabbit hole" and took the time to answer my questions on cyberwarfare, quantum computing, and artificial intelligence. You made me never want to send another email or text message ever again.

To **Kevin O'Malley**, **James Rupley**, **David Lehman**, and **Dan Gelston** for going through the early draft of this manuscript with red pens in hand. It is appreciated more than I can express. And to **Megan Gelston,** whom I forgot to thank last time.

To **Gavy Friedson** and his entire family for reading the chapters on Israel. I could not make it out in person due to the uncertainty in pandemic protocols, but something tells me James Reece will be back!

I've never been in a helicopter autorotating to earth, so for that section of the novel I relied on input from my friend **Don Bentley,** former U.S. Army Apache helicopter pilot and *New York Times* bestselling author of the Matt Drake series. Any mistakes made and/or liberties taken are mine alone. You can catch our conversation on the **Danger Close** podcast.

To **Dylan Murphy** for always going the extra mile in developing the fight sequences. They would not be what they are without his proficiency in the art and science of violence. And to **Elyse** for being such a good sport.

To **Clint** and **Heidi Smith** of **Thunder Ranch** for all your support over the years and for reviewing the weapons-centric portions of the novels.

To **Jeff Rotherham** for your time in uniform and for your expertise in all things that go boom.

To **Ian McCollum** of **Forgotten Weapons** for your help on the Galil. One day I will add one to my collection.

To **Jason Burton** of **Heirloom Precision**. I am fired up for that prewar .38 Super.

To **Larry Vickers** and **James Rupley** for the Vickers Guide series. They are never far from reach as I research the weapons in my novels. You can find them at vickersguide.com.

To **Rob Bianchin** at **Cabot Guns** for your years of support. *The Devil's Hand* custom 1911 is just awesome!

To **Jim Fuller**, AK connoisseur—I am fired up for our builds.

To **Monty LeClair** of **Centurion Arms** for his wealth of knowledge on sniper weapons.

To **James Rose** and **Jamie Swanson** and the team at the **Park City Gun Club** for always keeping a lane open for me.

To **Ron Cohen, Tom Taylor, Jason Wright, Samantha Piatt, Morgan Baker** at **SIG Sauer**. Thank you all for being such an integral part of this journey.

To **Evan Hafer, Logan Stark, Richard Ryan, Mat Best, Jared Taylor**, and **Tom Davin** at **Black Rifle Coffee Company** for your inspiration and support. Congratulations on going public! Keep an eye out for BRCC in the Amazon Video series adaptation of *The Terminal List*.

To **Daniel Winkler** and **Karen Shook** of **Winkler Knives** for your kindness and generosity. Get ready to build some RnD Tomahawks! When *The Terminal List* hits **Amazon Prime Video**, I have a feeling you are going to be very busy.

To **Mike Glover** and the entire team at **Fieldcraft Survival** for all you do to make citizens of this country more aware and prepared.

To **Donnie** and **Kathryn Edwards** and everyone who volunteers at the **Best Defense Foundation** to honor those who answered the call.

To **Dom Raso** of **Dynamis Alliance**—every American needs a Combat Flathead.

To **Andrew Arrabito** of **Half Face Blades** and **War Paw Wines** for making two of my favorite things.

To **Bill Rapier** of **AMTAC Blades** for your service to the nation and for an epic fixed blade.

To **Dory Schoby** and everyone at **Aimpoint** for the innovation and support.

To **Taran Butler** of **Tactical Innovations** for all the range runs on my weekends in LA and for the incredible pistol builds.

To **Tuck Beckstoffer** for your friendship and for fueling my late-night writing sessions.

To **Mike Pappas**, **Ernie Beckwith**, and **Tasson Nique** of **Dead Air Silencers** for an awesome product line.

To **Ray Porter** for continuing to crush the narration in the audiobooks.

To **Jon Sanchez** of the **Team Performance Institute** for being the person you are and for your role in making this dream a reality.

To **Chris Pratt**, **Antoine Fuqua**, **Jared Shaw**, **David DiGilio**, **Kat Samick**, **Max Adams**, **Jon Schumacher**, **Dan Shattuck**, **David Auge**, **Ray Mendoza**, **Indivisible Productions**, **MRC**, **Amazon**, and the entire cast and crew of *The Terminal List* on **Amazon Prime Video**. Thank you for being so welcoming and for knocking it out of the park. For the story on how my debut novel was brought to life, see the foreword to the new hardcover edition of *The Terminal List*.

To **Joe Rogan**—keep asking questions.

To **Katie Pavlich** for always being there and for sitting down as my first guest on the Danger Close Podcast!

To **David Bolls** for kick-starting the process that resulted in *The Terminal List*'s coming to screens. Thank you, my friend.

To **James Yeager** for your friendship and early support.

To **Jim** and **Louise Shockey** for your example and strength. Prayers inbound.

To **Ryan Steck**, aka The Real Book Spy. Congratulations on your debut thriller, *Fields of Fire*! I can't wait to see it on shelves.

To the hosts of **The Crew Reviews Podcast—Sean Cameron, C.E. Albanese,** and **Mike Houtz**—for highlighting the world of publishing through such informative and insightful conversations.

To **Eric Bishop**: Congratulations on the publication of *The Body Man*!

To **Dr. Robert Bray**—Not a day goes by that we don't think about all you and **Tracey** have done to make the transition from the military to the private sector happen. Thank you.

To **Frank Lecrone**—I'll never be able to thank you enough for everything you made possible for my family. It is an honor, brother.

To **Jon Dubin**—Thank you for answering my federal law enforcement questions and for Pineapple Brothers Lanai. Where are we going next?

To **Mike Stoner** of **Mike Stoner Photography** for great work behind the camera.

To **Ironclad** for being such an instrumental part of this journey: **Jeremy Carey, Ryan Berry, Jesse Carey, Matt Turley, Nico Johnston, Catey Carey, Jessica Collins, Brian Crouch, Noah Knight, Ashley Morrison, Danny McCusker, Kevin Kelleher, Daniel Peebles, Harley Taylor, John Aho, Noah Amedick, Elizabeth Swainston.** Let's go!

To all those who have supported this effort along the way: **Mark Owen, Mike Schoby** at **Field Ethos, Christian Craighead, Kyle Lamb** of **Viking Tactics, Andy Moeckel**—the Flip Flop Guy, **John Devine** of **Devine K9s** and the **Rescue 22 Foundation, Rick** and **Esther Rosenfield, Lucas O'Hara** of **Grizzly Forge Knives, Isaac Aleman, Trevor Thompson, John Dudley** of **NockOn, Nick** and **Tina Coussoulis, Chris Hunt** of **Code of the West, Cole Kramer** of **Kramer's Kodiak Guide Service, Isaiah Washington, Tim Fallon** and the team at **FTW Ranch, Rich Zeoli, Eric** and **Sarah Cylvick** of **ZipRider, Bert Sorin** of **Sorniex, Jocko Willink** of **Echelon Front, Eric Anderson** at **Salomon, Stacy Wenger, Josh Smith** of **Montana Knife Company, Mark Bollman** and the team at **Ball & Buck**, **Jonathan Hart** and **John Barklow** at **Sitka Gear**, **Jon Edwards** and the team at **Schnee's**, **Matt Graham** at **ARES Watches**, **Andy Stumpf** of **Cleared Hot**, **Jeff Kimbell** at **Safari Club International**, **Tucker Carlson**, **Lexi Ciccone**, **Mike Bursaw** of **Mystery Mike's**, **Tetiana Gaidar**, **Tom Flanagan** of **Eagles & Angels**, **Barbara Peters** at **Poisoned Pen Bookstore** in Phoenix, **Michaela Smith** at **Dolly's Bookstore** in Park City, author **Desiree Holt**, **Nick Siefert** at **Athlon Outdoors**, **Jeff Kimbell**, **Elaine Ryan** and **Rick Kaiser** at the **UDT SEAL Museum**, **Ross Kaminsky**, **Rihana Cary** at the team at **MTN OPS**, **Jack Daniels**, **Elias Kfoury** of **Seven Sages Health**, **Tyr S.**, **Steve "Mato" Matulewicz** of **Sentry**, **Jimmy Spithill**, **Trig** and **Annette French**, **Martin** and **Kelly Katz**, **Patrick Hemingway Adams**, **Razor** and **Sylvia Dobbs**, **Mike Atkinson** of **T3 Gear**, **Mike Comacho**, **Damien** and **Jen Patton**, **Alec Wolf** at **Zev Technologies**, **Adam Janke** of the **Journal of Mountain Hunting**, **Marcus Torgerson** at **IKMF Krav Maga**, **Amy Robins** at **Alexo Athletico**, **Rick Stewart** at **American Zealot Productions**, **Mike** at **Last Line of Defense**, **Wally McLallen** and **Keith Walawender** and the team at **Tomahawk Strategic Solutions**, **Mickey Schuch** at **Carry Trainer**, the legendary **Ken Hackathorn**, **Jeff Houston** at **TAC 7**, **Chris Osman** at **Rhuged**, **Eli Crane** at **Bottle Breacher**, **Jeff Reid** at **Frozen Trident**, **Brent Gleeson** at **Taking Point Leadership**, **Lacey Biles**, **Garry** and **Victoria Peters**, **Shane Reilly** (I finally did a move without you), **Michael Davidson** and **Natalie Alverez** at **Gen Next**, **Jeff Crane** and **P.J. Carleton** at the **Congressional Sportsman's Foundation**, **Joe** and **Charlotte Betar** at the **Houston Safari Club**, **Ryan Michler** of **Order of Man**, **Hoby Darling**, **Herman Achteruis** at **Achter Knives**, **Brian Call** of the **Gritty Podcast**, **Clint Emerson** of **100 Deadly Skills**, **Mike Sauers** and **Samantha Bonilla** of **Forged**, **Jared W. Ogden** of **Triumph Systems**, **Erik Snyder**, **Chris DeWitt**, **Damien Clapper** at **Lead Nav Systems**, **Kurt Schlichter** of **Townhall**, **Maddie Taylor**, **John Nores** at **The Thin Green Line**, **Dana** and **Chris Loesch** of **The Dana Show**, **Aron Snyder** at **Kifaru Interna-**

tional, **Sean Haberburger** at **BlueCore**, **Eric Frohardt**, **Billy Birdzell**, **Shahram Moosavi** of **Phoenix JKD Institute of Mixed Martial Arts**, **Josh Waldron**, **Ed Byres**, the team at **MTN TOUGH**, **Phil Hoon** of **Capitol 6 Advisors**, author **Rob Olive**, and **Fred Burton** at **ONTIC**.

To **Taylor Matkins** and **Katie Manhart** at **Lucky Ones Coffee** for all you do for my family and for the community in Park City.

To **Negar** and **Jean-Marc Chevre** for finding us the perfect spot.

To **Craig** and **Heather Flynn** for allowing me to use your barn as a storage facility. I'll get everything moved out in the next year or two . . . or three . . .

To **Mike Mitchell** and the crew at **Majestic Canyon Creations** for all the work on the new podcast studio. It is looking great!

To **Andrew Kline** for always being there for my family.

To **Bill Crider**—Can't wait for our next adventure.

To **James Jarrett**, a warrior of **Project Delta**, for your mentorship.

To **Jimmy Klein**—Let's get afield soon!

To **Chris Cox** of **Capitol Six Advisors** for your years of friendship and support. Thank you for everything.

To **Graham Hill**—You finally got that character. Thank you, my friend.

To **Brock Bosson**, **Ted Lacey**, **Tina Davis**, **Alexander Haberman**, and the legal team at **Cahill Gorden & Reindell** for going above and beyond at every turn.

To **Norm Brownstein** and **Steve Demby** at **Brownstein Hyatt Farber Schreck** for always making time for me.

To **Mitch Langberg** at **Brownstein Hyatt Farber Schreck** for continuing to have my back as a friend and on the legal front.

To **Garrett Bray**—I certainly would not be where I am today with you. Thank you.

To my agent, **Alexandra Machinist** at **ICM**, for guiding me through terrain on which you are a tier-one operator.

To my agent at ICM in Los Angeles, **Josie Freedman**, for navigating the world of Hollywood.

To the magnificent **Emily Bestler** for having taken a chance on me and giving me my shot. Not a day goes by that I do not count my blessings that you are such an integral part of my life. I am forever grateful.

To **Lara Jones** for your undying patience and for keeping this venture on the rails.

To my publicist, **David Brown**, for your friendship and for making this journey so much fun! I look forward to our every encounter!

To **Al Madocs**, whose work in turning my manuscript into the book in your hands is nothing short of miraculous.

To **James Iacobelli** for crushing another cover. Can't wait to see what you come up with for book six!

To **Jen Long** and the team at **Pocket Books** for the incredible series of James Reece paperback thrillers!

To **Jon Karp**, president and publisher of **Simon & Schuster**, for your leadership.

To **Libby McGuire**, senior vice president and publisher of **Atria Books**, for all your support.

To **Dana Trocker**, **Suzanne Donahue**, **Paige Lytle**, and **Iris Chen** for all your efforts. Thank you.

Thank you to **Sarah Lieberman**, **Gabrielle Audet**, **Chris Lynch**, and **Tom Spain** at **Simon & Schuster Audio**. There is not a day that goes by where I do not receive compliments on the audiobooks. That is all due to your efforts. Thank you.

To **Karlyn Hixson**, **Liz Perl**, **Sue Fleming**, **Sienna Farris**, and **Saimah Haque**, whose work introduces James Reece to readers across the world.

To **Gary Urda**, **Colin Shields**, **Chrissy Festa**, **Paula Amendolara**, **Janice Fryer**, **Leslie Collins**, **Gregory Hruska**, and **Lexi Dumas** for all you do in Accounts and Sales to put these novels on shelves. It is sincerely appreciated.

To **Tom Pitoniak**, whose efforts in copy editing this manuscript will not be forgotten. I owe you a drink.

And finally, to my amazing wife, **Faith**—what an insane few years it has been! Thank you for holding down the fort while I was deployed and now while I'm locked down to write. I am more in awe of you with each passing day.

And to our three children—I love you with all my heart!

Turn the page for an exclusive look
at Jack Carr's next James Reece thriller,

ONLY THE DEAD

Only the dead have seen the end of war.
—George Santayana, commonly misattributed to Plato

I do solemnly swear that I will support and defend the Constitution of the United States . . .
Against all enemies . . .
Foreign . . .
And domestic . . .
—Oath taken by members of the United States armed forces, the vice president, and every member of Congress

"Against all enemies, foreign, and domestic"
is not included in the president's oath of office
as specified by Article II, Section 1, Clause 8
of the Constitution of the United States.

PROLOGUE

Newport, Rhode Island
1980

WALTER STOWE DEFTLY PILOTED the thirty-six-foot trawler through Vineyard Sound past Nashawena Island and into Rhode Island Sound. He kept Castle Hill Lighthouse to the boat's starboard side as he navigated a northeasterly course toward their destination. He had become quite adept at maneuvering small watercraft in dangerous waters, though the seas between Edgartown Yacht Club on Martha's Vineyard and Station 10, the New York Yacht Club's property in Newport, were not nearly as dangerous as the waters he had been navigating ten years earlier, inserting and extracting Navy SEALs in the Mekong Delta.

The route ahead clear, Walt turned from the helm to look at his wife. Martha sat behind him on the flybridge, her tan legs outstretched on the cushioned aft-facing bench seat, her face upturned to catch the fading rays of the late summer sun.

"Trawler" was a bit of a misnomer. It was a Grand Banks 36 and though it resembled the trawlers of Walt's youth, this vessel was built with comfort and touring in mind, not hauling in a catch in the hopes of making ends meet. A more than capable craft, bloody decks were foreign to her. This boat was built to impress the East Coast's prestigious yachting community.

The boat was hers, or, to be more precise, it belonged to her family, a family of means. A family with history.

Martha's grandfather had made his money investing in commodities. He had then used that fortune to purchase commercial real estate in New York City. It was rumored that he had run a profitable bootlegging business during Prohibition. That mythology naturally led to whispers of mob connections in Manhattan and Chicago. Her family had even been accused of delivering the Windy City vote in a presidential election for another high-profile Massachusetts family two decades earlier, when Martha was still in middle school. She had never witnessed her father or grandfather dispel those rumors. She suspected that a connection to the mob, real or imagined, didn't hurt in certain business dealings.

While blue blood ran strong through her stock, Martha had diluted the perceived nobility of the line when she married Walter.

The Stowes were seafarers. Walt and his brothers had grown up fishing and checking traps off the coast of Cape Cod. Most people associate lobsters with Maine, but as Walt and his brothers knew, wooden lath traps were first used in their home waters in 1810. The traps Walt would use over a century later operated in much the same fashion as their predecessors: A lobster would be lured through a funnel, unable to resist the temptation of the mackerel and herring bait. The smaller crustaceans could escape through vents, but the larger ones would remain imprisoned in their wood and metal cells until Walt and his brothers pulled them to the surface.

Wychmere Harbor in Harwich Port was their base of operations, and in a fickle industry with innumerable variables, Walt learned that in some years the catch was not enough to feed a young family. He watched as his father took odd jobs around town to make ends meet, working as a handyman and bartender as finances and seasons dictated. The man never complained. From bullraking for littleneck clams to chasing striped bass to roofing, shingling, and a bit of carpentry, the elder Stowe put food on the table and a roof over the heads of his wife and sons.

All three Stowe boys believed their paths were pre-ordained. The sea was calling. That was, until they started hearing about a country called Vietnam.

Because the United States never formally declared war on North Vietnam, Walt's older brother was one of the 2.2 million Americans conscripted for service in Southeast Asia under the peacetime draft established by the Selective Training and Service Act of 1940. The working-class Stowe family knew it was only a matter of time before Walt was drafted, so his father recommended his middle child volunteer in the Navy. Rather than rolling the dice with the Army, the elder Stowe believed a ship off the coast would be a much safer way to ride out a tour in Vietnam. Neither Walt nor his father had ever heard of the Brown Water Navy.

Within the year, Walt found himself on a Mark II PBR in the Mekong Delta, learning the ropes from a weathered first-class petty officer—the boat's captain. Walt and the captain were augmented by a gunner's mate to run and maintain the twin .50-caliber machine guns and an engine-man to keep the new Jacuzzi water jet propulsion system operational.

With the .50s in the bow and a .30-caliber M1919AH mounted to the stern, along with a hand-cranked Mk 18 40x46mm grenade launcher, the patrol boat and crew of river rats operated throughout South Vietnam's extensive river systems, which cut through the country from the South China Sea all the way to Cambodia. With roads and rail lines still in rudimentary stages of development, it was the veins of rivers and canals that provided the lifeblood of Vietnam's economy via access to resources. Those who controlled the waterways controlled the country. It was upon returning from a patrol that he received a letter from his mother letting him know that his younger brother had been drafted by the country's first lottery. He wouldn't last three weeks in Vietnam.

Walt's commanding officer summoned Walt to his hooch in April 1970 to inform him of his brother's death. That same officer would summon him back a week later with news that Stowe was going home; his older brother was also dead, one of 1,448 service members to be killed on their last day in country and making the Stowe family one of thirty-one families to lose two brothers in the conflict.

Walt had a mission growing up in a family of lobstermen, and he had a mission in the Navy; the deaths of his siblings changed the course of his life and gave it new purpose. He returned from Vietnam and made use of the GI Bill, going to the State University of New York while working odd jobs in the city and earning his degree in less than three years. Walt could smoke dope and protest, or he could make changes from the inside. He was headed into government. He thought his path to instigating change would be through the State Department, believing he could work his way up the ranks and help prevent another war that he viewed as a waste of blood and treasure, needless and avoidable, a permanent scar on the nation. He soon learned that ascension to a position of influence would take longer than patience dictated and that coveted ambassadorships were, for the most part, reserved for campaign donors and for people with recognizable last names. They did not come from families who trolled and checked traps; they came from those who paid top dollar for the catch to be served at private dinner parties in second, third, and fourth homes from the Hamptons to Martha's Vineyard. He needed another avenue if he wanted to keep his government in check. He found it in politics. The State Department had opened that door, as it was at a State Department function that he met Martha Stirling. Looking like she would rather have been anywhere else, her outward demeanor matched Walt's internal disposition. They hit it off immediately.

All Martha's sisters had been married off to suitors approved of, and possibly arranged by, her father; suitors from other prominent, connected East Coast families of means, influence, and generational wealth. Martha was the problem child: Brown University, a Peace Corps mission to India, and antiwar protests across the nation formed the foundation of her rebellious tendencies. Men with what her parents and grandparents considered the "right pedigree" bored her to tears. Walt was the one. Plus, he was a lobsterman. Her parents would *hate* that. But, rather than be disavowed, Walt was accepted into the family. Martha suspected it was because her father thought he might end up being useful. It couldn't hurt to have a politician in the family, especially if you funded his campaign. *Favors.* Walt proposed under a tree she had climbed as a child on the Stirlings' Martha's Vineyard estate and they were married on the property the following spring. Walt knew less than a third of those in attendance, but he was well aware that he was marrying more than Martha. He was marrying into something bigger.

Martha tilted her head back, admiring her husband at the wheel. They had been married for just over six years and had two children to show for it. As a congressman from Massachusetts's 12th district, elected to the House just two years prior, Walter's star was on the rise. His background resonated with blue-collar workers and his new affiliation with one of America's wealthiest and most connected families immersed him in the world of the political elite. He had already made waves as a staffer for Representative Otis Pike of New York, who led the United States House Permanent Select Committee on Intelligence. Better known as the Pike Committee, it was established to investigate overreach by certain agencies of the federal government to include the FBI, NSA, and the CIA. The Pike Committee was the House's answer to the Senate's Church Committee, a key difference being that while the findings of the committee chaired by Senator Frank Church were made public, the findings of the Pike Committee were suppressed for reasons of national security. It was as part of those investigations that Walt began to meet with someone. At first, Martha thought he might be having an affair. That would not have been unusual for a man in his position. Martha's father was a well-known philanderer. Both of her sisters' husbands had strayed but her sisters had, of course, looked the other way, as had their mother, following Jackie Kennedy's, now Jackie O's, example.

Secrets.

Martha despised secrets. She came from a family of secrets and swore she would not continue the tradition with her own. They were partners. With Walt's reputation as a "man of the people," along with his political instincts and her family's fortune, they were a team. She was not about to be relegated to the backseat, as her mother and sisters had been.

As the former navy man guided the boat around Fort Adams and into Brenton Cove, she thought back to the night she had begun to unravel the mysteries of his clandestine world. They had been staying in her family's Upper East Side building when he abruptly announced that he needed to meet with a potential donor late one evening. He had been having more of those recently; meetings at odd hours meant a mistress, in her experience. She was disappointed but not surprised. She hailed a cab, seconds behind his.

"Follow that cab."

"Are you serious?"

Her look told her driver that she was.

"Okay, lady."

Walt's cab headed west through Central Park via the 79th Street Transverse and then took a right in the direction of the Upper West Side.

Where are you going?

A few blocks later, his cab pulled over. She watched her husband exit the yellow vehicle and run across the street, quickly ducking into another taxi. Thrusting a twenty-dollar bill at her driver, she asked him to make a U-turn.

"That's illegal," he said.

She shoved another twenty in his face; he cranked the wheel to a chorus of blaring horns.

Walt's new cab maneuvered through traffic toward the Hudson River, turning south onto State Route 9A. Fortunately for Martha, she was in the most common vehicle in New York; she was invisible.

Who is she?

Do I confront her? Him?

Of course I do.

Bastard!

They continued south past Hell's Kitchen, Chelsea, and the Meatpacking District before making a U-turn on Clarkson Street and cutting right on Morton into Greenwich Village.

Walt's cab then took a left on Bedford Street and came to a stop in front of a lime-green building sandwiched between two brownstones, marked only with the number 86, in the West Village.

"Keep driving," Martha ordered, turning in her seat as her husband exited his cab and stepped onto the curb.

"Pull over here," she said.

"Whatever you say."

She watched Walt approach the dark wooden door and disappear inside.

"Meter's running, lady."

"Keep it running."

Stay? Go inside? Leave? Turn a blind eye?

She glanced down at the gold Girard-Perregaux watch on her wrist.

Ten minutes.

She snatched two more twenties from her purse, handed them to her cabdriver, and pushed open the door.

Martha walked to the nondescript structure and closed her eyes to steady herself in preparation of what she was certain she was about to witness. Then she reached for the handle.

What greeted her was not row upon row of doors to apartments, nor a foyer, as she expected. Instead, she heard the hum of conversation, not between a man and a woman, but the low, steady drone of a crowd.

She pushed the heavy red velvet curtain in front of her aside and stepped into a dark, smoke-filled room poorly illuminated by dim lights on the walls and ceiling. Two bartenders mixed drinks for patrons across a weathered wooden bar and Martha noticed framed dust jackets adorning the walls of works from Fitzgerald, Hemingway, Salinger, Steinbeck, Cather, and Cummings. Tables lined the establishment, with drinkers who looked to be regulars deep in conversation. Very few were women. One man with a stack of legal pads next to him seemed to be writing.

What is this place?

She took in the scene, her eyes shifting from the bar to the tables until they settled on the corner booth. Walt's back was to her, but she recognized his jacket. She locked eyes with the man sitting across from him. The stranger wore a dark wool coat, its collar turned up, obscuring the lower part of his face. He zeroed in on the newcomer and then looked to Walt, who turned around. An expression of surprise was quickly replaced by resignation, and he waved her over. Stale air, thick with the smells of tobacco, sweat, and the damp, musty odor of whiskey barrels, parted way as she crossed the room.

Walt scooted to the side under a framed dust jacket of Theodore Dreiser's *An American Tragedy.*

"Martha," he said, as she slid into the booth. "Welcome to Chumley's."

"Hello, darling," she said. "Charming place. Old speakeasy? It's good to see your meeting is not with a woman ten years my junior."

She took stock of the man across the table. He wasn't smiling. The eyes weren't so much cold as they were perceptive and alert. *Penetrating.* She had not seen eyes like that before.

"I'm Martha Stowe," she said, more of a pronouncement, reaching across the table. "And you are?"

The man's left hand was on the table attached to a coffee mug. His right was out of sight. A stainless-steel Rolex was on his wrist. When you grew up the way she did, you noticed things like that. The Rolex was becoming popular with Hollywood stars like Newman, Redford, and McQueen. The dive watches were even starting to adorn the wrists of New York City's financial class, but unlike the ones she had seen worn by Wall Street bankers, this crystal was worn and scratched.

Walt looked at his companion and raised an eyebrow.

The man nodded.

"True name?" Walt asked.

The man's eyes had not left Martha's. He nodded again.

"Martha, this is Tom Reece."

"Mr. Reece, I'm Martha Stowe. It's a pleasure to meet you. What, pray tell, are you and my husband discussing this evening?"

Tom had hesitated, then reached his right hand across the table.

"Mrs. Stowe," he acknowledged, clearly less than pleased at the intrusion.

"Call me Martha, please. If you are working with my husband on what I think you are, you can use my first name."

"Martha," he said.

"May I call you Tom?"

"You may."

"Are you married?"

"Martha, *Jesus*," Walter said, shaking his head.

"Well, if you are meeting surreptitiously with someone who I can only assume is either a reporter or works for one of our government agencies, I'd like to know what he has to lose. He doesn't look like a reporter." She turned back to the man across the table.

His eyes took measure, evaluating, thoughtful. She caught a flicker of acceptance as he moved his left hand to his coat pocket and removed a pack of Marlboro Reds. He shook out a cigarette and placed the filtered end between his lips. He then tossed the pack on the table and pulled a worn silver Zippo lighter from his right pocket. As the flint wheel ignited the wick, she noted an insignia on its side, a red shield highlighted in yellow with what looked like a skull wearing a green beret. She couldn't quite make out the letters at its base but the last three appeared to be SOG.

"Well?"

"Well?" Tom asked back before taking a long drag on his cigarette. "Am I married? Not yet."

She thought she caught the hint of a smile, as if a fond memory had risen from his subconscious.

"I see. So, you have nothing to lose."

"We *all* have something to lose."

"How right you are. I'll be direct. Anything you are doing, any trouble you may cause, doesn't just impact you. It impacts me. It impacts my children. It impacts my family. I just want us to be clear. Are we clear, Tom?"

"We are."

"Good. Now, what do I need to know?"

That had been five years ago. Tonight, Walt would give a speech at the New York Yacht Club's Newport clubhouse. He was young, but there were already talks of his future as a presidential hopeful, so campaigning outside of Massachusetts was good business. The comparisons to Camelot were not unfounded; an attractive political couple, a war veteran who happened to have served on the modern equivalent of a PT boat, and a family connected to bootlegging and the mob. If they played their cards right, there was the possibility of a run for the White House; the country missed Camelot. It was still two, possibly even four election cycles away, but in politics you had to play the long game.

After the speech and an hour of shaking hands, she planned to retire to their room while Walt would excuse himself and relocate to the

White Horse Tavern for a drink and a bite to eat. There he would meet with Tom Reece.

Walt did not share everything with his wife, but he shared enough. He thought it would alleviate her worries. In fact, it did the opposite.

The Church Committee's report and what had been leaked from the Pike Committee had exposed the dark underbelly of the intelligence community to the American public. She knew that it had also illuminated something more.

Martha understood that she did not have the full picture of what Walt was doing in his meetings with the man she now knew worked for the CIA, the very agency at the center of the investigations. Her husband had emerged as a strong and ardent voice for reform on the campaign trail for the passage of FISA—the Foreign Intelligence Surveillance Act. The threat was communism and those in power at the highest levels of the country's intelligence apparatus would stop at nothing to curtail its advance; to include encroaching on the rights and privacy of U.S. citizens, politicians, reporters, and Supreme Court justices.

What else had Walt learned in the course of the House investigations? What was it that kept him awake? She had arisen in the middle of the night on multiple occasions to find him standing at the window, a bourbon in hand, staring into the night. Was it nightmares? The war? Work? What was it that scared him enough to go outside of official channels to meet with a renegade CIA officer? What was he doing with Tom Reece?

She knew they had met in Vietnam when Tom was a SEAL and had reconnected in the course of events surrounding the Pike Committee. She assumed him to be a source, but Walt kept the specifics of their dealings close. There were some matters he was not allowed to discuss with her, or so went the line. She could tell he was keeping things from her for her own protection. He promised he would tell her one day soon, that he just needed a little more time, an explanation she accepted as much as she disliked it.

Walt pulled back on the throttle and decreased speed, first to ten knots and then to five as they approached the long dock extending from the manicured grounds of the club. Martha stood and joined her husband at the helm.

"Want to dock her?" he asked.

"You know I do." She smiled.

With the children in the care of multiple nannies at her parents' estate on Martha's Vineyard, they were free—well, almost free. It was still work but she knew it was in pursuit of the ideals she had shouted for in the antiwar rallies of the late 1960s. Rather than just be the recipient of the wealth her family had accumulated and live a life parading from one social event to the next, she would have real influence. They could prevent conflicts like the war in Vietnam from happening again. They could fight to ensure that her children, and one day her grandchildren, would not die in an ill-conceived war, as had Walt's brothers.

Martha was confident behind the controls of the yacht and knew the waters in between the island and Newport the way most people know the roads of their hometowns.

Slipping the boat into neutral, she coasted toward the berth while Walt descended to the starboard-side deck, pushing rubber fenders over the side to prepare for docking. They were an hour early, which would allow them time to freshen up before the evening's event. She then moved the throttle into reverse and guided the craft alongside the pier.

Walt leapt from the boat to the dock, pulling the bowline taut and expertly lashing it to a cleat. He did the same with the stern line, examining his work to be sure the boat was secure before reboarding the vessel.

"Great job," he called up to his wife on the flybridge.

"I know, dear."

Walt disappeared below deck to retrieve their overnight bags. Martha shut down the engines.

"Ready?" Walt called up as he emerged from the trawler's interior.

"Give me a minute," she said, rummaging through a storage compartment in search of her purse.

She heard the gate to the pier open and glanced up to see a man with a clipboard walking down the dock, the harbor master coming to greet them.

"Hello," she heard her husband say. "Mind if I pass you these bags? Alan not working tonight?"

When Martha turned and looked back down at the dock, the harbor master was no longer holding a clipboard. In his outstretched hand was a pistol with a long cylindrical attachment she knew as a silencer.

Walt slowly raised his hands and shook his head.

"Don't."

The assassin fired. Due to the downward angle, the round entered near the top of Walter's head. It cut its way through the frontal, parietal, and occipital lobes, removing a large portion of the back of his skull on the way out, coating the lower portions of the side bridge windows with gray brain matter and bone fragments. Martha heard her husband's lifeless body drop straight to the deck.

Visions of her two young children overwhelmed her and locked her in place. Paralyzed and unable to react, she witnessed the assassin fire two additional suppressed rounds into her husband.

As the business end of the weapon swung upward, she gazed from the black pistol to her executioner's dead eyes. *Italian? Russian?* Martha was a good fifteen feet above the assassin. The setting sun was to her back. He held the pistol at her head and then dropped it to her upper chest and pressed the trigger.

It felt like she had been hit with a sledgehammer, her body contorting around the entrance wound.

The kids.

Walter.

Her parents.

As her body twisted, a swell rocked the boat and her knees buckled, which caused her to stumble backward and to the side. She felt another bullet impact her left arm and then had the brief sensation of falling. She collided with the safety rail that extended from the bulwark of the main deck before crashing into the waters of Brenton Cove.

As Martha sank into the darkness, she found herself thinking of someone else. A man she knew had experience with violence. A man her husband would have seen later that evening. A man with ties to the military and to the Central Intelligence Agency. A man named Thomas Reece.